Blood Sea Tales
Book One

The Pirate's Scourge

D1593366

Chris A. Jackson

Copyright © 2018 by Chris A. Jackson

Published July 2018 by Jaxbooks Publishing
Previous version of this story was published under the title *Stormtalons: The Queen's Scourge*

Cover design by Natania Barron
Cover background image courtesy of Iván Tamás
Images for interior from Pixabay have been altered for use

ISBN 978-1-939837-19-6 (paperback)
ISBN 978-1-939837-20-2 (ePub)
ISBN 978-1-939837-21-9 (Mobi)

jaxbooks.com

Acknowledgements
Special thanks to Ed Greenwood for his
imagination and generosity.
And as always, thanks to my wife, Anne, for her
help, patience, and passion for the sea.

This novel is dedicated to all our friends
who are battling for their lives against
the most dreadful foe imaginable.
We fight at your side, shipmates.

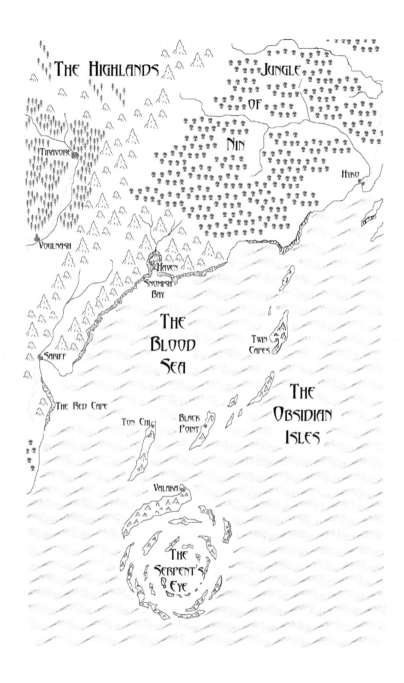

Chapter One
Scourge of the Sea

Few things are what we first perceive them to be.
The Lessons of Quen Lau Ush

From the diary of Kevril Longbright –
Every time I look in the mirror I'm reminded that scars are lessons. They are flesh memories that fade but never fully vanish. When I look at my scars, I remember who gave me each one and what I learned. Some lessons are easy, like never turn your back on an angry man with a shovel. Others are subtler. I have yet to forget any of the lessons carved into my flesh, but I long for the day when remembering them is no longer necessary.

"Dragon Mists, my arse." I pulled my jacket closed against the chill sea fog. "Maybe ice drakes, but not *real* dragons."

When cold air spilled down from the mountains to clash against the warm water of the Blood Sea, the result was a fog so thick it's said you can drown just by taking a deep breath. Sailors call this fog

1

the Dragon Mists because of the legends of dragons living in the coastal cliffs. There may well have been dragons here once long ago, but they've all flown away to the Serpent's Eye, thank Odea.

"Some call this fog the Pirate's Blanket, you know," Miko said. My first mate hated sailing through fog as much as I did, but neither of us wanted to admit it, so we told each other tales. "A more appropriate moniker for what we're about, don't you think, sir?"

"True enough."

I found a fingernail that hadn't yet been bitten to the quick and sheared it short with my teeth. A bell tolled two notes from somewhere ahead, and the lookout waved a white flag three times to starboard. Our quarry was out there, anchored safely and alerting other ships to its presence with its bell. A good practice safety-wise, but to pirates like us, it was like ringing a dinner bell. Come and get it.

The patter of bare feet on the deck heralded Tofi, one of the ship's brats, as he dashed up. "By the mark ten on the lead, sir." He kept his voice low, for I'd ordered a quiet ship, and scampered off at my nod.

The wind howled a shrieking gust overhead, heeling *Scourge* over a strake, but while her topgallants were drawn into hard planks and the topsails bellied full, the lower reefed mainsail and forecourse flapped and backfilled. The sheltering cliffs were making the wind fluky, allowing the mists to hang low over the water. From the quarterdeck I could make out *Scourge*'s bowsprit and the signals of the lookout there, but the rocks that could rip us to pieces remained a mystery.

"Sailing into a windward, cliff-shrouded cove in fog, Captain?" Miko's pearly teeth gleamed against her nut-brown skin like a lighthouse on a moonless night. "I hope we're getting *paid* enough for this."

"Could be worse. Could be *leeward* cliffs." I grinned to banish my nervousness. It didn't work.

The roar of the surf set my teeth on edge, waves pounding on reefs that could grind *Scourge* to kindling if these fluky winds denied her steerage. The distant bell tolled again, our only guidance through the fog.

Sane mariners, like our quarry, drop anchor in any one of the dozens of bays along the coast and ride out these foggy blows in the shelter of the high cliffs, ringing the ship's bell every quarter glass to warn off others. Those caught unawares by the fog at sea run well offshore under reefed sails, sounding a horn at intervals and praying to Odea for guidance, protection, or salvation. Personally, I've never found the sea goddess very forgiving, though that doesn't stop me from praying to her on occasion.

Then there are those of us who are less than sane, desperate, or seduced by rewards that exceed the risk. Either way, they don't call it the Pirate's Blanket for nothing, and I had a job to do.

A job… The notion still stuck in my craw, but I had no choice in the matter. I'd gone into my partnership with Jhavika with eyes open and couldn't balk now. Just like I couldn't stop pirating.

An honorable occupation at this point in my life was not an option, and pirate was better than shit-kicking farmer or dirt-side bandit. The former…well, there's the shit-kicking part, but other factors had driven me off my family farm. The latter usually ends up with said bandit dangling from a tree or gallows. A pirate's really just a bandit afloat, but nooses are easier to evade at sea. Besides, there's a living in it, and freedom. I was my own master, or more-so than most men or women could claim to be. *Scourge* was mine, free and clear; I owed no tithe to lord or master. I did pay Jhavika a fair percentage of my take, of course, because we were partners. She picked the targets and told me where to find them, and I did the pirating. Call me what you will, but I'll ride anyone's coattails to wealth, and Jhavika had very long coattails indeed. That woman's aspirations knew no bounds.

The lookout on the bowsprit madly waved a black flag. He'd spotted a reef or rock ahead, though I could still see nothing.

"Wear ship, Miko." I looked aloft. The topsails now flagged, only the topgallants drawing. "No wind to tack. This isn't the place to be stuck in irons, and we aren't in a hurry...yet."

"Aye, Capt'n." She gave a quiet order to bring *Scourge* off the wind and jibe sails. As the helmsman spun the wheel, she whispered to me, "Not enough wind to blow away a decent *fart* in here!"

"True enough." As *Scourge* came about, I stared hard into the fog off our starboard quarter. My blood chilled as I spied a line of white breakers amid the horizonless steel-gray of sea and sky.

Every eye on the ship watched that line with their hearts in their mouths, rocks barely a ship-length away that would have meant our end if we hadn't shifted course.

"A biscuit toss is as good as a league, I suppose." Miko ran a hand over her shaven pate and grinned.

The helmsman chuckled nervously.

I was out of fingernails to chew. "Remind me to give that lookout a bonus."

Tofi ran up again, panting from his dash. "By the mark *five*, sir." He sounded nervous, too.

"That's fine, Tofi." It wasn't fine. *Scourge* drew three-and-a-half fathoms and there was a four-foot swell running. With this steep shore, I needed quicker soundings. "Tell Wix to run a second lead line."

"Aye, sir!" Tofi cringed and darted off.

I knew Wix got the message when I heard a snarled curse from forward. My bosun is both the least-popular and most-respected member of my crew for two reasons. Firstly, he's in charge of maintaining crew discipline, and backs up that authority with the quickest left jab I've ever seen. The second reason is that he's an ill-tempered bastard who loves his work and violence—a trait of his part-ogre heritage—more than strong drink and fornication. His response to laggardly behavior involved the knotted end of a rope, and insubordination triggered that left jab. I sometimes had to curb

Wix's enthusiasm—too many broken noses—but for the most part I let him have free rein.

As *Scourge* began making way on her new course, close-hauled on the opposite tack and away from the reef, Tofi returned. "By the deep eight, sir, and Master Wix says two leads his pimply arse, and why for fook's sake are we flyin' the fookin' courses if there ain't no fookin' wind?"

"Tell him to furl the courses and thank him for his opinion of my seamanship, Tofi." I grinned at the boy and added, "And tell Master Wix to keep his fookin' voice down."

Tofi paled anew. "Aye, sir."

As he dashed off, another ship's brat, Boxley, ran up. "Four knots by the log, sir!" She grinned enthusiastically at my nod and darted away.

Recruiting eager young boys and girls for a life on the sea was simple. There were always starving urchins loitering around waterfronts, willing to work for three meals a day and a place to sleep. Boxley had gutted a man who tried to rape her when she was eight and stowed away aboard *Scourge* to avoid a hangman's noose. After five years, she was the toughest of my ship's brats, and every sailor aboard knew it. I wasn't supposed to know that Miko doted on her, sneaking her extra rations and teaching her to read and write. My bet was I'd have a new midshipman out of the deal, a welcome addition to the worthless gaggle of laggards I had now. I'd just as soon throw the lot of them over the side, but I desperately needed another one or two officers, and training youngsters was safer than hiring strangers, albeit slower and harder on my nerves.

The bell rang again, clear and pure, now off our port beam.

"She's sitting in Weatherly Cove." I reviewed the chart in my mind's eye. I knew these waters like I knew the chips in my teeth. The bay we were edging into sported three coves, each separated by a rocky outcrop and shoal. The westernmost, Weatherly Cove, had a tricky entrance bracketed by hard bars, difficult to negotiate with these contrary winds and impossible to do in haste, which our final approach would require. "Bugger!"

"Boats?" Miko asked, one brow cocked.

Sometimes I think she reads my mind.

"Yes." Attacking a merchant ship from boats was chancy, but not as chancy as blundering into Weatherly Cove in fog and fluky wind like a blind man looking for quicksand. "One more tack and we'll anchor in six fathoms. *Quietly*, mind you! Then lower three boats. Tell Wix to handpick the boarders."

Miko grinned. "You just made his day."

Wix loved nothing more than a brisk boarding action, probably because it gave him the opportunity to hurt people. "Make sure he knows we aren't out for blood on this one."

Her grin turned to stone. "I'll tell him personally." Miko hurried off the quarterdeck, leaving me alone with my anxiety.

Out for blood... I'd seen too many boarding actions where blood was all we got for our trouble.

Don't get me wrong, I'll kill if provoked, or if there's money at stake, but slaughtering innocent sailors only buys trouble. While it's true that dead men tell no tales—unless a necromancer is involved—I learned long ago that it was preferable to be wanted for piracy than hunted as a murderer. The *Scourge*'s former captain never learned that lesson. His penchant for wholesale slaughter precipitated his own death, and nearly mine. Captain Kohl and his first mate lost their lives in a trap. The rest of us were lucky to escape. I fingered the scars I'd earned that day, determined not to make *that* mistake.

Tofi and another brat fed me continuous soundings, running between the foredeck and the quarterdeck as fast as the leadsmen could throw their leads and pull them in. I kept an eye on the forward lookout and ordered course changes when he waved his flag. We brought *Scourge* around once again, avoiding a craggy black rock jutting out of the sea to windward.

"By the deep six!" Tofi reported, his breath coming short. "Black sand and shell, sir!"

"Helm to windward and slack sheets. Relay forward to lower the anchor, Tofi."

"Aye, sir!" He dashed off.

Scourge came upwind, sails luffed and were furled, and we lowered our best bower into the sea like a babe being nestled into its crib. The crew knew this drill well; every command passed in a whisper, sails furled without flapping, and lines and blocks ran smoothly with no squeaks or clatter. Boats were lowered into the sea without so much as a bump or bang of an oar on a gunnel.

My tension eased a trifle. For some reason, running my ship onto rocks in a fog caused me more anxiety than the pending boarding action. I don't know why. Maybe I value my ship more than my skin.

My bosun climbed the steps to the quarterdeck and pressed one scarred knuckle to his thick brow. Miko followed, looking as anxious as I felt.

"All secure, Capt'n." Wix grinned—a horrific sight, considering he had only three teeth in his head, not counting the two prominent tusks jutting from his lantern jaw—and nodded to the sailors lined up along the ship's waist, their cutlasses, boarding axes, and pikes at the ready. "Picked you out some right dandies."

"They all know my preferences on this operation, Master Wix?"

"They know, sir." He curled his lip, cracked his walnut knuckles, and spat over the rail, clearly displeased by my order.

"Good." I turned to my first mate. "Miko, would you please appoint one of our fine young midshipmen to command *Scourge* while we attend to a little mayhem?"

Many pirates don't bother with a midshipmen's berth, but advance capable seamen directly to officer rank when necessary. I prefer to train my future officers personally. A few years wearing a jacket, giving orders, and learning the finer points of mathematics and navigation *before* becoming full-fledged officers works far better than after. It not only allows me to train them properly, but gives me time to weed out those who can't make the grade.

"*Nothing* would make me happier, sir." Miko turned to the four pimple-faced mids sulking around the helm. "Mister Geit, you'll command *Scourge* in our absence."

"Aye, sir!" Geit, a gangly redhead of eighteen years with a nasty disposition, grinned at his peers, suddenly his subordinates.

"And if I hear of any nonsense upon our return…" Miko let that hang.

"No nonsense. Aye, sir." Geit snapped a salute, still grinning malevolently. Though he tended to hate everyone indiscriminately, he was particularly cruel to his fellow mids. He'd recently ordered one of them to shinny up to the topgallant and fly his pants from the pennant halyard for no reason other than spite. Unfortunately, he was also senior and the best navigator among them.

"Let's go." I led the way down to the middle deck, Miko and Wix at my heels. "We'll each take a boat. Hand signals only once we're away."

"Bout fookin' time," Wix muttered. "All this prancin' about like a flock of concubines on a fookin' ballroom floor…"

I knew Wix was just working himself up for the fight. When my bosun was truly upset he went scary quiet and all the Gods of Darkness wouldn't cross him.

Hemp, my steward, slouched up with a disapproving scowl, holding out my old patched jacket. "Be *careful*, sir!"

His concern didn't fool me; Hemp cared more about keeping my clothes free of gashes, bloodstains, and holes than he did about my tender skin. I relented, doffing the good jacket and donning the worn, then allowed him to sling a baldric over my shoulder and affix my worn but serviceable cutlass—he was probably afraid I'd nick one of my finer blades.

Finally ready, I strode to the main hatch cover, surveyed the weaponry arrayed there, and chose a pair of boarding axes to tuck through my belt. Miko had already armed herself with a boarding pike, cutlass, and her two wakizashi for close work. Wix rarely used anything but his daggers in a fight. They had heavy bronze guards with inch-long spikes that he preferred to punch with instead of using the blade. I'd seen him punch through chainmail with them.

We boarded the boats and shoved off, quiet and efficient, a dozen seasoned pirates in each. *Surely more than enough for a merchant*, I thought. Our target was the merchant junk *Yellow Blossom*, owned by Lord Fa-Chen of Haven. *Yellow Blossom* sported a complement of no more than two dozen, I'd been told, and they'd be sailors, not fighters. Surprise should give us an even greater advantage.

Oars dipped and pulled with barely a ripple and, thanks to canvas-padded oarlocks, no sound could be heard over the roar of the nearby surf. Our prey's bell tolled again, this time closer, though its direction was still hard to discern in the fog.

I squinted into the mists and whispered, "Two points to port."

A black cliff coalesced out of the fog, the merchantman's high transom. She was as pretty a junk as ever I'd seen—sea-worthy, spacious, and well cared for, with gilt scrollwork in the likeness of yellow roses entwining her stern gallery windows. *A damned shame.*

We eased forward. A sharp-eyed lookout could cost lives at this point, but we'd gotten lucky coming up on her stern; the high sterncastle hid us from the crow's nest. Above us loomed two rows of stern gallery windows. The higher, narrower windows were dark, but light glowed from the lower great cabin.

"Bugger!" If we climbed the ornate transom, whoever was inside might see us and raise an alarm. I motioned Miko and Wix to port and starboard. They could make their ascent up the quarter galleries to the poop deck, then fight their way forward with height as an advantage. I decided to take the fight right to the captain's cabin. If we took the captain prisoner, the conflict would end without undue killing. Or so I hoped.

I tapped a sailor on the shoulder and pointed up the transom. He nodded, grinned, and started climbing, nimble as a monkey and quiet as a mouse, a coil of knotted rope over his shoulder. At the lit windows he paused and peered over the sill, then looked down and made a suggestive gesture. Evidently, Captain Tan was entertaining.

Perfect... A distracted captain would be easier to capture. I motioned for the sailor to continue up and secure the line. When the knotted rope fell down into eager hands, I took it and climbed to the lower stern gallery windows.

Within, glistening flesh moved in rhythmic enthusiasm, grunts and moans audible through the stern glass. *No better way to pass the time while waiting for weather, they say.* Deciding on the direct approach, I gripped the line hard, kicked out from the transom, and swung back toward the window boots first.

Odea help me, but I love this part of my job.

Glass shattered, and I managed not to cut myself too badly or bash my head on the sill. I rolled to my feet and drew my cutlass, but the captain was quicker than I'd guessed. She vaulted from the bed fully naked, dagger in hand.

"Captain Tan." I saluted with my cutlass as pirates scrambled into the cabin through the windows to back up my swashbuckling ploy. One of them whistled long and low, and I had to admit that the captain cut a dashing figure in naught but her skin and a bared stiletto. "Pardon our intrusion. I can see you're busy with..." I glanced at the young man lying shocked on the bed—*Impressive*—and couldn't help myself. "...with *weighty* matters, but I must insist you drop the knife and put some clothes on."

Captain Tan glanced at the knife, then at her lover's flagging ardor—the dagger's blade was shorter by half—then glared at me. "Who the *hell* are you?"

"Captain Kevril Longbright of the *Scourge* at your service." I bowed with a flourish. "Now, the *dagger* if you please, Captain."

Her eyes widened a trifle in recognition, and the dagger fell from her grip. Snatching up a blue jacket, she flung it on, then reached for trousers. Her paramour hadn't moved, apparently too scared to even reach for a blanket.

She glared at him and snapped, "Oh, stop gaping and get *dressed*, Maurice!"

"Maurice?" He didn't look like a Maurice. To me, a *Maurice* is pale, portly, and pompous. This fellow sported a lithe chest, muscular legs, and an abdomen as flat as a table, with skin the hue of burnished teak. Islander blood mixed with Chen or Toki, I guessed, likely a pleasure slave or trollop, considering his good looks and magnificent proportions. The captain apparently like them young; Maurice looked to be in his late teens at most.

Sounds of scuffles could be heard from above and forward, then one cry, a scream, and a clash of arms.

"If we hurry, Captain, we can avoid unnecessary bloodshed." I gestured to the door.

"Gods-damned pirate!" she spat, fastening her trousers and slamming her feet into boots.

Her lover managed to draw up the blanket and fumble from the bed. Macie Moll, one of my more competent boarders, stepped forward to steady poor Maurice, a lascivious grin on her face.

"Is he a slave or a guest?" I asked the captain as she struggled with the second boot. The young man didn't bear a slave's mark, but some slavers didn't tattoo their stock.

"Why does it matter?" She glared at me.

"If he's a slave, I'll be taking him as plunder. If he's your guest, he'll go with you." That, of course, meant she'd claim him as her guest. It didn't really matter; I didn't need any slaves and knew he'd be a distraction, gifted as he was. Rumors spread quickly aboard a ship, and *Scourge* was no exception.

"Maurice is Lord Malchi's son. He's been assigned as my midshipman for training in seamanship."

My pirates chuckled, and I raised an eyebrow. "And I can *see* he's progressing well." I wasn't worried about retribution from Lord Malchi. A score of rich merchants in Haven styled themselves as lords, a fancy designation but lacking any authority. *Crime* lords was a more apt title. I worked with one, in fact. I waved at the door. "*Shall* we, Captain?"

Tan glared again and strode for the door.

11

"Macie, see that the lordling is properly dressed, but *no* liberties are to be taken. Understand?"

"*Aye*, sir." She looked crestfallen. "C'mere, *Maurice*! Grab your drawers and put that spar away!"

Captain Tan opened the door to find herself facing my bosun. He filled the portal like a nightmare in the flesh, the spikes of his dagger guards dripping blood. She stumbled back a step. I couldn't blame her; Wix can be startling.

"Wix? Any trouble?" There was blood on his shirt.

"No, sir." He tore his eyes from the gap in the captain's jacket and swallowed. "A few scuffles is all. One dumb fook tried to poke me with a sword. He won't be eatin' solid food for a span, but he'll live."

"Good. Bring everyone together on the middeck and search the ship for anyone hiding."

"Aye, sir." He hurried off, casting the captain one more glance.

"Shall we join your crew, Captain?" I nudged her between the shoulder blades with the tip of my cutlass.

"You're poking a sleeping dragon here, Captain Longbright." She started forward. "There'll be repercussions for this."

"These *are* repercussions, Captain Tan." In addition to directing me to richly laden ships for our mutual profit, Jhavika occasionally tasked me with discouraging her competition: a threat here, some mayhem there. This was one of those assignments. I'd intended to give the message when the whole crew was assembled, but now would do just as well. "The dragon's awake, and its fire is stoked."

The captain glared over her shoulder. "What in the Nine Hells are you talking about?"

"I'm talking about your master, *Lord* Fa-Chen." I gave her a wolf's grin. "This is in retaliation for his meddling in business that isn't his. Jhavika Keshmir is paying him back, Captain. We'll be putting you off in boats so you can deliver the message personally."

"Keshmir's nothing but a pir—" Biting off the word, she whirled around and slammed open the door to the middeck.

"*Lady* Keshmir *was* a pirate once, Captain, and takes no offense at the moniker, but she's moved up in the world since going ashore. She's now a...*business* woman." I prodded her toward the crowd of nervous sailors surrounded by heavily armed pirates. Only a couple of the sailors were injured; one sported a deep stab wound to the shoulder, and another—obviously the man whose jaw had been destroyed by Wix—wore a bloody cloth wrapped beneath his chin and knotted atop his head. "Have a care with that tongue of yours. I'll put you ashore in the condition I *found* you if you keep wagging it heedlessly."

The captain joined her crew and kept her mouth shut. A wise woman.

Miko caught my eye, her usual gleeful smile after a relatively bloodless operation conspicuously absent. That meant a problem. As the last of the stragglers were herded together, I motioned her aside.

"What?"

"Cargo's crap. Nothing but baled hemp and coarse-wove muslin." She made a face. "This shows up in Haven, it won't be worth the spit it takes to shine a boot."

"Damn Jhavika to…" I let that drop. Jhavika had promised me a rich cargo, but cursing her now wouldn't do me any good.

I glared at the captain and crew, then up at the rigging, spars, fittings, and cordage, and made some calculations. It would take time, but we weren't in a hurry; the north winds would howl for another day at least. Jhavika might be satisfied with mere vengeance, but I needed profit. I made a decision and turned back to Miko.

"Fuck the cargo. Take a launch back to *Scourge* and bring her in slow and careful. We raft up, strip this ship for every scrap of canvas, bronze, block, and line."

"Aye, sir."

"And have Wix post someone trustworthy at the captain's door. I'll go through Tan's things myself."

"I'm on it!" She still didn't look happy, but that was the best I could do.

As Miko relayed my orders, picked her crew, and set off in one of the boats, I turned to the ship's captain. "Captain Tan, I'll put you and your crew ashore with your boats and whatever provisions you wish to take with you."

"How *magnanimous* of you." The mists carried more warmth than her voice.

"Or I could strip you all naked and throw you in the sea." I pointed my cutlass between her eyes and grinned. "Your choice."

The muscles of her jaw bunched and relaxed several times. I could do worse than I'd threatened, and she knew it. "I'll choose the former option."

"Good. This isn't about you, Captain. It's about your lord and his recent actions. Our intent is to hurt *him*, not you. We'll take everything valuable from this ship and burn her to the waterline. Please let Lord Fa-Chen know *why* this happened when you next see him."

She smiled tightly. "I'll be sure to give him your name."

The implied threat stoked my temper. "And, considering the piss-poor excuse for *cargo* you're carrying, if *Maurice* here..." I pointed to the shivering young man who had recently been warming her bed, "...truly *is* Lord Malchi's son, perhaps I'll take him to ransom."

Maurice's eyes widened and his mouth opened.

"He's not," Tan said before the young man could answer for himself. "He's not a slave either. Just a hired trollop to keep me company."

"I surmised as much." Too bad; a fat ransom would have compensated for the lack of cargo. "Don't worry; I won't take your *toy* from you."

"Thank you, Captain." Her chin rose an inch and I could see that her estimation of me rose with it. She knew I could have taken him anyway. There were slavers in Haven who didn't ask questions. "I've heard of you, but you're not what I expected."

"*None* of us are what other people expect we are, Captain." I sheathed my cutlass and nodded toward the ship's boats. "Master Wix, put them in the boats with provisions and water. Canvas and cordage, too. There's enough driftwood on the beach to rig shelters. When the weather clears, they can coast-hop for Haven."

"Aye, sir!"

The crew moved with a will, and *Yellow Blossom*'s four boats were in the water and loaded within minutes. We shoved them off with a cheer, good wishes, and a few cat-calls. As they pulled away, Macie Moll pleaded with poor Maurice to take up the life of a pirate and share her hammock.

"Master Wix! Put someone on the bell so Miko can find us in this soup, then take this ship apart!"

"Aye, sir!"

As Wix shouted orders and my boarders fell to plundering, I went aft. Amid the shouts, clatters, crashes, and laughter of pirates doing what they did best, I meticulously inspected the captain's cabin. Tan had a nice set of silver plate, some jewelry, dresses, a fine set of navigational instruments, and a pair of matched daggers with ruby-pommeled hilts. Worth a tidy bit, but not enough to make up for the lack of cargo. I laid it out in piles and started rummaging through the hanging lockers and drawers. There had to be more.

I reached back into the dark beneath a shelf and felt a stab of pain. *Shit!* With visions of traps and poisoned needles in my head, I jerked back. The end of my finger was bleeding, but it felt like any other mundane cut, not stinging with poison. I sucked my lacerated finger and felt again more carefully, then dragged out an old strongbox with metal reinforcing, one corner bent and sharp. *This is more like it.* It was locked, but the pommel of my cutlass knocked the padlock free. I opened it to find rows of newly minted Toki imperial crowns. *Thank Odea.* Perhaps Tan had been sent to buy more valuable cargo in Hyto for the return trip. We'd do okay on this take after all, it seemed.

As I closed the strongbox and fitted the bent lock back together, movement outside the stern gallery windows caught my eye, *Scourge* emerging from the fog. Miko brought her alongside with the skill of a ballroom dancer gliding into a promenade, with barely a bump as the ships were rafted together. I went back to my work. There came a knock on the door as I was perusing the captain's small library, mostly poetry, none of which I cared for, though they might sell for a few pennies to a lord with high aspirations and bad taste.

"Come in."

Hemp entered, scowled at the hodgepodge piles of finery, and sighed. "More *junk* for me to cart around like a pack mule, I see, sir." He threw down a roll of canvas and light line to bale it all up.

"Only as far as Haven," I said. "Be careful with the silver and the dresses. Put the strongbox in my quarters. If you pick the lock, I'll know." Of course, it wasn't locked anymore, and I didn't really need to threaten him anyway. Hemp was good with locks, but he knew better than to steal from his captain.

"I wouldn't *dream* of it, sir!" He looked indignant and picked up one of the dresses, holding up the fine silk kimono as if it might look good on him.

"Not your color, Hemp." I endured a glare with good humor.

"Just wonderin' how women dress in such things." He started packing it all up.

"Don't wonder, Hemp, just thank the Gods of Light that they do." I slipped the two jeweled daggers into my boots and strode from the cabin, confident that Hemp would do his job well.

I leapt down onto *Scourge*'s lower deck. Miko was busy directing the stowage of loot, everything from tools to canvas to spars and provisions. My greasy-haired purser, Quibly, stood nearby, peering over the spectacles perched on his hawk nose and logging every parcel in his ledger. I smiled at my first mate, but she didn't smile back.

"Cheer up, Miko. I found a strongbox that will tip the scales in our favor quite nicely."

"Oh?" Her dark brows rose. "How nicely?"

"Well, we can't *retire*, but we won't starve either."

"Wonderful." She turned back to her task.

"Oh, and if you're interested, the captain had some nice dresses."

She looked at me like I'd told her she might like to light her pants on fire. "You *know* I don't—"

I held up a hand. "I know, but I *also* know a young lady in Haven who might appreciate a present."

Miko gaped as I grinned. She obviously didn't know that *I* knew she was seeing someone, and the look on her face was worth the price of fifty fine dresses.

"I…um…thank you, Captain."

I waved her off and headed for my cabin. "Pick one out for her and give her a kiss for me."

"I will, sir."

"Send word when we're done." I stopped at the sterncastle door and looked back at *Yellow Blossom*, a pang in my heart. It was a shame to destroy such a fine ship, but orders were orders. Though we could move illicit cargo easily enough, a ship is impossible to sell anywhere along the Blood Sea without prompting a slurry of pointed questions. "Then breach a cask of oil in her hold and torch it."

"Aye, sir!" Miko saluted, her eyes shadowed with the same regret.

I went to my cabin and doffed my slashed jacket. Shards of glass fell from the pockets and cuffs as I shook it out and hung it up. Hemp would curse me for not shaking it out the stern gallery windows, but I didn't care. Striding to my sideboard, I poured a lead-crystal tumbler half full of fine malt whiskey. A sip of the fiery liquor eased the unexpected lump in my throat.

Getting sentimental about a gods-be-damned merchant ship, Kevril? I sighed, set down the glass, and went to my quarter gallery to wash up. The mirror hanging there showed me the same middle-aged face I saw every morning. The tiny cut on my forehead from today's encounter paled next to the three parallel scars that slashed from my ear to chin, souvenirs given to me by my current business associate. *Lessons carved into my flesh...* That fight had made me captain, but the scars reminded me not to underestimate people.

I washed the cut with water from my basin, then dabbed it with a towel soaked in wood alcohol. My shirt had a tear in the shoulder, but no wound beneath. I took it off and draped it over a chair by my chart table, donned a fresh one, recovered my drink, and went to stand by the stern gallery windows.

Shouts and cries from the pillaging wafted in as I stared out at the mists and sipped from my tumbler, wondering why I didn't feel better about the day's work. Not a single pirate had been killed and we'd make a profit, albeit a small one after ship's expenses. My thoughts were interrupted when the door to my cabin opened and Hemp entered with the strongbox. Putting it down, he muttered at the glass shards scattered across the cabin sole, but he could read my mood. He swept it up without a word, and left, taking my jacket and shirt to mend.

Why? I wondered again, sipping my whiskey. Wix had vented a bit of his bottomless temper, and Miko had a dress for her lady ashore. I had had the pleasure of a daring bit of swashbuckling, receiving only a cut on the forehead for my stupidity. And the crew was in high spirits. They'd be telling tales of Captain Tan's interrupted tryst for weeks, not to mention the heroic proportions of her paramour, Maurice.

So why do I feel like shit?

I finished my whiskey and stared out into the fog. *Empty...so empty...like looking into the soul of a dragon, they say.* I felt like that inside. Sometimes it seemed there was no end to it, mission after mission, all to feed Jhavika's appetite for riches and power. Lately, *Scourge* had been at sea far more than she'd been ashore. My crew needed some time to unwind, spend their money, and remember why we were pirates. So did their captain.

Maybe that's why I feel lost. I fingered the scars on my face. Jhavika was riding *Scourge* like a rented mule, climbing to the top of the pile of lords and criminals who ostensibly ruled Haven on the strength of our backs. She wanted to be queen one day, she'd said, and queens needed navies. She'd promised that I would rule Snomish Bay with a score of ships, taking tithe from every merchant who came and went.

A tax collector, I realized with a snort of disgust. *She'll make a tax collector out of me.*

There was no doubt that we were both profiting by our partnership, but maybe it was time for a change. Maybe it was time to end it. I went to my sideboard and poured myself another whiskey, resolving to demand some time ashore for the captain and crew of *Scourge*. It couldn't come soon enough.

Chapter Two
Haven

Is it better to bend like the willow or stand firm like the oak? The answer lies not in adherence to a philosophy, but in knowing how hard the wind will blow.

The Lessons of Quen Lau Ush

From the diary of Kevril Longbright –

I remember thinking that the day I won the fight with Jhavika was the day I became my own master, beholden to no one, free at last. Some days I wonder who really won that fight. Other days, I wonder if either of us did. Each of us is a slave, after all, I to my ship and she to her avarice. I wonder, truly, what freedom is, what it would feel like, and if it would make me happy. Is it possible to be a slave to one's own freedom?

"They're like gods-damned sharks with blood in the water." Miko curled a lip in distaste at the flock of merchants descending on the Haven quay as the first bales of our ill-gotten cargo were offloaded.

"That they are, but they bleed gold when you harpoon them."

She barked a laugh. "Where's my harpoon?"

Haven is like no other city in the world. A long-abandoned gnomish stronghold—and yes, some git of a sailor saying "it looks gnomish" is how Snomish Bay got its name—resettled by warlords, refugees, pirates, criminals, and bandits. My kind of folks.

The city touts itself as the freest place of business in the Blood Sea, if not the entire world, a city state with no central government, no taxes, and few, if any, laws. Delve below that façade, however, and the seedy truth is revealed. The self-styled Council of Lords serves as a de facto government dealing with city-wide issues, but only when problems threatened their own livelihoods. There are no "taxes" per se, so funding for these projects derives from tithes, tolls, dues, and exorbitant rents. And laws? Well, each man, woman, and child is the law unto themselves. Want to kill someone? Go ahead; there is no city guard to bring you to justice. But be aware that the next knife might be thrust into your own back.

As such, Haven is the best port on the sea for any pirate.

Our potential customers poked and prodded the arrayed bundles skeptically, sneering and commenting that we must have looted a sunken wreck. Considering we'd stripped *Yellow Blossom* of everything but her hull and masts, they were pretty much right, except for the sunken part.

"Just be thankful Quibly does the haggling."

My purser strode back and forth with his thumbs in his belt, ignoring the pre-haggling banter. The haggling wouldn't begin until the crew finished unloading. That was when Quibly's skills would shine. The man's tongue fenced with a mastery unmatched by the most seductive courtesan in Haven. By the end of the day, the evidence of our piracy would be gone, transformed into gold as if by an alchemist's magic. Quibly had already assessed the value of our haul, and I'd paid the crew from the strongbox of coin. Throughout the ship, all conversation focused on how to spend it.

"I thank the Gods of Light every day for that, sir." Miko sighed and abruptly changed the subject. "Are you going to see her?"

The question took me by the lee, but I knew who Miko meant. We'd already agreed that the crew needed a break. Of course, it fell to me to apprise Jhavika of the situation.

"Yes, as soon as I scrub a week at sea off my salty hide and put on some decent clothes." I brushed at my salt-stained jacket. "Jhavika's particular about her guests these days."

"I think she'd make an exception considering what you're bringing her."

"You'd think," I agreed. I'd mulled over a potential break in that partnership during our voyage home, but didn't like the alternative. Too much work was better than not enough, and pirating was easier when I had someone handing me juicy targets.

A carriage arrived on the quay, like a fat rat crawling from a hole in the wall of warehouses. The conveyance disgorged three more plump merchants adorned in rich robes and glinting rings, and protected by a squad of beefy bodyguards. Shoes that rarely touched earth scuffed along the flagstones of the quay as they perused our goods. I had no interest in watching the spectacle.

"I need to get ready to go."

As I turned away, Miko asked, "What about shore leave?"

I paused, tempted to tell her to set the crew loose in shifts, but I didn't know what Jhavika would say yet. *Why should I care what she says? They're my crew.* My gut twisted abruptly, easing as I relinquished the thought. *Don't burn any bridges yet, Kevril.* "Take on fresh provisions and water, and serve out grog when the off-loading's done, but no leave until I get back."

Turning to go below, I spied half a dozen sailors with sour faces. They'd apparently heard the exchange and were displeased with my answer. Striding toward my cabin, I wondered if I'd have a mutiny on my hands if leave was denied.

In my cabin, I found Hemp laying out clothes on my bunk: gold-trimmed red velvet jacket, ivory shirt with ruffled collar and sleeves, black pants and boots, all freshly cleaned. Not my very best, but a far sight better than I'd intended to wear. He'd even laid out the daggers

I'd claimed from our recent prize, the gems in the hilts matching the jacket nicely, along with my dress cutlass.

"What's all this?"

Hemp wiped a nonexistent smudge from the sword's scabbard. "Jhavika appreciates somethin' easy on the eyes as much as the next woman. After all, it takes bait to hook a shark, don't it, sir? Might get the answer you want if you ask right."

"So, the whole crew knows I'm going to ask her for some respite, do they?" I doffed my jacket and muttered an oath beneath my breath. There were few secrets aboard a pirate ship.

"Well, we was hopin', sir." Hemp poured steaming water from a pitcher into a basin. "Let me just give you a proper shave and a trim, then you wash off the salt and get gussied up. You'll feel like a new man!"

I keep my face clean because it's easier than keeping a beard in trim, and I don't like the way my beard looks with three streaks of gray running through it. Call me vain, but I think a ship's captain shouldn't look like a vagabond. Generally, I shave myself, but Hemp did a better job, and his notion had some merit. He'd be insufferable if I told him so, however.

"Since arguing with you will only buy me grief, I might as well give in."

"Too right you are, sir." He grinned and stropped my razor, nodding to the stool beside the basin. "Have a seat."

I stripped off my shirt and sat down, allowing my steward to shave the whiskers off my face. If mutiny was afoot, he could have ended the affair right then, but Hemp had been shaving me for years and I wasn't worried.

Nerves of steel, right?

Actually, Hemp cared more about his reputation as my steward than the complaints of any whining foremast jacks and janes. If he cut my throat, he'd never be a steward ever again. Hell of a note when the only thing keeping me alive is the reputation of a man who thinks the height of culture is a brothel with clean sheets.

When my face was whisker free—and my throat still uncut—I endured a swipe with a towel soaked in wood alcohol and managed not to scream.

He'd just finished trimming my hair when there was a knock at the door, and Hemp hollered, "'Bout damned time!" Four sailors entered carrying buckets of steaming water. Hemp pointed to the quarter gallery and gave me a grin. "Now for a good scrub!"

That, at least, was one task he'd never suggested I needed help with.

For a sailor, a hot bath is a luxury like no other. Fresh water is always at a premium aboard ship and rarely used for other than cleansing a wound, diluting grog, or drinking when there is no grog on hand. But we were at the quay and would be taking on fresh water anyway, so I luxuriated.

By the murky hue of the water sluicing out the scuttle, I had needed the attention. Funny how you don't notice the salt-crusted filth on your skin until it's washed off. When I was done, I felt as fresh as a new-born babe. I toweled dry and dressed in the finery Hemp had laid out, buckled the thick leather money belt containing Jhavika's share around my waist, tucked my shirt over it, and looked in the mirror one last time.

I fingered the scars that marred my face, Jhavika's handiwork.

After the untimely deaths of Captain Kohl and his first mate, she and I, as the two senior officers, had had a disagreement over who should be *Scourge's* next captain. Already injured and exhausted from escaping the trap, we fell to a quick exchange of blows, then circled each other warily. During the second flurry, I knocked her sword from her grasp. Thinking I'd won, I lowered my cutlass. That was when she taught me the lesson, snatching up Captain Kohl's cat-o'-nine-tails and slashing out. Three of the barbed lashes tore through the flesh of my face even as my cutlass slashed across her stomach. Both clutching our injuries, we might have continued to the death, but Jhavika called a truce.

"Give me a share of Kohl's fortune," she'd bargained. "I'll take my stake ashore and you keep the ship."

Best deal I ever made. After she'd carved out a name for herself, she'd offered me a few jobs, then a full-time partnership. We'd both profited handsomely. Hopefully, she'd see the wisdom in granting some down time to continue that partnership.

Shaking off the memories, I stepped back to consider the whole view in the mirror. I'd never pass for one of Jhavika's fancy *lord* friends, but I looked respectable. Hemp might be a whore-mongering scallywag, but he has good taste in clothes and is deft with a razor and scissors.

Damn it! I'm going to have to either thank him or increase his pay. With a choice akin to death or dishonor, I opted for the easy way out.

"Hemp!"

He was through the door before the echo died. "Sir?"

"Good suggestion. I do feel better." I shot my cuffs and glared as he opened his mouth to comment. "One word and I cut out your tongue and feed it to Wix."

He closed his mouth, but couldn't keep from smiling.

As I strode past him, he glanced down at my glossy footwear and sighed. "Just *try* to keep those boots clean, sir. Took me *hours* to get the bloodstains out."

"No guarantees on that count." I was going to see Jhavika, after all, and blood was one of her favorite pastimes.

On deck, I ignored the low whistles from my crew at my attire and hailed Miko. "I'm heading up. How's the trading going?"

"Nearly done." She waved at the sparse remainder of crates and barrels on the quay, the rest having vanished as if by magic, levitating up the cargo lifts lining the warehouses to be stuffed away and shipped out or sold to merchant captains to refit their vessels.

"If I'm not back in a couple hours, come looking." I strode down the gangplank and across the quay.

"Keep your boots clean, sir!"

"Always," I replied with a wave. Unlike my steward's comment, Miko's had less to do with preserving my footwear than my life. The streets of Haven were some of the poorest, filthiest, most dangerous places I'd ever seen. No one walked the streets if they didn't have to, not unless they had a death wish.

I had no intention of walking those streets today. Fortunately, I didn't have to.

The former gnomish stronghold was carved right into the rocky shore of Snomish Bay, sheltered on the landward side by an impenetrable mountain range, with seaward access guarded by fortified headlands. From the sea, the city is beautiful; sturdy stone buildings cling to slopes that angle steeply up to sheer cliff faces, and the torrent of White Rock Falls cascading from the mountains, bathing the heights in mist. Get closer, and you see the tangled network of bridges and catwalks connecting the buildings like the blood vessels of a vast beast. Some residents of Haven spend their entire lives without ever touching solid ground.

A stevedore manning one of the cargo lifts opened the gate and waved me aboard. The gnomish contraptions made me nervous, but they were the only way into the city without slogging through the filth-mired streets, which would risk both my life and the wrath of my steward. I handed him two pennies for the ride, and the lift elevated me above the festering underbelly of Haven.

As we rose, we passed the gaping portals of each successive level, giving me glimpses inside. The lowest two floors were actual warehouses, stuffed to the gills with all manner of goods and guarded night and day by grim mercenaries. The next levels housed myriad unsavory inns, flesh houses, and taverns common to most waterfronts. I bypassed more upmarket accommodations and eateries above those, but my destination was yet higher. When the lift jerked to a stop at roof level, I stepped off into a light breeze that wafted beneath taut canvas awnings sheltering shops, cafés, and opium dens. Hawkers cried out the virtues of their wares—colorful cloth and beadwork, silver trinkets and charms, scantily clad slaves of all varieties, spices, soaps, and an endless assortment of food and intoxicants—while pickpockets targeted the intoxicated, distracted, and unwary.

Jhavika's estate was about a mile away as the crow flies, but much farther with the circuitous route I'd be taking. Though wealthy, she wasn't yet a member of the Council of Lords, so she still lived within the city proper and not in one of the exclusive keeps perched upon the cliffs.

After traversing the rooftop without incident, I paused with some trepidation before starting across the first bridge. Strange how I'm entirely comfortable a hundred feet up the rigging of my ship, but Haven's lofty neighborhoods unnerve me. Perhaps it's because nobody tries to push me out of *Scourge's* crow's nest. Gnomish stonemasons evidently didn't believe in guardrails, and a preferred method of assassination in Haven was a careful nudge over the side. I'm well known as Jhavika's business partner, and one of her competitors might try to foil her by eliminating me. I kept a hand on my sword and stayed as far from the edge as possible.

My third traverse was a cable bridge that swayed under my feet. I found the motion oddly comforting, more like a ship than land, and the span sported wrist-thick lines I could grab if someone tried to pitch me over.

By the time I reached Jhavika's walled estate, I was nerve-wracked and slightly footsore. Hemp must have overdone the cleaning of my boots; they were stiff, and I was unused to walking so far. *Scourge's* quarterdeck is only thirty feet by thirty feet and, though I do tend to pace, I don't put in more than about a mile a day.

Unlike most of the bridges, the span to Jhavika's estate is private and protected by a locked gatehouse. I pulled the rope and a bell chimed. The door opened without so much as a "Who goes there?" It didn't surprise me; Jhavika had spies all over the city and undoubtedly knew when we arrived and maybe even when I left the ship to meet with her. My spirits sagged as the door opened to reveal one of my least favorite people in all of Haven.

"Captain Longbright!" Ty-lee's teeth gleamed ivory and gold, his smile far brighter than my arrival warranted. It made me want to mine his mouth for the precious metal with a pair of pliers. Jhavika's steward pressed his palms together and bowed, his topknot wobbling, then gestured me through the door. "You're looking lordly today!"

"And you're looking exactly the same as always, Ty-lee." I stepped through and nodded to the guards dressed in Jhavika's livery. "Your mistress is expecting me, I gather."

"Of course." He closed the door and ushered me onto the cable bridge before him. The narrow span lurched with a motion not unlike the pitching of a small skiff. "She's looking forward to your visit."

"I'll *bet* she is." How not? The two hundred Toki imperials around my waist had her name on them.

"I trust your voyage was successful?" Ty-lee's smile remained undaunted by my sarcasm.

"I'll discuss my successes with *Jhavika*, if you don't mind." I'd be damned to the Abyss before I'd discuss my business with a servant.

His smile wavered, then steadied. "Of course, Captain."

A light rain began to fall, one of the splash-and-dash showers Haven is known for. I quickened my pace, which made the bridge swing and the cables squeak. Ty-lee maintained his position at my side, smile intact, constantly glancing at me. Perhaps that was why I didn't like the man; he always seemed to be staring at me. I tried to ignore him.

The bridge led to a vestibule nestled into the fourth floor of Jhavika's estate, a high-walled stone keep. The entire city was stone, of course, typical gnomish construction, solid as the mountains themselves, but not fit for anyone over four feet tall. Most buildings had been converted by knocking two floors into one and enlarging the doors or gates. Few actual gnomes still lived in Haven, and those that did kept to themselves. I asked one once why Haven had been abandoned by its original residents, and he just stared at me like it wasn't my business. Maybe it isn't.

My point is, though some renovations are shoddy—obvious seams, slap-dash plaster to disguise imperfections, negligent cracks—Jhavika's home was flawless. Not the finest estate in the city by far, but it was both impressive and impregnable. I had to admit that she'd done remarkably well for herself in the short span of years since she moved ashore. To me, it seemed as splendid an estate as any lord could wish for, but Jhavika wanted more. No matter how much she got, she always wanted more.

Ty-lee opened the door and gestured with a short bow. "After you, Captain."

I stepped into the entry chamber. Columns of rose marble cunningly hewn in the likenesses of comely men and women soothed my eyes. Elvish tile smoother then my freshly shaven face brushed the soles of my boots. Silk tapestries, curtained alcoves, porcelain vases filled to overflowing with aromatic blooms in a riot of color and fragrance…an oasis of beauty and peace. It was almost enough to make me forget the cesspool of Haven just outside the door. Almost…

"This way, Captain," Ty-lee waved me down one of the three branching hallways.

As we walked, I wondered if I might one day retire from pirating and move ashore. If I could afford a place like this, it wouldn't be torture, certainly.

We walked down a sweeping stair and a long hallway, stopping before a pair of ornate double doors, blazing white with gilded filigree and gleaming fixtures. Ty-lee opened them without knocking and waved me into the morning room. Floor-to-ceiling windows and glass-paned doors admitted the feeble morning sunlight that struggled through scudding clouds. The doors led onto a wide patio of white marble that overlooked Jhavika's cherished gardens. Today the doors were closed and a merry fire burned in the grating of a cavernous fireplace, giving the room a cozy feel. Artwork and furnishings that would have bought me a new ship if I sold them on the open market graced the walls, tables, and even the floor—a rug of fine Fornician silk that I always hesitated to walk upon.

Jhavika stood with several people near the windows, dressed for business in kidskin breeches, boots, and a blousy shirt of rose-hued silk. As always, her looks disconcerted me—her dark eyes and olive skin suggest Morrgrey heritage, but her honey-gold hair and brows streaked with even lighter highlights were more typical of northern climes—not unattractive, but incongruous. Though rich women paid good money to have their hair dyed a similar shade, I knew that Jhavika's was natural. One slender hand rested idly on the cat-o'-nine-tails at her hip.

Doesn't she ever put that damned thing down? Of its own volition, my hand raised to my face and rubbed my scars.

Jhavika kept the lash as a remembrance of her days at sea, or so she'd told me, though she seemed to have adopted it as a symbol of her authority. She often joked that she had two scourges to enforce her will; I was the other one.

I recognized the finely dressed man she was speaking to, a slave merchant I'd done business with. The other five were slaves. Jhavika looked to be augmenting her household staff.

"Ah, Kevril!" Jhavika smiled at me. "I'll be right with you. Just some domestic business."

"Of course." I turned half away as if to appreciate the view of the gardens, irritated that she obviously knew I was coming, but was making me wait while she conducted such mundane household affairs.

"Ty-lee, bring us some refreshment." She dismissed the butler as easily as she had dismissed me and returned to her business.

I stood with my hands clenched behind my back, facing the rainy gardens but watching Jhavika out of the corner of my eye. She rarely did anything without a purpose and this smacked of a power play. I rocked from my heels to my toes—the phantom motion of the ship lingering beneath my boots—and girded my temper.

"So, Lady Keshmir," the slave merchant continued, "observe the quality of the merchandise I bring you: exquisite stature, perfectly proportioned, fair of face and form without the slightest mark to mar their beauty. The *very* finest."

She's no lady, I thought with an inward smirk. Jhavika might style herself as an up-and-coming power in the Haven hierarchy, but she'd never pass as a fine lady. There would always be a bit of the pirate in her that could never be scrubbed away.

Examining the slaves with a sidelong glance, I had to admit that they were quite fine. Three men and two women, tall and straight, clean-complexioned and well-proportioned. These weren't common house slaves or laborers. I wondered what Jhavika wanted with them.

"As a matter of fact, I *can't* see, Master Heldech." Jhavika paced before the slaves, eying them from head to foot, one hand poised at her chin. "Disrobe them."

"Of course, milady." Heldech ordered the slaves to strip, and they complied without hesitation. Their eyes were cast down, and one fair young man blushed furiously, but they knew better than to protest. "They are well trained, as you can see, and without flaw."

"Can they dance?" Jhavika walked slowly around the five as clothing piled at their feet.

"With the grace of doves in flight, milady." Heldech was laying it on a little thick.

I looked more closely at the poor unfortunates. Two, a man and woman, were dusky skinned and so similar that they might have been siblings. The other three were pale: one red-headed man with barely any body hair, the other man and woman fair-haired. They all bore tattoos denoting the reasons for their slavery: the two fair-haired were criminals, the redhead was a debtor, and the two dusky ones had been convicted of sacrilege. If Jhavika wanted dancers, she was planning to use them for entertainment for herself or her lordly friends. I didn't care—it wasn't my business—but it didn't surprise me. Like the expensive rug beneath my boots, appearances were important to her. Only the best would do.

31

"Which two are the *best* dancers? I want a matched pair, mind you, a man and a woman."

That leaves the redhead out, I thought, turning away.

Ty-lee returned with a crystal decanter of auburn tea and limes. He poured a glassful for me. I added a lump of sugar and sipped it with pleasure, the spicy concoction of herbs and bite of lime redolent of warm summer winds and lush green growth. In truth, it tasted like of my homeland. Tira was blessed with the finest farmlands south of the Bitter Sea, graced by the magic of wood sprites, they say. Sometimes I miss it, but most times not.

Heldech expounded on the grace of the slaves, and Jhavika finally chose the dusky pair. After a short bout of haggling, they settled on a price. Jhavika paid the merchant, and he ordered the slaves to don their clothes.

"Not you two," Jhavika instructed her new purchases, dismissing the others with a flip of her hand. She accepted a glass of tea from Ty-lee. "Stay a moment, Ty-lee. I'll need you to show our new additions to their quarters."

"Of course, milady." He bowed from the waist, palms pressed together, his ivory-gold smile gleaming.

When Heldech had gone, Jhavika plucked the lash from her hip and shook out the thongs. I cringed at the familiar gesture, recalling the sting against my skin. It was a nasty weapon, crafted of the finest leather woven with tiny barbs at the tips of the lashes, made to harm as much as inflict pain.

Flicking the thongs back and forth like a cat might twitch its tail, Jhavika circled her new slaves. "I want to make clear to you that you have nothing to fear from me as long as you do my bidding."

The two stood as if carved from dark stone. Though the woman remained utterly still, but the muscles of the man's jaw clenched. He knew what was coming.

"However, if you stray *once* from performing *exactly* as I say, this will be your punishment." With two flicks as deft as a fencer's thrust and parry, Jhavika lashed the scourge across their bare backsides. The man winced. The woman didn't even flinch.

Jhavika strode around in front of them and held the scourge before their downcast eyes. "If you stray twice, I will personally flay the flesh off your backs with this and sell you to the vilest brothel I can find. Do you understand?"

"Yes, mistress," they both said.

"Good. Now take your clothes and go with Ty-lee. Follow his instructions."

"Yes, mistress." They snatched up their clothes and hurried out, the stripes from Jhavika's lash vivid on their flanks.

When the door closed I found Jhavika staring at me. I didn't care for the look in her eye as she gently swung the scourge. "Do I shock you, Kevril?"

"Shock?" I shrugged as if I didn't care what she did with her whip or her slaves, which I didn't...much. "No. Now put that thing away and let's discuss business."

Jhavika cocked one pale eyebrow, but hung the lash at her hip before striding to the fireplace and picking up a poker. "You took care of *Yellow Blossom* for me?"

"Yes. She was right where you said she'd be, but the cargo was trash. Hemp and muslin. The take was barely enough to cover my costs." I put my glass down and untucked my shirt to unbuckle the money belt. "Here's your cut." I put the belt on the table.

"Hmmm, that's a shame." She didn't even look back at me and didn't sound terribly disappointed.

"It *is* a shame. My crew won't be satisfied with their percentages. They've been hard at it for months now. We need some time ashore or I'm going to have trouble."

"Really?" She turned to me, the poker still in her hand. "I don't recall ever getting a *vacation* when I served aboard *Scourge*."

"I'm not talking about a vacation and you know it. I'm talking about a few days ashore to kick up their heels and spend their money." I stared down her scowl. "I'm *sure* you remember shore leave."

"Yes, I remember shore leave. I also remember months at sea without a decent prize to be had." She stirred the fire, then racked the poker. "I'm handing you prizes every other week and you're *complaining?*"

"We've had no time ashore in more than three *months*, Jhavika. If I don't give them some soon, I'll start losing people."

"I see." She strolled over to the table while sipping her tea and looked down at the money belt. "Things are going well, Kevril, but I need you to do one more mission for me. After that, you can give your people some time off."

"There's *always* one more mission, Jhavika. Give me a week now, then send us out again."

"This one is *important*, Kevril, and it will be lucrative for you."

"All of your missions are important, and you said *Yellow Blossom* would be lucrative. It wasn't."

"Listen to me!" She fixed hard eyes on me. "Lord Balshi is foremost on the council and he's opposing my inclusion. His brother-in-law, Aldaur Nightspinner, captains one of his finest merchantmen. The *Hymoin* left this morning for Mati loaded with spices, silk, and fine wine. Nightspinner takes the usual winter route, using the westerly cape-effect winds off of Sariff Bay to make his southing into the trades. If you leave tonight, you'll be able to catch him before he's across the Blood Sea."

I knew *Hymoin*. She was a fat prize indeed, but that didn't solve my problem. "Jhavika, if I leave tonight, I could have a *mutiny* on my hands by morning."

"Ha! Ridiculous!" The laugh was forced and her knuckles shone white on the lash at her belt. She was angry.

I didn't care. "It's *not* ridiculous. Line up something else in a week or wait until *Hymoin* makes her next run."

"No, Kevril." Jhavika spoke through a smile that bore no humor at all, her voice tight and low. "You will take *Hymoin*, you will kill

Aldaur Nightspinner, and you will put the ship's crew into boats with a message to Balshi letting him know that his political machinations cost his sister her husband. Then you'll take the cargo, pillage the ship for every last penny, and burn her. You will do this as soon as you are able, and you will *not* argue with me about it!"

I opened my mouth to tell her that I certainly *would* argue, but then reconsidered. My partnership with Jhavika *was* lucrative, and if I told her to piss up a rope, it would be over. I'd be looking for my own targets instead of having her hand them to me like treats on a silver platter. The silks and spices that *Hymoin* carried would bring in a good return and, if we left straightaway, we'd only be out a week or so. It made sense. Killing Balshi's brother-in-law might be a mistake, but it was Jhavika's mistake, not mine. Her ascent to the Council of Lords would benefit us both, and she couldn't do it if I didn't help her.

"Fine, but *Scourge* gets some shore time when we get back," I insisted.

"Of course." Jhavika smiled genuinely this time and raised her glass. "Here's to another successful mission."

"To a *quick* and successful mission." I touched my glass to hers, drained it, and put it down. "I'd best get back before I have people jumping ship." I turned to go.

"Kevril?"

I stopped with my hand on the door latch. "Yes?"

Jhavika opened her mouth, then closed it and nodded, waving a finger at my attire. "You look quite dashing in red and black. I like it."

Fat lot of good it did me, I thought, but spurning her compliment would only breed ill will. "Thank you. I should go. Time and tide, you know."

"Safe voyage, Kevril."

I left Jhavika with a long stride, for there truly was no time to lose if I was to catch *Hymoin*. I guess I really shouldn't have been surprised at the outcome. The meeting had gone like all my meetings with Jhavika go; she'd gotten her way. Crossing the span back into Haven, I glared over my shoulder. *How does she* always *convinced me to do things her way?* The question plagued me all the way back to *Scourge*.

Chapter Three
Hard Propositions

Is it better to whip the mule or tempt the mule with a carrot?
Whip him and he will kick. Tempt him and he will expect
reward for breathing.
The Lessons of Quen Lau Ush

From the diary of Kevril Longbright –
I despised Captain Kohl with a passion. We all did. Why he
wasn't stabbed in the back is a mystery to me. But then, after
a fashion, he was. I took a hard lesson the day he died, for
when the trap was sprung, not a jack or jane aboard leapt to
his defense. Never be a tyrant, I tell myself. Discipline is one
thing, sadism is another. Even a beaten cur will bite
eventually.

During the walk back to the quay, my temper percolated like a
pot of blackbrew simmering on the stove too long, more bitter and
acidic with every step. By the time I boarded the lift to be lowered
down to the quay, I was cursing Jhavika and muttering to myself.
Partnership, my arse. She was treating me like one of her house
slaves, a rented mule to be whipped without mercy. *So why didn't you*

tell her to stick that lash up her ass and walk away, Kevril? That was the question that vexed me beyond reason. *If you don't like her orders, sail away and pick your own targets!*

The trouble was, she was right about one thing; piracy was a dangerous and often sparse existence without a port like Haven to come back to. If I thwarted Jhavika and she *did* eventually claim a seat on the council, Haven could well be closed to me. A pirate had to sell plunder somewhere, and there were few ports as well-suited as this one. Only here would merchants meet ships at the dock and buy illicit cargo with no questions and ready gold. There was no formal government to tax me, no barons or kings to send constables or soldiery, no navy to dodge, and no harbormasters to bribe.

Haven was perfect.

So I had to do as Jhavika said or settle for less than perfect. Unfortunately, she knew that, too, and it put me over a barrel.

So quit bitching about it and do your job, Kevril. It's not like you're starving here! I stepped out of the lift onto the quay and strode for my ship, determined to make the best of the situation.

"So, *that* didn't go well, I see."

I glared at Miko as I traversed the gangplank. She was reading my mind again, and half the deck crew were lingering nearby to catch our conversation. There was no dodging this and only one way to deal with a disgruntled crew.

"We sail on the evening tide, Miko. We'll be out for a week to ten days. Make sure we have enough fresh provisions and water." I turned for the sterncastle.

"Captain! We need some time ashore!" There was a burr in her voice I didn't like. "The crew's been—"

I whirled, my hand clenched on the hilt of my cutlass. "I don't want to hear it!" The faces of the crew were grim, some outright belligerent. I pointed to the gangplank. "We've a fat prize waiting for us a four-day sail away. Follow my orders or get off my ship, but if *any* of you walks down that gangplank, you'll not be walking back aboard, *ever!*"

Miko glanced down at my white-knuckled grip on my sword and closed her mouth. She nodded once and touched her forehead with one knuckle. "Aye, sir."

I raked the deck with a glare and not one pair of eyes lingered on mine. "Six hours and we're under way."

"Aye, sir." Miko turned and waved a hand in a broad arc. "Wix, six hours."

"Aye, sir!" Wix turned and drew a deep breath as a prelude to his bellow. "You heard the captain! Six hours! Provisions and water! Move your salty arses or I'll cut a new butt-crack in 'em!"

I turned away and strode for my cabin. I'd barely doffed my dress jacket and shirt before there was a knock on the door.

"Come in." I'd expected Hemp coming to take care of my clothes before I managed to soil them, but it was Miko. I snorted a laugh and pulled on a plain shirt. "So, are they abandoning ship like rats from a flaming hulk?"

"No, sir." She cleared her throat. "We may lose a couple, but no one I'd give a damn about."

"Well, that's something, anyway." I tucked in my shirt and reached for my jacket. "Then what is it?"

"I need to talk to you about this situation, sir." Miko's voice was controlled, her stance exact, her hands behind her back. That was bad. She gets all formal when she's really upset.

"Am I facing a mutiny, then?"

"Not right away, sir, but things aren't good. Wix'll keep them in line for a while longer, but we can't keep at this without a break. Three months without more than a day ashore is asking too much. They'll not go on without some leisure. There's no point to pirating if you can't spend your pay."

"Exactly my words to Jhavika, but she said this mission was important and I agreed with her. I asked her to put it off a week, and she said no." I shrugged. "End of argument."

"Yes, sir, but…" Miko sighed and shook her head. "Can I ask you one question without being put ashore for being insolent?"

"*One* question?" I cocked an eyebrow at her. Was she really thinking I'd kick the only decent officer I had off *Scourge*? "Ask as many as you like, Miko. I need you, and you know it."

"Yes, sir." She took a deep breath. "Are you fucking her or something?"

"Jhavika?" My jaw dropped and I barked another laugh. Nothing could have been further from my mind. We'd had a few tumbles back when we were junior officers together, but that had been nothing more than an intermittent physical attraction. Truth be told, it had been something to do when we were bored. Trying to kill each other after the captain's death had put a damper on any potential ardor, as well. "No, I'm not fucking Jhavika. Why would you think so?"

"Because it's like she's got you by the balls or something!" Miko shook her head again, looking honestly puzzled. "I can't figure out why you jump whenever she says 'frog'. Is she blackmailing or threatening you?"

"No and no, but you have to understand something. If I tell Jhavika to take a flying leap off her balcony, we'll be looking for our *own* targets, and might not have Haven to come back to." I fixed my first mate with a steady stare. "Hunting merchantmen off the isles of Toki or in the North Sea Reaches doesn't leave a lot of time for shore leave either. Our take would probably be cut to a third of what we're making now, and we'd have three different navies hunting us as well. Yes, we're being pushed hard, but too much work is far better than none."

"I understand that, sir." Miko shook her head again. "But Jhavika was a pirate once. Surely she understands we need time off."

"Yes, she understands, and she said we could have time ashore when we get back from this run." I hung up my dress cutlass and pulled down my old one. "It *is* a fat prize, by the way."

"Oh?" She arched one dark eyebrow. "How fat?"

"The *Hymoin*. She's reaching for Mati as we speak, loaded with silks and spices."

"That's Balshi's pride and joy," Miko said, her eyes squinting in a mixture of avarice and suspicion. "They'll be armed and wary."

I nodded. "Commanded by Balshi's brother-in-law and loaded to the gunnels with the best he can buy." I shrugged. "Balshi's been blocking Jhavika's ascension to the Council of Lords, and she's had enough. She wants me to make his sister a widow."

"*Kill* his brother-in-law?" Her suspicion doubled. "That's a dangerous ploy."

"But it's *her* ploy, not ours. We send *Hymoin*'s crew off in boats with a message from Jhavika, just like we did with *Yellow Blossom*. Then we take every last bale, barrel, crate, and fitting off that ship and burn her."

"And she doesn't think Balshi will retaliate?"

"I don't *know* what Jhavika thinks, Miko. Maybe she's trying to draw Balshi into an open confrontation. Maybe he doesn't like his brother-in-law and asked her to have him killed and make it look like piracy. Maybe dragons will lay eggs in the bilge and we'll all ride the hatchlings into the sunset!" I slapped my arms against my sides in frustration. "Speculating about Jhavika's motives is pointless, but you can take one bet and double down on it—she's as ambitious a woman as I've ever known, and she won't stop until she's either dead or the queen of Haven."

"And if she gets us killed in the process?"

"We're *pirates*, Miko. Since when is that a safe profession?"

"Good point." She bit her lip. "But the crew…"

"Yes, the crew. Don't think I didn't argue with her on that score, Miko, but she was adamant and I could only go so far."

"Can I tell them we'll have time off after this run, sir?"

"Yes, and sweeten it with this." I went to my cabinet, retrieved a pouch of spending money, and tossed it to Miko. "Buy a cask of Highland Dragonspit for them and tap it once we're in the offing. We won't find *Hymoin* for three days at least. That'll give them time to sleep it off."

"Good idea, sir." She touched the pouch to her forehead and turned for the door, but then turned back. "Answer me one more question first."

"Sure."

"Why can't you tell Jhavika to fuck off?"

I opened my mouth to answer, then realized that I didn't have one. "I don't know, Miko. She's just... It always seems like she's *right*, I guess. It's hard to argue with her when she lays it all out like sums in a purser's account book."

"That's what worries me, sir. It's not *her* as much as it's *you*." She shrugged and frowned. "I've never known you to *always* agree with *anyone*."

"I don't *always* agree with Jhavika. I just have to weigh the cost of *disagreeing* with her, and that cost is getting too big to pay."

"Too *costly* to disagree with?" Miko looked at me like I'd just told her I'd traded my testicles for a pair of dream crystals. "That makes her one *dangerous* woman, sir."

"There's no doubt of that." I waved her out, wondering after the door closed why I didn't have a better answer.

There's something to be said for drunken sea chanties. They serve one purpose, to raise your spirits. This they accomplish through sheer disregard for key, melody, rhyme, and meter by those drunk enough to sing them properly. It is absolutely impossible to be downcast when a sea chanty is being sung with all heart and soul by properly inebriated sailors.

Consequently, my spirits had risen since we'd sailed into the offing and set a course two points west of south. I was on watch and therefore sober as a magistrate on sentencing day, but I could appreciate the bawdy disregard of my crew as they belted out verse after chorus of "The Bald White Whore of Hiko."

Snickers broke out at the helm station from Boxley and Quiff, the midshipman assigned to steer. As the crew broke into the verse about the phallus of a ship's cook being substituted for a longboat's tiller, the two elbowed each other and giggled.

Scourge veered to leeward.

"Eyes on the compass card, Mister Quiff, or I'll nail your nose to the binnacle!"

"Aye, captain!" Quiff knew by my tone that the threat wasn't serious, but he paid closer attention, and *Scourge* steadied back on course. He was a good-natured lad, albeit prone to laziness and definitely not the sharpest sword in the armory.

I listened to the off-key singing, watched the capering youngsters, and could not for the life of me suppress a smile. We were at sea. That, for me, more than riches or power or a noble title, meant freedom. My crew was at least temporarily happy, and we were sailing on a broad reach in brisk winds hunting a fat prize. I was lord of my own fiefdom girded by four-inch planks below and canvas above, and I wouldn't have traded it for Jhavika's fancy estate, her money, or her lordly friends.

The ship's bell tolled eight notes, and I checked my pocket watch. Time for the midnight watch change. As if by some wizard's conjuration, Miko strode up the stairs to the quarterdeck, teeth gleaming white in the darkness. She sketched a salute and glanced at Boxley at the helm in passing.

"Captain."

"Miko." I nodded and grinned like an idiot as the crew broke into the verse about the gull's egg and the water spout. "Quite a row from forward."

"Aye, they're in high spirits." She gave me a wink. "A wise choice on the cask of Dragonspit."

"I do have a good notion occasionally." I stretched and looked up at the few stars and the moon visible through the scudding clouds. "Shall we try for a moon sighting? Unless my watch is fast, she'll peak soon."

"Yes, sir." Miko fetched the ship's sextant from the deck locker and began sighting the moon with it.

I sat down on the bench locker with my back to the mizzen mast. In the light of the oil lamp I looked to my pocket watch, pulling the pin and moving the hands. The watch was about as accurate as a blind marksman, so I set it whenever I can. I had our position fairly well fixed by dead reckoning, and my almanac provided the adjustments for the time when the moon would be highest.

"Time?"

"Still rising…" Miko stood like a statue, eye fixed to the sextant and the moon.

I waited.

"There, sir! She's peaked!"

"Set." I pressed the pin and my watch started back up. "You shoot and I'll mark."

I pulled a lap desk and notebook from the bench locker and sharpened a pencil with my boot dagger. Without a timepiece that can maintain its accuracy aboard a lurching ship—something even the gnomes haven't perfected yet—we could only estimate our east-west position. Latitude was a simpler affair; the angle of the Pole Star would give us our distance south of the equator. I'd been doing these calculations for three decades now and could run the numbers in my sleep.

"Aye, sir." Miko strode to the taffrail and raised the sextant to her eye. "Pole Star, on my mark."

"Ready." I kept my eyes on the face of my watch.

"Mark!" Miko said, and I marked the time on the log as she read the dials on the instrument. "Fifty-eight degrees, twelve seconds."

"Got it." I glanced at the helm out of habit. Quiff was studiously ignoring us, probably due to his inability to grasp the rudimentary mathematics required for navigation and afraid I'd quiz him on it. Boxley, however, sported a lively look of interest. I thought about Miko's doting on the girl, the sorry state of the midshipmen's berth, and made a snap decision. "Boxley, have you ever handled a sextant?"

Her eyes widened like I'd caught her dipping into the ship's grog. "Um, *no*, sir!"

"Mister Quiff, do you think you can manage the helm alone for a few minutes?"

"Of course, sir!" The little git shot a glare at Boxley that might have earned him a black eye if she'd noticed. Quiff was a head taller than Boxley, but I wouldn't have given him odds in a fight with her.

"Good. Miko, please show Boxley how the sextant works and help her shoot the moon. Also explain how we set the time at peak."

"Happily, Captain!" Miko grinned and motioned the girl over.

I waited several minutes while Miko showed the girl the basic operation of the sextant, how to sight a heavenly body, align the image in the mirror with the horizon, and read the angle. I caught another glare from Quiff as he manned the helm. With four midshipmen already, adding Boxley would certainly shake things up. They would give her hell, but if anyone aboard could dish hell back on a silver platter, I felt that Boxley could. Still, elevating Boxley from the deck to midshipman would have to be done carefully. Ideally, one of the four current mids would pass for lieutenant soon, but none of them showed much promise.

"Mark!" Boxley cried out, grinning like an idiot, which she most certainly was not.

"Good, now read the dials," Miko coached.

"Thirty-two degrees, six minutes, and...um...twelve seconds, sir!" Her grin widened until I thought her face would split.

"Got it!" Of course, I didn't need the information, but I checked my almanac and deemed her reading quite close. "Back to the helm with you now, Boxley." I continued my calculations. I was halfway through when Miko sidled up next to me and leaned down as if to inspect my work.

"Thank you, sir," she whispered.

Chris A. Jackson

"Thank me when she makes the grade, Miko," I whispered back, finishing up my calculations. "Just make *damned* sure she doesn't murder one of my midshipmen. They're liable to give her a hard time."

"She won't stab anyone." She gave me a grin and a nod. "Well, not *lethally*."

"All right, then start teaching her." I wasn't fooling Miko by making like I didn't know she was already schooling the girl, but aboard a ship that which is known isn't always openly discussed. There were proper ways to elevate someone from the lower decks. "She's got to read and write legibly before we put a jacket on her and bring her aft of the foremast. With a full midshipmen's berth, we could have—"

"I did *not*!"

At Boxley's cry, *Scourge* veered off the wind. I looked up from my calculations to see Geit lying on the deck clutching his crotch. Quiff and another midshipman, Rauley, were dragging Boxley off the groaning Geit. Meanwhile, the wheel spun free.

"The helm!" I abandoned my lap desk and lurched up, but Miko was already on her feet and quicker.

Quiff released his hold on Boxley and reached for the spinning wheel. A spoke cracked his wrist, eliciting a yelp, and Quiff clutched his hand. Miko snatched the wheel a moment later and heaved back to starboard, but it was too late. The spanker jibed hard, something overhead parted with a hard *snap*, and the sail tore from luff to leech just below the gaff. I grabbed the mizzen sheet and hauled it in. The topping lift kept the boom from crashing to the deck, but the spanker flapped and flagged as we jibed back on course.

I cleated the mizzen sheet and grabbed the gaff halyard. We weren't flying the gaff topsail, thank Odea, so I slacked the halyard as fast as I could without tearing the flesh from my palms. Two sailors dashed past to gather the falling canvas. When the gaff reached the boom, they lashed it down. I tied off the halyard and turned to the helm.

46

Miko and Quiff were on the wheel, the latter favoring his injured wrist, while Geit still lay on the deck clutching his groin. Rauley held Boxley by the shoulders, but she wasn't fighting him much. Her eyes were spitting daggers down at Geit.

The sea chanties had fallen silent.

"What in Odea's tits is going on here?" Before I got an answer, Wix stormed up the steps from the middeck with mayhem and murder written all over his face.

"Torn fookin' sail! Helm fookin' abandoned! I'll have the hide off the lot of you!" He grabbed Geit by the collar of his jacket and jerked him to his feet, though the young man didn't seem capable of standing upright quite yet. "Stand up *straight*, you little—"

"Master Wix, hold fast and let me get to the bottom of this." I raked the midshipmen and Boxley with a glare. "First things first! Mister Quiff, you left your post at the helm and are responsible for damaging my ship. Why did you abandon your duty?"

"It's Boxley's fault, sir! She kicked Geit right square in the nuts! I *had* to help!"

"Breaking up a scuffle is not sufficient reason to leave the helm unattended!" I gritted my teeth and turned to my volatile ship's brat. "Boxley, did you kick Mister Geit in the testicles?"

"I did that, sir!"

"Why?"

"'Cause I didn't have my knife to *gut* him!"

"Be glad that you didn't. Gutting a superior officer is a bit more serious than a kick to the testicles. Now, *why* did you assault him?"

"He said…" Her eyes flicked to mine, then to Miko at the wheel, then down. "…something bad."

"What *exactly* did he say?"

"He…" She swallowed hard and straightened, obviously trying to master her temper. "Mister Quiff told them I'd just used the sextant, and Mister Geit asked me…what I…did to get to do that."

"What you *did*?" I looked to Geit, who had finally managed to stand on his own. I knew from his face that I wasn't going to get a straight answer from him. "Mister Rauley, you seem to be the only person here that I can't find a reason to fault in this debacle. If you wish to remain so, you'll tell me *word* for *word* what Mister Geit said to Boxley."

"Yes, sir." He stiffened, looked to Geit, then back to me. "He asked Boxley if she sucked your dick or licked Miko's crotch to get to be your favorite, sir."

A low growl rumbled in Wix's chest, and Geit's face drained of color in the lamplight. My own simmering temper threatened to boil over, and Miko looked ready to kill the young man for the implication. I clamped my rage and made a decision.

"This may be a pirate ship, but there will be *discipline* aboard or I will drag the offenders behind the ship for fish bait! Is that understood?" They all nodded and muttered agreement. "Master Wix, Boxley will receive ten strokes with a rope's end for striking a superior officer."

"Aye, sir." Wix snapped his fingers and pointed to the deck beside him.

Boxley saluted me and said, "Thank you, sir," before taking her place. She knew it could have been twenty with a lash instead.

"Mister Quiff, you left your post for no good reason, which resulted in damage to the mizzen and risked much more." The young man swallowed and nodded. "You'll receive ten lashes well marked, and you will, under Master Wix's direction, repair the spanker stitch by stitch. You will not eat, sleep, or rest until that job is done to his satisfaction."

"Yes, sir!" Quiff looked miserable, but knew he deserved every inch of that punishment.

"Mister Geit!" I took a step closer and glared into the unruly midshipman's face. "Unfortunately, an out-of-earshot comment to a ship's brat that disparages both the captain and the first mate in the same breath is *not* a punishable offense." His face brightened, but I wasn't finished. "*However*, the implication that *anyone* can garner favor from an officer of this ship in the manner you suggested is unforgivable. If I learned of such a vile action, the perpetrator would be keel-hauled in a full gale. I will *not* have the suggestion that this has occurred voiced aloud, even in jest, aboard *my* ship." I took another step forward until our noses were a hand-span apart. "Do you *understand* me, Mister Geit?"

His eyes flicked to Miko, then to Boxley, then lowered. "I understand *perfectly*, sir." He said it through clenched teeth, and I knew that he did actually believe what he'd said to Boxley. It wasn't true, of course, but even the rumor of it would damage morale.

"You will go to the foremast topgallant yard and stay there until I summon you. You will not come down for watch changes, to take meals, or to relieve yourself. You will keep a sharp eye out, and you will report any and all sightings to the foretop crow's nest lookout. If that lookout spots anything before you do, your tenure on the topgallant yard will be extended by a half day."

He swallowed, and hatred flickered in his eyes. "Yes, *sir*."

"Get out of my sight."

"Sir!" He saluted and hurried forward.

"Mister Rauley, man the helm. Master Wix, carry out the punishments after breakfast. See that Mister Quiff knows what to do."

"Aye, sir!" He shoved Boxley forward and gathered up Quiff in one meaty hand. "C'mere my lovely, and tell me where you want your stripes while I teach you a little stitchery."

"Miko, walk with me." I turned and strode aft.

Miko joined me at the leeward taffrail. I stood for a moment staring out at the dark sea, deciding how to ask her the impossible question, but once again, she read my mind.

"It didn't happen, sir. You know it didn't."

"I know." I'd known the moment I saw the open rage on her face when Rauley related the incident. "But I needed to hear you say it. Thank you."

"I'm sorry, sir. It's partly my fault. I *have* been playing favorite with Boxley, teaching her a few things. She's smart as a whip and tough as nails. She's got *real* potential." It all came out in a rush.

"I know, and there's no problem with nurturing that potential, but it *has* to be done in the open so everyone can see there's nothing…like that going on." I looked at her and she nodded. "Lucky she didn't have a knife."

"Yes, it is. I told her not to carry one, that she was safe from rapists aboard *Scourge*."

"She *is*!" I clapped my first mate on the shoulder. "Don't worry. If she's half as tough as I think she is, this won't set her back."

Her eyebrows shot up. "You still want me to teach her?"

"Of course!" I laughed loud enough for Geit to hear from the foremast. "I'm not likely to let a slip of a girl willing to kick a grown man in the nuts to defend *my* honor go by the board."

Miko smiled. "Thank you, sir."

"Thank me when she passes for midshipman." I started forward. "I'm going to my bunk. I'll be up by the morning watch to supervise the punishment. See that Wix knows I don't want any permanent damage to either of them."

"What about Geit?" His name dripped like venom from her lips. Maybe she thought I let him off too easy.

I stopped, glanced back at her, and then looked up at the foremast. "Let him *rot* up there for all I care."

"At least we agree on *that*, sir."

Chapter Four
Surprise Cargo

The only thing sure in combat is that it will not go as planned.
The Lessons of Quen Lau Ush

From the diary of Kevril Longbright –
I always wonder at myself, a pirate who doesn't care for violence. I know people who delight in mayhem so much that I wonder if they're sane, and others who shy from it to the point of utter cowardice. I dislike violence, perhaps, because I've been on the receiving end far too many times. I can tolerate pain better than most, but there's something unsettling about facing a man or woman and knowing to the depths of your bowels that the next three seconds will end with one of you dead.

Three days later the prevailing north-westerlies waned; Midshipman Giet was down from the foremast, suffering from thirst, hunger, and exposure, but contrite; our spanker was repaired; both Quiff and Boxley had recovered from their punishment— Boxley had born hers without so much as a whimper, put her shirt back on, and reported for duty five minutes later; Seriff Bay had opened to starboard; and we caught first sight of our quarry.

"Sail off the port bow! Hull down, flying all plain sail."

"Strike the topgallants and flying jib, Master Wix. We need to keep our profile down." I looked around the quarterdeck as Wix ordered the topcrew aloft. Rauley manned the helm alongside my youngest midshipman, a lass named Kivan who could do navigational calculations in her head, but would shirk duty at any provocation. I often thought if I could take all four of my mids, wad them up into one fleshy mass, and wring out the crap, I'd have one decent officer. "Rauley, take a glass to the fore topgallant and tell me what you see. We're looking for *Hymoin*, a three-masted junk."

"Aye, sir." He took up a spyglass from the deck locker and dashed forward to clamber up the foremast ratlines.

Kivan immediately began to struggle with the wheel. She was as skinny as a split rail, but as stubborn as a mule, too. *Scourge* wanted to round up as her topgallants were furled. I wondered if Kivan would tell me she was having trouble before the ship veered to windward or wait until it was too late. I watched Rauley climb and ignored her. *Just one more lesson...* Sometimes I think I should have been a tutor for rich nobles who wanted their snot-nosed children to learn the rudiments of mathematics and navigation. No doubt I could make a living at it, but I would probably cut my own throat inside a year.

Rauley took up position where Geit had spent the last seventy-two hours and peered forward. "I have her, sir! Three masts, but I can't see her transom. She's heading maybe three points south of west."

"Picking up the cape effect off Sariff Bay already," I thought aloud.

From her course and position, I would have bet the ship was *Hymoin*, but there was no way to be sure until we were closer. Unfortunately, striking our topgallants would cost us a knot or two. *Scourge* was faster than any slug of a junk sailing the Blood Sea, but *Hymoin* was a fine ship and had just picked up at least ten knots of wind that we wouldn't encounter for another two hours. I had to close the gap before dark to make sure it was *Hymoin*, but couldn't fly anything above topsails. There was only one solution.

"Rig studdingsails on the courses, Wix! We need another two knots out of her."

"Aye, Captain! You heard the man, studdingsail booms out of the fookin' hold or I'll ram the fookin' things right up yer arses!" The crew responded to Wix's colorful encouragement, rigging the slim booms outboard of the main and forecourse yards. The light sails billowed and caught the wind, heeling the ship over another strake.

"She's griping, sir," Kivan said, now having to brace her slim shoulder to the spokes of the wheel to keep the ship from rounding up.

About damn time. "Wix, send me someone to help on the helm!"

"Aye, sir! Camoin, get yer arse aft and lend Mister Kivan a hand on the wheel."

The seaman ran aft and took station beside my midshipman. She stopped struggling and heaved a relieved breath.

Learn anything today, Kivan? I waited until the ship settled, then ordered, "Tofi, Boxley, run the log."

The two leapt to comply, pulling the knotted string and minute-glass from the deck locker and dashing to the leeward rail. Tofi pitched the weighted disk over the side and called, "Run!" when the first knot passed his hand. Boxley flipped the glass and watched until the last grain fell, then shouted, "Stop!" Tofi pinched the line and measured back to the nearest knot. "Ten and a half, sir!"

"Thank you! That will do nicely, Wix. There's not a junk on the sea that can match that in less than a gale."

"Too fookin' right you are, sir!" Wix's grin scattered sailors like leaves on the wind.

"Sir?" Miko climbed the steps to the quarterdeck rubbing her eyes. "Is she *Hymoin*?"

"We don't know yet, but we're closing." I looked her over. "You look beat. Hit your bunk. We won't know for at least an hour and won't close to striking distance until well after dark."

"Aye, sir." She saluted and headed for her bunk.

One trait all true sailors share is the ability to sleep whenever they can and wake up quickly. Miko and I were the only two senior officers aboard, so we stood watch-and-watch whenever course, speed, weather, or any other hazards warranted. The schedule took its toll, which was one reason I was so disgruntled with my midshipmen's berth. *Scourge* could use one or two competent lieutenants, and had in years past sported as many as four. Attrition due to injury, illness, and one case of falling ass-over-tea-kettle in love, had whittled us down to just Miko, and I'd burn in all Nine Hells before I'd promote one of the four current candidates to lieutenant before they were ready.

I paced the quarterdeck as the afternoon wore on. Hemp brought me blackbrew and biscuits, and I drank and ate because I knew I should. Finally, when the sun was halfway to the horizon and my patience was wearing thin, Rauley called down that our chase was showing her upper transom as she topped the swells.

"Strike tops'ls, Wix. We're close enough and showing too high a profile. We'll rig black sails and crack on after dark."

"Aye, sir." He shouted orders and the topcrews started drawing in the topsails.

I grabbed the ship's best spyglass from the quarterdeck locker and told my midshipman, "Mind the helm, Mister Kivan. I'm going to have a look from the foretop. If you round her up while I'm aloft, I'll be *very* cross indeed."

"Aye, sir."

I tucked the spyglass in my belt and made my way forward, then up the foremast ratlines. The topcrew was still busy furling, but greeted me in passing, some even risking a fall by saluting. Morale, it seemed, wasn't so bad after all.

At the topgallant yard, I threw a leg around the mast and drew my spyglass. "Where away, Rauley?"

"Two points port bow, sir." He pointed and nearly lost his grip.

"Easy now, lad. One hand for the ship and one hand for yourself." I wrapped an arm around the pennant staff and brought my spyglass to bear. The pyramid of canvas shone clearly, then the hull rose atop a swell, leaving a broad, foaming wake. I waited for a set of swells to peak before I saw her transom clearly. I couldn't read the name placard, but I recognized *Hymoin*'s ornate sternpost lanterns and arched windows. "That's our prize, Rauley. Well done. Back on deck with you. We'll watch from the crow's nest from now on."

"Thank you, sir." He smiled and hurried down.

I followed at a leisurely pace, enjoying the exercise. Of course, I had tar streaks on my trousers and shirt when I returned to the quarterdeck. Hemp would give me three shades of hell for it, but I didn't care. I felt the age-old elation that only comes when a chase is in sight.

"Wix, that's our prize. We pace her until dark, then bend every sail she'll bear. Keep a sharp eye on her; we can't lose her now."

"Aye, sir!"

The deck crew let out an impromptu cheer. They felt it, too.

The chase was on.

"Couldn't ask for better timing, sir," Miko hissed in my ear. "An hour after moonset and we just lost the swell behind Red Cape. Odea must have started listening to you or something."

"Or Jhavika's smarter than either of us give her credit for."

"Nobody's *that* smart." Miko made a warding sign that would have cost her a finger for blasphemy in Toki.

I raised my spyglass and watched *Hymoin* grow larger by the second. The junk had lost much of her speed as the cape-effect winds that had sped her along through most of the night diminished in the lee of Red Cape. *Scourge*, a much lighter ship than the beamy junk, and unladen to boot, made better way in the lighter air. We were bearing down on her fast and they still hadn't shown any sign of spotting us. The glow of the city of Sariff had just vanished behind the cape, rendering starlight and our quarry's own lamps all the brighter. *Hymoin*'s stern gallery windows were lit, and running lamps shone high on the mainmast.

Hymoin turned two points to starboard, bringing the lighter winds onto her beam as she reached for her destination: Mati. The sea between the isle of Ton Chi and the continent was a busy stretch of water, Mati being the gateway to the empire of Tira and the last real city before the Leviathan Reaches and the Great Circle Sea to the south. Consequently, and much to my advantage, most ships cruised with lights at night to avoid collisions.

We were actually *planning* a collision, albeit a soft one.

"Ready port-side fenders and grapples, Miko. Let's try not to splinter *Scourge* too badly, shall we?"

"Got to keep the carpenter busy, sir." She grinned at my well-known dislike for scratching my ship.

"Fine. I'll take the repairs out of *your* percentage." She snorted a soft laugh, knowing I wasn't serious. "On your way forward, tell Wix to make damn sure we're secure once we board. The last thing we need is to get separated." Being stranded aboard *Hymoin* with nobody to manage *Scourge* but my inept midshipmen would be disastrous. The little ingrates might get the notion to sail off and leave me.

"Aye, sir." Miko saluted and hurried forward to join her boarding party, her boarding pike at the ready.

I glanced aloft to make sure my two squads of archers, each commanded by one of my midshipmen, were ready in the crow's nests. I'd put Rauley at the helm with Tofi, with Boxley standing ready to assist. The mid couldn't manage to grasp navigation, but he had a deft hand at the wheel. And yes, I'm a sentimental git and try to keep my youngsters out of the fray. They'd have plenty of opportunities to get killed later in life.

"A point to starboard, please, Mister Rauley. I'd rather not put our bowsprit through their transom." I suppressed the urge to take the helm myself.

"Aye, sir." *Scourge* edged to starboard.

I glanced at my squad of boarders, a score of seasoned pirates armed to the teeth—those who had teeth—and ready for mayhem. I wiped the sweat from my palms. The moments just before a fight are always the worst for me. This was not likely to be as bloodless an engagement as *Yellow Blossom* had been. Such a prize as *Hymoin* crossing the Blood Sea would be armed and wary. They'd put up a fight.

"Ready, boys and girls?" I asked.

They murmured assent, hands on weapons and grapples. Hemp stood among them, crossbow at the ready, probably more intent on keeping me from damaging my clothing than killing anyone.

I gauged the angle again and deemed it good. Rauley was grinning at the helm. Maybe he'd make a better pilot than officer; it required fewer mathematical calculations, and he seemed to be enjoying himself.

Hymoin was barely a ship-length away when a cry of, "Ship astern! Black sails!" went up from her poop deck.

"We've been spotted!" Miko bellowed from forward.

"Shit!" I leapt up to the railing and grasped the mizzen shroud, leaning out for a better view. A figure moved in *Hymoin*'s stern gallery windows, and several more on the lofty poop deck. One shouted something unintelligible and waved to leeward. "She'll veer to port, Rauley. Cut them off!" The last thing I wanted was a downwind chase. It would give *Hymoin*'s crew time to arm themselves and mount a coordinated defense.

"Aye, Captain!" Rauley hauled the wheel to port, and *Scourge* veered with an agility that no junk could match.

"Starboard boarding," I called out forward.

"To starboard, you fookin' scallywags!" Wix roared, and the crew surged from one rail to the other.

The junk's tactic to veer downwind made sense; they couldn't point to windward worth a damn, and *Scourge* had the weather gauge, a distinct advantage that meant we could dictate the engagement. My choice to give up that advantage, veering hard across their stern to come up on her leeward side, was reckless, desperate, and, best of all, unexpected. It would get us aboard quickly, but risked a hard collision with a much heavier ship.

"Mind their transom, Mister Rauley!"

"I'm on it, sir!"

Once again, I clenched my teeth and resisted the urge to take the wheel. A captain has to show confidence in his young officers, after all. I breathed a sigh of relief as our bowsprit cleared *Hymoin*'s shiny windows by a good twenty feet. Rauley brought us into their lee, then, as *Hymoin* veered away in panic, hauled the wheel back to starboard before I could even give the order. The two ships came up into the wind and lost speed, our starboard rail barely fifteen feet from *Hymoin*'s port rail.

"*Damn* fine job, Mister Rauley! Grapnels away!" I heard a buzz and felt a tug at my jacket. Someone had shot at me. They were playing for keeps. "Archers!"

Thirty stout hooks sailed across the gap, and pirates hauled madly on the ropes while our archers raked *Hymoin*'s deck to keep her crew from cutting the lines. Wix bellowed orders to haul and make fast, and the two ships came together with a staggering crunch. I should have ordered fenders on both sides. The carpenter would have some work do to after all.

"Boarders away!" I leapt the narrow gap and clambered over *Hymoin*'s higher rail onto their quarterdeck.

Two sailors lay on the deck with arrow wounds. A third thrust a boarding pike at my face. That was a sign of a novice or someone too frightened to remember to aim for the center of mass. I ducked under the weapon and slashed him across both thighs. I could have gutted him just as easily, but we weren't out to slaughter everyone. He dropped the weapon and went down screaming and clutching his legs.

A man in a jacket with gold braid on the cuffs dashed up the steps to the quarterdeck, several more sailors at his heels. "Do you know who I am, you bloody pirate?" The officer drew a cutlass and dagger, his face a rictus of rage.

"Well met, Captain Nightspinner." I saluted with a flourish and remembered Jhavika's command...*You will kill Aldaur Nightspinner.* Orders are orders...and it wouldn't be the first time I killed at her behest. "Lady Keshmir sends her regards."

His eyes widened, then narrowed. "That *bitch*!" He brandished his weapons and advanced. "After I take your head, my wife's brother will—"

Something buzzed past my ear, and Captain Nightspinner's head snapped back. He fell with a crossbow bolt buried to the fletching in his eye.

I looked back as Hemp lowered his weapon. "Bugger might have cut up your fine jacket, sir." He shrugged. "Teach him to marry for money anyways, it will."

"Enough!" I whirled and leveled my cutlass at the rest of the sailors facing us. "Your captain is dead! Don't be fools. We're not here to slaughter, but to send your lord a message!"

They stopped and looked dubious. That was all the incentive I needed.

"Drop your weapons or die!" I bellowed. A glance forward confirmed that little resistance remained anyway. "Your captain has paid for his foolishness with his life! Don't make the same mistake! We'll set you off in boats if you lay down arms. Fight us, and you'll feed the sharks!"

That was enough. First one, then several more sailors dropped their weapons and backed away from the fight with their hands raised. The eyes of the rest glittered with doubt—except for those facing Wix, which widened with stark terror. Weapons drooped, then clattered to the deck.

A sweeter sound I've never heard.

"Master Wix, secure their weapons and line them up amidships! Their wounded, too!" The deck shuddered beneath my boots as *Scourge*'s cap rail ground against *Hymoin*'s thick timbers. "And slash their sheets. We're starting to roll in the trough and we've no fenders out."

"Aye, sir!" Wix waved his boarders forward and inspected the bloody spikes of his dagger guards with a grin. "Nice little tussle!"

"Miko! Take your squad and search from forward. I'll search aft."

"Aye, sir!" She waved and grinned.

I turned back and called over to my own quarterdeck. "Heave us to, Mister Rauley, and call the archers down to help with the cargo. Oh, and rig some fenders!"

"Aye, sir!" The young man grinned as if I'd put him in command or something.

Simple pleasures... "Come on, Hemp. Let's see what finery they have aboard."

"Right behind you, sir!" He'd reloaded his crossbow and held it at the ready.

"Don't shoot anyone unless I tell you to."

He looked crestfallen. "Take all the fun out of piratin' you do sometimes, sir!"

"Yes, I'm a spoilsport that way, I know."

I took my squad through the sterncastle one cabin at a time, weapons bared and ready for anyone stupid enough to oppose us. Two passengers cowered in a cabin, and I sent them forward under guard. In the galley we found a vast woman sporting short gray hair, a flushed face, and an apron. Between her glare and the two cleavers in her hands, she looked like she could stand toe-to-toe with Wix.

I surveyed the orderly galley appreciatively—herbs and sausages dangling from hooks, pots and pans stowed shipshape—and breathed in the heavenly aromas. "You're the cook?"

"No, I'm the ship's bloody *physician*, you foul git!" She brandished her cleavers.

I snorted a laugh and traded a glance with Hemp. "We could *use* a proper cook, couldn't we, Hemp?"

"You tired of my cookin' sir?" He feigned a hurt expression, but winked at me. "Might be nice to have a decent meal aside from spotted pickle pie and biscuit."

I checked my gag reflex at the mention of Hemp's spotted pickle pie. "Right." I pointed my cutlass at the huge woman. "I'll give you a choice, madam. You can fight us and die, get into one of the boats with the crew and be set adrift with nothing, or accept a paying job as my cook."

She affected a dubious scowl that doubled her number of chins and made her nose almost vanish beneath her curled upper lip. "How *much* pay?"

"What do you make now?"

"A gold imperial a week, my own cabin, and all I want to eat."

From her girth, the last went without saying. *Never trust a skinny cook, I always say.* I considered Hemp's cooking, which only confirmed that old adage, and made another snap decision. "One imperial a week, one one-hundredth share of our plunder after ship's expenses, including what we take from *Hymoin*, your own cabin, and...*three* square meals a day plus grog."

"Done!" She nodded and lowered her cleavers. "Need a diet anyways! I'm Bert Cutworthy."

"Captain Longbright." I hooked a thumb over my shoulder. "My steward, Hemp, will get you and your gear over to *Scourge*."

"I will?" He raised an eyebrow at me. "Sir, my back..."

"You don't have to *lift* her for fucksake!" That brought a jolly cackle from Bert and a chuckle from the rest of my squad. "Just get it done, Hemp. You three, come with me."

"Aye, sir!"

Three sailors accompanied me through the rest of the sterncastle until we finally reached the great cabin. The door was locked, but yielded to my boot readily enough. What we found inside took me by the lee like a summer squall.

"By Odea's green garters…"

A dusky-skinned young woman sat on a pile of satin pillows beneath the stern gallery windows. Scratch that, she didn't just sit there, she was *chained* there, her wrists bound by golden manacles attached by gold chains to her waist. Orbs of ebony swimming in pools of cream stared at me, wide with fear. She didn't speak, but that might have been due to the band of ivory silk that girded her mouth. She wore green silk pantaloons and a matching strip of cloth elegantly wrapped around her torso. Her hair was bound back in a tight braid with green silk ribbon, and her feet were bare. She was breathing hard, obviously terrified.

Prisoner or bait? I glanced left and right to make sure we weren't about to be ambushed and, finding no lurkers, stepped into the cabin.

"Check the quarter galleries," I ordered my squad.

I ventured closer and noticed a dark tattoo between her ebony eyebrows. It was a character I didn't know, some foreign script maybe, but its meaning was clear enough.

"You're a slave?"

She nodded, which also meant she understood me.

The tattoo wasn't the only mysterious symbol. Her manacles were etched with silver inscriptions, and her gag embroidered with arcane runes. There was magic afoot here, which made her potentially dangerous…and extremely profitable.

"All clear, sir," Macie Moll reported. "Some nice trinkets." She frowned down at the chained slave. "What's she got a gag on for, sir?"

"Hell if I know. Start packing up the finery. I need to find out what we've got here." I wiped my cutlass on my pant leg and sheathed it, then squatted down before the woman for a closer look. She cringed away, staring at me wide-eyed. I held my palms out. "Don't worry. I'm not going to hurt you."

She didn't look convinced, though she should have been. I had no intention of hurting such an obviously valuable piece of plunder. It would be like smashing a priceless vase or slashing a beautiful painting. But there was something amiss here. Slaves generally weren't garbed in silk and bedded on pillows, and *certainly* didn't wear rune-etched manacles and magical gags. The question was, what *was* she?

"Sir, I heard you found a..." I turned to find Miko standing there staring, her mouth open. "What in the name of..."

"I don't know yet, Miko, but I'm thinking it might be dangerous to take off her gag and ask her." I pointed to the ivory silk binding the slave's mouth. "It's enspelled or I'm a eunuch."

"That tattoo..." Miko leaned down to examine the woman, who seemed just as afraid of my first mate as she was of me. "That's a Toki character, I think."

"Can you read it?"

"No. It's not one of the typical marks, but she's definitely a slave."

"Yes, but what *kind* of slave?"

"A *dangerous* one if she's bound by magic." Miko pointed to the silk gag. "Take that off and she might charm you with her voice or turn you into something small and slimy."

"Which is why I haven't taken it off. But that raises the question: if she's *that* dangerous, why would the captain keep her here in his cabin?"

"Well, she'd have to be valuable."

"Or useful."

"Maybe, or he wanted to keep his crew from...um...spoiling her."

"There is that." I stood. "Well, we're not going to figure it out by staring at her, and we've got work to do." I looked around and summoned a pair of pirates who were busy looting the captain's valuables. "You two, take her to my cabin and put her in my bunk. Be *careful* with her and whatever you do, do *not* take off her gag! You understand me?"

"Yes, sir." The two looked dubious, but complied, lifting the young slave with little difficulty.

She didn't struggle, but her eyes wept fear like a gash to the scalp weeps blood.

"Careful with her, sir," Miko warned me after they'd left. "I've heard of demons and worse in the guise of beautiful women."

"So have I. Don't worry on that count, Miko." I scratched the scars on my face. "I'm used to dealing with dangerous women."

We pillaged *Hymoin* at our leisure. She carried bales of silk and satin, crates of spices, and casks of aged wine. I found some very nice things in the captain's cabin, including some high-quality navigational instruments, a Tsing-made chronometer worth a king's ransom, nautical charts, and elegant clothing that would fit me after a few alterations. That last find would elate Hemp more than a chest of diamonds. In a drawer I discovered a set of keys, one of which was gold and inscribed with the same Toki character I'd seen tattooed upon the beautiful slave's brow. I'd have bet my mother's honor that the key fit the manacles girding the slave's waist and wrists.

Plunder is plunder, I thought, pocketing the keys. The slave was valuable, no doubt, and would fetch a fine price…once I figured out what in the Nine Hells and Seven Heavens she was.

Chapter Five
Truthsayer

For facts, seek a sage. For truth, seek a prophet.
Know the difference between them.
The Lessons of Quen Lau Ush

From the diary of Kevril Longbright —
I both curse and bless the day I found her. Who knew the truth could be so damning, so freeing, and so seductive. Whoever coined the phrase "ignorance is bliss" had it right.

Dawn brought a brisk northeasterly breeze right in our teeth, a cloud-streaked sky, and a well-satisfied captain and crew aboard *Scourge*. My ship was stuffed to the gunnels with prime plunder. We were beating close-hauled east-southeast under reefed topsails into choppy seas, with spray lashing the decks due to our low waterline. The log showed barely five knots, but I was in no hurry. Once we neared the isle of Ton Chi, we'd get some shelter and hopefully some land breezes to clock the wind. My crew was sleeping off mild inebriation from a cask of Marathian red that I ordered broached in celebration of our victory and mourning over the two crew who had died in the fighting. Moreover, my new ship's cook, Bert, laid out a fine repast for my breakfast, the likes of which I hadn't seen in months.

Worth every imperial, that one, I thought, sopping up the last bit of poached eggs served under crispy cheese alongside a lightly toasted piece of fresh bread. I'd even forgiven her for calling me a foul git. I washed the bite down with a swallow of blackbrew as strong as a cyclone and patted my taut belly. It was a good morning to be a pirate.

Still, my sleep had been troubled by the mystery I'd encountered on *Hymoin.* Of course, part of that might have been being displaced from my customary sleeping arrangements by that very mystery. The slave lay in my bunk now, staring at me as I ate. Hemp had all but called me an idiot for not stuffing the "admittedly attractive, but dangerous as a viper by the look of her" slave in a barrel and stowing her the in the hold, but I wasn't going to let her out of my sight until I figured out exactly what I had on my hands. I'd asked Bert if she knew what this slave was. My cook just shook her round head with a frown.

"Nobody knew but the captain, and we didn't ask no questions, neither," she'd said. "He took her on more'n a year ago and she never left his cabin. We all thought he just…you know…used her."

Never left his cabin… That brought up all kinds of questions in my mind. Was she really a pleasure slave? I'd never heard of one needing to be bound by magic, but there were stranger things in the world.

I stood, stretched, and strode to my bunk. The slave lay there staring up at me, evidently comfortable enough, though I noticed that her wrists were red from her manacles. I bent to look more closely and saw old scars beneath the metal. She'd been a slave for some time, then. No calluses on her hands or feet, so she performed no manual labor. She wore no jewelry at all, not even an ear or toe ring, though her clothes were finely made. I'd seen the like before on both women and men from Fornice, usually on courtesans or performers. Considering her closely, I nodded; she could be

Fornician, though her skin was darker than usual. The unknown Toki character tattooed on her brow puzzled me.

Her eyes never left mine as I examined her. There was still fear in them, though less than before. If it was feigned, she was very good at it. I didn't think so. I hadn't questioned her directly yet—the enchanted gag gave me pause—but as Hemp clattered the breakfast plates and cups onto a tray and left, I thought of one pertinent inquiry.

"Do you eat?"

She nodded.

"Are you hungry?"

Another nod.

We wouldn't be in Haven for at least four days with this wind against us, so I'd have to give her water at least, and should probably feed her as well if I wanted to get the best price for her. I couldn't trust her to tell me the truth, of course. For all I knew she was indeed hungry, but fed on human souls. Mine could be her breakfast if I took off her gag, though I couldn't imagine Captain Nightspinner keeping such a dangerous creature in his cabin.

"Hemp!"

"Sir!" He was in my cabin in an instant.

"Tell Bert to send in a pot of tea and a bowl of porridge."

"Aye, sir.

"And send for Miko."

"Straightaway, sir!"

When he'd gone, I leaned down to look into the slave woman's dark eyes. "What in Odea's name *are* you?"

She couldn't answer, of course, but her eyes widened in fear again. Not the same kind of naked terror as the night before, but it was there. Was she less afraid because I had rigged a hammock for myself and hadn't ravaged her? Only a fool would have done that, in my opinion, but there are fools aplenty in the world.

"I'm going to feed you, but I don't know what you are, so I'm going to be cautious. Do you understand me?"

She nodded again.

I stared into her dark eyes, watching for any hint of evasion or deception. "If you try to cast a charm on me or make some kind of magic, I promise you, you won't live long enough to regret it."

She nodded.

A knock sounded, and I told Miko to come in. Hemp followed her, bearing a pot of tea and a steaming bowl that filled the cabin with the scent of spiced oat porridge, dates, and apples. My mouth watered even though I was full. Damn, Bert could even make porridge a treat.

"Sir?" Miko nodded to the slave as Hemp put the tray on my table and left, muttering an oath under his breath. "What's the plan?"

"I'm going to feed her and you're going to watch from the door with waxed cotton in your ears." I pulled a crossbow from my locker and handed it to her. "And this trained on her head."

"How about I feed her and you watch," she suggested.

"No, I want to ask her some questions while she eats."

"Captain..." Miko nodded past me to the slave.

"What?" I looked back. Those dark eyes were wide with fear again. They met mine, and the slave shook her head in a quick, almost frantic motion. She hadn't objected to being fed before, so this had to be about the questions. "You don't want me to ask you questions?"

She nodded with that same quick, birdlike motion.

"Well, that's too bad, because I've got to know more about you." I motioned Miko over to my locker.

"So, if she grows fangs and rips your throat out, I'm supposed to shoot her, right?" Miko cocked my crossbow, a gleaming weapon that I enjoy hunting and fishing with, though I prefer sword and dagger for fighting.

"No, if she grows fangs, you're supposed to shoot her *before* she rips my throat out."

"Oh." She smirked and fitted a bolt, looking around my cabin with a wistful sigh. "Shoot *before* the throat ripping… I'll try to remember that."

"Remember, if I die, *you* have to deal with Jhavika."

"May Odea *forbid*!" Miko grinned.

I just glared at her and cut two swatches of soft cotton cloth from the piece I use to clean and oil weaponry. Dabbing them in the soft wax at the base of a candle, I handed them to her. "In your ears."

"Aye, sir." Miko rolled the cloth and stuffed it in her ears.

I didn't know if it would protect her from a spell, but it's said that you have to actually *hear* a charm for it to take effect. Deafness wouldn't protect her from a bolt of lightning or firebreath, but Miko has a quick finger and is a crack shot.

I held up a finger, and Miko freed one of her earplugs. "And remember," I instructed, "she's valuable. Don't kill her unless you're sure it's necessary."

"And *before* she rips your throat out. Got it." She sighed again, stopped up her ears, and took a position at my door barely fifteen feet away from my bunk. "All these *conditions*…"

I glared, which checked her mirth as much as a butterfly would the path of a charging bull. Turning back to my bunk and the slave, I considered how best to do this. She was already chained, so restraining her further seemed foolish. Her legs were free, so she might kick me, but if she did, she had to know that it would be the last thing she ever did. I slipped my arms under her legs and back, and lifted her into a sitting position. She weighed no more than a whisper and didn't struggle. I caught a faint muskiness from her, the sweat of fear, perhaps.

Nudging her to lean forward, I reached for the knot of her gag, careful not to get between her and Miko. The cloth came away easily to reveal a pair of full lips set in a frown of consternation or worry. Well, mine probably sported the same look.

At least she didn't grow fangs and rip my throat out. Not right away, anyhow.

"Tea first?"

She nodded.

I poured a cup and tested it to make sure it wasn't scalding. It was hot, but not burning, the steam lightly scented by cloves. I tilted the cup at her lips, and she slurped, swallowed, and nodded. She didn't thank me, which I thought a little cocky for a slave. Maybe she knew how valuable she was. I'd seen haughtiness before in high-priced pleasure slaves and performers, but I didn't think that was the case here.

I put the cup down and reached for the bowl of porridge. "You're a slave, not a captive, is that right?"

She nodded, but still didn't speak. I wondered if she could. If not, what was the gag for? I stirred the porridge and worked up a spoonful. "What *kind* of slave are you?"

She frowned and looked down. "Nothing. I'm nothing." Her voice was deeper than I'd imagined, husky with a hint of an accent. It was also lying.

"Bullshit." I put the bowl down. "If you want to eat, you'll tell me the truth. What kind of slave are you?"

"I am…" She looked up. "I *was* for the captain's pleasure. He bought me only to please him."

I frowned. She was still lying, but more convincingly. She was certainly lovely enough to be a pleasure slave, but magical gags and manacles belied that.

I leaned down until our eyes were only inches apart. "Listen carefully. If you don't cooperate, I can make your passage to Haven very unpleasant, and once there, even *more* unpleasant. A slave master I know will find out what you are, and you'll like *his* questions much less than you like mine. Now, let's try this again. What are you? What is that tattoo you bear?"

"It…means Flame of Truth." She cast her eyes down. "I'm a truthsayer."

"A wha…" I stared at her open mouthed.

Truthsayers were the stuff of legend, kind of like a magic lamp that you rub and a genie pops out, ready to grant you wishes. There are charlatans and fakes aplenty, tattooed savages who will speak in tongues then go into convulsions to be interpreted by their masters for a modest sum. Trickery and rubbish. I'd never seen a real one or even heard of anyone who had. Genuine dragon eggs are more common by far. Truthsayers were *supposed* to be able to answer any question posed to them truthfully, but they weren't reputed to be dangerous.

"I don't believe you. If you're a truthsayer, how did you just lie to me?" I picked up the rune-inscribed gag. "Why this? Why the manacles? Why—"

"Please, sir!" She cringed as if I'd slapped her. "Your questions…they…endanger my life."

"*What?*" I almost asked how, but then thought better of it. If questions were dangerous, prudence seemed wise. *Fine*, I thought. *I won't ask. I'll demand*. I picked up the gag and held it before her face. "Explain this."

She nodded, trembling, eyes still down. "To keep me from speaking, from answering incautious questions. The…ability is not voluntary. It's only invoked if I'm asked something I don't know the answer to, something that is beyond my knowledge. Asking my opinion or what I *think* of a subject is safe, but asking for specific facts I don't know invokes the…magic. I'm *forced* to answer. Answers…tax me. A simple one will put me into a sleep of no waking for half a day, longer if it's a trying question. If another is asked too soon, I'll fall insensate and die."

I'd never heard that, but then, I'm no sage. I wondered if she was lying again, but couldn't think of a reason why that particular lie would benefit her. I needed to think about this and I needed to be careful, keeping my questions to things I knew she would know the answers to. I repeated my earlier question. "If you're a *truth*sayer, how can you lie to me?"

The slave shook her head gently. "When asked a question I don't know the answer to, the magic compels a truthful answer; I have no say in what that answer is. When I'm asked a question for which I *do* know the answer, well..." She shrugged. "...my words are my own."

I didn't really like that answer, but she did seem to be telling the truth about her ability to lie. I touched the manacles that encircled her wrist and waist. "Do you know why your master put these on you?"

"Yes." She clenched the chains. "To prevent me from...doing myself a mischief."

"A mischief?" I thought I knew what she was talking about, but I had to be sure. I took her hand and pushed the wide gold bracelet up her arm as far as it would go, then examined the tender flesh on the bottom side of her forearm. Aside from the old marks of restraints, she bore three long scars from the heel of her palm up her wrist. "Odea's scaly hide..." The manacles were to keep her from killing herself.

I released her wrist and picked up the bowl of porridge. "Has your life as a truthsayer been so horrible?" I stirred the warm food and stuffed a bite into her mouth.

"I..." She chewed and swallowed. "I'm nothing but a tool, sir. I sit and I answer a question, then fall into a dreamless sleep, only to wake and answer again as soon as I'm able." She accepted another bite. "I've been a slave since I became a woman. My own parents...sold me. I will be a slave until I die."

I considered that as I fed her. Hers seemed a bleak existence, but far better than many slaves endured without attempting to take their own lives. Then again, I'd never been a slave. But there was one other thing I had to consider. If she truly was a truthsayer, I could learn the answer to any question I wished. My pulse quickened as I considered the implications. What questions I might ask her? What mysteries might I learn? What unknowable things could I discover? And how might much she be worth?

I didn't need a truthsayer to answer the last one.

I knew one thing for certain; if she was telling me the truth, I didn't want the entire crew to find out. Powerful magical abilities draw thieves, assassins, and the attention of very powerful people like shit draws flies. If the crew started spreading rumors ashore, I'd have the High Priests of Toki hunting me like hounds after a fox, not to mention every crime lord in Haven. I motioned to Miko, and she pulled one plug from her ear.

"You spelled yet?" She looked at me as if considering whether to shoot or not. "You're acting pretty strange. Never known you to spoon feed a slave before."

"No, I'm not spelled. Now, aim that thing somewhere else and come over here. You need to hear this." I trusted Miko to keep her mouth shut. "Pull up a chair."

She did so, but kept the crossbow in her lap. "So, what is she?"

I kept feeding the slave, interspersing sips of tea. "She *says* she's a truthsayer." That got about the same response from Miko as it had from me. "I know. I don't know whether to believe her or not. She also said asking her a question she doesn't know the answer to will knock her unconscious for half a day, so be careful what you ask."

"I never heard of that, but sure." Miko touched the ivory silk gag. "Why the gag and the manacles?"

I told Miko what the slave had told me and showed her the woman's scars in between bites of porridge. "So, she's telling the truth about wanting to kill herself at least. But she did admit that she can lie."

"Hmmm." Miko rubbed her chin as I continued shoveling porridge. "If she *is* telling the truth, she's worth a fortune."

"I know, but we have to be sure, and we have to be damn careful about who we sell her to." I shook my head. "If Jhavika found out…" Jhavika obviously hadn't known that Captain Nightspinner possessed a truthsayer.

With such a talent at her disposal, Jhavika could learn every sordid detail of every lord on the Council. She could blackmail them at leisure, murder them when they thought they were safe, and find their hidden treasures. If she'd known, she would have told me to bring the slave back at all costs.

Miko chewed her lip and scratched her bare scalp. "She'd stop at nothing to have something like this, and she wouldn't want anyone to know. Our lives wouldn't be worth spit if she found out you had one. Damn, that's a bugger."

I scooped more porridge, but the slave turned her head away. "Well, we've got a few days to decide what to do, but we should…I don't know, test her somehow." I offered the cup of tea, but the slave shook her head, never looking up. "We have to confirm this…talent."

"You mean ask her a question?" Miko glanced to the truthsayer and shrugged. "It'd have to be something she couldn't possibly know that we do. For that matter, I don't suppose she can answer *any* question. If truthsayers could do that, every dragon that ever flew would be in someone's keeping, tamed, or bespelled by whoever asked a truthsayer how it could be done."

The slave glanced up at Miko, then away again.

What a miserable existence, I thought. But all slaves bore hardship, and hers really didn't seem as horrible as many endured. Anyway, it wasn't my job to decide which deserved to be freed and which didn't. I was a pirate, not a magistrate.

I probed some more. "Do you know what limitations your talent has?"

"Not all," she said without raising her eyes.

"Tell me the ones you know of."

"I have no control over the answers I give. Even if I'm asleep, I'll answer. I may not even understand the answer, but it will be true as far as it goes. Ambiguous questions generally receive ambiguous answers. I can't answer specific questions about powerful magical things or beings," she glanced at Miko, "like dragons. I don't know why, but the answers just don't come. I can't answer questions about the future or what another person thinks or intends to do, only what currently is or has already happened."

"Do you know if it would it be safe for you to answer a question now?"

"Yes."

"What do you mean *safe*?" Miko looked at me suspiciously.

"Answering questions taxes her. Asking another too soon will kill her."

"Maybe that explains why there aren't many truthsayers," Miko said with a chuckle. "Like the old story about the dove that laid diamond eggs."

"Right."

I looked at the slave and realized that she hadn't said it would be safe to ask a question, only that she knew if it would be safe or not. For that matter, if she wanted to kill herself, she might lie to me. The manacles probably restrained her from physical attempts, but I couldn't depend that they would prevent her from tricking me into killing her. I had to convince her to play along, at least for now.

"Listen to me." I put a finger on her chin and raised her face so she was forced to look me in the eye. "We're not going to hurt you, and I swear on my name that I'll do my best to sell you to someone who will treat you well. If you're lying to me in hopes that I'll ask a question too soon and end your life, I'll just wait a few days to ask."

She blinked and nodded. "I'm not lying to you. It's safe. The day we left Haven, Captain Nightspinner asked me who his wife was having an affair with. Four days is plenty of time."

"Seriously?" I flopped back in my chair. "He has a truthsayer, and *that's* what he asks you?"

"That is all he ever asked me. Actually, his usual question was 'What is the name of the man my wife is having an affair with?' There was never an answer. This time he phrased the question differently, said 'person' instead of 'man'. I was compelled to provide the answer."

"A woman, not a man." I chuckled. "And you told him who it was?"

"Yes." She shrugged. "It was several names, actually."

75

"Really?" I glanced at Miko. "Maybe Nightspinner's wife *did* ask her brother to have her husband killed to keep her liaisons secret."

"Could be, but if it's true, don't let Jhavika know you found out."

"Right." This was getting complicated already and we hadn't even asked a question. "So, do you have any ideas what we could ask her?"

"Something simple, like..." Miko looked to the slave and opened her mouth.

"Wait!" The slave shifted on my bunk and gazed imploringly at me. "Um...I would ask a favor first that would be a benefit to you, sir."

"All right. What?"

"I have to...pee very badly. I don't want to soil my clothes or your bed when I fall insensate."

"Ha! Well, that's easily solved!" I lifted her up and put her on her feet—she barely reached my shoulder—and pointed to the quarter gallery. "In there."

"Thank you, sir." She nodded and went to the door, walking stiffly with the roll of the ship and her wrists chained to her waist.

"You don't think she'll do something desperate like wiggle out through the scupper, do you?" Miko asked when the door closed.

"I don't think the manacles will *let* her try to hurt herself," I said.

"Hmmm, no wonder Nightspinner put them on her." Miko frowned. "What are we going to tell the crew? There's already talk, some of it rather...saucy."

"Maybe it would be easiest to tell them she's a pleasure slave and I've decided to keep her for myself for a while." I considered the implications of that. "She's certainly attractive enough, but I don't want to start the wrong rumors flying around."

"Why not?" Miko grinned. "Might further your reputation as a rake."

I glared at her. She knew damned well that I valued my reputation. "Those *are* the wrong rumors, Miko."

She looked disgusted. "Some pirate *you* are."

The quarter gallery door opened, and the slave came back out, fumbling with her limited reach to secure the latch.

I got up and gestured to my bunk. "You may as well lie down and get comfortable if you're going to be out cold all day."

"I..." She looked around the cabin, then nodded. "Thank you, sir."

"Don't thank me. I sleep better in a hammock while underway anyway." I watched her struggle a little to get over the leeboard into the bunk without using her hands. When she finally lay back, I asked. "Ready?"

"Yes, sir. Please remember to put the binding back on my mouth afterward."

"Right. Ask away, Miko," I said.

"What is the number of crew aboard *Scourge*?"

The truthsayer stiffened, her back arching, hands jerking against her restraints, and her eyes rolling up until only white shone. I stepped back from the bunk, a little unnerved and also rapt at the spectacle. Her voice came in a dull rasp totally unlike her previous dulcet tone. "Ninety-seven." The slave's eyes closed and she went limp, her head lolling side to side with the roll of the ship.

I looked at Miko. She gazed unseeing at the bulkhead, her lips moving as she silently tallied our complement. "Well?"

"Ninety-eight if we subtract the two we lost in the fight and add in that cook you just took on, and not including you, of course, since you're the captain, not *crew*," Miko finally said.

So, our mysterious slave hadn't hit the mark. Still, her answer was awfully close. I wondered if she could have somehow learned the number before, but then, she couldn't have had any idea what Miko would ask. I thought about it for a moment while I secured the gag back in place. "Make sure for me, would you? Gods forbid someone fell overboard while we've been sitting here and we just don't know about it yet."

"Sure, sir." Miko handed me my crossbow and headed for the door. "Be careful, she might be dangerous." She laughed as she closed the door behind her.

I slipped the bolt, uncocked the weapon, and put it away, then came back and considered the strange creature lying in my bunk. Was this real? Was she really a truthsayer? How could I be sure she'd told me the truth about any of it?

I took up her hand and pressed my thumbnail hard into the bed of her own thumbnail. She didn't even stir. Either she had a very high tolerance for pain or she was truly out cold. I dropped her hand and looked her over, wondering why Nightspinner would garb her in silks. Maybe to perpetuate the rumor that she was his pleasure slave, an ornamental diversion. She was certainly beautiful enough to pass for one. And who knows, maybe he used her for his own pleasure as well as to answer his questions. Perhaps the dusky beauty sequestered in the captain's cabin was *why* his wife had so many lovers, a sort of payback in kind. How ironic it would be if Nightspinner's wife had her powerful brother contract Jhavika to murder her husband because she believed he had a pleasure slave, not a truthsayer. *Sometimes*, I considered, *having all your questions answered might be more of a curse than a blessing.*

At the knock on the door I said, "Come in."

Miko stepped inside and closed the door behind her, an odd expression on her face. "Damned if she wasn't right. Moopi Tanse died during the night from that belly wound. The carpenter didn't even know until he checked on her after I asked."

"Well, I'll be." I looked again at the sleeping woman in my bunk. "An honest-to-Odea truthsayer. What do you make of that?"

"A *fortune* if you play your cards right, sir."

"Right you are, Miko." I brushed a stray hair from the truthsayer's smooth forehead and thought of all the possibilities. A truthful answer to anything I wanted to know. I could find the richest prizes on the sea without Jhavika's help, be truly free, not to mention rich beyond my wildest fantasies. "A treasure indeed."

"We have to be careful about this, sir." Miko joined me beside my bunk. "I mean *really* careful."

"Right again." Powerful people would kill or worse to get their hands on something like this. "We sell her on the open market, we're dead. If we keep her and rumors get out, we're dead."

"I know it'd be dangerous, but could you sell her to Jhavika?"

"Also dangerous. She'd probably have us killed to keep the news that she has a truthsayer a secret."

"Sell her to someone far away, then. Someone who can afford to pay what she's worth."

"Someone like the emperor of Chen or Tsing?" I chuckled dangerously. "Talk about playing with fire…"

"Hmmm, yeah, we need to think about this all right."

"Yes, we do." I sighed. "Tell the crew she's a pleasure slave, but dangerous, violent, and able to charm with her voice. That'll keep them away from her and explain the gag and manacles. I'm keeping her in my cabin to keep her safe, which is true enough."

"Okay."

"And start making a list, Miko."

"A list of what?"

"Questions." I gave her my most avaricious smile. "We may as well get a few answers before we figure out how to safely sell her, don't you think?"

"Answers, indeed, sir." Her dark eyebrows arched. "Like where the richest lord in Haven hides his money?"

"Or who knows I have a truthsayer in my bunk."

She looked at me and blinked, her smile fading. "Yeah. That's a *good* one."

Chapter Six
One Man's Treasure

That which we covet, we esteem too highly.
That which we have, we esteem too little.
The Lessons of Quen Lau Ush

From the diary of Kevril Longbright –
I like to think I've learned from my mistakes. I've been
fortunate enough that none of them have killed me yet. I rue
no mistake more, however, than not recognizing Preel for
the treasure she truly was the moment I saw her. I should
have known from the beginning that such a treasure would
rain fire and damnation down on me. Even knowing,
however, I fear I would have endured it.

I paced the quarterdeck throughout the forenoon watch,
considering the treasure asleep in my bunk and what questions I
might ask a truthsayer. There was no doubt in my mind that her
talent was genuine. She was real. She couldn't have faked that
answer.
My own truthsayer...

But just having her was dangerous. Could I risk keeping her, even for a while? A pirate's life is hardly risk-free, but this was something above and beyond leaping onto the deck of a merchantman with swords and pikes to greet me. Part of mitigating the risk of being a pirate was anonymity. If anyone in Haven learned I had a truthsayer, I would have to sail for the Northlands, grow a beard, change my name, and maybe even my ship.

No, that won't do… I scratched my stubbled face in irritation. *I'll not be growing a beard.*

"Captain!" Geit called to me from the helm. "The wind's clocking, sir. I can't make our course."

Damn! I was hoping for the wind to shift, but not so soon. "Steer south a point. We'll tack in the lee of Ton Chi Isle and ride the coastal wind for Snomish Bay."

"Aye, sir." Geit eased the helm, and the topsails filled once again.

The circuitous route would delay our return to Haven, but that was fine with me. I had a truthsayer aboard and didn't know what under the Seven Heavens to do with her.

Yet…

Haven…a pit of thieves, murderers, cutthroats, and swindlers, and those were the pillars of the community. It might be the perfect city to sell *most* ill-gotten merchandise, but probably not a truthsayer. If I tried, I was as likely to end up dead as rich. But where else could I go?

Not Toki. The god-emperor had spies in every port ready to confiscate any and all magical trinkets and *anyone* with magical talent for his own personal use. That made charlatans rarer in Toki. If you tried to sell your palm-reading skills or claimed you could cure boils with a touch, you would be dragged before the god-emperor and forced to demonstrate. If you failed, you were burned as a heretic. If you succeeded, you were "collected" for the god-emperor's benefit and never seen outside the palace again.

Some said burning was the kinder fate.

Mati wasn't much better. The king was avaricious, commanded a navy of two dozen war junks, and cursed the name of *Scourge* for reasons that were not entirely my fault. The legacy of Captain Kohl came back to haunt me occasionally. Ta Chin? Too big, too far, and their tithe inspectors would search the ship from the bilges up. The Northlands or Tsing were weeks away across the ocean to the east, and the North Sea Reaches were dangerous in winter.

That, of course, brought another question to mind: *How had a merchant captain found, purchased, and kept a gods-damned truthsayer a secret?* Nightspinner had either been brilliant or foolish...or both.

So which am I, genius or fool? I laughed to myself. It hadn't been genius that brought me the truthsayer, but blind luck. Well, I've always said I'd rather be lucky than talented. Still, luck couldn't tell me what to do with this windfall.

Looking out across the sea, I tapped my knuckles on the salt-crusted taffrail as I considered, then sighed. A quick sale to Jhavika seemed the safest option. Though Jhavika with a truthsayer would be a force to be reckoned with, she *was* my partner. With such a boon, she'd soon find herself atop the Haven hierarchy like a crow perched atop a pile of rotting corpses. I'd just have to be damned careful that *my* corpse wasn't among them.

"My watch, sir!"

I looked up to find Miko standing only a step away, regarding me like an ill-dressed courtier at a royal ball. I'd been so deep in thought I hadn't even heard the ship's bell.

"Right!" I wiped the salt spray from my eyes. "Well rested?"

"Not really." Miko flipped up the collar of her weather cloak and scowled into the wind. "Couldn't stop thinking about..." She glanced around at the sailors and midshipmen. "...things."

"Me too." I grinned and waved off my worries, or tried to. "We'll figure it out, Miko. Don't obsess."

"I'm not, sir, I just...wonder what—"

I held up a hand and shook my head. "Later. We'll talk later."

"As you wish." Shivering in the brisk wind cutting across the deck, she fished a biscuit from a pocket of her weather cloak, gnawed off a bite, and looked up at the rigid sails. "I hate beating to weather."

"Unless you want to sail to Mati, we'll be tacking against this for days. The wind should clock tonight, and we'll get some shelter from the Ton Chi coast." I scratched a stay for luck. "You know what they say: the only thing sure about the wind is that it will eventually shift."

"Ah, well, now it'll shift for sure, right on our nose!" She grinned and reached out to scratch the same stay. "Maybe not so bad anyway. Gives us more time to think."

"Too right." I stretched and gave her my watch report. There wasn't much to say. We were well out in the offing, only one sail sighted and that one headed southwest, passing behind us without changing course. We were all alone. "Wake me for the first dog watch."

"Aye, sir."

I went below and doffed my weather cloak, stowing the salt-caked garment in the wet-locker just inside the sterncastle door. Salt draws moisture, which means mold aboard a ship. Even with constant cleaning, leather and cotton are hard to keep in trim. I was lucky; I had a steward to do my scut work.

I entered my cabin to find Hemp laying out lunch and the truthsayer still passed out in my bunk. The aroma of food made my mouth water, and I peered over my steward's shoulder at the huge plate of braised beef and onions with mustard on soft tack and a mound of fried potatoes, peppers, and garlic on the side. If Bert kept this up, I'd gain weight.

"Mind the boots if you please, sir!" Hemp glared at my boots shedding salt onto the rug. "Here, I just got that clean and now it'll mold for sure, but don't you mind old Hemp, he'll just scrub it again. Not like he's got nothin' *better* to do."

"You *don't* have anything better to do." I kicked off my boots by the door and went to the quarter gallery for a quick rinse of hands and face. I decided to forego the shave until evening. "Just leave the boots there, Hemp. I'll change back into them for the dog watch. We're beating to weather, and I may as well get only one pair wet."

"As you wish, sir." He fussed over the rug, then brushed the salt from my boots with a damp cloth.

Clean and feeling refreshed, I returned to find Hemp hovering like a nervous waiter. "A touch of something to stave off the chill, sir?" The neck of a bottle hovered over the cup of steaming tea beside my plate.

"No." I wasn't cold or chilled, just tired and hungry. "The tea's fine." I tucked into my lunch with a will, blessing my luck for finding Bert. A decent cook might turn out to be a greater boon than a thrice-damned truthsayer.

"So, the um...your guest is right out cold, she is." Hemp fussed about, putting the bottle away and tiding things that weren't in disarray. "I knocked about and she didn't even stir. You must of plum tuckered her out this mornin'."

"Not your business, Hemp." I ignored his suggestive comment, too busy with my lunch to care much. "Carry on and tell Bert to lighten up on my fare. There's enough here for two."

"Aye, sir." He nodded to my bunk again. "Will there be nothin' for her?"

"I said carry on." I couldn't very well explain to him why she was asleep and wouldn't be eating. "She's a slave, and dangerous. I'll feed her something for supper, but don't you go near her. You hear me?"

"Aye, sir." He trudged out, glancing back once more as the door closed.

I knew Hemp would be spreading rumors about the slave and had little doubt they'd grow in the telling. There was trouble brewing over her already and it hadn't been a full day yet. I finished my lunch at a relaxed pace, groaning as I chased the last bite with a swallow of tea. It really had been enough for two, but I'd eaten every bite. Bert might be a curse as well as a blessing, just like the woman occupying my bunk. I loosened my belt to ease the tension in my gut.

"Hemp!" I stood as he came in. "You can clear and pull the shades. I'm going to sleep until the dog watch."

"Plum tuckered out, too, ay?" His grin vanished with my glare, and he cleared the table double quick, muttering under his breath about touchy ship's captains.

With the shades pulled, the great cabin was dim, but not really dark. Not bothering with a lamp, I rigged my hammock and climbed aboard with a practiced flip. I lay there for a while swaying with the motion of the ship, listening to the working of the timbers, the creak of the rigging, the groan of iron. *My ship...my little world...* Who would have thought that it could be threatened by the invasion of a woman who couldn't even speak unless I allowed her to?

I looked toward my bunk and watched her breathing for a time. *A treasure...and maybe a curse.* She shivered, and I could see gooseflesh risen on her shoulders.

"Bloody idiot." I flipped out of my hammock, cursing myself for a fool.

It would serve me right if the most valuable bit of plunder I'd ever taken caught lung fever from a simple chill. I drew a blanket over her, tucking it around her shoulders. She stirred slightly, her eyes moving under her lids. *Something* was going on behind that tattooed brow of hers.

"Probably dreaming of gutting me in my sleep." I picked a dagger from my cabinet and flipped back into my hammock, grasping the comforting hilt as I swayed. I was tired from the night's exertions and the tumultuous morning watch, but sleep came hard. My mind wouldn't be quiet, nagging me with questions...

Questions that I might finally have answers to.

Tired and irritable after an afternoon of poor sleep and a squally dog watch, I stomped to my cabin trying to think of nothing but dinner and bed.

"Supper, sir!" Hemp greeted me at my door with a grin and a mug of hot tea smelling of rum. "Somethin' to banish the chill, here, and Bert said she'd feed you as she saw fit, and if you don't like it, send it back."

"She said…" I accepted the tea and stopped, staring at my table where two place settings flanked several covered platters. "Did I invite someone to supper?"

"Um, no, sir, but your guest is awake and you said you'd feed her some—"

"She's *not* a guest, Hemp!" I kicked off my boots and glared at him as I downed the cup of spiked tea at one swallow, determined to nip this problem in the bud. "She's a *slave*! I do not *dine* with slaves."

"Sorry, sir. I just thought…"

"Stop trying to think, Hemp. It's not your strong suit." I handed him the cup and my jacket. "Open a bottle of the Beriknor red that we got from *Hymoin*. I'm tired and want to eat in peace."

"Aye, sir."

The truthsayer blinked at me from my bunk, but looked down as I strode past her for the quarter gallery. I doffed my salt-caked shirt and washed up quickly, dousing my head with fresh water to get some of the salt out of my hair. A fast shave with only one nick and a swipe with a damp towel, and I was back in the cabin. I pulled out a clean shirt and drew it on while Hemp fussed over the table, removing one place setting and drawing the cork from the bottle. I sat down with my back to my bunk.

"Here you are, sir." Hemp poured a measure of wine, dark and aromatic, into my cup.

"So, my uppity cook thinks she knows better than her captain, does she?" I lifted one cover to reveal some manner of stew on rice noodles. The scent made my stomach growl. Lifting the two others revealed a dish of roast fowl and a bean salad. "Odea's scaly tits, there's enough here for the entire midshipmen's berth!"

"Like Bert said, just eat what you want and send the rest back." Hemp tossed a suggestive glance toward my bunk. "No point wasting it, is there?"

"No, you're right, there's not." I loaded my plate with liberal servings of each dish and put the covers back on the platters. I'd be damned before I let my steward and cook dictate how I treated a slave. "Send the rest to the midshipmen with my compliments. They're pulling double watches with this blow and could use the extra energy."

"The..." Hemp clapped his gaping jaw closed. The midshipmen ate crew fare by tradition. Hemp would liken my giving over my meal to them to throwing it overboard. "Aye, *sir*." He picked up the platters and hurried out.

I ate, reveling in Bert's prowess with simple ship's fare. The sauce of the stew was sublime, savory with a hint of sweet pepper. The fowl was done to a turn, the skin crispy and wonderful; it must have been roasted half the day and basted within an inch of its life. Even the bean salad surprised me, tart and sweet with bits of pickled beet and sweet onion. I would have to be careful or I'd get fat, slow, and spitted by a merchant captain's sword. My plate was still half full when I forced myself to stop. A sip of wine and a sigh of contentment; the meal had sated not only my appetite, but also my temper. Though my ire with Hemp and Bert was justified, the truthsayer didn't deserve my wrath. I'd eaten right in front of her, and she had missed lunch. Feeling like a heel, I poured another cup of wine and glanced with exaggerated nonchalance over my shoulder. She lay there unmoving save for her eyes, which looked quickly away from my gaze.

"Are you hungry?"

She nodded, her dark eyes downcast.

"Fine. You can eat something while I ask you some simple questions." I lifted my plate and cup and strode to the bunk, shaking my head at the concern in her eyes as they rose to meet mine. "Nothing that will invoke your talent, so don't look like that." I put the plate down and unfastened her gag with one hand. "Can you sit up?"

"Yes." She scooched around until her shoulders were braced against the bulkhead and crossed her legs tailor fashion. She'd obviously grown accustomed to maneuvering herself with her hands bound.

"Do you have a name?" I skewered a bite of fowl and held it for her.

"Yes." She took the bite and chewed without elaborating.

"Tell it to me." I prepared another bite, bean salad with some of the stew on noodles.

"Preel."

"Preel, do you know where you're from?" I had been thinking all day how to phrase questions so they wouldn't invoke her magic.

"Yes. From Fornice originally, but when I was young we moved to Chen, northwest of DinJa. The mountains." Preel cleared her throat. "May I have some water please, sir?"

"Of course." Absurdly pleased that I had correctly deduced her ancestry, I put the plate down and emptied my cup, then went to the quarter gallery and filled it from the wash ewer. I sat back down and held the cup for her to drink. "Do you know how old you are?"

"Not exactly. About twenty-five summers, I think."

"Twenty-five." I would have guessed about that. I continued to feed her, considering my next question. During the dog watch I'd started thinking that, if I was to get the most from this truthsayer before I sold her—learning her limitations and how best I might invoke her talent—gaining her confidence would help. Also, I was curious. "You said before that you've been a truthsayer since you became a woman. Do you remember how old you were?"

"Yes. I was twelve."

"Tell me how it happened. How you found out about your talent."

Her eyes flicked up, then dropped again. "I'd just had my first bleeding a month or so before. My father asked me where the spotted goat had gone. I started to say I didn't know when I fell down and...words just came out of my mouth. I couldn't stop them. I blurted that a snow-cat had taken the goat from the byre the night before and carried the carcass to its den under the old willow tree. Then I fell into such a deep sleep that my parents worried that I'd become ill. But...my father found the cat's den and the remains of the dead goat. When I awoke, Father asked me how I had known about the snow-cat. I didn't know, of course, so the question invoked my...ability. I blurted that I was a truthsayer and fell unconscious. I was insensate for five days." Another quick glance up, perhaps to see if I was listening. "They sold me on my thirteenth birthday to a local lord."

"For quite a sum, I hope." I could hardly fault them if they were poor goatherds.

Her eyes shot up to mine, her gaze smoldering. Hatred maybe, for me or her parents, it didn't matter. She was a slave, but that wasn't my fault. I didn't enslave her. Still, it wasn't her fault either. She hadn't broken any laws; she'd just been unlucky enough to be born with a valuable talent.

"And this lord, he had you tattooed?" I fed her another bite.

She chewed and swallowed before answering. "Yes."

"Do you know why a lord from DinJa would tattoo you with a Toki character?"

"Yes. His mother was from Toki. He studied Toki lore and worshiped the Toki god-emperor. He said it was...traditional for truthsayers to bear the mark of the Flame of Truth." She took another bite when I offered it. "He spent the next three years *conditioning* me."

"Conditioning you?" My stomach knotted. *Thirteen years old...* I had no idea why she was telling me this; it had nothing to do with what I'd asked. Maybe to garner sympathy, but I didn't think so. "You mean he..."

"He taught me some lore and…what it meant to be a slave." She shook her head at the next bite of food and looked away. "He was…careful not to damage me…permanently. He said it would lessen my value. I got away once and…" She shook her wrists in her manacles, and a tear slid down her cheek.

"And you were thirteen." It occurred to me then—I was probably the first person since her enslavement who had really *talked* to her, taken an interest in who she was, not just in what she could do. Musing on that thought, I took my plate back to my table and filled my cup with the hearty Beriknor red. I drank it down, then refilled it and returned to my bunk. "Here." I held out the cup.

She took a swallow of the wine and hiccupped, then cleared her throat. "I need to…use the pot please, sir."

"You mean empty your bowels?" She hadn't said pee like she had before.

She nodded.

I considered her manacles, her clothes, and the necessities involved. "Well, I'm not going to wipe your ass for you, so I'll have to unlock you, I suppose." I watched her closely, thinking this might be a ploy to escape, but she seemed more embarrassed than eager or evasive. Though her skin was dark enough to hide a true blush, I thought her cheeks darkened a shade.

I went to my cabinet and retrieved the key I'd taken from Nightspinner's cabin. The locks on the wrist cuffs also linked the cuffs to the chain encircling her slim waist. Chain and cuffs fell away, and she rubbed her wrists.

"Preel, I'm trusting you not to hurt yourself or try anything foolish. There's no way out of the quarter gallery except that door and the window. We're miles out to sea and downing is not the worst that can happen to someone who goes overboard."

She looked up at me, still rubbing her wrists. "It's not the worst that can happen to a slave, either."

There was a tone of defiance in her voice I didn't like, but she was right. She'd been abused in ways that had nothing to do with her supernatural talent. It hardly seemed fair. That gift was priceless, and foolish men had soiled it with their baser instincts.

Pity for a slave? Perhaps. But I also didn't want to lose her; she was too valuable. To that end, I needed her to trust me not to similarly abuse her. "You've been wronged by your former owners, Preel, but I'll make you a promise."

She blinked at me, her full lips pressing tight together.

"You might have guessed that I'm a pirate, and you might have heard that pirates are rapacious scoundrels and worse. I won't lie to you. Some of them are all that and far worse than you can imagine." I leaned close. "I, however, am not."

Her lips parted and she blinked at me again, probably unsure if she could believe me.

I stepped back and pointed to the quarter gallery. "Go do your business, but know that you need never fear that I'll abuse you as others have. I may be a pirate, and I may sell you for a king's ransom, but I'll do my best to make sure your next owner won't abuse you either."

"I won't hurt myself," she said, her voice a plea.

"Then go."

She got up and hurried to the quarter gallery, nimble and lithe as a cat now that she was unfettered. The door clicked closed. I prayed to Odea that I was right about her. I thought of Jhavika and knew that she would see Preel's potential. She was far too intelligent to squander such a prize. Preel would be still be a slave, but she'd be safe with Jhavika. I would be rich...or dead.

It was the dead part that worried me.

I topped off my cup and drank it down, despite having to go on deck shortly. We were beating into weather and I needed the fortification, both from the chill sea and Preel's revelations. What a turn of events... Why did I give a shit about the trials of a slave? She was worth a fortune and I could live like a king on the proceeds of her sale if I just played this right. But I'd told her the truth. I was not a rapacious scoundrel, and I'd not just sell her to the highest bidder without consideration of her wellbeing. By Odea, I'd treat her like the treasure she truly was, albeit a slave.

The door to the quarter gallery opened and Preel stepped out.

"Thank you, sir," she said with a nod over her shoulder. "For trusting me, I mean."

"And thank you for trusting me." I pointed to the bunk. "I've got the first watch, so I won't be back for four hours. Do you need anything else before I go?"

"No, master." She sat on the bed obediently.

"Don't call me that." I picked up her manacles. "Call me sir or captain. I'm used to that."

"Yes, sir." The flicker of a smile crossed her lips.

I closed one manacle around her wrist, then considered the other. If I asked her if she would hurt herself if I left her unchained and she was unsure, the question might invoke her talent and kill her. But she'd said she couldn't foretell the future or the intent of people. Did that include her own? This was getting complicated again.

I settled for closing the other manacle around the sturdy post of my bunk.

"There. That'll leave you free to move around a bit more." I pocketed the key and went to retrieve my salty jacket.

"Sir!"

"Yes?" I looked back.

Preel held up the ivory silk band that prevented her from speaking. "Please. Your steward comes in. He might ask me something I can't answer without..."

"Right you are." I returned and affixed her gag.

I couldn't tell if there was a smile beneath that band of enchanted silk, but her eyes narrowed and she nodded. I took that as a thank you and left my cabin to spend four hours in the salty spray on deck, beating into the slashing winds.

Chapter Seven
Wrath and Ruin

*Beware the aged warrior, for they have paid for their years
with the blood of many.*
The Lessons of Quen Lau Ush

From the diary of Kevril Longbright –
I don't like to think of myself as a vengeful man. That my
father was still alive when I left home is evidence of this. It's
also evidence that I loved him and hated him at the same
time. There's no forgiveness behind the pain a child endures
at the hand of a parent, only confusion. A ship, I have
learned, is very much like an extended family, and I'm like a
father to my crew. Sometimes, like a farmer culling a herd of
the sick and infirm, a captain must cut away the sickness that
threatens his entire family.

At midnight, Miko relieved me. I was cold, wet, salty, and longed
for a warm cup of tea, my hammock, and deep sleep. Trudging
belowdecks, I found the great cabin dark. Thinking Hemp must have
turned the lamp down to allow Preel to sleep, I crept over and struck
a match. The flame sizzled on the lamp's wick and caught. Turning

the light low, I headed toward the quarter gallery to wash up. The wan light flickered across my bunk, and I froze in my tracks.

Preel lay curled into a ball, the sheets stained with blood, her torn pantaloons bunched about her ankles. A pit of rage opened in my gut and exploded into an inferno.

"HEMP!" My bellow must have shaken the deck halfway to the beak head.

"Sir! I just—"

The back of my hand cuffed the tea service out of his grasp and sent it smashing against the wall. He gasped in shock as I grabbed his shirt and slammed him against the bulkhead.

"Who *was* it?" I growled, my nose an inch from his, spittle flying from my clenched teeth. I prayed to all the gods that Hemp didn't know what had transpired in my cabin while I'd been on watch.

"Who..." His saucer-wide eyes stared into mine, terrified, confused, and utterly lacking in guile or guilt. He didn't know.

Thank you.

I yanked him off the wall and pointed him toward my bunk for an instant, long enough for him to see and comprehend. Then I lifted him and pinned him back against the bulkhead.

"Who...*did*...this?" I thought my teeth might shatter from the pressure I was putting on them. "You're my gods-damned *steward*, Hemp! You are in *charge* of this cabin! Who came in here and *violated* her?!"

"I...don't know, sir! I swear it! I was sleepin'! Ask...ask *anyone*!"

I released him and looked back to Preel. She huddled in a fetal ball, shivering, either unconscious or too traumatized to even pull up the blanket. I went to my bunk and covered her with the sheet. She flinched and jerked back. Her eyes were squeezed tightly closed, one swollen shut and mired in blood from a bad cut. Blood soaked the silk band that girded her mouth, but whoever had done this hadn't removed it.

Of course not... Why let her scream? I wanted to kill something—no, I wanted to kill some*one*—more than I've ever wanted to kill anyone before in my life.

"Hemp, get Bert and Miko." I whirled on him with death in my eyes. "I want them here *now*!"

"Aye, sir!"

I thought about what I had to do. "And bring me Wix as well."

"Aye!" The door slammed and Preel winced.

"Preel," I said softly, kneeling beside my bunk. She didn't respond. "Preel, it's the captain. I don't know who did this, but I need to find out. I need you to tell me if you can." Still, she didn't respond, only lay there shaking. "Nod if you can hear me. I *promise* nobody will touch you again. I'll post a guard and make sure of it."

Fat lot of good your fucking promises did her before, I thought.

Her head bobbed ever so slightly, but her eyes remained tightly closed.

"I need you to—" A knock at the door interrupted me. My vengeance would have to wait a moment. "Come in."

Hemp ushered them all in at once, Miko at the fore, then my vast cook, then a wide-eyed and bristling Wix. Hemp looked utterly miserable and scared for his life, which well he might.

I stood. "Bert, come over here and have a look at her. She's been..." I could barely say it. *My fault...all of it.* "...beaten, probably raped. I think she'll let you touch her more readily than..." *Than me, than any man...* My teeth chirped as I ground them together. "Do what you can for her, but don't remove her gag without me or Miko here."

"Gods and demons!" Bert hustled over, wide eyed. "Who would..."

"I don't know, but I'm going to find out." As Bert ordered Hemp to bring warm water, towels, unguent, and bandages, I gathered Miko and Wix on the far side of the cabin. "I'm going to find out who did this. I don't know yet if she saw who it was. As soon as she's able to answer, I'll find out."

"Captain, can't we..." Miko shrugged and glanced to the bunk. "...I mean...you know."

"By Odea, we *can!*" I had a truthsayer. I could just ask, but not for at least a couple of days without risking her life. And as traumatized as Preel looked, I probably shouldn't risk the strain even then. "We'll try the old-fashioned way first, Miko. She might have seen his face."

"Sir?" Wix looked confused at our conversation.

"Never mind, Wix. I want to find out who broke into my cabin and beat and raped her, and I want to find out now. It happened within the last watch. I know she's a slave, but I'd promised her my protection, and since I failed *miserably* at that, I'll settle for vengeance."

"Aye, sir." Wix nodded, murder smoldering in his eyes. He cracked his scarred knuckles. "If he beat her...assumin' it *was* a he, the bloke should have marks on his hands. She might even have marked *him*."

"Maybe, but we just took *Hymoin* and there was fighting, so more than a few of the crew have marks here and there."

"He'll tell someone," Miko said, her tone as cold and hard as a mountaintop in winter. She glanced at Wix. "*Assuming* it was a man. Anyone who does this does it to feel strong or powerful, or just hates women. I don't know anyone aboard who fits that last one and wouldn't have them on the crew if I did."

"Aye to that, sir." Wix nodded past my shoulder.

"Captain?"

I turned to find Bert up and walking toward us, her face flushed and tears streaking her cheeks.

"How is she?" I asked, feeling stupid for the question.

"Beat up and raped. She's got marks on her arms and face, and one eye swole shut, but no broke bones as far as I can tell." She sniffed and wrung her hands. "I'd like to take the gag off, sir, if you'll allow it. Don't know why she has to wear such a thing, but she may have a broke jaw or teeth."

"All right." I turned to Wix and Miko. "Start asking questions of crewmembers you trust. Find out if anyone's bragging or sporting new scratches. Don't tell *anyone* what happened, just that my cabin was broken into...for now, at least."

"Aye, sir." Miko nodded and Wix followed her out, as grim as I'd ever seen either of them.

I was feeling pretty grim myself.

I followed Bert back to my bunk. Preel still huddled on her side, knees drawn up under the blanket, but she'd stopped shaking. The manacle around her wrist was bloody where it had cut her. She must have put up a fight. I fished the key out of my jacket and unlocked it. Preel's hands were clenched, her nails bloody, and her forearms red with contusions.

"Hold on, dearie, we'll just get this off." Bert's nimble fingers worked the knot free of the silk gag. It came away with clotted blood on the inside. "By all the demons, if you ever find the bastard who did this, Captain, just give me five minutes with him."

"There won't be anything left after I'm through, Bert." I took the silk gag and handed it to Hemp. "Wash this out. We'll have to put it back on when we're done."

"Sir I..." He looked at the bloody cloth like it was a viper. "Yes, sir." He took it and went into the quarter gallery.

"Sir." Bert looked to me, her fingers bloody from examining Preel's battered face. "Nothin's broke, but she bit her cheek when she was hit. She'll be okay with some water or weak tea. For the rest..." She looked down at Preel's huddled form. "Time...maybe...if she's strong."

"She's strong. She's *got* to be." I don't know what possessed me to say that.

Preel was a slave. I really shouldn't feel any worse than if someone had beaten my dog or destroyed some valuable possession, but she was also a human being. Unlike most slaves, she'd committed no crime to earn her fate, but had merely been unlucky enough to be gifted with a talent coveted by the powerful. She'd paid for the avarice and lust of fools for half her life, and had even tried to take her own to escape, but she was alive. She *had* to be strong.

"Bert, I'll want you to tend her as best you can. Food and drink, whatever she needs, but I need to warn you: do *not* ask her any questions while her gag is off."

"Warn me?" Her face clouded over. "Why?"

"Because it's *dangerous*." I nodded to Preel. "For *her*. So choose your words very, *very* carefully."

"Yes, sir." Bert still looked confused, but bustled off. "I'll get some tea and some more water. Back in two shakes."

"Thank you." I knelt beside the bunk. "Preel, it's the captain." I reached out to brush her hair away from her battered cheek, but stopped my hand before I touched her. "I'm sorry this happened. I should have thought to post a guard. It's my fault." I gritted my teeth again. "I need to ask you about what happened."

Her eye that wasn't swollen shut blinked open. Tears spilled onto the sheets. "N...not..."

I didn't know if she was saying it wasn't my fault or that she couldn't tell me what happened. If she meant the former, she was wrong. If she meant the latter, that was a problem.

"Did you see who did this? Can you recognize him?"

"No." Her eye closed and her jaw trembled. "D...dark."

I remembered that the lamps had been out when I came into the cabin. Damn, that would make this harder. "Did he say anything? Would you recognize his voice?"

"Yes..." She trembled again and drew in a wracking breath. "He...said... He called me...whore. Fancy...bitch...who needed...a lesson. A real man...inside...m..." her voice trailed off to a moan.

That moan stabbed me like a knife in the gut.

"Shhh, Preel. That's all for now. You rest. We'll find who did this and he'll pay for it. I pro—" I clamped my mouth shut. I couldn't promise her, not after my first promise failed so miserably. I brushed her disheveled hair aside, wishing I could ease her pain. "We'll find him."

Her eye opened again and her hands unclenched to reach for mine. "Ask me!" she blurted, bloody teeth gritted between her lips. She grasped my hand with hysterical strength, blood caked under her nails. "Ask me his *name*! Ask me now!"

I knew what she was asking me to do, and it revolted me. If I asked her the assailant's name now, she would die. She wanted me to discover his name and kill her in the process. I couldn't. I wouldn't.

"No, Preel. We'll find out who…"

She let out a wracking sob and pulled her hands away from mine.

I let go and stared down at the blood on my hand…and the tuft of curly red hair stuck to it. Was it actually red, or just colored with blood? I peeled it away and held it under the lamp. Yes, red hair, and curly. He'd have scratches on his face from her nails and he had red curly hair.

I *knew*… I would check the watch schedule to make sure, but I knew who it was.

Bert came back in with a tray of tea and a bowl of soup, a stack of towels under her arm. She put them down on the table and fixed me with a look that said she saw on my face what I'd discovered. Her chin folded inward with her frown.

"Do me a kindness, Captain Longbright. Just one, if you please, and I'll never ask you another."

"I'm going to kill him, Bert." I strode past her to the cabinet and pulled down my cutlass and daggers. "*Me. I'm* going to do it, because *I'm* the one at fault for this!"

"No you *ain't* at fault, and I ain't gonna stand in your way." She stepped over to me, her lower lip trembling with rage. "Just do me the kindness of makin' it *hurt*." She looked back over her shoulder at Preel, then back at me. "A lot."

"I can guarantee you that." I headed for the quarter gallery. "Hemp, when you're done washing that, wring it out and put it back on her as soon as Bert's done. Then stand at my door with a sword in your hand until I come back."

99

"Aye, sir." My steward wrung bloody water from the white silk and looked down in misery. "I'm sorry, sir."

"Not your fault, Hemp. It's mine." I headed for the door. "I should have keel-hauled Geit's worthless arse five days ago."

Geit was exactly where the watch schedule said he would be, standing by the helm station with two crewmen. I had Miko precede me up the steps to the quarterdeck. It was her watch and her presence wouldn't alert him that anything had been discovered. Of course, he had to know I would find Preel in the condition he'd left her, but he probably didn't think I would discover who was responsible so quickly. Regardless, the moment he saw me he backed away from the helm, his hand dipping under his weather cloak.

His eyes darted right and left. The wind pulled back the hood of his cloak, revealing the scratches along his brow inflicted by Preel's nails. An inch lower and she'd have taken an eye. He dashed for the windward-side stairs, but Wix was already there, grinning gape-toothed, his daggers in his hands.

Geit drew a long dirk from under his cloak and brandished it. "Stay back!" He backed and dodged away from Wix, correctly assuming that he had a better chance against his captain and first mate both than the bosun.

"Midshipman Geit, stop there and drop the dirk!" I drew my cutlass, stepping past the helm and the two wide-eyed sailors on the wheel.

"So you can murder me? Go fuck yourself and your whore slave, captain. She's an easier target for your tiny little cock!" He spat at me, but the wind was against him. "Or do you prefer ship's brats? Are they small enough to give you a tight fit?"

I knew he was trying to goad me into doing something stupid. I wasn't stupid, but at that moment I really wanted to be.

The ship veered as the two sailors at the helm turned to gawk. Geit dodged, trying to get around me. I sidestepped and slashed with my cutlass, missing taking his weapon hand off at the wrist by bare inches.

"Eyes on your course, you two!" Miko barked to the sailors at the helm, drawing two wakizashi from her cloak and stepping over to cover my left side. "We've a matter of *discipline* to discuss with Midshipman Geit."

"You've got nowhere to go, Geit. Drop it." I really hoped he wouldn't.

"Take it from me, old man." His mouth stretched in a rictus of desperation as he lunged.

He was quick, and he was right, I *was* older…which meant I'd been fighting with cutlass and dagger when he was still kicking in his mother's belly. Just because I avoid violence when I can doesn't mean I'm not good at it. I'm *very* good at it. I parried, feinted low, and slashed high at his eyes. When he parried, I drew my dagger, stepped inside his guard, and drove it into his stomach. His eyes widened in surprise.

I stared at Geit, face to face. "Beware the old pirate, boy. He's old for a *reason*." I twisted the blade and sliced him open like a codfish.

Geit screamed and dropped his dagger, clutching at his open belly with both hands as he staggered backward. His legs failed him and he landed hard with his back to the taffrail. I strode forth with naked steel in my hands, rain and spray running in crimson rivulets down my left fist. I stared down at him, longing for nothing more than to put eight inches of steel through his eye.

His screams faded and he glared up at me. "Finish it! Or have your bitch do it for you if you don't have the—"

I drove the tip of my cutlass into his knee and twisted it.

When his screaming stopped again, I pulled the blade free and leaned down to look him in the eye. "You can die fast or slow, boy. That's your only choice now."

"Fuck you, old man." He spat at me again and this time hit his mark. "Just like I fucked that whore of yours. She couldn't even scream with that gag on her mouth. Not quite as much fun as I hoped it would be."

Goading me again, this time for a quick end. I grinned at him.

"Oh, you want *fun* do you?"

I dropped my weapons and drove a punch hard into his nose. While he reeled, I reached into the wet mass of his open belly and grabbed a handful of slithering viscera. His shriek shivered the air as I wrenched out a yard or two of ropy intestine, increasing in pitch as I whipped a messy clove hitch around the taffrail baluster. He was still screaming when I lifted him by his lapels and brought his face to mine.

"Now get off my ship."

I pitched him over the rail.

Geit wailed and grabbed at the railing, but his gore-slickened grip failed. Then he grabbed at the only other thing he could, his own bowels. The ropy mass slipped through his grasp and he hit the water, still screaming, pleading, wailing. I watched him fall back into the ship's wake. Miko joined me at the taffrail and handed me my weapons, her face like stone as we watched and listened.

I wondered how Preel might have screamed if she had been able.

"Fookin' artfully done, sir!" Wix stepped up to my other side and stared down at the midshipman flailing in the foam. The screams were getting weaker. "Artfully done indeed."

"I promised Bert I'd make it hurt." I sheathed my dagger and cutlass, refusing to look away from my handiwork.

"I think you kept your word, sir." Miko clapped me on my shoulder. "I couldn't have done better myself." She cocked her head and listened to the gurgling shrieks. "Well, maybe I could have made it last a bit longer, but Wix was right, it was artfully done."

"When he stops screaming, cut him loose, Wix, then have someone swab this deck. I don't want any trace of that raping piece of shit on my ship." Geit's shit was just about all there was left of him still on my ship, slithering under my boots.

"Aye, sir." Wix grinned and sheathed his daggers.

"Miko, make gods-damned *sure* every foremast jack and jane aboard knows what happened here and why." I looked to my first mate. "And that I'll treat any more such vile acts in similar fashion."

"They'll know, sir."

"Good."

I turned and strode forward, ignoring the stares of the sailors manning the helm. I realized at the sterncastle door that I hadn't donned a weather cloak. I was soaked to the skin, my shirt mired in blood. I peeled off my jacket and tried to wipe away most of the gore. It was pretty much useless; Hemp was going to have some washing to do. I flung my jacket in the wet locker and made for my cabin. Hemp stood at the door with one of my cutlasses in hand. He didn't say a word about the salt water or blood I dripped on the rug.

Preel was at least sitting up, wrapped in blankets and wedged into the corner. Bert perched like an overgrown songbird on the edge of the bunk, spooning soup into her charge. She stopped when I entered, and I met her eyes.

"It's done." My bloodlust seeped away like the bloodstained water dripping from my clothes. "The man who assaulted you is gone, Preel. The whole ship will know what happened to him by morning. It *won't* happen again."

Preel just stared at me, a strange look in her one unswollen eye; fear maybe, or something else. Thanks, perhaps? I didn't feel like I deserved her thanks.

"We heard, Captain." Bert put the bowl aside and stood to face me. "We... She saw him fall past the windows."

I hadn't considered at the time that Geit would fall right past the stern gallery on his way to the sea. "Then you know I kept my word to you, Bert. He died screaming." I looked into Preel's battered face. "It was less than he deserved."

"Thank you, sir." Bert nodded and turned back to her patient.

Preel just stared at me.

"Hemp, get me some dry clothes. I need to wash this off." The thought of Geit, any part of him, still touching me made me feel like retching.

I went to the quarter gallery and stripped, sluicing cold fresh water over my head and scrubbing away the salt and blood. As I was toweling dry, Hemp handed in a fresh shirt and trousers. I donned them, picked up my wet sword and dagger, and stepped back into the cabin. I hung the sheath and scabbard upside down to dry and picked out a stone, oil, and cloth from my cabinet. Bert had gone. Preel lay curled up with her back to the bulkhead watching me. The white strip of silk girded her mouth once again. I considered the golden chain that had bound her wrist. It hung from my bedpost empty.

I stepped over to the bunk. "If I leave your manacle off, do you promise to stay put and not hurt yourself?"

She blinked at me, looked at the dangling golden band, then wormed one arm out from under the blanket and extended it toward me. A strip of clean cotton girded her wrist where the manacle had cut into the flesh during her ordeal. My bedpost was scarred by the other end, a testimony to her struggles.

"Very well." I put my weapons on the deck beside the bunk and clipped the manacle around her wrist. The chain was long enough that she could pull it back under the blanket.

I sat on the floor with my back against the bunk and cleaned, oiled, and sharpened my cutlass and dagger. I knew Hemp would do it, but I took some comfort in the familiar task. I owed him an apology anyway for manhandling him. If I had only put a guard on the door in the first place, none of this would have happened.

When dagger and sword were shaving sharp, I put them away and climbed into my hammock. It took me a long time to fall asleep, and when I finally did, I dreamt of screaming.

But the voice wasn't Geit's or Preel's.

It was mine.

Chapter Eight
An Unpleasant Truth

Have a care what you ask for. You may get it.
The Lessons of Quen Lau Ush

From the diary of Kevril Longbright –
I am ever amazed at the resiliency of the human body and spirit. I've seen men and women so injured and beaten that one more blow would have ended them, and I've watched those same men and women laughing and joking days later as if they hadn't stared death in the face and walked away. I've felt that giddy relief myself more than once; the amazement that I was alive, the relief that I would have another chance, the resolve that I wouldn't let it happen again. I wonder if there will ever come a day when I give up and quit fighting. I both dread and long for that day.

Three days later we were still beating to weather, but the winds and seas were finally slacking somewhat. Snomish Bay opened before us, Haven only a day away. Never had I been so ready for a voyage to be over. The morale aboard *Scourge* had never been lower. Even Wix's customary railing was half-hearted.

The midshipmen's berth remained as silent as a tomb, its three surviving occupants solemn and close-mouthed. I learned from Tofi that Geit had bragged to Quiff and Rauley that he'd gotten even with me for exiling him to the foremast for three days, though he'd told them no details. They were walking on eggshells, probably worried that I'd punish them for knowing something and not telling me. I wasn't in much of a disciplinary mood.

The only bright spot was Bert.

My new cook bustled about her galley with abandon, impervious to the mood of the ship, surprising the crew with meals the like of which they had never tasted aboard ship, and tantalizing the ship's officers with cuisine just this side of paradise on a plate. She also proved to be quite a proficient nurse, tending Preel and seeing to the crew's injuries with a brusque motherly manner that far exceeded the rough treatment of our carpenter, who had previously served as our ersatz surgeon. She seemed able to get along with anyone and even coaxed a chuckle out of *Wix*.

Preel responded quickly to good food and care. The swelling around her eye was down only a day after the attack. The dark bruises were muted by her natural dusky coloring and looked better every day. She continued to sleep in my bunk, taking her meals there as well. I wasn't about to let her out of my protection, for Geit had not been without friends aboard, and there had been grumbling about my murder of the midshipman over the mistreatment of a slave. Two stern-faced bosun's mates stood guard at my door watch-and-watch.

I still didn't know quite what to make of Preel. I only removed her gag for feeding, and what little conversation we had consisted of necessities. Was she hungry? Yes. How did she feel? Fine. Did she need to use the head? Yes. I couldn't make myself question her further on the nature of her talent. I kept the key to her manacles on a chain around my neck and released her only as long as necessary. Hemp discovered that we had a chest of her garments that had been pillaged from *Hymoin*. They were all similar, made to be doffed and donned without removing the chain that had encircled her waist.

Today, finally in calmer seas, morale began to lift as the crew anticipated pay, respite, and shore leave. A few of the foremast jacks even broke out in song during the dog watch. Considerably cheered by their heightened spirits, I went to my cabin to find Hemp arranging my table for supper, laying out plates and silver between covert glances at the truthsayer.

I stopped and stared.

Preel contorted herself into a strange pose beside my bunk, standing on one foot with the other leg extended behind her, toe pointed, her torso as flat as a board to balance. She remained impressively still, even with the pitching of the deck. I watched her as I removed my salt-crusted boots. Slowly, she twisted into another pose and held it for several seconds, amazingly graceful. She glanced at me, but continued, the fluid moves seemingly choreographed to prevent the chain on her wrist from coming taut. Her skin shimmered with a light sheen of sweat.

"She's been doin' that fer hours, sir." Hemp whispered to me as he took my boots and jacket, glancing at her sidelong. "Can't figure out if she's prayin', doing some kind of magic, or just stretching herself like a cat."

"Exercise, I imagine." I didn't bother to keep my voice down for a slave. This was my cabin, after all. "She's been cooped up her whole life and learned how to keep in trim."

"And a nice trim it is, too," Hemp said, then cleared his throat and added, "if you don't mind my sayin', sir."

"I do mind." I rinsed my hands and face in the quarter gallery and returned to find Hemp holding a clean shirt. I glanced at Preel. She stood on one foot, her free leg wrapped around the supporting one, her arms likewise entwined, her palms pressed together. She looked like a one of the sinuous statues so common in the northern temples. Hemp was right. She'd obviously kept fit.

Preel's eyes flicked over as I sat down. She stopped her contortions and sat tailor fashion on the bunk, eyes closed, hands on her knees, torso swaying slightly with the ship's motion. While Hemp went to fetch my supper, I moved my chair to face forward, the bunk now to my left, and regarded her for a moment. She'd recovered remarkably for such a short time and seemed to have no lasting physical deficit from the trauma. I'd taken enough beatings to know how she felt on that score, but the other... She'd said that she'd been abused before. I couldn't imagine what was going on behind those dark brows.

Maybe it was time to talk to her some more. I'd been putting it off until she was at least physically recovered, but we'd be in port tomorrow. And I had questions.

"How do you feel today, Preel?"

She opened her eyes and blinked at me, then shrugged.

I took the rebuke. *Stupid question...*

Hemp came back with a platter supporting a single covered dish and several small bowls. Bert had taken the hint and reduced my portions. The bowls contained various garnishes for the main dish, a fillet of searaker surrounded by sautéed onions and peppers. The voracious, and very tasty fish often follow merchantmen. In decent weather we usually trail lines to catch what we can to vary the diet of salt meat, hard tack, rice, beans, and dried peas in all their varied forms.

"Plate something for Preel, Hemp." I shook out my napkin and took up my knife and fork. "I want to talk to her while I eat."

"Aye, sir!" Hemp filled my cup from a bottle of soju, a mild fermentation of rice that complemented the fish, then hurried out.

Turning back to the table, I tucked in, trying first one garnish, then the next. Sweet, spicy, savory, tart... Damn, Bert was amazing. Where had she gotten all these flavors? I wondered if she might be a closet alchemist. Then again, all good cooks are alchemists, after a fashion.

Hemp returned with a bowl of some of the same fish in a stew over rice. I suspected this was officer fare, not the common crew meal, but let it go. I'd told Bert to feed Preel whatever she saw fit, and the slave could probably benefit from a little coddling. Hemp put it down before her and handed her a spoon, then poured some water into a cup for her. Lastly, he reached behind her head to unfasten her gag.

"Thank you, sir." Preel nodded to me and lifted her bowl.

"As you may have heard, we'll be in port tomorrow." I continued my meal, enjoying the mixture of flavors. "We'll have some time ashore."

She ate slowly, eyes down, uninterested or unsure of how to respond. Of course, she could hardly expect shore leave for herself, so whether we were in port for a day or a month didn't affect her in the slightest. What she didn't know was that I planned to use the time to ask her a few questions and maybe find a buyer for her. I hadn't yet decided whether or not to sell her to Jhavika.

"Before we arrive, I'd like to know more about you and ask at least one more question that will require your…talent."

"My *curse*, you mean."

That surprised me. Not that she considered her talent a curse, but her acerbic tone. No doubt she still bore some harsh feelings toward me for her ordeal. I could hardly fault her, but I wasn't going to take ridicule from a slave. I opened my mouth to tell her to soften her tone when she spoke to me, but couldn't make myself say it. Levying rebuke for her bitterness at being mistreated seemed petty.

"Call it whatever you like." I flipped a dismissive hand and chased another bite of fish with a sip of soju. "Those exercises you were doing… I'm curious where you learned them."

Her eyes rose to mine for a moment and I could see the unspoken "Why do you care?" written plainly there.

"It's called Yamshi. My second master insisted that I learn it to stay fit." She returned to her meal.

"And you continue to practice it, even though he's not here to enforce his will upon you?"

"Yes." Again the short, almost biting answer.

"Why?"

She looked up and shrugged. "It gives me something to do, something to occupy my mind."

"You said you read, yes?"

"Yes."

"Good." I got up from my meal and went to my bookshelf. I picked out two books of poetry that I liked and put them on the bunk by her knee. "There. If you don't like those, there's more." I sat back down to my meal.

"Why…" Her hand reached out to brush the cover of one of the books. "Why do this, sir?"

"Because you're a priceless treasure, Preel."

Her eyes darted up to mine, her cheeks darkening. "A *what?*"

"A treasure." I ate and considered her reaction. "Whether you consider your talent a gift or a curse, it's an invaluable ability. You must know this."

"I understand, but why does my value as a truthsayer prompt you to give me…" She touched the books again. "To loan me your books?"

What a crop of fools her previous masters must have been to treat her so poorly, I thought.

"Because, Preel, mistreating something, or some*one*, of such value is foolish. Consider my crew; I can either beat them into submission or encourage them to perform their duties well by treating them well. Which do you suppose provides me with a better crew?"

"The latter."

"Exactly. So just like keeping my weapons polished and clean, keeping the ship's rigging in trim, the sails in good order, swabbing the decks, and careening her twice a year for bottom cleaning and caulking helps me in the long run, keeping you healthy and as happy as you can be also benefits me."

"Why?" She looked puzzled. "I'm not a ship or a sword, sir. You may treat me as you will and the answers I yield will be the same. You could abuse me as your crewman did as often as you like, and still I would be forced to answer your questions. I have no choice."

I frowned and chewed another bite, then shook my head. "Until you found a way to kill yourself, or tricked me into asking you a question too soon, as you tried to do before." I pushed my plate away. "Only a sadist or an idiot treats another person poorly when it serves no purpose. I've seen the results of that type of *discipline* first hand. It ends badly."

She stared at me for a moment longer, then attended to her meal.

"Hemp!" He entered, and I gestured for him to clear away my empty dishes, but leave the bottle of soju. When he'd gone, I filled my cup and turned my chair to face Preel. "After your meal, I wish to ask you a question that's been plaguing me for some time, but I want to make sure I get the answer I need."

She didn't respond, so I continued.

"You said before that you can't foretell the future or what someone *will* do. But do you know if you can say *why* someone already did a certain thing?"

"That would depend on the thing that was done, sir, and why it was done." She shrugged. "If the reason was merely personal satisfaction, then the answer might just be because that person *wanted* to do it. If there was a specific goal achieved by that action, the answer might be more precise."

"Interesting." I rubbed my jaw, fingers tracing my scars. "And quite a conundrum."

I'd had three days to craft this question, and still felt like a blind man. I thought about my dealings with Jhavika—her goals, her ambitions—and shook my head. She'd always been ambitious, but since she'd moved ashore, her ascent into the higher echelons of

Haven business and society had been nothing short of meteoric. If I sold Preel to her, Jhavika's success would compound exponentially, but might also get me killed.

The real question was, how the hell did Jhavika always get her way.

"Do you know if you'd be able to tell me about methods? If I asked *how* someone managed to do something, do you know if that would receive a good answer?"

"Again, it depends, sir. A vague question is more apt to elicit a vague answer, whereas a specific, *focused* question is more likely to provide a specific, focused answer."

"All right." I finished my soju, corked the bottle, stood, and started to pace. Discovering what I wanted to know about Jhavika was going to be tricky. If I asked Preel how Jhavika did *anything*, the answer might be, "She's persuasive," which would do me no good at all.

From the day we formed our partnership, it seemed to me that I'd done her bidding, sometimes against my better judgment. But asking how she always convinced me to do what she wanted rather than what I wanted seemed a very nebulous question. Again, Preel might simply tell me that Jhavika is persuasive.

From overhead I heard a roar from Wix, then a yelp from a crewman who obviously had vexed the bosun. *Thank the gods we'll be in soon.* Another day out and I might indeed have had a mutiny on my hands, just as I'd told Jhavika. I halted mid-pace and considered. The mission to take *Hymoin* was a perfect example of her convincing me to do something against my better judgment. My crew had been disgruntled, we needed time ashore, but I'd done what she told me to do, *knowing* I was risking mutiny. That had to be my specific, focused question.

When next I looked at Preel, her bowl was empty.

"Hemp!"

"Sir!" He was through the door in a heartbeat. Sometimes I wondered if he stood there with his ear pressed to the wood, but I'd never caught him at it.

"Clear Preel's dishes and take the bottle and cup. I've got the first watch, so I'll be going on deck in an hour or so." I nodded to my bunk. "Preel will be sleeping, so don't come in here while I'm on watch."

"Tired is she?" He smiled as he picked up her bowl and cup. "All that twistin' and turnin' maybe got her tuckered plum out, it does. Exercise is a sure way to an early grave, I say. Nobody ever died of a seizure from sittin' on his bum with his feet up, ya know."

"Thank you, Hemp. That'll be all."

"Very good, sir."

He left and I turned to Preel. "Do you need to use the head?"

"Yes, please."

I unlocked her manacle and she hurried to the quarter gallery. After she'd begged me to end her life once, releasing her from the magical binding made me nervous. I'd locked my razor and daggers in my cabinet, but if she chose to kill herself, crawling out the quarter gallery window while we were underway would probably do the job. Finding a man overboard in even mildly choppy seas would be like finding an honest merchant in Haven. I paced and waited, gnawing on a fingernail. I tried to listen, but could hear nothing over the rush of the sea past the hull and the working of the ship.

I was about to call her name when the door opened.

Preel stepped out, looked at me strangely—did I actually look as worried as I felt?—then hurried back to the bunk.

"All right, get comfortable, and I'll ask my question."

"Yes, sir." She lay down, her head on my pillow, legs braced against the roll of the ship.

I felt curiously reluctant to ask, but I didn't know if it was fear of what I might discover or a reticence to use Preel like this so soon after her ordeal. It felt like forcing a horse to gallop when it had a lame hoof or ordering a crewman to dive into shark-infested water to

113

retrieve sunken treasure. But this wasn't something that would be easier if I put it off or that I could do myself. Preel had a talent, god given perhaps, and that talent was meant to be used. Using it did her no harm.

So I asked.

"How did Jhavika convince me to hunt down *Hymoin* when I didn't want to?"

Preel stiffened, and her eyes rolled back as they had before, her voice a harsh rasp. "The scourge has tasted your flesh. You must do its master's bidding." She went limp.

"What?" *The Scourge?* I leaned over her and grasped her shoulders. "What the hell are—" I bit my lip and released her. I'd very nearly asked her what she was talking about, which might have invoked her talent again. Without her gag on, it would have killed her.

I snatched up the silk band and affixed it over her mouth. I don't know why, but my hands were shaking. I clipped the manacle around her wrist and backed away from the bunk, staring at her as if she'd caught fire.

"What the *hell* are you talking about?" I whispered. "The *Scourge?* My *ship?*"

I looked at the timbers over my head, the planks beneath my feet. *My ship...* Her words rang in my mind... *The Scourge has tasted your flesh. You must do its master's bidding.* It didn't make sense. Even though I'd certainly spilled blood and torn skin aboard *Scourge*, I was her master, not Jhavika.

"Fucking truthsayer my ass!" I whirled, grabbed up my jacket, stomped into my boots. "Hemp! Place a guard. I'm on deck!" I strode past before he even responded. I needed air and time to think about this, and more room to pace than my cabin allowed.

I grabbed a weather cloak at the wet locker and flung it on. The night air was bracing, whipping my hair into my face as I climbed the steps to the quarterdeck. Miko blinked at me and I could see in her face that she knew something was wrong. I waved her away. I had to think. I had to make sense of this, but how?

You must do its master's bidding...

What the hell...

One thought recurred to me. Maybe it *was* a sham. Maybe Preel was lying. Maybe she wasn't a truthsayer at all...

But that didn't make sense either.

My temper rose and fell with each swell and trough. I paced before the taffrail, trying to piece the mystery together, but however I tried, I couldn't.

"Sir?" I turned to find Miko staring at me, worry writ large on her features. "What's wrong?"

"I asked." I didn't have to elaborate. She knew what I meant.

"And you didn't get the answer you wanted?"

"I didn't *understand* the gods-damned answer!" I bit back another surge of temper. "Maybe I asked the wrong question. I don't know."

"You mind telling me what the question was?"

"Not at all." Two heads were better than one, after all, and Miko was sharp. "I asked how Jhavika talked me into going after *Hymoin* when I didn't want to." I shrugged. "Seemed simple enough, right?"

She nodded. "And the answer?"

"Cryptic as hell!" I barked a laugh. "Let me get this word for word. 'The scourge has tasted your flesh. You must do its master's bidding.'"

Miko blinked. "The *Scourge*?"

"That's what she said. Makes no sense at all, right? I mean, I'm master of *Scourge*, not Jhavika!"

Miko pursed her lips and shook her head. "I don't know, sir. Maybe she didn't mean *Scourge* the ship, but some other scourge."

"What other *Scourge* is there?"

"Every ship has one. You had Wix stripe Quiff's back with ours after that fiasco with Boxley, remember?"

"But Jhavika's not the captain of a ship! What scourge—" I stopped cold, a knife of pure ice slipping between my ribs to touch my heart. *The* scourge, *you idiot! The scourge that used to belong to Captain Kohl! The scourge he applied liberally to the backs of every single crewman, offense or no, then slept like a baby at night without fear of mutiny. The scourge that Jhavika picked up when we fought over the captaincy and lashed across my face. The scourge that she now wears on her hip and lashes her new slaves with.*

"Shit!"

"What?"

"Captain *Kohl's* scourge."

Miko looked confused. "What about it?"

"Remember when Jhavika and I fought after Kohl died?" I fingered the scars on my face. "She lashed me across the face, then yielded. When she left, she took it. She still has it."

"The captain's cat-o'-nine-tails?"

I nodded. "And Miko, the thing never leaves her side! She has it with her all the time. I watched her lash two brand new slaves with it like she was *indoctrinating* them or something!"

"Some kind of enchantment?" Miko gaped like she'd been knifed. "Could Jhavika have some kind of magical *control* over you? Over *us*?"

"No." I shook my head. "It's not possible. I disagree with her all the time! This is a *partnership*!"

"She tells you where to go, what ships to take, and who to kill for her." Her face turned to stone, hard and impassive. "And you do it, every single time!"

"No." I tried to remember one time I'd refused Jhavika…but couldn't. "I entered into this partnership willingly. We've all profited by it!"

"You entered into this partnership because she *told* you it would be a good idea. Do you remember what she said?"

I fingered the scars on my face. "She said she'd be queen of Haven when it was all said and done, and that she could use a pirate on her side. Queens have navies and I could be her admiral. It would be a good partnership."

"And you agreed."

"It seemed like a good idea, Miko, and it *has* been a good partnership."

"As long as you do what she tells you to do."

"It's not *like* that!" I flexed my hands at my sides as if straining for something to grasp, a lifeline. "She's just so gods-damned persuasive! She told me taking *Hymoin* was important, and I agreed."

"Did she tell you why? Did she really explain why, or just tell you it was important and you believed her?"

"Of *course* I believed her, Miko! She's not going to…" I stopped myself from finishing that thought. Why *wouldn't* Jhavika lie to manipulate me? I recalled the encounter. "She told me it was important, and then told me what I had to do: take *Hymoin* and kill Captain Nightspinner. Then…she told me I wouldn't argue with her."

"She told you not to *argue*?"

"No, she said 'And you won't argue with me on this.' I remember thinking, 'Like hell I won't,' but then I just…agreed. I thought if she was so hell-bent on taking *Hymoin*, it *must* be important, and I should go along. Then I insisted we get some time off when we came back."

"But that had nothing to do with taking *Hymoin*! She told you not to argue, and you *didn't*!"

"No, I…didn't." It was hard to wrap my mind around the possibility. It couldn't really be an enchantment, could it? Wouldn't I feel something? Some compulsion?

"Kevril!" Miko rarely used my given name and it brought me up short. "Preel *couldn't* have lied to you. Not if she's really a truthsayer. Think about it. The scourge has tasted your flesh." She reached up and ran three fingers down my scarred face. "You must do its master's bidding. Jhavika is the scourge's master and she lashed you with it. It answers everything."

It felt like a boot slamming into my gut. I knew that feeling well. It meant you were helpless, and the next blow would put you down.

"I have to be sure." *Before I kill her…*

"That should be easy, just try to tell her to fuck off." Miko grinned. "But that'll be dangerous."

"Too right, though we do have one advantage."

"And what's that?"

"The one passed out in my bunk."

Miko grinned again, ivory teeth flashing. "Right you are, Captain."

Chapter Nine
Compulsion

The only revelation greater than the slave realizing that he is free,
is the freeman realizing that he is a slave.
The Lessons of Quen Lau Ush

From the diary of Kevril Longbright –
I never thought that I could become a slave to the truth as a
drunk is a slave to drink. Yet so have I become. May Odea
help me...

After more than a week at sea breathing nothing but salt air, the
reek of Haven hit me like a slap across the face. I wouldn't even
notice the funk in a day or so, and I wasn't sure if that thought
bothered me more than breathing the foul air in the first place.
Sailors tend to be attuned to smells, as they're attuned to the
vibrations of working timbers and the groan of rigging. At sea, a
whiff of rot in the bilge or mold in a compartment meant someone
wasn't doing their job properly. Docked in Haven, a corpse could rot
down to bones in the main hold and nobody would smell it.

"Necessary evils," I muttered to myself as I gauged the
waterfront.

"What's that, sir?" Miko glanced at me from where she stood at the quarterdeck rail, supervising the two boats nudging the ship toward the quay.

"I said that I forgot how much this place stinks." I wrinkled my nose in distaste.

"Smells like money to me, sir!" She grinned and snapped an order to one of the coxswains.

"I suppose." I let the crew do their jobs and watched the pier as *Scourge* neared, my mind whirling with trepidation.

As heaving lines were thrown and caught, and hawsers were passed to the bollards, I considered my options. I'd had two watches to think over my strategy to confirm whether or not Jhavika had some kind of hold on me. The easiest way seemed to be to disagree with her on something, to take a stand and not back down. Easy enough…maybe. The real trick would be not letting her discover that I suspected foul play. If there really was magic afoot, if the scourge gave her dominion over those Jhavika lashed with it, then she would hold that secret very close to her vest. If it became common knowledge, someone would either put a blade in her back to take it from her or kill her for having control over them.

Like I'm going to do, if it's true.

But I had to be sure.

The massive hemp bumpers that kept *Scourge* from grinding against the stone quay groaned in protest as the hawsers were snugged. The gangplank thumped down and Quibly strode across wearing his best, waving to the few merchants who had already begun to assemble. My purser had spent four days sequestered with our ill-gotten cargo and knew its value down to the last penny. He'd told me how much he expected to get for it, and I put aside Jhavika's cut from my own not inconsiderable stash. Then I deducted a third of it and put it aside in a red satin bag on my chart table. This was my first test of Jhavika's control over me. Never once had I shorted her on her percentage. If I could successfully lie to her about that, it would give me room to maneuver.

"Captain?"

I jerked out of my musing to find Hemp standing a step away with a cup of blackbrew and a huge pastry on a plate.

"Morning nibble from Bert." He grinned and handed me the scalding cup.

"I had breakfast."

"Aye, that you did sir, but Bert says yer too thin and you need to eat up."

"Tell her she can piss up a rope." I'd just about had it with people telling me what to do. I sipped the blackbrew and glared at the pastry. Hemp just stood there with a look of utter innocence on his face. I could have ordered him to take it away, but my mouth started to water. "Oh, fine." I picked up the gooey monstrosity and took a bite. The taste of nuts and spices, sugar, and some type of dried fruit exploded in one chewy, wonderful mouthful.

"Tasty, ay, sir?"

"Mmmm." I chewed and swallowed, chasing it down with another sip of blackbrew. "And if she keeps this up, I'm going to need a longer belt!" I took another bite and put the rest on the plate. "Take it away."

"Aye, sir." Hemp eyed the leftover pastry, and I knew it would never make it back to the galley. "Oh, thought you'd like to know that Preel's awake."

"Fine." I finished the blackbrew and handed over the cup. "Feed her. I'll be down to change shortly. We're in no rush, and I want to watch the cargo offload." That was a lie. I was putting off talking to Jhavika.

"Aye, sir." Hemp hurried off.

"Shore leave, sir?" Miko asked, one eyebrow cocked.

"Damn *straight*, shore leave!" I said it loud enough to get the attention of half the crew. "The moment the cargo's sold, the off watch goes ashore. And tell them I've got a bonus for every jack and jane aboard. I'll give it to you to distribute before I go." It was the best use I could think of for the money I'd cheated from Jhavika.

Miko's eyes popped in surprise and a grin lit her face. "Aye, sir! You're getting soft-hearted."

"That's a filthy rumor that I will deny to my grave!" I snapped in blatantly false indignation. "I'm a rotten bastard, and don't you forget it!"

"You'll always be utterly vile and repugnant in my book, sir!" She snapped a salute and hurried forward to spread the good news.

The mirth and surprise spread through the crew like ripples on a pond, and the cargo came out of the hold with a vigor I hadn't seen in weeks. The laughter and tomfoolery among the crew lit my heart with a warmth I'd forgotten I could feel. Morale problem solved. When the last crate had been lifted from the ship's hold and deposited on the quay, I finally went below to my cabin.

Preel sat on my bunk spooning porridge into her mouth with a will. Evidently the use of her talent stoked her appetite.

"Thank you, sir," she said, lifting her bowl and hazarding a weak smile between bites. Evidently the long sleep had also improved her mood.

"Not at all." I doffed my shirt on the way to the quarter gallery and did a quick swipe with a washcloth. I looked in the mirror and decided not to shave.

As I toweled dry, I frowned at the finery that Hemp had laid out. I wasn't trying to impress Jhavika this time. She'd already agreed to give us some time off. In fact, finery might send the wrong message. If anything, I wanted to incite a confrontation so I could disagree with her; looking a little sea-worn might help there. I picked a plain white linen shirt from my locker and a black jacket with wide lapels and cuffs. One dagger in my boot and another clipped to my sword belt, then I added my favorite cutlass.

"May I ask a question, sir?"

Preel's voice surprised me. I think that was the first time she'd initiated any kind of conversation. As usual, she sat tailor fashion, back straight, her dark eyes clear and fixed upon me, the empty bowl by her side. I wondered at the slight change in her, the faintest hint of boldness, maybe, and considered whether to encourage or discourage it.

"Yes, you may." I finger-combed my hair and shot my cuffs.

"Do you go to confront the master of the scourge?"

"You remember?" I looked at her as if she'd asked me for a kidney, so shocked by the question. "You recall the answer to my question?"

"Yes, sir. This woman, Jhavika, I think, must be the master of the scourge my answer referred to."

"Yes, I figured that out." I didn't need a slave to tell me that.

"And you go to confront her?"

"Not exactly. I'm going to find out if she *does* actually have some kind of hold on me."

"And if she does?"

"I said you could ask *one* question and I've answered it." A little boldness was fine, but too much would cause problems.

Preel looked down. "I'm sorry, sir. I overspoke."

"That's all right." I pursed my lips in annoyance. Why did I say that, when I'd just told myself that she was being too bold? *First Jhavika, then Bert, and now a slave...* I waved my hand impatiently at Preel. "Do you need to use the head before I go?"

"Please, sir." She held out her manacled wrist.

I worked the key in the lock, and she scurried for the quarter gallery. While she was gone, I belted Jhavika's percentage around my waist and tucked my shirt over it. Preel was out in moments this time and hurried back to the bunk. She sat obediently and held out her wrist, and I clicked the manacle closed around it. Snatching up the bag of money I'd deducted from Jhavika's cut, I stuffed it into a pocket and started for the door.

"Sir?"

I turned, surprised again that she'd spoken without my leave. I supposed the dove had flown on that score, since I didn't rebuke her for it the first time. "Yes?"

"Please be careful with Jhavika. If she learns that you know of her control over you—"

"I figured *that* out by myself, too, Preel."

"I'm sorry, sir." Her gaze dropped to her lap and remained there. "I don't mean to be presumptuous. I'm simply concerned for you."

"You shouldn't be." I gripped the door latch, then looked back. "If Jhavika has me murdered, Miko will take care of you."

"Yes, sir." She didn't look up.

I left the cabin and found Miko on deck. The cargo looked to be selling briskly, and half of my crew were making ready for their shore leave, as primped and combed as five minutes with lye soap, salt water, and a straight razor could make them. They'd started lining up beside Miko, waiting expectantly for their bonus money.

"Here." I fished the bag from my pocket and handed it to her. "Two imperials each."

"Thank you, Captain!" a foremast jack shouted from the front of the line, grinning gap-toothed.

"Aye! Thanks, Captain!" another said with a salute.

Before I could open my mouth, the deck erupted in calls of thanks and cheers.

"Avast that caterwauling!" Wix's bellow cut the noise like a broadsword cleaving flesh. In fact, it doused the chatter between Quibly and the merchants as well.

"Thank you, Wix." I stared at my crew with a stern mien. "Don't get used to this treatment. If you get falling-down drunk and knocked on the head by some press gangers, don't expect me to come get you."

"That's right. The captain's a right bastard, and don't you forget it!" Miko added with a grin, earning a glare from me and a chuckle from my crew.

"Anyone not back in time for the next shift to take their leave will be docked the amount of this bonus." I put a hand on my cutlass and glared. "Now, go kick up your heels, you scallywags."

"A cheer for the captain!" cried a crewman far enough from Wix to avoid a drubbing.

The cheers echoed off the warehouses, probably scaring half the whores of the waterfront right out of their beds.

"You old softie," Miko said low in my ear as I started for the gangplank.

I turned to her with a grim smile. "Tell that to Mister Geit."

The look on her face made my morning.

I strode off the ship and took the first empty cargo lift, settling my mind onto the less pleasant task of dealing with Jhavika. My walk to her estate was uneventful, with only one attempted pickpocket and a dozen or so offers for various intoxicants, entertainments, and sexual favors. A slow day for this den of iniquity.

I rang the bell at the gatehouse guarding the bridge to Jhavika's estate and looked out over the roof-top crowds while I waited. The door creaked open to reveal the ever-grinning Ty-lee.

"Captain Longbright! We were afraid you'd fallen prey to pirates!" He laughed at his little joke and motioned me through.

I didn't laugh. "Ty-lee. I trust your mistress is home."

"Quite at home, Captain, and positively on pins and needles to meet with you." His smile remained undaunted by my lack of mirth.

I resolved to try harder and glared fixedly, imagining how his face would look if I cut that smile off.

It didn't work.

Smile still intact, he led the way across the bridge, glancing back. "Is there a problem, Captain?"

"Yes, there is." I didn't elaborate. I'd decided that coming into this confrontation with a smoldering temper would suit my purposes nicely.

"I pray it's nothing to do with Lady Keshmir." Ty-lee's smile faltered.

"*Lady* Keshmir?" I snorted a laugh that had no more mirth in it than the look on my face. "I don't discuss my business with *butlers*, Ty-lee. I thought I made that clear."

125

His smile vanished utterly. Score a victory for the vile and repugnant Captain Longbright.

"You did." He nodded solemnly. "My apologies, Captain."

We arrived at the vestibule of Jhavika's manse without another word, and Ty-lee opened the door for me. I stepped through and waited for him to usher me to his mistress. He did so silently. Evidently even butlers can learn new tricks.

Ty-lee took me down two flights of stairs to the second floor and out onto the back terrace. Jhavika stood beside the marble balustrade sipping from a crystal tumbler, a wedge of lime floating amid ice chips in the clear liquid. As she turned toward me, my eyes immediately fastened on the cat-o'-nine-tails coiled on her hip like a viper ready to strike. I struggled to avoid staring at it, deepening my frown. Jhavika's glance took in my mood and the conspicuous lack of a smile on her butler's face, and her welcoming smile thinned.

"Kevril."

"Jhavika," I stopped just out of striking distance and crossed my arms, resting my hands on the pommels of my blades.

"I expected you days ago. Was there a mishap?"

"No. Just weather." I cast a pointed glance at Ty-lee, then looked back to her. "Can we speak in *private*?"

"Of course." She swirled her glass so the ice chimed against the crystal and gestured to the stairs leading down into the gardens. "Walk with me."

I followed her down the stairs, wondering if I could escape the grounds if I clove her from collar to navel with my cutlass. *Probably not...* Besides, I had to be sure of my facts before I did anything so drastic. Cleaving is generally considered drastic. I settled for walking along in silence.

We strode side by side between rows of flowers I had no idea the names of. I never really understood gardens. You have to support half a dozen slaves to create and maintain an enclosed area that simulates nature. Why not simply walk through a real forest and see real nature? Yes, the flowers are pretty, I suppose, but so is a needle fish before you pick it up and feel its pretty spines piercing your flesh. Then your hand rots off while you scream and beg to die. I've learned not to trust pretty things just because they're pretty.

"Is something wrong?" Jhavika asked finally.

"Yes. *Hymoin*'s cargo wasn't as fine as you told me it would be. Our take was little more than half what you said, and my crew are fit to be keel-hauled." I glanced at her. "And as far as the morale situation, I was forced to execute one of my midshipmen on the return trip because he attacked someone. That's twice in a row you've been wrong about cargo, Jhavika, and I'm a hair's breadth from a full-blown mutiny. Our *partnership* is becoming a little one-sided."

"That's strange. My intelligence informed me that *Hymoin* purchased a cargo of fine silks, wine, and spices."

"Then your intelligence isn't very *intelligent*, is it?" I put as much venom as I could manage into that. I was pretty proud of that venom, but it had little effect.

"Apparently…" Jhavika paused to bend and sniff a flower, one hand resting idly on the coiled scourge. "But you *did* kill Captain Nightspinner, didn't you?"

"No. One of my crew beat me to it."

"Good enough."

"Why kill Balshi's brother-in-law other than to piss him off even more than he will be for losing *Hymoin*?" I gave her an accusing look. "Is this actually business, or are you risking our necks for a personal grudge?"

"You don't need to know, Kevril. Knowing *why* I send you on these missions would only put you in danger." Her smile held all the warmth of the ice in her drink. "And I *do* care about your safety."

"Don't feed me that bilge water, Jhavika!" If I was going to start a real argument, I was going to have to crank up the invective. "I'm in danger every time I leave port and doubly so sitting in port. Haven is full of spies, assassins, and worse, most of them working for your competitors. And the sea, you might remember, has its own hazards.

I risked my life to take *Hymoin*, against my protestations, I might add, and I didn't make *half* what you promised I would. *Scourge* needs repairs and I gave what was left of my cut to my crew to keep them from jumping ship the instant we returned."

"Kevril, I understand—"

"No, Jhavika, you *don't!* You've been ashore too long to understand half of what we go through. You sit here in your stone fortress and sip iced drinks and sniff flowers while I risk my life, my crew, and my ship! For you!"

My tirade wasn't all feigned; I was trying to test Preel's prophecy. I could obviously lie to Jhavika and rail at her with no inhibitions. Maybe she didn't have control over me after all. But I needed her to order me to do something so I could turn her down flat. Only that would truly test this supposed enchantment.

"Kevril, please calm down. You're upset. I understand. You and your crew *have* been working hard and deserve some time to yourselves. I've delayed some of my operations enough to give you ten days, at least, before your next mission. How's that?"

"That should do." Her conciliatory tone sucked all the vitriol out of my rising temper, and it was damn hard to disagree with someone when they gave you exactly what you'd asked for. Maybe all I needed to do all along was stand up for myself. "But our take…"

"Keep my percentage on this one, then." She waved a hand as if the money riding around my waist didn't matter at all. "Enjoy it. You've earned it."

"I…" This was unprecedented. Jhavika *never* gave away money. "I don't know what to say. Thank you."

"You're welcome." Her smile warmed, and she cocked her head for me to follow as she continued her stroll. "*Scourge* was damaged, you say? How badly?"

"We came rail to rail with *Hymoin*, a much heavier ship than *Scourge*. We need a new cap rail and a few knees and planks. Quite a lot of joinery damaged, but nothing structural below the waterline."

"Well, *that's* good, at least." Jhavika strolled again, pausing time and again to admire the beauty of a bud or inhale a flower's fragrance. She stopped finally and turned to me. "I won't lie to you, Kevril, I'm not pleased with your…attitude."

"My *attitude*?" *Here it comes*, I thought, *my opportunity to get in a pissing contest.*

"Yes." She fixed me with a regal stare and continued. "I tell you I understand your difficulties and you tell me I'm full of shit. I give you time off and don't even get a thank you. I *do* understand the difficulties you face. What *you* don't understand are the difficulties *I* face."

I opened my mouth to protest, then realized I didn't have a leg to stand on in this argument. Jhavika had been a pirate and a seafarer once; she *did* know what that entailed. I, on the other hand, had no inkling of the struggles she faced in climbing the web of crime, corruption, assassination, and intrigue that seethed beneath the surface of Haven's upper class. But then again, I didn't know because she kept me in the dark.

"I'll grant you that, but it's hard for me to empathize when you won't tell me the reasons for my missions. And don't give me that 'I fear for your safety' crap."

Jhavika raised an eyebrow. "You want *in* on this? Is that what you're saying?"

"No." I could think of nothing worse than becoming embroiled in the morass of criminal politics that permeated Haven like pus in a suppurating wound. "No, I don't want in on your dealings. I want you to respect my assessment of my own ship and crew, not fan it away like smoke on the breeze. I don't understand your problems because you don't tell them to me. I expect you to listen to mine because you *were* a pirate once and *should* understand!"

She frowned, but more in consideration than disapproval. Obviously, there was no magic prohibiting me from disagreeing with Jhavika. I was beginning to wonder if this truthsayer's revelation was nothing but smoke and mirrors.

"What you're saying, I *think*, is that each of us has to trust the others' judgment with regard to their own expertise."

"Yes, I suppose that *is* what I'm saying. That's how partnerships are *supposed* to work." I was actually starting to feel good about this discussion. "You listen to me and I listen to you."

"Fair enough." Jhavika looked at me sidelong, then smiled and gestured toward a hedge of bright red flowers. "Walk with me, then, and listen to this. I have something coming up that you may be able to help me with. Something that might...fit you nicely."

"Oh?" I had no interest in helping Jhavika with one of her plots, but she was being so agreeable, telling her to piss off would be overtly rude. I couldn't risk her suspecting I was picking a fight on purpose. Besides, listening wouldn't hurt. I could always say no. "What *something* is this?"

"I little thing, really. I'm entertaining two of the lesser lords on the council, Getashi Temuso and Ursilla Roque. They need wooing and I think having you there would...impress them."

"I'm *impressive*?" I gave her an incredulous look.

"Whether you know it or not, yes, Kevril, you are." She reached up to finger the lapel of my plain black jacket. "Especially when you're cleaned up and wearing your best. You're intimidating as hell and have a...dangerous quality that might bolster their opinion of me. I've arranged to have them over for dinner and entertainment, but have no one I trust to balance the table. You'll be bored by the conversation, but the food will be excellent and the entertainment will be...well, I think you'll like it."

I didn't like the idea of posing as Jhavika's pet pirate for her lordling friends, but I had to have a good reason to bow out. "When?"

"Tonight. Your arrival is serendipitous."

"Tonight's out of the question. I have plans for the evening." Not exactly untrue. I had a date with a meal in my cabin and a bottle of something mind-numbing.

"Kevril, I *need* you *here*. If you want me to meet you halfway, you have to help me, too. This is important for *both* of us." Her eyes hardened. "Cancel your plans. I want you to wear your finest and make yourself as presentable as you can. Be ready at sunset. I'll send a carriage and escort."

I opened my mouth to protest—this was exactly the opportunity I needed to take a stand against her on a simple matter—but then I considered our previous conversation. I'd look like an ass refusing something as simple as a dinner after agreeing to respect her judgment with regard to her business as she respected mine in matters of seamanship. I didn't want to look like a hypocrite. Besides, it was just a dinner.

"All right." I nodded to her respectfully. "In the interest of our new understanding, I accept your invitation."

"Excellent!" Jhavika beamed and turned back to her flowers. "Thank you, Kevril. I appreciate it."

I glanced down at her hand resting on the grip of the scourge and felt a chill. *The scourge has tasted your flesh. You must do its master's bidding.* Preel's words rang in my mind like a discordant bell tolling my fate. I replayed Jhavika's invitation in my memory and realized that it sounded more like a command than a request. Had my capitulation been my idea or induced by magic?

I could think of only one way to find out, but it was too soon to ask Preel another question. I couldn't risk her life. That truthsayer was the only card I had in this game.

Chapter Ten
Dangerous Questions

The truth is a double-edged sword.
The Lessons of Quen Lau Ush

From the diary of Kevril Longbright –
I laugh to myself now every time I hear the old adage "What's the harm in asking?" Watching Preel convulse and fall senseless after a simple question took me aback like nothing else. When she begged me to ask her who had assaulted her, I realized in my soul that a question is never simple. The consequences of asking can be unforetold and have nothing to do with the answer. The question itself can inflict harm. And not just to a truthsayer.

Miko met me at the gangplank when I arrived back at the ship. Our cargo had vanished into the warehouses of the waterfront. The deck was spotless, sails furled in tight bundles, lines coiled, and bronze fittings gleaming. After five days beating to weather, putting the ship to rights couldn't have been an easy task, but my crew seemed to have done it in short order. The inducement of pending shore leave, no doubt. The carpenter and his mates were working on the starboard cap rail, and the sweet, dusty pall of fresh-cut teak filled the air. Only a few sailors still lounged around on guard duty or busied themselves with minor tasks. The off watch had been ashore for an hour now and wouldn't be back for several more. The orderly, calm surroundings should have been soothing, but the quiet unnerved me.

"Well?" Miko asked, her brow furrowed.

"Come aft with me. I need to talk this over with you." All the way back to the ship I'd pondered my exchange with Jhavika, the truthsayer's prophecy, and this supposed enchantment. I needed a second opinion.

"Yes, sir." Miko followed me aft without further comment.

We entered the great cabin to find Preel doing her exercises, twisting and turning like a slow-motion warrior fending off attacks, dodging and weaving, feinting and striking. Of course, it was just exercise; nobody would train a slave in a martial discipline. She stopped when she saw Miko behind me.

"What's that she was doing?" my first mate asked as she closed the door.

Preel sat on the edge of my bunk, her skin sheened with a light sweat, her breathing deep and regular.

"Just exercise." I stowed my cutlass in the locker and sat at the chart table, waving Miko to a chair at the dining table. I wrenched off my boots and flexed my aching feet.

"So, how did it go?" Miko's gaze lingered on Preel. I couldn't blame her for looking. May as well tell a starving man to ignore a sizzling beefsteak.

"Strangely." I recounted my conversation with Jhavika as best as I could remember, word for word, action for action. Miko listened attentively, and I also noticed Preel hanging on every word I said, as if any of this pertained to her in the slightest. When I got to the part about Jhavika donating her cut of the profits to me without my even asking, I untucked my shirt and removed the money belt. "So why would she do such a thing if she's got *control* over me?"

"That's...bizarre." Miko eyed the heavy belt as if it might morph into a serpent. "Since when does Jhavika give away *anything*?"

"Exactly." I dropped the belt onto the table and shrugged. "It was almost like she was trying to woo me. If she had *control* over me, all she'd have to do is tell me to shut up and do my job. I'll have another opportunity to test this...thing again tonight. She invited me to dinner with some friends of—"

Preel shook her head, quick and jerky, her eyes wide. We both looked at the truthsayer, then at each other.

"I think she's got something to say."

I frowned and got up. "Very well, Preel, I'll let you speak." I removed her gag and dropped it to the bunk. "Careful with any questions, Miko."

"Absolutely, sir," Miko agreed.

"Please, sir, I think you might be misinterpreting Jhavika's largesse."

"Oh?" I shared a glance with Miko, but she just shrugged. "You don't even know Jhavika. Explain how you think I'm misinterpreting her."

"She's giving you what you want to make you *believe* you have free will. Only when something truly matters will she invoke the scourge."

"Why do you think she'd do that? If she could control me, she could just command me to do as she wants and order me to forget that it was her idea, not mine."

She shook her head. "Magic cannot alter your memories, sir. At least, none that I've learned about. She has to worry that you could discover that she's manipulating you. She's being careful."

"You're educated in magical lore?" Miko asked.

"Yes. My second master insisted that I learn as much as I could about how magic works, what it can and cannot do. He...wanted magic for himself, you see, but my...talent is unable to discern the locations of powerful artifacts."

"Then how..." I stopped myself from asking the question outright and killing Preel with my carelessness. "How do you *think* your talent told me that Jhavika controls me using the scourge?"

"Because your question was not about the scourge, it was about Jhavika." Preel shrugged. "If you asked me what abilities the scourge bestows upon its master, I would probably be unable to answer. You see the limitations?"

"I think so." I chewed a thumbnail and started pacing. "So, if she can't change my memories, but *can* make me obey...she'd be careful not to push the control too hard. If I guessed what was happening, I would be less...useful."

"Yes." Preel nodded.

"Or you'd put a blade through her skull when she wasn't looking," Miko added.

"Which begs the question: why hasn't she— Damn it! This is too dangerous." I whirled back to Preel and picked up the silk gag. "I have to put this back on or risk your life with my imprudence."

"I understand, sir." She held still while I fixed the band of silk over her mouth.

"If you have something to say, just rap on the edge of the bunk. You've brought up an interesting point, Preel, something I hadn't thought of." I stepped back and she nodded in understanding. "This is *complicated*."

"Like a puzzle with poison pieces, sir," Miko agreed. "So, what was your question?"

"Oh, right. So why hasn't she just ordered me never to harm her? I couldn't raise a hand against her if she did that."

"I don't know. Maybe she didn't want to risk that command. It would be a bit suspicious." Miko frowned, and we both looked to Preel.

The truthsayer simply shrugged.

"Damn..." I started pacing again. "So, she can't risk ordering me to do something I wouldn't normally do as part of our partnership or

135

I'd get suspicious. She's being careful, using the thing only when she has to."

"Right." Miko chuckled. "If she ordered you to stand on one leg and cluck like a chicken, and you *did* it, you'd know something was up."

"Right." I snorted a laugh at the image, then felt a knot tighten in my gut. "But if she can't change my memories of what she's ordered me to do, how can she make me think it was my idea to comply in the first place? When she ordered me to go after *Hymoin*, I thought about arguing, then reconsidered. She'd said it was important and I believed her. It seemed like a reasonable request, so I agreed."

"And you didn't argue, because she told you not to."

"Yes…" I thought about that. "I remember wanting to tell her I'd damn well argue with her if I wanted to, but then thought it wasn't worth it." I looked to Preel. "So if this really is some kind of magical control, it *is* changing the way I think, but it *can't* change my memories of how I…*came* to think that going after *Hymoin* wasn't such a bad idea."

Preel nodded.

It was a fine distinction. I had absolutely no experience with magic, so I had to trust Preel's assessment. I rubbed my temples. "This is giving me a headache."

"You should get some rest if you have to socialize with her this evening." Miko got up. "You're short on sleep and you need to be sharp to spar with her."

"You're right." I nodded and sighed. "Hemp!"

"Sir!" He was through the door in a flash.

"I'm dining at Jhavika's tonight and I need to be ready by sunset. Lay out my very best, everything spit and polish. My hair could use a trim, too."

"Aye, *sir*!" Hemp grinned like I'd just given him the day off. He hurried to my locker and took down several garments that he kept wrapped in linen and packed with bay leaves to keep the mold and moths at bay.

"Sir?" I turned to find Miko nodding toward Preel, who tapped her knuckles frantically against the edge of the bunk, her eyes wide.

I held up a finger and cast a pointed glance at Hemp. The last thing I wanted was to discuss this openly in front of my steward. Preel nodded in understanding. Of course, Hemp was so occupied with picking out my finery that I probably could have lit his hair on fire without his notice. He left the cabin carrying an armload of things to brush, polish, shine, and stitch, happy as a lark, muttering about tarnished buttons, lint, and boot polish.

I removed Preel's gag again and nodded, "Go ahead."

"This social engagement she invited you to. Did you truly want to go or did she order you to go?"

I opened my mouth to say that I could hardly turn down an invitation to dinner when she'd just gifted me eight-hundred imperials, but then I remembered that I had *not* wanted to go and that I'd made up an excuse not to.

"Bugger!"

"What?" Miko looked at me like I'd suddenly grown horns.

"I told her no, that I had another engagement. It was a lie, but I have *no* desire to go to this dinner. She's entertaining her lordly friends and only wants me there because I'm intimidating and balance the table." I made a face. "Then she told me it was important, and to cancel my plans and be ready at sunset...dressed in my best." I looked at the locker where Hemp had just retrieved my best clothes...at my orders.

My very best...

"Shit," Miko agreed.

"Please, sir, try to remember what you thought when she ordered you to attend. Did it seem like you simply changed your mind, or did you feel something else?"

"I didn't feel anything." I swallowed hard, trying to recall what had gone through my mind. "I just thought that she'd been so fair with me before, agreeing to give us some time ashore and her share of *Hymoin*'s take, that I'd be petty if I spurned her invitation. I'd just told her we needed to trust each other's judgment, and I couldn't back down from that. It made perfect *sense!*"

"Yes," Preel said, worry edging in her voice. "Yes, it *would* make perfect sense. The scourge made you incapable of refusing, so your mind made it seem like a good idea. You're captain. You're used to *giving* commands, not obeying them. You rationalized it."

"Maybe…" I gritted my teeth against the rising probability that I was being controlled through magic by one of the most avaricious people I'd ever known. "Gods and demons!"

"Please, sir, listen to me. You must be *exquisitely* careful tonight. You mustn't let her know you've learned of this control. If she does…"

"She'll order me to fall on my sword." I looked into Preel's dark eyes, dread wafting through my chest like a chill wind. "And I'd do it."

"Yes, sir, you would."

"Miko," I said, turning to my first mate.

"Yes, sir?" The same dread edged her voice.

"If I don't come back tonight, take *Scourge* and sail away."

"What?" She rocked back on her heels as if I'd slapped her.

I laughed, though there was more nervous fear than mirth in it. "I said sail away! You've been lashed with that damned thing, too. I don't know if Jhavika has control over you as well, since it was Captain Kohl who lashed you, but I don't want to take the chance. If you try to kill Jhavika, she might be able to enslave you as she has me."

"I understand that, but…" Miko blinked hard and swallowed. "Yes, sir. I'll sail away."

"Good." I gave her a smile. "Don't worry. I'll be careful. She won't know I'm onto her."

"What would…" Miko turned to Preel and cringed. "What do you *think* would happen if I tied the captain to a chair so he couldn't go to this dinner?"

"I don't know." Preel glanced to me, then back to Miko. "But Jhavika would know something was wrong."

"She's right," I said, running a hand over my stubbled jaw. "It's not worth the risk." I sighed and shrugged. "Don't worry, I'll just eat and smile. It won't be that hard. Besides, Jhavika said the food would be excellent!"

"Not better than Bert's, I'd wager." Miko patted her flat stomach. "I swear I've put on a stone in just five days."

A strange sound touched my ears, like the soft coo of a dove cut short. I turned to my bunk to see Preel hiding a smile behind her hand. The sound had been her laughter.

How, by all the gods of heaven and hell, can she ever laugh again after what's befallen her? I tried to smile at her, but I saw in her face that it came out as a grimace. I picked up the silk gag.

"We'd best put this back on before someone asks you a question by mistake."

Preel nodded and held still while I tied the thing in place.

"Is that all, sir?" Miko asked.

"Yes. I need some sleep before I get cleaned up for tonight. See that the watches change smoothly. There're likely to be a few fuzzy heads coming back from shore."

"No worries, sir." Miko sketched a salute and left the cabin.

I turned to the quarter gallery, but caught Preel staring at me. Her gaze fell to her lap before I could comment. I don't know why the gaze of a slave would unnerve me, but it did.

When Hemp touched my shoulder, I came instantly awake. The sun shone low through the stern gallery windows.

I'd slept *hard*.

I don't know how I managed it, with all the worries trundling through my head, but after a delicious lunch of shellfish stew, fresh bread, and a cup of light wine, I'd rolled into my hammock with the shades drawn and fell right into a dreamless and restful slumber. *Thank Odea for Bert...*

"It's time, sir," Hemp said apologetically. "Water's hot for your bath and the razor's honed and ready."

"Right!" I rolled out of my hammock with practiced ease and found Preel looking at me from my bunk, one of the books I'd loaned her in her lap. I gave her a nod and went to the quarter gallery while Hemp stowed my hammock and prepared for my primping.

Hot water, soap, and a vigorous toweling did wonders. When I stepped from the quarter gallery wearing naught but a towel around my waist, I felt like a newly minted imperial. I caught a wide-eyed look from Preel as I passed my bunk, but ignored it. Reluctantly, I'd allowed Miko to spread the rumor that she was some kind of enchantress pleasure slave that I'd taken for my own. Showing modesty in her presence would sweep that fallacy over the side like yesterday's bilge water.

"Here you are, sir!" Hemp dusted off the chair before my vanity and waved a welcoming hand. "Let's just see to your hair first."

"Right."

Hemp draped a towel over my shoulders and deftly trimmed my wet hair. My mind strayed to the coming ordeal, and I wondered if I would survive it. Hemp hummed as he worked, one of the sea chanties the crew sang. I caught my mind humming along and my spirits rose. Such a simple thing... The snipping scissors fell silent and he shook the towel out the stern gallery windows. Done with my hair, he whipped up soap with my shaving brush and applied it to my stubbly face. The razor scraped smoothly along my flesh without the slightest nick. Lastly, he doused a cloth with wood alcohol. I braced myself for the sting and managed not to jump.

"Slick as a merchant's conscience, sir!" Hemp cooed, shaking out the towel and stepping back. "I laid out the blue brocade and your best shirt, clean linens, and those black trousers with the silk stripe down the side."

"Very good, Hemp. Thank you." I glanced at the clothing and gleaming weapons precisely arrayed on my dining table. "Boots?"

"Just finishin' the shine on 'em now, sir." He stowed my shaving things and scurried for the door.

I kept the towel wrapped around my waist while I pulled on my linens and trousers. The waist felt snug, and I had to tug the last button into place. *Damn Bert into the Serpent's Eye!* I'd have to be careful not to overeat tonight or risk popping a seam. I checked my face in the small mirror beside my locker and caught sight of Preel behind me, sitting on the bunk like a temple statue with a book in her lap, her dark eyes watching me.

Just a slave, I thought as I turned to pick up my shirt.

A soft rap, like someone timidly knocking at my door, drew my eyes to the bunk. Preel raised a hand to her face and drew three fingers down from her ear to her chin, repeated the motion over her shoulder, then raised both hands palm up. The meaning was clear; she was curious about my scars.

"Yes, they're from that scourge Jhavika carries. She gave me these," I indicated the scars on my face, "when we fought over the captaincy of *Scourge*. The previous captain, Kohl, gave me the ones on my back. Well, most of them. My father had a deft hand with a willow switch, and I was a…rebellious youngster." Unbidden, a distant memory rose of the day I told my father that if he ever whipped me again, I'd kill him. He'd knocked me unconscious with a shovel for the threat. It was my first lesson in combat: never threaten, just kill. "No worse than most foremast jacks and janes bear after a career at sea."

Preel nodded and looked back to the book in her lap while I finished dressing. She couldn't speak with the gag on, and right now I didn't want hear anything she might say. I was nervous enough. Hemp arrived with my glossy dress boots. I donned them and let him fuss over the lay of my clothes. Lastly, I buckled on my dress cutlass and a silver dagger that complemented the glossy thread of my jacket's cuffs.

"That's enough, Hemp." I brushed away his fidgeting fingers and he stepped back, grinning with satisfaction.

"Ya look as sharp as yer best dagger, sir!"

"Yes, well, thanks to you." I looked out the stern gallery windows again. The sun was nearing the horizon. "You're going ashore with the second shift, aren't you?"

"Aye, sir." He brushed his hands on his shirt and straightened. "Got that bonus burnin' a hole in my pocket and I know just how I want to spend it! That was right kind of you to give us extra coin, sir."

"Well deserved." I tugged my jacket straight once again and thought about the pending night. "Just keep your wits about you ashore, Hemp."

"And you, sir." Hemp brushed non-existent lint from my shoulder. "Jhavika's dinner table's probably more dangerous than most the brothels in Haven, and not near as much fun."

"I can't argue with that."

A knock rattled my door and Miko leaned in. "Jhavika's escort's here, sir."

"Thank you." As I started for the door, her eyes roved over me from head to toe. A grin spread across her lips and she opened her mouth, but I forestalled her with one raised finger. "Not a word, Miko. I'm not in the mood."

"Not a word, sir." She sketched a salute and tried to suppress her smile as I passed.

The escort surprised me. I'd expected a few thugs on horseback and a hired hackney, but an elaborate coach and four matching horses awaited me on the quay, surrounded by a dozen liveried horsemen, all armed to the teeth. The horses were already mired to the hocks from the filthy streets of Haven, but their tack and harness gleamed. I wondered why Jhavika was going to such an effort for me.

Probably to impress her fancy friends.

"Keep your boots clean, sir," Miko said at the gangplank.

Her mirth had devolved into concern. "I will." I paused and regarded her, realizing how lucky I was to have a first mate I could trust implicitly. "Remember my orders."

"I will, sir."

Suddenly I realized that she'd been on deck all day, standing my watch as well as her own. "Sorry you're pulling double watches here. You can take off as soon as I get back. I'm sure there's someone ashore who's eager to see you."

"Thank you, sir." Miko's skin was dark enough to hide a blush, but I was sure it was there. "I sent her the dress."

"Good." I strode off my ship and stepped aboard the carriage. Adjusting my cutlass, I sank into the plush seat as the door clicked closed, and the coach lurched into motion. I felt like a ship running before a gale with a lee shore looming.

Chapter Eleven
Painful Answers

One does not know fear until one lies at the mercy of a pitiless soul.
The Lessons of Quen Lau Ush

From the diary of Kevril Longbright –
I wonder sometimes about Haven, how long the city can survive like this with people dying of hunger, neglect, disease, and malice in the streets every night. Where do they all come from? Is there an endless supply of human refuse just waiting to fill the gutters and alleys, working their way into the city from outside like worms boring into a rotten apple, finding nothing to feed upon inside but each other? Will I be one of them someday?

I actively avoid the streets of Haven; even pirates have standards. A few times early in our partnership, back before she had an estate and her own private soldiers, Jhavika sent me on occasional missions into this festering pit of refuse, blood, and misery. With thirty seasoned pirates at my side, I'd not feared the rabble of the streets. This time, I was just along for the ride, shuttered up tight in a carriage and surrounded by a squad of cavalry. I was supposedly safe, so I sat back and girded my tightening nerves.

The carriage driver skirted the worst of it, I think. I tensed a few times as shouts and catcalls rang out, and a few bottles and stones were thrown from the shadows. The outriders bellowed for people to get out of the way. More than a few times they drew steel to give the bolder ones incentive. Once, a scream rang out, and the carriage jolted over an obstruction. The driver didn't slow, even though I felt sure he'd ridden someone down.

Such is life and death in the streets of Haven...

The ride did little to improve my mood.

I had never seen the street-level entry to Jhavika's estate, so when the procession cleared the inner city and the shouts and catcalls fell silent, I slid open one of the shutters and ventured a peek. A stone ramp centered upon the north wall led up one level to a portcullis flanked by rounded barbicans. The portcullis rose at our approach and rumbled closed behind us. Evening cast the small courtyard in shadow, but scores of bright lanterns drove off the gloom. The carriage stopped before a tall double door flanked by more of Jhavika's liveried guards.

How many does she employ? I wondered, as I stepped down. A man head and shoulders taller than I stepped forward and gestured me toward the portal.

"This way, Captain." The fleshy mountain's voice rumbled like distant thunder. "The mistress and her guests await your arrival."

"I'll bet they do." He cocked an eyebrow at my muttered comment, but I ignored him.

Shut up and make the best of this, Kevril, I told myself as I strode through the door. If I came off as belligerent or ungracious, Jhavika might suspect I knew something, so I painted on a false smile and prepared to face the woman who could command me to fall on my sword.

"Kevril!" Jhavika whirled around to face me, a beaming smile on her lips and a crystal glass in her hand.

145

"Jhavika." I strode forth, trying to look elated. I felt like asking who the hell she was and what she'd done with Jhavika Keshmir. I'd never seen her so bedecked in finery.

Her gown squeezed her torso into an hourglass of golden satin the exact hue of her intricately coifed hair. Topaz dangled from her ears and encircled her throat in a V that delved her daring neckline. Matching elbow-length silk gloves concealed the scars of dozens of sea battles that marred her hands and forearms. The hem of her dress brushed the floor, but a slit up the side revealed a shapely curve of leg as she flowed forward to greet me.

"Right on time, too!" She leaned in to kiss my cheek and whispered, "Loosen up a little, Kevril. You look like you're ready to leap into battle."

"Isn't that what this is?" I whispered back, but I eased the tension in my shoulders and neck by sheer force of will. Raising my voice to a more conversational volume, I said, "You look lovely this evening. That color suits you perfectly." *The hue of gold...and avarice...* At least she couldn't carry that gods-cursed cat-o'-nine-tails in that getup.

"And you look positive *delicious*!" She took my hand and pulled me forth. "Come meet my friends."

Jhavika was playing it up, of course, putting on a show for her crime-lord friends on the council. She positively bounced with eagerness as she dragged me toward them, like a little girl showing off a shiny new toy.

Which is exactly what I am, if Preel's right, I thought. *Nothing but her marionette...*

"Lord Getashi Temuso, Lady Ursilla Roque, I'd like you to meet Captain Kevril Longbright." Jhavika beamed at me in well-feigned pride. "A former shipmate of mine and current business associate."

"Ah, yes, the pirate." Temuso extended a hand. He looked Chen, but with some mixture of highland or horse-lord blood, swarthy and dark-eyed. "Well met."

"And you, Lord Temuso." I took his soft hand in mine and resisted the urge to crush it. Jhavika wouldn't approve. "Though I prefer *former* pirate, if you please. Now that I work with Jhavika, my pirating days are over."

"Of course." He nodded graciously, his immaculately trimmed goatee bobbing, pearly teeth glowing beneath his waxed black moustache. I don't think he believed me. Maybe he was brighter than he looked.

I released his hand and turned to the other. "Lady Roque."

"Captain Longbright." She extended a manicured hand. Bending to kiss it, I felt calluses along her fingers. The lady exerted herself in some way other than counting money. Looking me up and down, she smiled in approval. "Jhavika's told us about you. I must say, though, you aren't what I expected."

"Am I *not*, Lady Roque?" I smiled amicably. "What did you expect?"

"Oh, something more piratical, I suppose. Your finery and…well, general appearance are more lordly than any sea captain *I've* ever seen."

I barked a laugh. "Lordly?" I scrutinized the lord and lady. They looked exactly as I'd expected: rich, vain, and shrewd.

Roque wore a deep green gown that rivaled Jhavika's at the neckline and plunged far down her back. Emeralds graced her ears, throat, and two of her fingers. She was slim, shapely, and stood a hand shorter than Jhavika. Her jet-black hair looked dyed, but it was full and styled in an intricate coiffure that emphasized her shapely neck with a few dangling curls. She had a tiny scar on her left cheekbone that was partially concealed by rouge. I guessed her age at no more than thirty-five, but I've never been good at that. Her arms were bare, and I noticed muscles playing along her right arm that were absent from the left. *She's a fencer, then,* I reasoned. *Probably a long, light blade with reach to offset her lack of height.* I wondered if she'd ever put her blade into a living opponent, one who was trying earnestly to kill her.

Lord Temuso, however, looked as soft as a freshly landed sole. He wore a blue brocade jacket a shade lighter than mine and a frilled shirt of lily white, a broad blue sash girding his slightly pudgy middle. He wore a katana through the sash, a pretty dueling blade that might be worth its metal or might be simply for show. The scabbard showed no signs of wear, and the hilt reflected the light evenly with no glossy patches where a hand would have worn the braided silk grip. His hands bore no scars, but I glimpsed one on his neck just under the edge of his beard as he turned to smile at Ursilla. I wondered how he'd gotten it.

"Kevril has a sense of style and a taste for the finer things, Ursilla." Jhavika flicked a hand and a footman approached with four full glasses on a silver tray. My three companions exchanged their nearly empty drinks for full ones. "And he cleans up nicely." She winked as she handed me a glass.

"I could say the same for you, Jhavika." I grinned like a wolf, more for show than out of sincerity. If she wanted me to play the intimidating pirate, I could do that. "Quite nicely indeed."

The two lordlings laughed politely.

"Why, thank you, Captain Longbright." She raised her glass. "Here's to the finer things."

We all drank. The beverage fizzed as it went down, light as air and heady. *Careful, Kevril. The last thing you want to be is out of control tonight.* I trusted my conscience and took another careful sip.

"But you are a fighting man, are you not?" Temuso asked, nodding to my cutlass. "I mean, Lady Jhavika employs you for...certain activities that require armed conflict, isn't that right?"

Certain activities that require armed conflict? I bit back a snort of derisive laughter. I couldn't call him a pompous prick, as was my reflex, but I could certainly set him straight.

"Lady Jhavika doesn't *employ* me, sir." I gave him a tight smile. "We have a partnership and share in the profits."

"But it *does* require fighting," Lady Roque said, her plucked brows knitted between her kohl-lined eyes.

"Not as often as one might think," I said, as if admitting a sad truth. "I haven't killed anyone in…" I thought of Geit screaming as I pitched him over the side. "…well, *days*."

The two of them blinked at me as if I'd draw steel and start slashing, but Jhavika laughed and they joined in.

"Yes, Kevril's reputation is such that opponents often surrender without a fight." Jhavika swept a hand gracefully in an inviting arc. "Shall we ascend to the dining room?"

I started for the stairs, but the two lords followed Jhavika in the opposite direction. Blinking in confusion, I turned to follow, wondering how we would get upstairs without actually *using* stairs. Seeing Jhavika's dress from the rear for the first time, however, I was taken up short. The scourge rode at the base of her spine, its barbed tips dangling over the curve of her ass, swaying suggestively as she walked.

Ice shivered up my spine, reminding me of how I came to be here. I quelled the urge to drive my sword into her daringly exposed back.

Jhavika led us to a small pair of doors manned by an attendant. He opened the doors and motioned us into a room barely larger than my quarter gallery.

"What's this?" I asked.

"Oh, I'd forgotten that you haven't seen this, Kevril." Jhavika stepped inside and waved the rest of us to follow. "It's a new device, all the fashion. An indoor lift."

"I see. Like the cargo lifts at the waterfront." I squeezed inside with the rest of them, and the attendant closed the door.

"Precisely." Jhavika pulled a cord and a bell rang high above us. The floor lurched upward.

"Easier on the legs than *stairs*," Temuso said, as if climbing stairs was for menials.

"Quite," Rogue agreed, her shoulder brushing my arm as we rose. "And rather cozy."

I returned her smile and gritted my teeth, feeling as if the walls were closing in on me.

The floor steadied, and the doors opened into a familiar corridor, white stone with gold accents. Two liveried footmen framed a pair of doors that opened onto a wide canopied balcony. Lamplight and torchlight both illuminated an ornately set table, a uniformed servant standing behind each chair. Pungent lemon grass scented the torch smoke. Crystal, silver, and porcelain gleamed on the white linen tablecloth, and a bouquet of pastel flowers centered the arrangement. The chairs were cushioned with silk. Lilting string music rose on the air from beyond the balustrade, musicians on the balcony below.

I like finery as much as the next man, but this seemed overly extravagant. I felt like I'd soil the cushions just by sitting down. I did, however, and managed not to flinch as an attendant shook out my napkin and placed it in my lap. Other attendants brought carafes of libation and the first course of our meal, tiny crustaceans arrayed in crystal bowls like the petals of a flower, a spicy sauce at the center.

I sat with Jhavika to my left and Ursilla—she insisted I call her Ursilla—to my right. My view of Lord Temuso across the table was partially blocked by the centerpiece, which excused me from talking to him overmuch. I'd have to thank Jhavika for that. I found Ursilla tolerable, but Temuso struck me as a merchant with more money than sense and a bloated self-opinion. Ursilla seemed to like him, however, and, as the meal progressed, the two exchanged sultry glances.

The food, at least, was excellent, with a different wine for each course. I ate carefully but with appetite, and barely touched the drinks, firm in my resolve to stay sober. The others drank steadily as they ate, and the conversation evolved from polite drivel to a vehement discussion of business, and finally to a surprisingly saucy analysis of the social interactions among their peers. I nodded, smiled, and laughed politely when appropriate, but didn't have much to add to the conversation.

Until the discussion turned to the unhappy fate of *Yellow Blossom*.

"Malchi's absolutely livid!" Temuso exclaimed as his attendant removed the second meat course. "He accused Fa-Chen of endangering his son's life! Ha! He sends a boy to sea in an effort to make a man out of him, and he thinks it'll be perfectly safe?"

So young Maurice was a noble after all. I shook my head and chuckled.

"You find that amusing, Captain? You earn your living on the sea and know its dangers."

"That I do, Lord Temuso, but young Maurice was *hardly* in danger." I nudged my plate away, settling back while the attendant removed it and swept away the few crumbs with one gloved hand.

"You know of what befell *Yellow Blossom*?" Ursilla's eyes widened, then narrowed, flicking between me and Jhavika.

"Let's just say that I have it on good authority that the only danger the young lord might have faced was a pulled *groin* muscle." I smiled at Ursilla and sipped the heady red liqueur newly poured to accompany the final course. "Captain Tan performed valiantly in the boy's...*education*, though I don't know how much of it was nautical."

"Kevril?" Jhavika narrowed her eyes and gave me a tight smile, clearly a warning not to give too much away. "Where did you hear *that* rumor?"

"Sea captains trade tales like trollops trade the pox, Jhavika. You know that."

"True enough." She sighed. "Well, it seems the boy has no aptitude for seamanship anyway. Malchi pulled him ashore after the loss of *Yellow Blossom*."

"The boy's got other talents," I said, pushing my nearly full glass aside, "from what I hear."

"*I* hear he's hung like a stallion," Ursilla stated with a saucy smile.

"Considering a liaison?" Temuso asked with a laugh. "The boy's a bit *young* for you, my dear, isn't he?"

"A few years difference in age didn't bother Captain Tan." I raised an eyebrow at Ursilla.

The music rose in pitch, lilting and rhythmic.

"Exactly." Ursilla leveled a steamy stare at Lord Temuso. "Maybe I'll seduce the boy and form an alliance of marriage. Pull Malchi over to our side by his youngest son's cock."

"A worthy goal," Jhavika said, raising her glass in toast with a lascivious grin. "But be careful not to bite off more than you can chew, my dear."

"Oh, I can *chew* quite a lot." Ursilla raised her glass in return.

Temuso and Jhavika laughed openly at the retort. I just smiled and sampled my dessert, a chocolatey baked concoction topped with sweetened cream. Two figures moved fluidly through the doors to the corridor and past us, a man and a woman dressed in flowing translucent silks. Upon the broad expanse of the balcony, they began to move to the rising music. I recognized the two slaves I'd seen Jhavika lash with her whip. The significance of those lashes now crashed into me like a runaway coach. *The scourge has tasted your flesh.* Had she been lashing them to control them? It made sense, and the notion sent a chill up my spine.

The rich dessert set my teeth on edge. I pushed it away.

"Too sweet for you, Kevril?"

"Yes, and I'm overfull already." I sighed and patted my stomach. "I recently hired a new cook for *Scourge* and I'm afraid I'm gaining weight."

"An ample middle is a sign of prosperity, Captain Longbright." Temuso patted his stomach and smiled.

"Perhaps, but for a man who relies on agility and fitness to stay alive, it's a death sentence."

"That may be true, but a man *or* woman," he raised his glass to Ursilla, then to Jhavika, "of *true* power may rely on others to provide such services."

"Until someone sneaks up on you with a dagger in their hand," Ursilla retorted. "Personally, I rely on no one. I find it safer that way."

"Everyone relies on *someone*, my dear." Temuso narrowed his eyes at me from around the flowers. "Even the captain here must rely on his crew. Isn't that right?"

"Yes, that's right, but going into battle *with* them, instead of behind them, shows them that they can rely on me as well." I shrugged. "A ship is a very tightly knit community, Lord Temuso. As Jhavika knows, it can't be ruled by utter tyranny."

"Is that right, Jhavika?" Temuso looked genuinely surprised. "I've always heard that a captain is utter lord and master aboard ship, judge and even *executioner* when necessary."

"Both are true, Getashi, as I'm sure Kevril would agree." Jhavika nodded to me. "Tyranny aboard a ship can lead to mutiny, but a captain must maintain discipline. Loyalty through mutual trust and respect makes that easier."

"Interesting." Temuso sipped his liqueur and eyed me.

"Our captain is full of surprises." Ursilla drained her glass and held it out for a refill. "And no wonder Jhavika is so successful, if she follows that philosophy."

Or she uses that gods-damned whip riding on her ass to assure obedience through magic. I smiled at Jhavika, trying to remain calm and keep my true emotions hidden. The music picked up in tempo, and my eyes were drawn past our hostess to the undulating dancers. I decided to try for a change of subject.

"Those are the two new slaves you recently purchased, aren't they?" I waved off my attendant's attempt to refill my glass.

"Yes, they are." Jhavika smiled at me and turned. "Lovely aren't they?"

"They are," Ursilla agreed.

"Beautiful indeed," Temuso complimented.

"Shall we relax and enjoy the dance?" Jhavika rose and we with her. "I've arranged an extended performance."

We moved to the two low divans that had been placed to view the dancers. A ring of aromatic torches burned around the periphery, casting the two slaves in a wavering light that enhanced their graceful and sinuous movements. I sat beside Jhavika, and Ursilla beside Lord Temuso on the opposite divan. I'd left my glass behind, but attendants stood beside each seat, offering cordial, liqueur, and pungent plum brandy.

When I declined the offering, Jhavika interjected.

"Oh, have *something*, Kevril. Don't be a stick in the mud." She waved the attendant forward. "We're all friends here."

No, we're not, I thought, but I saw little harm in having one more drink, and I didn't want to cause a scene. "Brandy, then."

I sipped amicably as we watched the dancers in the torchlight. They were truly gifted—lithe, muscular, and graceful—moving as though the music itself played their limbs as a minstrel plays a lute. They slid along one another sensuously, effortlessly. Backlit by the torches, the sheer silk became transparent, and as he pirouetted, twirling her over his head, it became obvious that neither wore undergarments. The music changed tempo again, building in urgency, and their movements evolved from sensual to outright erotic. Their hands brushed at breast and groin, lips met and passed with the hint of promised kisses.

"Lovely *indeed*, Jhavika," Ursilla purred, one hand pressed to her bosom while the other traced circles upon Lord Temuso's leg. "Where did you find such a perfectly matched pair so well formed and skilled?"

"A local supplier," Jhavika said.

The male dancer lifted his partner high. Wrapping her legs around him, the woman slid down his body like a pole, her diaphanous garment riding up to expose her dusky legs and flanks. She arched her back, her nails raking at his costume. The cloth tore, revealing his chest and rippled abdomen, then tore further to reveal even more.

"Oh…she's woken the serpent now," Temuso chuckled.

"And a mighty creature it is." Ursilla caught her breath as the female dancer caressed her partner's manhood. "Oh, Jhavika, how deliciously decadent."

"I thought you might enjoy it." Jhavika's fingers played with the hairs at the back of my neck, sending shivers down my spine.

"Oh, I *am*." Ursilla leaned against Temuso's chest, his arm around her shoulders, her nails tracing lines up his thighs. "Might I...borrow them some time?"

"I'm sorry, Ursilla, but they're not for loan." Jhavika's fingers tickled through my hair, then clenched it tightly just as the male dancer did the same with his partner, clutching her close enough for her lips to brush his phallus, then pushing her away. "I've taken great pains to...train them properly."

"So I see." Ursilla squirmed on the divan as Temuso's hand slipped beneath her bodice to fondle her breast.

"But you can enjoy them as much as you like tonight, my dear." Jhavika's other hand slid up my leg toward my crotch. "One or both of them."

The female dancer reclined on the floor raising a shapely leg, and her partner took it, pulling her up. Her back arched, but her legs remained rigid, one up, one down. He grasped her by the hips and yanked her to him. She cried out, her face contorted in a mixture of pleasure and...something I couldn't name as he entered her.

"Oh, Jhavika, I may have to take you up on that offer." Ursilla gasped at Temuso's caresses.

"Please do." Jhavika's nails raked the bulge in my trousers, sending jolts of sensation through me.

No...

I shifted and disengaged myself from Jhavika's questing grasp, rising from the divan. I knew where this was going and wanted no part of it. I like a romp as much as the next man, but I couldn't do this, not with Jhavika, not with these two lordlings whom I didn't know and certainly didn't trust.

"Kevril, where are you going?"

"I'm leaving." I downed my brandy and dropped the glass on the divan beside her. "This isn't my...type of entertainment."

"Oh, sit *down*, Kevril, and *enjoy* yourself." She nudged the glass aside.

I opened my mouth to tell her no, then found myself sitting back down. My gut clenched in fear. I'd had no intention of sitting, but my body complied without hesitation. I strained to get up again and couldn't. The erotic dance continued, the pair contorting and writhing in imaginative poses of copulation. Ursilla's dress had slipped off her shoulder to expose her breast, and Temuso's soft fingers teased her taut nipple as she caressed his crotch. Jhavika's hand quested up my thigh again.

And I found myself enjoying it, all of it.

No! By the gods...I will not!

"Kevril, you're trembling." Jhavika leaned in to nuzzle my neck and whisper in my ear. "Don't worry. Just relax and enjoy this. It's just play."

Even as I felt the tension ease away at her command, my worries vanishing like mist in the sun, I opened my mouth to protest. "Jhavika, I—"

"Shhh." Her tongue flicked my ear. "Don't speak, just relax and *enjoy* this. You *want* to."

And to my own rising horror, I *did*.

Preel's raspy voice in the throes of her talent rang in my mind— *The scourge has tasted your flesh. You must do its master's bidding*—and I knew it was true. I was a slave.

Chapter Twelve
The Deal

Nothing is more dangerous than a warrior enslaved.
The Lessons of Quen Lau Ush

From the diary of Kevril Longbright –
I remember the day I left home, the feeling that I was finally free. Free of my father's tyranny, the beatings, the ridicule, the helpless anger. I remember thinking that I would never let that happen again. What an ignorant fool I was. Now it seems that I have been nothing but a slave my entire life, from a helpless boy to a witless ship's brat to a sniveling midshipman, all the while enslaved. Even as captain I'm a slave to Jhavika's lash, her will, her debasement. I wonder if I might have been better off staying at home and enduring my father's beatings. At least there I could fight back.

My knees very nearly folded as I stepped from the carriage onto the quay. I slammed the door and cursed under my breath at the trembling muscles of my legs, back, and stomach. Walking a straight line to the gangplank challenged my nerves and had nothing to do with alcohol. I gripped the railing with white knuckles and crossed to my ship, teeth gritted against the weakness, the helplessness, and the memories of the evening.

I'm going to kill her... That had become my litany during the ride home, and I intended to bring it to fruition. *But not now. Not yet.* Right now, I needed to expunge every memory of the last six hours.

I stumbled as I stepped through the boarding hatch down onto the deck, but the sailors on watch must have seen something in my face that warned them off. Or they thought I was drunk, which would serve just as well. They both just saluted and kept their faces neutral. I would have thanked them had I been in a thanking mood.

I'm going to kill her...

I flung open the sterncastle door and strode aft, feeling a little stronger. My legs had cramped during the ride back, fatigue followed by sudden immobility a dangerous mixture. By the time I reached my cabin door, I felt steadier. I nodded to the guard, opened the door, stepped through, and leaned back as it closed behind me, gritting my teeth against my memories.

"I'm going to *kill* her." The oath barely left my lips, a harsh whisper in the dimness of the lamps turned low. I didn't mind the darkness. I didn't want anyone to see me.

I lurched toward my locker, shaking fingers fumbling at my sword belt. I hung it up and eased my shoulders out of my jacket. The muscles of my lower back quivered. I flung the fine garment to the floor, then fumbled with the buttons of my shirt, reeking of perfume and the musk of sex. Jhavika had ordered me to enjoy it, and I had, but she couldn't command me to forget that I'd not *wanted* to, that I'd tried to leave and she'd commanded me to stay. I felt as if I would retch. I threw the shirt atop the jacket, then sat gingerly on my dressing stool. Removing my boots without passing out challenged my fortitude, but I had to get them off. My breath came in gasps as I eased out of my trousers and bloodstained linens. Not all of the blood was mine, but some of it was.

I'm going to kill her...

I kicked the clothes into a pile—I'd have Hemp burn them tomorrow, but I didn't want to face him tonight—and staggered to my quarter gallery. I had to wash off the stink of perfume, sex, and blood. Water, cool and clean, stung the lacerations on my flanks— *Beg me*, Jhavika had whispered in my ear. *Beg me to whip you as you fuck her.* I gritted my teeth against the pain, the memory worse than the actual welts left by Jhavika's scourge, the memory of my begging her to lash my ass as I fucked Ursilla Roque. That had been the tipping point, the cliff she had pushed us over. With utter control over me and her two pleasure slaves, she'd worked her two friends into a frenzy of lust, all the while whispering in my ear, *Enjoy it! You love it! Beg me for more...*

And, helpless, I had.

As the game of sex and pain escalated, she applied the scourge to both of the lords as well, lashing playfully at first, then hard enough to raise welts. That was when I finally understood her game. The whole evening had only been a pretense to give her the opportunity to do this. Once the scourge tasted their flesh, she would have two slaves on the Council of Lords who would never disagree with her...ever again.

Like me.

I'm going to kill her...

I scrubbed the stink from my body, reveling in the sting of soap on my welts. Drying myself, I hissed in pain and a deeper anguish as the towel came away bloody. I gritted my teeth and wrapped the towel around my waist. Back in the cabin I pulled a bottle and glass from my cabinet. I didn't even look at the label. I didn't care. My hand trembled as I poured, liquor slopping over the rim of the glass. I downed half of it, swallowing hard the spicy rum, willing it to burn away the shame, degradation, rage, and impotence.

It didn't.

I finished it and poured more, gulping it down, liquid fire filling my belly. I sat down too hard, winced, and poured a third.

I'm going to fucking kill her...

159

Movement caught my eye and I jerked around.

Preel sat up on my bunk, her eyes wide and black in the dim light. I glared at her, cold anger smoldering in me, and took another swallow of rum. *Her fault*, my conscience said. *If she had never told me about the scourge, I would have never known Jhavika was controlling me, and my memories of tonight would be very different.* My knuckles whitened on my glass as I raised it trembling to my lips. As Preel stared at me, a tear trickled from one dark eye into the white silk that bound her mouth.

"Don't look at me." I drank more, my head already swimming. I wanted to forget, to purge my memory of everything I'd ever known.

Preel looked down into her lap and sniffed, crying openly. I didn't understand why she should be crying. It didn't make sense. She was a slave; she should be laughing her ass off at me, the mighty captain brought low by a slave's truthful answer to his own question. I drank more and glared at her.

"Why the hell are *you* crying?" My hands shook as I poured more liquor into my glass. I didn't know why I was bothering with a glass at all.

Preel looked up at me again, tears streaming from her dark eyes, her brow knitted in a mask of pain. She couldn't answer, of course, but clenched her hands at her breast and bowed over them. The gesture was simple: I'm sorry.

"I don't need your fucking *pity*!" I lurched up and threw my glass, not at her, but through the stern gallery windows.

Preel flinched and looked down again, her hands clasped in her lap.

A knock at the door. "Everything okay, sir?"

The guard… Damn! I went to the door and opened it a hand span. "Everything's fine. You're off duty. I'm going to bed. No need for a guard."

She looked worried but saluted. "Aye, sir." Turning, she walked away.

Damn… There'll be rumors now.

I closed and locked the door, then turned back to the frightened woman on my bunk, the woman who had been raped on that very bed. *Gods, what a fool I am*, I thought, realizing that making her sleep in the very place she'd been violated must be torture. I don't know why at that moment I felt sorry for someone I'd cursed a moment before, but I did.

"I'm sorry." I lifted the rum bottle, staring at the amber liquid within. "I'm more than a little drunk and…"

I looked up to find her watching me, and I winced, shamed at my selfishness. She'd suffered more pain than I would ever know.

"You were right." I took a long pull from the bottle and stared at her as I forced it down my throat. A deep breath banished my hatred of her, the blame for telling me the truth. "Jhavika has utter control over me. She commanded me like a puppet tonight. She ordered me to…do things I didn't want to do and even told me to *enjoy* it."

Preel tapped the gag at her mouth urgently. She wanted to speak to me.

"No. No, I don't what to hear what you have to say." I took another swallow of rum and wavered on my unsteady legs. "She told me to…" I couldn't say it. "…enjoy it and I did. I did everything she commanded, and I loved it because I had no choice. I'm her slave."

Preel's tears continued to fall, her eyes pleading. She tapped the silk band again.

"I don't want to hear you say that it wasn't my *fault*!" I wobbled to my chart table and sat, hissing through my teeth at the pain of the lashes etched into my flanks, and the other, deeper pain. The memory brought a bitter laugh. "You should be *laughing*. I got fucked tonight just like you got fucked. Neither of us could stop it from happening. We're both slaves, Preel, but I'm a captain. Ha! What a fucking joke."

Preel shook her head, a quick jerk of negation, and tapped the silk band again. Her eyes shone like obsidian orbs in the dim light, hard and fragile, but as sharp as daggers. I stared into them as they welled with tears. Why was she crying…for me? It didn't make sense.

I had to know.

"What the hell. Who cares? I'm not going to remember any of this in the morning anyway." Smacking the bottle down the chart table, I lurched up, forgetting that I wore only a towel until it started to slip. I turned away and tightened it, then turned back to Preel. She sat like a statue as I reached behind her head and worked the knot loose. The band of silk fell into her lap.

I took a step back and looked into her upturned face. "Well, say what you want to say."

Her tongue darted out to moisten her lips. "I will help you."

"What?" I blinked at her, my rum-soaked brain trying to make sense of what she'd said. "You'll *help* me? How? Can you purge the last six hours from my memory? Can you take the pain from my ass where Jhavika lashed me because I *begged* her to? Can you stop me from shitting blood tomorrow from getting fucked, because I *asked* for it, because Jhavika *told* me to?"

"No." Her lower lip curled in a hard frown. "Though I wish I could."

I stumbled back a step. She cared.

Why?

Even in my state of rising inebriation, I knew I couldn't ask her any questions that would invoke her talent. To that end I snatched up the bottle and sat back down to face her. The rum was working; my ass hardly hurt at all.

"Fine." I took a pull and swallowed. "How can you *help* me?"

"I am a *truth*sayer." Her back straightened and shoulders squared, as if for the first time she took pride in her ability. "You wish to kill Jhavika? Ask me how it would be most safely done. You wish to escape her grasp? Ask me how you can do that. You wish to remove the enchantment that binds you?" She paused, and the muscles bunched at her jaws. "*Ask* me."

"Sonofa*bitch*!" I raised the bottle to me lips again. The liquor burned a track to my stomach, but the question in my mind burned even hotter. "Why? Why offer to help me? You're a *slave*, Preel. I can order you however I wish. I can ask you whatever I want, and you *have* to answer!"

"Yes, I have to answer." Her eyes hardened until I thought they might shatter. "But that doesn't mean I have to help you ask the right questions."

"Okay…" I swallowed hard, raised the bottle, then thought better of it and put it down. "Why, again, do you want to help me?"

"Because, Captain Longbright, I know what it is to be a slave. I know what it is to be violated against my will. I know what you feel right now and I find it *abhorrent!*" Tears coursed down her cheeks, but her eyes bore into me like dark daggers. "Also, you avenged me. I am a slave, and you killed a free man because he violated me while I was under your protection. In thanks, I would help you, but…" She swallowed and looked down.

"But?"

"But I wish to make you a deal, Captain Longbright."

"A *deal?*" Slaves didn't make deals… Slaves obeyed. But then, most slaves didn't wield the power that Preel did. "What *kind* of deal?"

"If I help you break this binding, or kill Jhavika, or whatever is your end goal in this…" She raised her manacled wrist. "Free me."

My inebriated mind spun like a child's top. *Free her? End her slavery? Throw away a priceless treasure?* Miko would gut me. *Talk about killing the dove who laid diamond eggs…*

"I…" I reached for the bottle again and only managed to knock it over. I caught it before much spilled and sat it upright, forgetting why I'd reached for it to begin with. I stared at Preel, her dark eyes seeming to swirl in circles, the golden manacle luminous in the dim light. "I'm drunk, Preel."

"I know."

"I probably won't remember our conversation in the morning."

"I know. I'll remind you." The corner of her mouth twitched.

I blinked at her. By Odea, she was a beauty. I cleared my throat, intending to tell her so. What came out of my mouth was, "My ass hurts."

"I'm sorry for that, sir. If I could take away your pain, I would."

"Why?"

"Because you tried to take *mine* away."

"Oh." I swallowed hard and tried to stand. My legs folded, cramped again, but at least the pain was blunted.

Preel lurched forward to catch me, but all she managed was to ease the impact. It didn't matter. The deck felt like a featherbed under my cheek and her hand the caress of a dove's wing on my aching shoulder. I wondered if her hand would lay diamond eggs. I felt something warm settle over me before my mind descended into darkness.

"Sleep, Captain Longbright…"

I rode the truthsayer's words into oblivion.

Chapter Thirteen
Cautious Questions

Only a fool or an idealist fights an unwinnable battle.
The Lessons of Quen Lau Ush

From the diary of Kevril Longbright –
I never understood slavery until I learned of my own.
Keeping slaves always seemed to me too dangerous for a sea
captain. Accidents are too easily arranged aboard ship, and
no slave is truly content with his or her master. Even a
beaten dog will bite eventually, and a slip over a railing at
night is easier and more lethal than a knife in the back. The
slave's choice is not whether to rebel or accept slavery; a
slave's choice is always *when* to rebel. My time is now. The
question is: how to rebel and survive. Fortunately, I have
someone who can answer that question.

"Captain?"
Something touched my shoulder, softly, tentatively, and awoke a
dozen hot knives in my flesh. A sound escaped my lips, a groan or an
unintelligible curse, I couldn't tell. My mouth tasted like a rat's nest in
the bilge. When I tried to open my eyes, they felt as if they'd been

sprinkled with shards of broken glass. Every muscle in my body cramped, and my head pounded in time to my ragged heartbeat.

"Captain, your steward is knocking at the door." The voice at my shoulder—so soft and mild—hurt less than opening my eyes.

"Captain! Are you all right?" The voice beyond the door boomed like a god's, and thunder erupted in my head, seeming to shake the whole ship.

Hemp... Gods preserve me from enthusiastic stewards.

I rolled over, igniting another dozen hot knives, and tried again to speak. Something more intelligible came out. "Fine, Hemp. Give me a quarter glass before breakfast." I sounded like I'd been gargling hot coals.

"Aye, sir." The answer sounded dubious, but I knew he'd follow orders.

"How do you feel?" The voice and the gentle touch were Preel's.

I rubbed the gummy residue from my eyes and blinked up at her. She peered down at me from the side of my bunk, dark eyes wide, her tattooed brow furrowed with concern. A blanket—her blanket—had been draped over me. I wore nothing under it, a towel stretched out flat beneath me.

What the...? Memories... My effort to expunge them had failed, of course. They crashed down onto me like an avalanche of jagged stone. *Oh, Gods of Light, take me now and end this...*

My stomach clenched in a rebellious spasm.

I lurched up, tried to stand, failed, then tried again and succeeded, but only by gripping the edge of my bunk. The blanket started to fall away and I snatched for it, but releasing my grip on the bed proved a bad idea. I cracked my knee against the leeboard. I let the gods-damned blanket go and staggered to the quarter gallery. Bile burned my throat as I emptied the contents of my stomach into the scuttle. I retched again, my head threatening to explode, then a third time, and I wished it would. If my skull split open like a dropped melon, maybe the pain would go away.

I'm not that lucky.

When my stomach finally settled, I stood and splashed tepid water on my face, rinsing my mouth and risking a careful swallow. The water eased the burn in my throat and my stomach seemed to accept it without complaint. Another splash and a quick finger combing of my hair helped my headache a little. I reached for my towel, then remembered that it lay on the cabin sole beside my bunk.

"Shit."

I looked down and cursed whatever capricious god caused men to wake up with erections. Even my hangover hadn't affected this, and I wasn't about to walk back into my cabin like this with Preel staring at me. Not after last night.

More memories crashed in, and I thought I might be sick again. I relieved myself and drank some more water, splashing a little down my chest to hopefully chill my unseemly state of arousal. A few more swallows of water, some stretches to alleviate the cramps of sleeping on the deck, then one more splash, and things began to recede to normal proportions. There was nothing in the quarter gallery to cover myself with, so I hitched up my pride and stepped back out into my cabin.

Preel glanced at me, her eyes widened, and she averted her gaze.

I strode to my locker without a word and pulled on fresh linens. The welts on my backside were still tender, but less so. The other pains, both emotional and physical, blazed like fire. I drew up my pants, cinched my belt tightly, and picked out a light shirt. Thus garbed, I turned to face my slave-turned-benefactor.

She sat tailor fashion, her gaze cast down, her usual pose. I wondered if, after a night's reflection, she regretted her offer to help. The rumpled blanket and bloody towel lay beside her...no, *my* bunk. I walked over and scooped them up, much steadier on my feet now. She looked up at me.

"Are you feeling better?"

"Better than a few moments ago, yes." I flung the towel onto the heap of discarded clothing from the night before. A bottle of rum sat on the table, barely two fingers of liquid left in the bottom. No wonder I felt like my head was stuffed full of nettles. "Better than last night? No."

"I'm sorry."

"Stop that." I snatched up the bottle and stowed it, refusing to meet her dark eyes. "You have nothing to be sorry for, and I *still* don't want your pity."

"I'm…yes, sir."

I looked around the cabin, saw the broken window, and winced. I'd forgotten about throwing the glass. "I'm sorry if my drunken raving scared you. You've been through enough already and shouldn't have to tolerate that. And thanks for the blanket." I dropped it at the foot of the bunk.

"And our deal?" Preel looked up at me again, determination firming her expression. "Do you remember?"

"I remember." I unlocked the door, then returned to the bunk. "I'm thinking about that. I need to speak to Miko and consider this carefully." I picked up the ivory cloth etched with silver runes and held it out.

"Of course." Her gaze fell, her voice solemn, defeated. She leaned obediently forward and I fixed the gag in place.

"I am *considering* it, Preel, but things are…complicated."

She nodded.

I retrieved the key to her manacles from my cabinet and unlocked her wrist. "Use the head."

She scurried off.

A knock sounded at the door, and Hemp poked his head in. "All clear, Captain?"

"All clear." I gestured to the table. "Go ahead."

Hemp entered bearing a large platter of covered dishes, a pot of blackbrew, and a brimming glass of some type of juice. He put it on the table and started to place things with military precision. His gaze darted about as I sat down, obviously taking in the broken window and discarded clothing.

"Everything all right, Captain?" He poured blackbrew, strong and dark, the aroma euphoric. "The guard said there was quite a row last night."

"Not your business, Hemp." I sipped the scalding brew and thought I might just survive the day after all. "A bit too much to drink is all."

"Yes, sir." He uncovered plates: smoked fish, sausage, eggs, fried potatoes, porridge, and toasted bread.

My mouth watered. *Thank the gods for Bert.*

Hemp lifted a second bowl. "Bert sent porridge for Preel as well, sir. Is it okay to…"

"Yes." I tucked in, knowing from years of experience and hundreds of hangovers that food would put me to rights.

Hemp put the bowl, a spoon, and a cup of water on the shelf beside the bed. I noted that he moved the book I'd loaned Preel to do it and blinked curiously at the volume of poetry. Hemp could read, but barely. What he thought of me loaning my books to a slave, I had no idea, and honestly didn't care to know. When he went to pick up the pile of last night's clothes, however, I interjected.

"I want those burned, Hemp."

"Sir?" He looked at me as if I'd asked him to cut off his testicles. "But this is your *best* jacket!"

"Not anymore it's not. I want all of it burned. Do it today." I fixed him with a stare that brooked no argument. "Understand?"

"I'll do as you order, sir, but no, I *don't* understand." He tucked the bundle under his arm and stormed from the cabin, muttering epithets I didn't care to hear. I wasn't about to explain my reasons for my orders to my steward, and he knew it.

I concentrated on my meal for a few moments, chasing each savory bite with a sip of blackbrew. By the time the quarter gallery door opened, I felt almost human and had reduced the gargantuan portions of my breakfast by half.

"Breakfast," I said to Preel, pointing to the bowl on the shelf.

She nodded, approached my table, turned, and knelt to present the knot of her gag for me to untie. I'd almost forgotten and smiled at my own stupidity. I untied it and tossed it onto the bunk. She sat down and picked up her breakfast.

We both ate in silence.

When my plates were empty, my belt straining, and my head only aching rather than pounding with my heartbeat, I leaned back in my chair with a cup of blackbrew and tried to think. Hemp came in, took my plates and Preel's bowl, and nodded to the broken window.

"You want me to tell Wix to send someone to fix your window, sir?"

"Yes. And send for Miko, if she's aboard and awake. I need to speak with her."

"Aye, sir." He left, still surly and muttering.

I turned to Preel. "Do you need anything before I put your gag back on?" I hadn't refastened her manacle either, but with me sitting here she wasn't likely to do anything foolish.

"No, sir." She kept her eyes down.

I affixed the silk band around her mouth and sat back down to sip my blackbrew and think. My temper smoldered as I reiterated my new mantra.

I'm going to kill her...

But things weren't that simple. Killing Jhavika might solve my problem, but would also be dangerous in the extreme. Trying and failing would be disastrous. And that was only half my problem. Even if I did kill her, what about the scourge? Would someone else pick it up? *I* certainly didn't want it.

A knock at the door came as a welcome distraction. "Yes?"

Miko opened the door, trying to stifle a yawn. "You called for me, sir?"

"I did." I pointed to the other chair at my table. "Sorry about calling early, but we need to talk. Have you eaten?"

"Not hungry, sir, but thank you. Late night last night. That blackbrew smells good, though."

"Hemp! Another pot of blackbrew!" My shout made my head pound.

"Aye, sir!"

"Oh, and thanks again for the dress." Miko smiled broadly. "Illian liked it very much."

"Good." I poured the last of the pot into my cup and wondered how much to tell Miko about last night. It was humiliating to even think about, but I had to be honest with her if I was going to ask for her help. "I learned a lot last night. Preel was right."

"Oh." Miko's smile dropped, her hand rising to rub her eyes. She looked around the cabin and spotted the broken window. "I heard you were in a temper when you came back."

"I was." I sighed, trying to keep the pain out of my voice. "I still am. Jhavika commanded me to do things I didn't want to do, Miko, and she ordered me to *enjoy* it. I *did*."

"By Odea…" Miko looked like I'd slapped her.

"She has complete control over me. The whole night was a pretense for her to use that damned scourge on two of her crime lord friends, and it worked. She's gathering an army of slaves who don't even know they're slaves."

"But…" Miko blinked and shook her head. "How can she—"

Hemp knocked and entered with a fresh pot of blackbrew and another cup.

"Thank the gods." Miko accepted a cup and raised it. "And thank *you*, Hemp."

Hemp pressed a knuckle to his forehead. "Obliged for the gratitude, sir." His gaze flashed to me, his frown pronounced. "More'n some." He turned to go, muttering, "Orderin' perfect good clothes burned like they was rags…"

The door closed.

"So," Miko continued after another sip of blackbrew, "how can she hope to keep the people she controls with this thing ignorant of it?"

"By being careful, like she's been with me. With her slaves, she can probably just order them never to speak of it. With her retainers and soldiers, I'm sure she's more subtle. Last night, she crossed the line with me. If she realizes that today, I'm in danger. If she thinks I suspect, I'm a dead man."

"So, do you intend to sail away before she orders you to fall on your sword?"

"I don't know." I poured more blackbrew into my cup and rubbed my aching head. "But that's not all."

"What else is there?" Miko looked dubious. "If you can't fight her, you *have* to run."

"Maybe… Preel's offered to help me." I nodded to the truthsayer and she looked up at us, her dark eyes wide. "Under certain conditions."

"What conditions? She's a slave, and her talent isn't voluntary." Miko's brow furrowed as she looked at Preel, then back to me.

"True on both counts, but she knows magic, and she knows how her talent works." I sighed and shrugged. There was no delicate way to put it. "She's offered to help craft the questions to best deal with this…situation however we decide, whether it's to kill Jhavika, flee, or somehow lift this enchantment."

Miko's dark brows arched. "*Can* it be lifted?"

"We don't know until we ask, do we?"

Miko looked at Preel, then her eyes snapped back to mine. "Why? Why does she want to help you?"

"Because, in return, she wants me to free her."

Miko's mouth opened, then slowly closed. She downed her blackbrew and poured more without a word, the muscles of her jaw working rhythmically. She sipped and swallowed.

"You're talking about killing the dove that laid diamond eggs, Kevril."

"I know, but if she can help lift this curse—"

A rap of knuckles on wood drew my eyes to my bunk. Preel was shaking her head. She tapped her gag. She wanted to speak.

I shook my head. "No, Preel. It's too dangerous. We might accidently ask a question that would invoke your talent."

She nodded, then pantomimed writing.

"You can write?"

She nodded.

"Huh." I frowned, chagrined that I hadn't thought of this earlier. If Preel could read poetry, then she could certainly write. "She's just full of surprises."

"That she is."

I retrieved a quill and blank parchment from my chart table and handed them to Preel. "Okay, what do you want to say?"

She dipped the quill and scratched hurriedly. Her hand was better than mine, the script flowing and elegant. She handed it over and I read it aloud.

"I will still be a truthsayer if you free me. You would not be killing the dove, only freeing it." I looked to Miko.

"What's she saying? That she'd stay aboard and...let us use her talent?"

Preel nodded and reached for the paper. She scratched and I read, "I'm safe here. I can't walk around ashore marked like I am and wearing a gag." She tapped her tattoo, then the silk band.

"She's right," Miko said.

"But it'd be dangerous keeping her here, free or not. If word got out..."

Preel shrugged and wrote, "No more dangerous than selling me."

"She's got a point," Miko agreed. "If we try to sell her to a slaver, word's bound to get out, maybe even to Jhavika."

"True." I sat back down and drank more blackbrew. My head buzzed already, and my tender stomach roiled, but it helped me think.

"What would *you* choose to do?" Miko asked curiously. "Kill Jhavika, run, or try to break the enchantment?"

"Last night I would have said kill Jhavika, but now...I don't know." I massaged my aching temples. "Unless Jhavika realizes that I know what she's done to me, we have some time to consider those options."

"True." Miko poured more blackbrew, and I could see the wheels grinding behind her eyes. "Damned dangerous no matter what you do."

"Yes, it is."

Preel's quill scratched, and I read her message aloud.

"First find out if the enchantment can be broken, then decide." I looked to Miko. "Seems reasonable."

"She's smart." Miko stared at the truthsayer with a mixed expression of admiration and worry. "So, are you going to take her up on her offer?"

"To free her?" I saw the hope in Preel's eyes and felt a pang. *Freedom...* I'd never truly had it. Offering it to Preel might mean finally achieving it for myself. It seemed apt. "Yes, I think so. If she intends to stay aboard once I do."

Preel nodded enthusiastically, her eyes crinkling above the band of silk with a hidden smile.

Miko chuckled. "I guess that's settled, then."

"I guess." I stood, trying not to visibly wince. The muscles of my back and legs still protested with every move and had cramped while I sat. Besides, I needed to pace; it would help me think. "Which means we need to plan ahead."

"Why?" Miko shrugged and reached for the blackbrew pot. "Until we know if the enchantment *can* be lifted, what plans can we make?"

"Because Jhavika could summon me at any time and renege on her promise to give us time off. Remember, she can order me to do anything she likes." I shivered as I considered the things she might command of me.

"We could sail away now and figure it out at our leisure."

"That's burning a bridge we can't rebuild, Miko. If we leave without her permission, she'll know something is up." I shook my head. "Once we do that, there's no turning back. Then, if we can't find a way to remove the enchantment, we'll *have* to run...or kill her."

"So we need to cool our heels and act like nothing's amiss for," Miko looked to Preel, "what, two more days at least?"

Preel nodded.

"That could be dangerous if Jhavika already suspects you know something." Miko gave me one of her looks, the kind she gives me when she knows I'm keeping details from her. "Do you think she does?"

"I don't know." I truly didn't, but filling Miko in on last night's goings on seemed prudent, despite my misgivings. "She'd had a lot to drink before things got really out of hand. She might assume I did, too, and that I won't remember...everything."

"What do you remember? How did you know for *sure* she had control over you?"

"Before things...escalated, I got up to leave." My stomach knotted at the memory of my helplessness, my futile struggle against feelings I knew weren't mine. "She told me to sit down and enjoy the entertainment, and I *did*, Miko. Everything she told me to do, I did without question. Things I'd *never* do on my own! I remember not wanting to, then doing it anyway. I felt like two people."

"That's...something." Miko obviously didn't know what more to say, so I said it for her.

"It's *terrifying*." I stopped and glanced at Preel, not sure why, but compelled nonetheless. The sympathy in her eyes twisted me inside. I still didn't want it, but maybe I needed it.

"If Jhavika can make you change the way you feel about something, about some*one*, she could order you to..." Miko's open-ended supposition hung there like a lance for me to impale myself upon.

Preel's quill scratched, and she showed me the page.

"So plan!" I read, nodding. "She's right. Dwelling on what *might* happen will only drive me crazy. I need to really think about this, and you obviously need about four more hours of sleep, Miko. Let's talk this over at lunch."

"All right." My first mate finished her blackbrew and stood. "I do need sleep, but I need to ask you one more question before I go, Captain."

"Yes?"

"What if Jhavika summons you? If she's figured out you know about her control, and you go to her, you either won't come back or you'll come back a different person." She shook her head. "She could order you to hate me, slaughter anyone who opposes you, burn *Scourge* to the waterline, or any one of a million things. What do I do if you come back from her spouting orders to set sail after another prize with no delay?"

"Knock me on the head, tie me down, and set sail for the Northlands!"

"But you'll remember giving me that order and you'd be ready for it."

A cold hand gripped my guts and squeezed. "I don't know, then, Miko. All I can tell you is to do what you think best. You know me better than just about anyone. If I start acting strangely, saying or doing things you know I normally wouldn't, assume its Jhavika controlling me."

Miko sighed and rubbed her eyes. "I don't like this, Captain. I think we should just run now."

I looked again to Preel. She shrugged.

"I don't like the idea of running before we have a plan, Miko."

"Running's not a plan?"

I barked a laugh. "No, running is a reaction to a threat. Sometimes it's the right reaction, but running blindly... I'd rather not."

"Your call, Captain." Miko went to the door and put her hand on the latch. "But you can bet your ass Jhavika's going to send for you soon. If she does before we can ask Preel our next question, you have to decide what you're going to do."

"I know." I nodded to her. "Get some sleep. I'll have Bert put lunch on for us and we'll talk."

"Yes, sir."

Miko left, and the scratch of Preel's pen drew me back. She handed the page to me and I read, "Miko is right about Jhavika. If she thinks you know she's controlling you with magic, seeing her will be dangerous."

"I know, but the moment we run, there's no turning back. She'll be an enemy forever and I'll be hunted; *we'll* be hunted."

She scratched a response. "And if she commands you to be in love with her?"

My stomach clenched on my breakfast as I read it, the combination of too much alcohol, too much blackbrew, and the gut punch of Preel's warning tipping me over the edge. I hurried to the quarter gallery, slammed the door, sat on the head, and gritted my teeth against the pain as my bowels emptied out through the scuttle.

I forced myself to walk the deck most of the morning, checking the work of the carpenter, talking to Wix about a dozen different details of maintenance and a few cases of insubordination. The activity eased the aches and pains of my strained muscles. By midday I almost felt human again. My stomach and bowels had settled down, and the copious breakfast and as much water as I could drink eased my aching head to a dull background irritation. I'd told Bert to prepare lunch for Miko and me in my cabin, so when a surly Hemp summoned me from the quarterdeck, I had an appetite and a clear head.

I entered the great cabin to find Preel exercising. I'd forgotten to refasten her manacle, but I didn't say anything. Hemp had set the table for two, but I realized that if I intended to free Preel, I had to start treating her like a free woman, not a slave.

"Put out a third plate, Hemp. I'm tired of crumbs in my bunk. Preel will eat at the table with us."

"As you wish, sir." He cast a strange look at Preel and went to get another place setting. I assumed he was still upset that I'd ordered him to burn my best clothes, but as he passed I picked up a few bits of his muttering. "Bloody prancin' about the cabin all hours, not even chained up like a slave ought to be, wearin' the carpet to tatters..."

Preel sat on the edge of the bunk breathing deeply, a questioning look on her face. I didn't know if she was worried that we might accidently invoke her talent with an incautious question while we ate, or if she was simply surprised that I'd decided to sit at the same table with a slave. Hemp returned before I could explain. I went to the quarter gallery to wash my hands and face before lunch and came back in to find Miko there and Hemp filling our cups with steaming spiced wine. Only two of the three cups, of course. Preel's he filled with water.

"Have a seat, Miko. Did you get some sleep?"

"Like the dead," she said, raising an eyebrow at the three place settings as she took her chair.

I motioned Preel over to the other chair and removed her gag after Hemp left. "I thought we could do with Preel's opinion and I don't like the idea of notes lying around for anyone to read." I sat, adjusting my backside to the least painful position. The welts didn't hurt much anymore, but they were in an awkward spot. "Just be careful what you ask."

"Too right, sir."

Hemp returned with a platter of serving dishes. He laid them all out with precision and left without a word.

"What's wrong with him?"

"He's mad because I ordered him to burn the clothes I wore last night." I lifted the covers, inhaling the wonderful aromas. One contained some kind of baked pie, the crust golden and crispy. Another brimmed with stewed greens studded with bits of pork and garlic. A bright orange mash of fire-root and butter steamed in the third. I plated my own—the pie turned out to be beef and vegetables in a spicy brown gravy—and nudged them toward Miko. When Miko had finished plating her meal, I pulled the platters close and nodded to Preel's plate.

"Preel, I'd like to explain why I asked you to eat with us. What would you like?"

Preel eyed the platters as if they might leap up and bite her. "Um...some of each, please, sir. Not as much as you. It looks delicious, but..."

"But you're not used to such rich fare and *certainly* not used to a captain serving you lunch."

"Yes, sir." She stared at me as I piled food onto her plate.

Miko chuckled and started eating.

"If I'm going to free you, you need to get used to acting like a free woman. We'll have to keep it quiet at first, just like your talent, but once you're free, you can't act like a slave." I indicated the tattoo on her brow and the gag lying beside her plate. "We'll have to figure out something to do about those later. For now, we'll be careful, but don't be afraid to interrupt us if you think we might say something that could invoke your talent."

"Yes, sir."

"Good! Now eat, and let's talk this over." I tried some of the pie and chewed blissfully. "Bert's going to double my weight in a month if I'm not careful."

"I meant to mention that the whole crew holds her in awe, sir." Miko raised her cup and sipped the spicy brew. "They rate her higher than any emperor or king, just short of a god."

"I'm beginning to wonder myself if she's not some kind of alchemist." I tried some of the other two dishes, finding them equally wonderful. "So, I think we've agreed that the next question we need to ask Preel is if there is any way to break this enchantment."

They both nodded.

"Okay, if the answer to that question is no, that narrows our options."

"Please remember," Preel said, "that specific questions about enchanted artifacts sometimes don't generate answers at all. If you asked me where Jhavika's scourge is right now, I probably wouldn't be able to tell you."

"But you could tell us where *Jhavika* is. She never leaves it behind, so where Jhavika is, so is the scourge."

"Yes." Preel ate daintily, tiny bites that she chewed carefully and thoroughly before swallowing. "You see, there's always a way to craft the question to get the answer you need."

"So, if the enchantment *can't* be broken, asking how to destroy the scourge might not get an answer at all."

"Yes, but I have no way to know until we actually attempt it."

"Asking the best way to kill Jhavika would probably get a good answer," Miko said.

"Perhaps not the 'best' way, but asking about the 'safest' way would probably receive a specific answer." When Preel spoke of her ability, her tone changed from that of a meek slave to a sage or scholar. "Phrasing is important. The word 'best' can mean many things: the surest to succeed, the safest, or even the least likely to be discovered."

"Pesky magic…" Miko muttered around another bite.

"Yes, it is," I agreed, wondering what forces governed how such things worked. "So, if we assume the enchantment *can* be broken somehow, the next question would be how."

"Yes, but again, you should try to be specific."

"How…" Miko paused and took a sip from her cup. "How do you *propose* we be specific when we don't know the first thing about the magic or how it works?"

"There are things you must consider." Preel spoke slowly and precisely, as if she carefully chose every word. "If you ask something ambiguous like how to break Jhavika's hold on the captain, the answer might be to kill her or destroy the scourge, both of which we already know would work, but not how we might accomplish them."

"And both of which are likely to get me killed," I added.

"Yes." Preel smiled at me. "Yes, we don't want *that*, do we?"

Her wry bit of humor startled me. I wondered if I'd heard her right, then barked a laugh.

Miko chuckled. "I certainly don't! That damnable thing has tasted *my* flesh, too. Not at Jhavika's hand, but at Captain Kohl's. I might be just as much her slave as the captain is."

"True." Preel looked from one of us to the other. "That would be a good question, if we have time."

"Yes, time…" I considered that as I ate. "Jhavika said we could have ten days or so before another mission, but if we discover that the enchantment *can* be broken, I think we should cut and run. We can take our time at sea figuring out how to do it."

"That could be problematic, too, sir," Preel warned. "If you later ask how to break the enchantment, and the only answer is more dangerous than the option of killing Jhavika, you may be in trouble if you've already fled."

"I hadn't thought of that." I ate, drank, and considered. "Bugger, this is getting complicated again."

"I think we could cut the 'can we break the spell' question by simply asking who we can ask or where we can go to get the enchantment lifted." Miko shrugged. "If there's no answer, it can't be broken. If we get an answer, we're good to go and we have a destination."

Preel cocked her head and looked doubtful. "What if the answer is to convince the God-Emperor of Toki to help you? That might not even be possible. The question must be precise."

"And, again, we need to find some way that won't get us killed." I thought some more, my frustration building. "And if we asked *where* we can go to get the enchantment lifted, the answer might send us into the Crown of the World on a pixie hunt."

Miko rolled her eyes, but persisted. "Okay, maybe we could ask where we could sail *Scourge* to find someone both able and willing to remove the enchantment. That's specific, refers only to destinations we can reach, and would give us time later to find out exactly who there can help us. If we don't get an answer, we at least know there's no one in any coastal location who could help us."

"That might do."

"But not what this person would want in exchange for helping you," Preel pointed out. "Be careful about asking people's intentions. A question about whether or not someone would be *willing* to help us might or might not work. And if the question failed, we might simply have to ask it again without any restrictions. If the enchantment *can't* be lifted, we have little option but to flee."

We... She said it like she was a part of the crew already, which, if I freed her and she intended to stay, she would have to be. I wondered how I would explain that to the crew.

Preel must have seen the consternation on my face. "I didn't mean to assume..."

"Never mind, Preel. I was just wondering how to manage the crew. We'll still have to keep your ability a secret."

"Yes." She looked down. Her plate was still half full, and she didn't look like she wanted any more.

"Don't worry. We'll figure that out later." I pushed my plate away. "So, even if we can find someone who fits the criteria of able and willing, I doubt they'll do it for nothing. I've got money and a few baubles from the prizes we've taken, but I'm not exactly rich."

"You've got a ship and crew," Miko said. "We could exchange our services for the cure."

"There is that." Seagoing vessels weren't uncommon, but hiring one outright was expensive. "We just have to find someone willing to barter."

"Then craft your question to stipulate that criteria," Preel suggested. "Someone capable of breaking the enchantment and willing to accept payment or barter to do so."

"Excellent!" I smiled at her in admiration of her quick wit. "You're good at this."

She smiled and looked down. "Thank you, sir."

"So, if we *can* find someone, *some*where who can—"

A rapid knock at the door interrupted Miko. Hemp poked his head through and hissed, "Captain! Jhavika's just arrived! She come up in a big fancy coach with a score of soldiers on horseback! She insists on seeing you and is already aboard!"

"Shit!" I lurched up from the table. The woman who could murder me with a simple command was here. There seemed only one reason: she had realized I might know I was a slave.

Chapter Fourteen
Delicate Negotiations

In negotiating from a position of vulnerability,
showing weakness is deadly.
The Lessons of Quen Lau Ush

From the diary of Kevril Longbright –
How strange that I faced the same choice twice: kill or run away. The difference between the two instances was only that I still loved my father to some degree.

"Stall her as much as you can, Hemp!"

"Aye, sir!" Hemp closed the door, but not before I heard Jhavika's voice from down the passage.

We had only seconds.

My first thought was to arm myself. Facing Jhavika without a weapon grated against every fiber of my being. Chairs scraped the deck as I hurried to my cabinet and picked out two daggers. I tossed one to Miko and tucked the other into my boot.

"If it comes down to it, don't hesitate," I told her.

"Aye, sir." She slipped the dagger under her belt at the small of her back and pulled her shirt down over it.

"Captain!" Preel held up the silk gag, horror writ large on her features. "And…" she pointed to the golden manacle fastened to the corner post of my bunk.

"Right!" I snatched the silk band from her hand and stuffed it into a pocket, then fumbled the key to the manacles from the chain around my neck and worked it in the lock.

"Are you sure you won't have a peck to eat, Lady Keshmir?" Hemp's voice carried through the door.

She's here!

I tucked the manacles under the mattress, flung the blanket flat over the bunk, then tried to assume a casual stance. A knock sounded at the door. Preel moved to stand near Miko, her eyes frantically flitting about the cabin as if searching for a place to hide. My first mate's features hardened into a mask of tension, the look she gets the moment before a fight.

I made a calming motion with my hands. They both nodded. We all looked at the door at the sound of a knock.

"Yes?"

Hemp opened the door. "Lady Keshmir to see you, Captain."

"Jhavika!" I painted on a smile as she came in. She wore a cutlass on one hip and the damned scourge on the other, but I forced my eyes to meet hers. I strode across the cabin and greeted her with a kiss to her cheek. We'd been far more intimate the night before, so holding back now would be ludicrous.

"Kevril, I…" She stopped, her gaze taking in the remains of our meal on the table, Miko, then snapping to focus on Preel. "I'm interrupting."

"Not really. We'd just finished lunch and were chatting." I waved a hand at Miko and Preel. "You know Miko, of course." My mind spun on how to introduce Preel and latched desperately onto the first idea to pop into my head. "This is her friend Preel." I grinned and gave Jhavika a broad wink. "Her very *special* friend, I might add."

"Oh, well, nice to meet you, Preel."

185

"Milady," Preel smiled and curtsied, pressing her palms together in the Toki fashion, then sidled up to Miko, clutching my first mate's arm possessively. "Thank you for allowing the *Scourge* some time ashore. I miss my Miko when she's out gallivanting across the seas."

Thank Odea for her quick thinking...

"Yes, I know that feeling." She smiled, but I knew Jhavika; there was suspicion behind it. "That tattoo on your brow... I've never seen one like it."

"Preel's..." Miko faltered. "...um...from Toki."

"It's okay, love," Preel said, hugging Miko close. She faced Jhavika with an unassuming smile. "I'm a truthseeker for the god-emperor."

My heart skipped a beat. That, too, was quick thinking, but far too close to the dangerous truth for my liking.

"Really! I thought all truthseekers were priests or priestesses."

"Not all. Some of us are simply devoted to our lord's reign." Her fingers brushed the tattoo on her brow. "The mark is the symbol of our life-long devotion, but that doesn't mean we can't devote ourselves to other things...and *people*." She nuzzled Miko's neck and pecked her on the cheek. "Isn't that right, love?"

"Too right, love." Miko wrapped an arm around Preel's waist and pulled her close. "But Lady Jhavika wants to speak to the captain, so we'll be off." She nodded respectfully to Jhavika, sketched a salute to me, and tugged Preel toward the door.

"Thank you for lunch, Captain," Preel said with another glowing smile. "Your cook is very talented."

"That she is. Nice to meet you, Preel." I silently thanked all the gods for her convincing performance.

The door closed behind them and I breathed a little easier.

"Well, Miko smitten by a truthseeker! I never thought I'd see the day." Jhavika looked around the cabin, then at me. "I'm glad to see you recovered from last night."

"Quite recovered." I turned to my cabinet. "Can I offer you something? Scales of the dragon that bit you, perhaps?"

"No, thank you, Kevril. My head still aches from the drink." Sighing, she strolled around the table to gaze out the stern gallery windows. One entire pane was missing, removed by a crewman and yet to be replaced, but she didn't mention it. "I came here to ask how you felt about what happened last night."

"How I *felt*?" I chuckled and hoped it didn't sound forced. "Other than having a sore ass and a hangover this morning, you mean?"

"Yes." She glanced back at me and I saw that her cheeks were actually flushed. "I didn't know Lord Temuso had such...appetites. Things got a little out of hand."

"With a head full of brandy and those dancers, it wasn't surprising." I forced a wry chuckle and took a step closer. With her back to me, I could put a dagger in her heart in a flash. "I've got to admit that I didn't expect to get buggered by a lord when I came to dinner, but we were all a little over the top of the hill and riding a runaway coach down the other side, weren't we?"

"We were." Jhavika turned around and leaned back against the sill beneath the windows, quirking an apologetic smile. "I didn't expect things to go so far. I just wanted to have a randy night with friends. You...seemed to enjoy yourself."

"What I remember of it, at least." I shrugged. If Jhavika was here to learn if I had any suspicions that she controlled me with magic, I had to put those concerns at ease. What better than a memory lapse? "That brandy had a kick like a mule. I hope your other guests had a good time."

"They certainly seemed to." Jhavika's gaze roved around the cabin again, taking in my rumpled bunk, the table...and me. "And you have no...regrets about it?"

"Regrets?" I frowned and gave her a quizzical look. "No. I don't relish another encounter with Lord Temuso soon, but it was all in fun."

"Good, I was worried that you might have taken offense."

"Is that why you're here, Jhavika? You're worried that you've offended my delicate sensibilities?"

She hadn't apologized, but I hadn't expected her to. An apology would have been admitting that she'd done something wrong. If she thought I didn't remember her ordering me to enjoy the orgy, to *want* it, even though I'd made clear by trying to leave that I hadn't, I might survive this encounter.

"You're saying I *didn't* offend you?" She cocked an eyebrow, and I wondered if it was in amusement or suspicion.

"I'm a *pirate*, Jhavika. I left my delicate sensibilities ashore when I left home."

"Oh, that's a big fat lie and you know it, Kevril!" There was an edge to her tone now. "You've always had...principals."

"Yes, I have principals, but you don't have to worry that a randy evening offended them, Jhavika. I was a little reluctant at first because I didn't know your other guests very well, but I had fun. It *was* a bit unexpected." I tried for a different tack. "Why are you so concerned about my feelings?"

"Because I value you as a business partner and..." She glanced around again, obviously reticent to say too much. "I don't want to ruin our relationship. That's all."

"I'm not about to sail off and leave the perfect partnership just because things got a little out of hand last night, if that's what you're worried about." I took a step closer, well within striking distance now. I wasn't likely to get my dagger out of my boot sheath before she ordered me to stop, of course, but I was ready.

"Good." Jhavika smiled and nodded, looked me over again, then reached out to straighten the laced neck of my shirt, her fingers brushing the fine linen. "You were very...enthusiastic last night."

Because you ordered me to be, you maniacal control freak! "Yes, I was." Swallowing my terror, I took her hand and rubbed the tiny calluses on her palm with my thumb. "So were you."

"I was." She raised her other hand and traced the scars along my face. "I'm sorry I ever gave you these."

"We'll, we were trying to *kill* each other at the moment, if you remember." I grinned at her. "Besides, they lend me a piratical look that inspires terror in my enemies."

"That they do." Jhavika bit her lip and ran her fingers down my neck and chest. "We could be very good together, Kevril Longbright."

"We *are* very good together, Jhavika." Was this *emotion* from the cold-hearted crime lord? The warning Preel had scrawled leapt into my mind. *And if she commands you to be in love with her?* That would destroy any chance of regaining my freedom. There was no way in the Nine Hells I could let her give that command. But how could I prevent it?

Easy... Give her what she wants before she asks for it!

I brushed a lock of hair from Jhavika's ear and ran my fingers down the nape of her neck. She shivered and bit her lip. "We have the *perfect* relationship."

"Is it perfect?" She blinked lazily and moistened her lips with her tongue. "Do you ever want...more?"

"I *always* want more, Jhavika." I nested my fist in the back of her hair, reminiscent of last night. "That's part of being a pirate, and why we're such good partners. We *both* want more."

"I *do* want more, Kevril." Her eyes widened then, a desperate look crossing her features. "I *always* want more and I can't control it! It burns in me like fire every waking hour and plagues my dreams! I want it all and I can't seem to get it fast enough!"

What the hells? Opening up like this wasn't like Jhavika at all. There was only one thing I could say. "We'll *take* it, Jhavika. We'll take the whole world."

"Yes!" She clenched her fists in my hair and pulled my face down to her. "Now!"

As our lips met, her tongue darting out to play with mine, I realized that this was my chance. With my mouth on hers, Jhavika couldn't command me. I could put a dagger in her back and there was absolutely nothing she could do to prevent it.

I dropped my hand from her hair toward the sheath in my boot. Jhavika bit my lip hard, and I tasted blood. *She wants blood? I'll give her blood...* I kissed her desperately, distracting her while I lifted my leg to reach my dagger. The blade slipped from its sheath. I raised it behind her back...and stopped. *Her escort...* How could I escape Haven after killing Jhavika? Her soldiers would board Scourge in a tide of steel and blood. And even if we could escape, I couldn't ever hope to come back. I couldn't kill her. *Not yet...*

"Do it, Kevril!" Jhavika moaned between our lips, ripping open my shirt.

I doubt she knew how close that command came to ending her life. Ambiguous commands, like Preel's ambiguous questions, could receive ambiguous responses. But I knew she didn't want me to plant eight inches of steel in her back.

"Do it now." She pulled away, a carnal fever burning in her eyes. "Take me right here on your bunk! I want it!"

I couldn't disobey.

I backed her over to the bunk and up against the leeboard, gnawing at her neck. We fell onto the rumpled blanket, and I slipped the dagger down between the pallet and bulkhead. Her shirt came apart in my hands, linens ripping to expose milky breasts, the wide scar I'd given her across her abdomen...and the scourge.

I reached for it and she shifted, intercepting my hand.

"Just let me drop this," she panted as she unclipped her sword belt, dropping it and the scourge over the leeboard. She grabbed me by the hair, her face aflame with raw lust. "Now, as you were, captain."

Ever obedient, I nibbled my way downward, pausing here and there as she gasped and writhed when tongue and teeth found sensitive spots. The buttons of her trousers resisted and I nearly reached for my dagger, but they finally yielded to my grasp. Then there was nothing but flesh and tastes and sensations, and the overwhelming desire to follow Jhavika's commands.

"Poetry and philosophy?" Jhavika's tousled bronze mop rolled toward me, her eyes narrow. She held up one of the books that I'd loaned Preel. "Kevril, you never cease to amaze me." Her other hand tickled its way down my stomach to my groin. "In *so* many ways…"

"I'm glad to keep you guessing." *Truer than she'll ever know…* I rolled out of the bunk and staggered, my strained muscles complaining again. I looked back at her. "You surprised me yourself. This morning I thought that last night was just a ploy to win over your lordly friends. This…" I waved a hand at her lying on my bunk, languid after our tumultuous romp. "…changed my mind."

That was no lie. Jhavika's unbridled enthusiasm told me one thing; this was no act. She wanted more than a partnership. All things considered, I'd have rather wed an ogre. Slavery was no basis for a relationship. But the things she said and the way she acted made me think that perhaps something else was going on. I've never known a more avaricious person than Jhavika, but this desire to have it all, to be queen, to take everything—including me—for her own, bordered on mania. A notion tickled my mind… Was it the scourge doing this to her? Was it having an effect on her as it had an effect on me? Was Jhavika a slave as well?

Or, like so many other rich people, did increasing power only feed a desire for even more? Regardless, I could hardly broach the subject at this juncture. In fact, the more she wanted from me, the less I wanted anything to do with her, as long as I was enslaved to her every whim, at least.

But how the hell do I get out of this?

Jhavika rolled and stretched on the bunk, the soiled sheets rumpling around her shapely ankles. "And you've changed my mind, Kevril."

"Oh?" I reached for my linens and pants. "How's that?"

191

"I used to think that I didn't need anyone. That I'd be better off alone. All the profits for me with no worries about being stabbed in the back by a jealous lover who couldn't play second fiddle to a queen."

The 'stabbed in the back' comment nearly undid me. I lost my balance putting one leg in my linens, but recovered.

She rolled onto her side, head propped on hand, a sly grin playing on her lips. "You don't seem to mind playing my fiddle at all, and I rather like playing your...instrument." She reached for me as I pulled up my linens, pouting as I stepped back.

"And I enjoy *you*, Jhavika, but let's not ruin the perfect partnership." I buttoned my codpiece as I explained. "I'm your admiral, and you're my queen. Too much...fraternization would interfere with our work, don't you think?"

"Oh, you're probably right." She sighed and lay back down, smiling at me like I was her favored pet and had just learned a new trick.

Then I remembered that I was, and I had. My stomach clenched on my lunch.

"But that doesn't mean I can't play with you when you're in port."

Like your favorite toy... "Not at all." I went to the table, poured two cups of the mulled wine, and returned to the bunk, holding one out to her. "Something to take the edge off?"

"Thank you." She accepted the cup and drank as I did. "Mmm, that's very good. Your new cook's recipe?"

"I suppose. Bert's quite a surprise. She's probably the only reason I didn't have a mutiny on my hands on this last mission." I leaned against the side of the leeboard, taking another swallow of the spicy drink and swirling it in my mouth to wash away the taste of Jhavika. Would that it would do the same to my memories... "She was cook aboard *Hymoin*. I convinced her to join us rather than fight Wix in a death match." Not true, of course, but it made a good story.

"Hmm, I may have to steal her from you."

Another case of Jhavika wanting everything. "Oh, I don't think she's up to the standards of what *your* chefs put out last night, but she's good at plain fare aboard a ship."

"Probably right again." Jhavika drank and sat up. "Mind if I use your quarter gallery?"

"Not at all. Let me get you some hot water and a towel." She strode for the gallery, not bothering with her scattered and torn clothing. I went to the door and leaned out. "Hemp, hot water and towels."

He stuck his head out of the larder. "Straightaway, sir."

Miko leaned out of her cabin door and gave me a clear "What the hell?" gesture. I made calming motions and closed the door, taking a few moments to tidy up the cabin a bit before my steward knocked.

"Come in, Hemp."

He opened the door and stooped to lift two buckets of steaming water. Two thick towels rode over his shoulder. His eyes roved expertly over the cabin, like an inquisitor inspecting a crime scene. I could see on his face that he could read what had happened. More rumors would spread around the ship like wildfire. *Just what I need.* "Put them by the quarter gallery door. You can clear the table on your way out."

"Aye, sir." Hemp put the buckets on the floor and the towels on the shelf, then cleared the table with practiced efficiency. "Anything else?"

"Not yet, but we may want a pot of tea in a while."

"Aye, sir."

After the door clicked closed behind him, I tapped on the quarter gallery door. "Water and a towel?"

The door opened. Jhavika looked shaken until her gaze alighted on the bunk, then she sighed in relief, a brief smile flashing. "Thanks!" She accepted a bucket and towel. "Such extravagant use of water for *me*?"

"You deserve it after such…strenuous activity." I leered at her, wondering at her oddly shifting expressions. "Take your time."

I closed the door and followed Jhavika's previous line of sight. The scourge lay atop the clothes I'd picked up, a viper waiting to strike. I hadn't even realized I'd picked up her fallen sword belt. I strode to the side of the bunk and stared down at the accursed cat-o'-nine-tails, considering the opportunity. Thus far I'd avoided touching it, but now I reached out a hesitant hand. If I took it up, claimed it for my own, would the enchantment be banished, ending my slavery? Then, when Jhavika came out of the quarter gallery, I'd lash *her* with it, and *she* would be *my* slave.

My stomach roiled at the thought, and I pulled back my hand, clenching my fists to resist the temptation. *It can't be that easy.* In freeing myself from Jhavika's control, I might merely enslave myself to the scourge. And there was no guarantee that just picking it up would work anyway. Would I have to kill Jhavika to gain control of the scourge? *Yet another question for Preel…*

The open stern gallery window beckoned. I could throw the lash into the sea. But again, I had no guarantee that discarding it would break the hold it had on me. It would, however, tip my hand, revealing that I knew of its power.

Water splashed in the quarter gallery. If I was going to do something, I had to do it quickly. The best action right now seemed to be to put Jhavika at ease. I took up her clothes and folded them, placed her sword belt on top, avoiding my braided-leather nemesis, then put it all on the table. Reaching to the far side of the pallet, I retrieved my dagger and Preel's manacles and tucked them in my cabinet. Pulling out two clean shirts, I donned one and lay the other beside Jhavika's clothes. It wouldn't fit her, but her own shirt was torn.

The quarter gallery door opened, and Jhavika emerged wrapped in a towel. Again, her gaze flicked to the bunk, and brief panic melted in relief when she saw her things piled on the table.

"Feel better?"

"I feel *cleaner*," she said with a smile as she approached the table, "but I don't know if I could feel much better than I did a little while ago." She picked up her scanties and examined the tear my teeth had left.

"Sorry about that," I said with an honest cringe.

"I'm not." Jhavika dropped her towel and pulled the scanties on, then stepped into her trousers. She pulled on her sword belt next, her hand caressing the leather of the scourge.

As she dressed I stripped the soiled sheets from the bed and piled them beside the door. "I'm afraid your shirt's a loss, but you can wear that one."

"Thank you." She slipped into her torn linen undershirt, then my shirt. It fit her like a tent, but tucked in readily enough.

"Can I get you anything else? A cup of tea, a pot of liniment for strained muscles?" I gave her another lascivious grin.

"No, thank you, Kevril. I really should go." Jhavika sat to don her boots. "I've got things to do this afternoon, and…well, I need to get myself together."

"Of course." I wasn't about to beg her to stay. "We'll be in port for a while, so…" I let that hang for her to interpret as she wished.

"So, we can get together a few more times before your next mission." She stood and reached out to finger the lapels of my shirt. "I'd like that."

I smiled. "So would I." Endeavoring only to keep her from ordering me to report at some specific future time, I pulled Jhavika in and kissed her hard. She reciprocated with enthusiasm. When we parted, I smoothed her rumpled hair.

She sighed and left my arms, then my cabin, casting back one last glance and a smile.

After the door had closed, I sat down before my legs collapsed, suddenly shaking with the released tension. Before the tremors subsided, a knock sounded.

"Yes?"

Miko poked her head in the door. "You okay, sir?" She took in the state of the room, the piled sheets beside the door.

"Come in, Miko." I poured one more cup of the mulled wine and drank it down, willing my nerves to calm. Preel followed Miko, and Hemp lurked behind them, his face clouded with worry. I made a decision and said, "You, too, Hemp. You'll find out soon enough anyway, and I don't want rumors spreading."

The door closed behind them and I noted Preel's wide eyed stare at the pile of sheets and stripped bunk. Realizing the danger she was in, I stood and fished the silk gag from my pocket. "Preel, we better put this on for your safety."

"Yes, sir." She came to me and turned around, her eyes cast down.

"That was quick thinking and good acting, though you scared me to death when you told Jhavika you were a truthseeker." She nodded and stepped away, hands clasped white-knuckled before her and eyes still down. I didn't know what to make of her mood, but mine wasn't much better. "You all need to know that we've got a serious problem with Jhavika. She wants…more from me than I'm willing to give, and I can't say no to her. If we don't get out of Haven before she summons me again, things could get a lot worse."

"I agree," Miko said, casting a glance at Hemp before looking back to me. "We should sail tonight on the falling tide. You'll have to speak to the crew. They won't understand."

"Pardon me, sir, but *I* don't understand this either." Hemp gestured to Preel. "What in the Nine Hells *is* she and why does she have to wear that gag? Why's Jhavika so dangerous, and what's the problem with givin' her a tumble now and then to keep her happy? It's not like she's an *ogre*."

"No, it's not that, Hemp, and I'll tell the whole crew tonight, but you have to keep what I tell you now a secret. If you let it slip, we're all dead, and I mean every officer, foremast jack and jane, ship's brat, and scullery swab aboard, do you understand?"

Hemp paled. "Aye, sir."

"Jhavika Keshmir is controlling me with some kind of magic we don't fully understand yet. Preel here has a talent that allowed us to learn of this...enchantment." Hemp paled further, but I emphasized my point with a jab of my forefinger. "Let me be clear, Hemp, if Jhavika had ordered me to cut my own throat while she fucked me on that bunk, I'd have done it. Do you understand?"

"Um..." Hemp swallowed hard and jerked a nod. "Aye, sir."

Preel's eyes flicked up to mine, horror filling those dark pools before she looked down.

"Couldn't you have killed her?" Miko asked.

"Not with her private army waiting for her on the quay. I don't know what orders she's given them. And I couldn't steal the...implement she uses to control me."

"She must have taken it off so you could...um...you know." Miko stuttered. "Couldn't you have used it on *her*?"

"Too risky." Preel's vigorous nod of agreement surprised me. "It might only work for Jhavika. There's no way to—"

"You're talkin' about that gods-damned cat-o'-nine-tails she carries on her hip, aren't you, sir?" The knowledge in Hemp's eyes burned like fire. "The one Captain Kohl used to carry!"

Shit! My steward was more perceptive than he looked. "Yes, Hemp. It seems that anyone lashed by that thing must do as its master commands, but that's got to stay a secret for now. We've got to get out of Haven without Jhavika catching wind of our plan. I want to speak to the entire crew, *everyone*, an hour after sunset in the main hold. Until then, we provision quietly. Once we're done talking, we sail on the falling tide."

Preel nodded, her eyes wide and glistening.

Miko also nodded. "It's the only way out, sir. We'll get our answers at sea."

"Agreed." I turned to my steward, who'd remained uncharacteristically quiet. "Remember, not a word of this to anyone before tonight, Hemp, or we're sunk."

"Oh, aye, sir." He sounded duly terrified. "That bloody thing's left marks on *my* hide. I want no part of it."

"Good man." I nodded to the pile of sheets by the door. "Burn those sheets and the pallet as well. Get me a new one. I don't want Jhavika's...scent on anything in here."

"Aye, sir." Hemp picked up the sheets and towel, and rolled them both up in the feather pallet. "Don't worry, sir. I'll keep this on the sly."

"Good." I waited until he left, then rubbed my hands over my face and scraped my nails through my hair. "She scared the shit out of me, Miko. I had to give her what she wanted before she...ordered me to feel something for her. Thanks for putting on a good show. I think she bought it."

"Thank Preel, not me." Miko smiled at Preel and chucked her on the shoulder. "Though the smooch was nice."

Preel's smile reached her eyes. Then she sobered and tapped the band of silk girding her mouth.

"Of course." I untied it and watched her moisten her lips as if preparing them to speak. She opened her mouth, then paused, obviously balking. "Now's not the time to hold back, Preel. You've got as much at stake here as the rest of us now. Maybe more. If Jhavika ever got her hands on you, the entire *world* would be hers in a year."

"Yes, that was what I was going to say, sir." Her gaze fell with the lie. "That is why you must promise me one thing."

"I *must?*" I quirked an eyebrow at her. She was growing bold indeed.

"Yes, sir, not for me, but for...everyone. For every*thing*." She looked deeply troubled now.

"And what must I promise you?"

"That you'll kill me before you let Jhavika take me."

I stared at her, stunned speechless for a moment. "Preel, I..."

"She's *right!*" Miko's normally somber voice bordered on hysteria. "Sir! She's right. Think what Jhavika could—no, *would* do with a truthsayer *and* that scourge."

"I know…" Something Jhavika had said came to me then. "She'd take everything. She'd have an army unparalleled and unable to mutiny. She'd rule Haven in a year, the Blood Sea in two, and then take the rest of the world. *No* one could oppose her."

"No one," Preel agreed sadly.

It was the truth, but to kill Preel, the dove that laid the diamond eggs…

Chapter Fifteen
The Better Part of Valor

Convincing warriors that a strategic withdrawal is not cowardice
is delicate business.
The Lessons of Quen Lau Ush

From the diary of Kevril Longbright –
What makes a good captain? I ask myself that every time I wonder if I'm making the right decision. The problem, I've found, is that so much of being a good captain has less to do with seamanship than with handling people, something young officers are ill-trained in. I like to think I'm good at gauging the mood of my crew and responding to their needs. Why is it that I can't seem to do the same with the women in my life?

"They're ready," Miko said from my doorway.

"Good." I noted with approval the wakizashi at her hip and dagger in her boot, and strode for my cabinet. Wearing a cutlass would give the wrong message, putting the crew on the defensive, but it would be best to have a weapon handy. There was no way to known how my crew would respond to what I had to say. I shoved the jeweled daggers into my boots and shrugged into a clean jacket.

"Ready." I turned to Preel seated on my refurbished bunk. "You should come along, Preel. Don't worry, I won't give away your secret, but the crew has to know first-hand where our information comes from."

She nodded and rose, her eyes filled with worry.

"Is Wix ready?" I asked Miko as we followed her out of the great cabin.

"Yes, but he's not happy about this, sir. The crew knows something's up and there are all kinds of rumors flying around." Miko sounded worried, too. "I just pray to Odea that none have gotten ashore."

"What kind of rumors?"

"Well, after your little tryst with Jhavika, one involves you giving up pirating to be her lap dog. Another is that you're going to sell Preel to her and you're using your…um…carnal favors to negotiate a better price." Miko glanced over her shoulder at me as she descended the companionway to the lower deck. "And then there's the one that suggests you learned a few new tricks from your pleasure slave and you're whoring to earn some extra gold."

I snorted a laugh. "Well, we'll set them straight soon enough."

"You're going to disappoint a lot of people, sir. There's quite a lot of betting going on and serious odds are being given." Miko grinned as she led us aft to the main hold. "I thought about placing a few of my own that you were enspelled, but they'd hang me by my ankles from a yardarm if they found out I already knew."

"And I'd haul the halyard to hoist you aloft!" I gave her a perfunctory glare. "Nobody's guessed, have they?"

"The truth? No, sir. Not a one. That struck me as strange, actually." Miko stopped at the door to the hold. "Magic's usually high on the list of things sailors blame when something goes wrong."

"Hmm, yes." Sailors are superstitious. If not the gods, they'd blame some wizard's curse or alchemist's potion. "Well, there's no putting it off. We've got a tide to catch." I nodded to the door.

Miko opened it and led us in. Divested of cargo, the main hold is a vast, open chamber, two decks high interrupted only by timbers supporting the weather deck. The entire crew of *Scourge* stood, sat, or sprawled around the periphery. Wix strode forward and pressed a knuckle to his forehead in salute.

"All present and sober, sir." He looked grim, but no more than usual. Wix tended to clench and relax his scarred fists when nervous, but wasn't at the moment.

"Good." I signaled Miko to stay with Preel and stepped forward to the center of the hold. "Lads and lasses, I'll tell you no lie. We are in a dire spot of trouble. There's foul magic afoot and the entire ship and crew is in peril, myself more than anyone else."

Unease rippled through the crew. Men and women shifted and fidgeted, glanced about, and even looked away, unwilling to meet my eyes. My midshipmen studied their boots, their company having so recently borne the disgrace of Geit's betrayal. The ship's brats stared in wide-eyed horror, and even Bert frowned so prodigiously that her mouth nearly vanished amongst her many chins.

"Many of you served with me aboard *Scourge* when Captain Kohl ruled us, and you remember his cruel hand." I raked them with my gaze, locking it upon those veterans I knew had felt his lash, and saw flashes of recognition. "I can't give you specific details about how this vile magic works, because I don't exactly know, but Captain Kohl used it to dominate his officers and crew alike and make them slaves to his will. No one aboard could raise a hand against him, though none loved him and many despised the very sight of him, as did I."

There were several nods among those faces now.

"He fell in battle because no man or woman would raise a hand to keep him from harm, either. When he died, that magic passed to another, and she's used it to make slaves of us."

Murmurs raced through the massed crew. "Jhavika…" rose on the lips of those who made the connection.

I nodded. "Yes, Jhavika Keshmir is the wielder of that magic now, and this is the reason we've been so hard set for so long. The enchantment won't allow me to disobey a single order she gives, be it to sail through a cyclone, battle a dragon, fall on my sword, or…" I lowered my voice and let my loathing slip into my tone like a knife through flesh, "…pleasure her."

"Hells and demons," Wix muttered, his knuckles now white on his dagger hilts.

I looked to him and nodded. "Yes, my friends, I'm a slave to her will, as many of you may be."

"But how do you know, sir?" Quibly asked, stepping forward with a hasty salute. "If you pardon my asking. We've been making a profit by her orders for near five years now. How did you find out about this enchantment?"

I understood his skepticism and knew others would wonder the same, though they might not voice it. Nothing would do except to address that doubt with cold hard facts…or at least, as much of the truth as I dared.

"A good question, Master Quibly, and one I'll happily answer." I gestured for Preel to step forward to my side. She did so, trembling. "You all know that we found Preel chained in the captain's cabin aboard *Hymoin*. Her fetters and the silken bond that prevents her from speaking are magic themselves, for she bears a powerful talent, which is also the reason for her enslavement. Her magic revealed this enchantment upon me, and will hopefully also tell us how to break it. I'd intended to rest here in Haven and let you all spend your pay ashore while we accomplished that task. Unfortunately, Jhavika has become more…direct in her demands of me, and I fear she may command me to become something that will destroy us all."

"Why does she wear that gag?" a crewman called out, provoking a storm of questions.

"Aye, don't she got no mouth?"

"Don't she talk?"

"Is she a witch, then?"

"Hang on! Hang on! I'll answer your questions, but let's be civil about it. No, she's not a witch, and yes, she has a mouth." I considered a moment, then reached up to unfasten the gag's binding. Preel's eyes widened and she shook her head, obviously afraid of some incautious question. "It's all right," I assured her quietly before turning back to the crew. "I'll show you the truth, but you *have* to remain silent while I do this, for her magic is dangerous. Do you pledge to hold your tongues?"

The all nodded solemnly, rapt as they waited for the secret to unfold.

"Very well." I unfastened Preel's bond to reveal her sensuous mouth. "Say something to them, Preel."

"I'm very pleased to meet you all." She curtsied gracefully. "I long to help the captain remove this accursed enchantment."

"Thank you, Preel." I replace the silken band over her mouth before anyone could call out an inopportune question. "Unfortunately, there are limits to what Preel's talent can do, and we can't stay here and wait for Jhavika to command me to cut my own throat if she suspects that I know what she's about."

That earned another murmur from the crew.

"We sail out of Haven tonight on the falling tide. We've got to get away before anyone notices and raises a ruckus. No word or messages to anyone ashore. If we're not over the horizon by sunrise, we're *all* as good as dead." Every jack and jane stared in slack-jawed silence, which I hoped meant that they concurred with my plan. "If any of you have any questions, I'll do my best to answer them now."

"Sir?" Midshipman Rauley stepped forward and saluted, a miserable frown on his face.

"Yes, Mister Rauley."

"With respect, sir, how do we know it's not *Preel* who's enchanted you and not Lady Jhavika?"

His question provoked a rash whispering and a few nods of agreement through the crowd.

"A good question. Truth be told, I was afraid of that myself when we first found her. Miko and I took every precaution in dealing with her until it became obvious that she was a slave and cruelly used by her previous masters." I took Preel's wrist and raised it so they could see the scars there. "So cruelly used, in fact, that she tried on more than one occasion to take her own life. The chains you saw her wearing when she was brought aboard prevented her from injuring herself, as the binding on her mouth prevents her from speaking. I promised to keep her safe—a promise destroyed by Geit's mutinous actions. I've renewed that pledge, and in return, Preel has agreed to help us. I'm trusting you with all our lives when I say that we *must* keep her nature a secret, for powerful people will stop at nothing to take her for their own, and this I've vowed not to allow."

"But she's a slave, sir," Rauley argued. "Why all the fuss? Just order her to help or punish her."

"Because, Mister Rauley, Preel is intelligent, well-learned in magical lore, and familiar with the limitations of her talent, all attributes that we can use to our benefit. I *could* order her to help, but her willing aid will be a thousand times more effective than coercion." I nodded respectfully toward Preel. "She is a treasure beyond price. Only a fool abuses something so valuable."

Rauley nodded and stepped back.

"More questions?" I scanned the faces, but the next question came from a quarter I hadn't expected.

"Sir?" Wix stepped forward, knuckling his forehead in salute. "I got one."

"Yes, Master Wix?"

"I don't understand why you didn't kill that witch, Jhavika, when you had her in yer cabin." The disgust on his face shone like a bonfire in the night. "I mean, you had the chance, didn't you?"

"Yes, I had the chance, Wix, and I nearly did." I fixed him with a level stare. "I had a dagger at her back and could have put it in her heart, but I weighed the danger of killing her and decided against it. It's better if we simply leave, find a way to break this enchantment, and have done with it all."

"But if she's dead, it's broken, ain't it?"

"That's a question we don't know the answer to and one reason why I stayed my hand." I shrugged.

"So you *chose* not to kill her, or you *couldn't* kill her because she ordered you not to?"

It was more of a challenge than question, but I swallowed my anger and endeavored to answer honestly. "I *chose* not to kill her because I had no way to know what orders she'd given. If I *had* killed her, her private army might have stormed aboard *Scourge* like a bloody tide. Even if we escaped, we could never have returned to Haven. This way, we can drift off without risking any lives and come back free."

"And what about Jhavika? You think she's likely to welcome us back with open arms after we sneak off like dogs?" Derision edged his tone now; Wix abhorred cowardice above all things.

"No, Wix, I don't think she'll welcome us, but she also won't have control over us." I stared straight into my bosun's eyes, willing him to understand that leaving Haven in the dead of night was not a craven act, but the first step of a plan. "We can't win a fight with her if she can command us to fall on our blades, and I will *not* be her slave any longer! Yes, she hands us fat prizes, which is a *far* sight easier than finding them ourselves, but if we come back to Haven, it'll be as free men and women, and this will be a *real* partnership, not us jumping to fulfil her every whim. To do *that*, we need to break this enchantment, then come back and tell Jhavika to either make us real partners or bugger off. She needs us as much as we need her, but I'll be damned to the Nine Hells before I'll live as her slave!"

Wix seemed to consider this, his scarred knuckles flexing and relaxing on the hilts of his daggers. Silence hung heavy in the closed space, the tension humming through the crew like the strings of a poorly tuned instrument. Though the crew worked for me, they'd follow Wix in a heartbeat, whichever side he came down on. The bosun wasn't particularly liked, but he was one of them, he represented them. I *had* to win this battle of wills; if I lost Wix, I lost the crew. So I stared him down, my hands empty and relaxed at my side, fearless and confident, though my gut clenched with trepidation.

"This is the *only* way I know to come out of this on top, Wix. If I'd killed Jhavika, Haven would be lost to us. I don't know about you, but I'd rather be welcomed here than banished to the North Sea Reaches, the Shattered Isles, or reduced to hunting the isles of Toki and dodging the Imperial Navy." I swept the hold with my gaze. "You've all had a couple days off, and more pay to spend in those two days than you'd have in two *years* pirating on our own. And with Preel," I gestured to the dusky woman and smiled with avaricious glee, "and her talent working *for* us, we'll have the upper hand."

Wix frowned, glared at Preel, then at me, but finally gave a curt nod. "Aye, sir."

Thank Odea! I let out a breath I didn't know I'd been holding. "Good!" Trying not to show my relief, I regarded the rest of the crew. "Any more questions?"

There were none.

"Very well. Now we've got to slip out of here on the sly." I swept my crew with a conspiratorial grin. "We've provisioned well enough and taken on water, so we don't need anything from shore. We prepare the ship as quietly as we can and, when the tide shifts, we cast off and drift out under reefed topsails, quiet as a cutpurse. Once we're in the offing, we set every stitch she'll bear and make a southeasterly course for open sea."

A murmur of ascent swept through the crew, but I wasn't through yet. I raised a hand and they fell silent.

"I have a couple of changes to make before we start getting ready." That brought them all up short, and every eye centered upon me.

"Mister Rauley, you've shown a remarkable aptitude for handling the ship and have an excellent eye for trimming sail, so I'm appointing you as the ship's sailing master in charge of all matters to do with rigging, sails, and spars above and below decks. You'll be rated as senior petty officer and stand watch as a senior-rated seaman and pilot when officers are on watch and your deft hand is needed. This, I think you'll agree, is more befitting your skills."

"I…um…*yes*, sir!" A relieved smile flashed across Rauley's face. He knew as well as I did that he'd make a far better sailing master than he'd ever make a lieutenant. "Thank you, sir!"

"Thank me after you talk to Wix about your new duties." I flashed him a grin, then turned to my other two midshipmen. "The midshipmen's berth will have a new addition. Boxley, front and center!"

"Sir!" Boxley leapt up and dashed forward, stiff as a board, her face glowing with glee.

"My first mate tells me your reading and writing are sufficient to qualify you as a midshipman. You are hereby so appointed on a *provisional* basis. As you know, mathematics skills are also essential for every officer. If, at the end of one month's time, you can adequately calculate a noon sighting, a lunar, and a proper calibration of ship's time with sunset and sunrise, I'll make this provisional assignment permanent." I fixed her with a hard stare. "Do you understand me completely, *Mister* Boxley?"

"Yes, sir!" She snapped a salute. "I won't disappoint you, sir!"

"If you do…" I leaned close and grinned at her, "I'll feed you to Wix for breakfast."

That earned laughter all around.

"Yes, sir!" The threat barely dampened her enthusiasm one whit.

I scanned the faces and found my steward. "Hemp, scrounge up some suitable attire for our trial midshipman."

"Aye, sir, though I don't know where I'll find anything small enough. Bloody runts they're breedin' these days…"

"I'm sure you'll make do, Hemp." I raked my gaze over the crowd. "The rest of you know your duties. Hop to, but quietly. We can't afford to let word get back to Jhavika that we're leaving before we're well and truly gone, and she could have people watching us from shore."

A hushed roar of ascent swept through them, and I nodded in satisfaction. As the crew hurried to their work, I motioned Miko and Preel to follow me to the great cabin. There I closed and locked my door and went to my cabinet.

"Miko, remove Preel's gag, please." I picked out a bottle and three tumblers. Placing the glasses on the table, I uncorked the fine bottle of spiced rum and poured a finger depth into each. I handed one to Miko and another to Preel, who looked a little terrified, then took the glass.

"Miko, Preel, I'm in your debt for this. I've just put us on a course that could mean our deaths or worse, but could also mean salvation. From now on, there's nowhere to go but forward." I raised my glass. "To our success."

They touched their glasses to mine. Miko tossed hers back and sighed happily. Preel sipped hers carefully, then hiccupped. I downed half of mine and enjoyed the warm glow racing down my throat.

"I've got to get to work, sir. Too many loose ends to tie up before we go." Miko put the glass down and nodded, grinning. "And thank you, sir, for Boxley. She won't disappoint you."

"She better not." After Miko had gone, I regarded Preel. "How do you feel?"

"Scared, sir, but...excited." She smiled and sipped her drink again, eliciting another hiccup.

"Good. I had to tell the crew as much as I did, but they know now that spreading rumors will cost them dearly. We should be able to keep the details of your talent a secret." I dropped into a chair and sipped my drink. "I hope you don't mind, but I dare not assign you your own quarters yet. Not until this is done."

"I don't mind, sir." She turned a circle, and a smile touched her lips. "I like it here."

That astonished me. "After…what happened, how *can* you?"

"I don't remember it that way. The *place* isn't bad. It was Geit who was bad and he's gone. Mostly I remember you giving me your own bunk, Bert tending me, and you sitting guard while I recovered." She smiled shyly and sipped again. "And now…I'm comfortable here."

Just as I'd suspected, she was a strong woman. "Good." I downed my drink, rose, and put the two empty glasses on the sideboard.

"If you want to have your bed back, I'd be fine with a pallet on the floor or a hammock, sir. I don't want to inconvenience you."

"Oh, no. I'm fine in a hammock." Truth be told, I *did* associate that bunk with my recent and rather disturbing experience with Jhavika, an experience I wanted to put out of my mind. Despite Hemp's attention, I could still smell Jhavika there. But there was something else disturbing me, too. "About the other promise you asked of me…"

"To kill me rather than let Jhavika take me." Though Preel's voice was steady, the liquor in her glass rippled.

"I'll do as you wish, but I'll fight like a dragon to make sure it doesn't come to that."

"Thank you, sir." Preel finished her drink and hiccupped once again, her fingers rising to cover her mouth. "And thank you for the drink. I'm not used to such things, I'm afraid."

"I know." I took her glass. "And I find it adorable."

"Ad…" She hiccupped again, her eyes wide in surprise. "Adorable?"

"Yes. Now relax and read while I get my ship ready for sea." I waved at my bookshelf. "Whatever you like. I'll be on the quarterdeck most of the night. I'll have Hemp bring you something for dinner."

"Thank you, sir."

"I'll keep a guard on the door, so you needn't worry." I turned to go, but she called me back.

"Sir?" She lifted the silk band from the table and held it out. "Please. I dare not risk someone asking me a question. Not now."

"Right." I affixed the band around her mouth and stepped back. "I'm sorry you have to wear that, Preel. I enjoy your smile."

Her eyes rounded into dark pools, then looked away.

"I'm sorry. I didn't mean to embarrass you." I left the cabin without looking back, kicking myself for being an ass. Preel had been through enough without having to deal with my clumsy compliments.

In the deep night, we slipped lines and drifted away from the quay under topsails and jibs alone, a ghost vanishing into the gloom. Not a single shout or cry rose from the shore as we bore away into Snomish Bay. At a safe distance we set more sail, bearing south, as far away from Jhavika Keshmir as I could get.

When the bell struck for the morning watch, and my first mate mounted the quarterdeck, I yawned mightily. "She's yours, Miko. I'm wrung out like an old swab. When we change watch at the forenoon, I'll ask Preel if she can answer another question. It's been four days."

"Sounds good to me, sir." She saluted and grinned. "I'll put Boxley on her first watch with you for the forenoon, if you don't mind. She'll need a firm hand the first few times."

"Good enough." I left the quarterdeck, fatigue wearing on me after such a long and strenuous day and night.

With mild winds well abaft the beam, *Scourge* corkscrewed gently down the long ocean swells in a manner that never failed to lull me to sleep. I tried to recount the details of the day, but my only coherent thoughts were of a snug hammock and a dreamless sleep.

Treading heavily aft to my cabin, I nodded to the guard I'd placed on my door.

"You're off duty."

"Aye, sir." She yawned mightily. "Goodnight, sir."

"Goodnight." I stepped quietly into the cabin and closed the door behind me.

At this hour Preel would be deeply asleep, but a low-burning lamp provided enough light to keep me from stumbling. I doffed my boots by the door, stripped down to my linens, and padded to the quarter gallery. I hadn't bathed and could still smell Jhavika on my flesh, but I didn't want to wake Preel with a lot of splashing and clattering about. I settled for a quick swipe with a damp cloth, a scrub of face and hands, and a hard brush of my teeth. Emerging from the quarter gallery, I felt somewhat clean and totally ready for bed.

I donned a nightshirt and quickly rigged my hammock, my eyes now well-attuned to the low light. When I started to climb into my gently swaying cocoon, however, my gaze fell upon the rumpled nest of blankets and sheets upon my bunk.

Preel wasn't there.

My heart plunged to my feet.

I lunged to the lamp and turned it up, casting about the cabin in a sudden panic. The stern gallery windows were open. Had she decided that a death at sea might be better than a life aboard a pirate ship? I stepped around the bunk to close the windows and nearly stumbled over her, curled under a single blanket beside the bunk, hidden deep in shadow.

"What the hell?" I knelt, suspecting the worst, but she lay there untroubled, breathing deeply, asleep and unharmed.

As my panic receded, I watched her breathe for a long moment, wondering what had possessed her to abandon the bunk in favor of the hard cabin sole. The blanket had slipped from her shoulder, and I noticed that she'd removed her clothes. It made me realize that she'd been wearing the same ones for days now, and I shook my head at my thoughtlessness. But soiled clothes didn't answer the question of why she'd chosen to sleep on the floor.

I can't very well leave her like this. I reached out and gently touched her shoulder. "Preel?"

Her eyes fluttered open, widened in a moment of panic, then blinked several times.

"Shh. It's okay, Preel. It's the captain. I need to speak with you." I reached out tentatively and she didn't withdraw, so I removed the silk band from her mouth. "Why in Odea's name are you on the floor?"

"I..." The truthsayer rubbed her eyes and looked around as if surprised to find herself where she lay. "I couldn't sleep...there." She struggled to sit up, clutching the blanket as it slipped. "I'm sorry, but...I couldn't stop thinking about...things."

"What things?" My brow furrowed as I tried to make sense of what she'd said, but I was tired. "You said you were comfortable here."

"Yes, in the cabin, and I am, but..." Her gaze dropped, and she climbed up to sit on the bunk. "I'm sorry, sir. I'm being disrespectful. You lent me your own bed. I'll use it."

"Not if you don't *want* to, Preel, but why? Why now? Did my foolish questions remind you of what happened to you here?"

"No, sir, it's...something else." Preel sighed at my obvious confusion. "I couldn't stop thinking about you...that you were with Jhavika here only hours ago, and I thought...and it made me uncomfortable."

"Oh." I hadn't thought that would have made Preel uncomfortable, only that it made *me* uncomfortable. *Thoughtless bastard...* "Would you rather sleep in the hammock, or would you like me to move the feather pallet to the deck?"

"No, sir. I'll be fine, truly. I'm sorry." Her eyes remained down, though she still seemed troubled.

"Preel, I'm too tired to think straight. Please, just tell me what you want."

Her eyes snapped up. "What *I...*" Her voice broke, and she looked down again.

What the hell had I said now? "Preel, what's *wrong?*"

"Sir, I...I'm sorry." She looked up again slowly. Unshed tears glistened in her eyes. "Nobody, since the day I was made a slave, has asked me that. What *I* wanted. You've already given me so much, and I'm being ungrateful. Now you ask me that, and I... I don't know what to say."

My mind spun like a maelstrom, spiraling into darkness. I was too tired to figure this out. I needed sleep.

"Preel, I'm going to sleep in the hammock. I don't want to sleep in the bunk either, for the same reasons as you, evidently. Sleep wherever you like, but if you don't want to use the bunk, at least move the feather pallet down to make yourself more comfortable. It's a new pallet, not the one that Jhavika and I...used."

"Yes, sir." She nodded again. "I'm sorry."

"Don't be." I turned down the lamp and rolled into my hammock. Exhaustion dragged me down into sleep, but for some reason—concern for Preel, perhaps, or some sound she'd made—I opened my eyes.

Preel sat on the edge of the bunk, the blanket still clutched to her breast but drooping off one shoulder, her smooth skin fairly glowing in the starlight through the stern gallery windows. Then she stood and unwrapped the blanket from about her, draping it across the bunk before climbing beneath the covers.

I closed my eyes against the vision of dusky curves in starlight, praying for sleep and oblivion.

Chapter Sixteen
Unfettered

The light of morning answers many questions.
The Lessons of Quen Lau Ush

From the diary of Kevril Longbright –
Freedom has always meant so much to me. To see Preel taste it for the first time in her adult life changed me in a way I can't even try to explain. To this day, I don't know why.

A knock woke me from a deep sleep to the bright morning light. I rolled out of my hammock with the ease of long practice and found Preel smiling at me from my bunk, seated with one of my books in her lap. She wore her old clothes again, but not the silk band. I'd forgotten to put it back on.

I rubbed my eyes and blinked them awake. "Come in!"

"Half a glass to the forenoon watch, sir!" Hemp entered with a bucket of water in one hand and a tray in the other. "Just time enough for a nibble and a pot of blackbrew."

"Good!" I pulled trousers on, then pulled off my night shirt. "By Odea's scaly tail, I could eat the south end of a north-bound mule!"

215

"Got no mule for you this mornin', sir, just porridge, eggs, and bacon." He put the tray on the table and the bucket by the quarter gallery door. Steam rose from it. "A shave?"

"Not this morning, but…" I glanced at Preel. "Would you like to bathe, Preel, and maybe put on clean clothes?"

Her eyes widened and blinked in surprise. "Yes, please, sir." She got up and hurried to the quarter gallery.

Hemp scowled and muttered as he fussed about the cabin, "Takes the captain's shave water… Porridge'll be cold by the time she's done, and I'm *not* gonna fetch no more. More washin' too. Never gonna get done if I don't get someone to—"

"That's enough, Hemp. Just lay out some clothes for her." I donned a shirt and sat down to my breakfast. "Wash her clothes when you do mine. You can have one of the scullery swabs help. There's no extra work."

"Aye, sir." He went to Preel's chest and pulled out the first pair of pantaloons and matching halter he came to, holding the curious garment up with a skeptical look. "Can't imagine who in the name of all the tailors in the world would make such a thing. No sleeves, no buttons, not even a proper draw string. Barbarians!"

I ignored him and attended to my breakfast. Hemp muttered incessantly, a surly tirade of all the ways the world didn't conform to his high expectations. He straightened the bunk and laid out Preel's clothes, then fussed about a bit more before leaving. I poured myself more blackbrew and ate, considering precisely how to word the question I'd ask Preel this evening.

From behind the quarter gallery door came the sound of splashing and…humming? The lilting musical tune was the last thing I'd expected to hear from her. *After all she's been through…* I listened to Preel's lovely voice as I finished my food, my mind wandering to the starlit curves I'd spied last night. *A treasure, indeed…*

"Sir?"

My gaze snapped up to the quarter gallery door. Preel peered from the narrow gap, her damp skin dark against the white towel wrapped around her, wet, tousled hair draping her shoulders in ebony ringlets.

I caught myself staring and cleared my throat. "Yes, Preel?"

"My clothes, if you please, sir. I didn't want to…um…"

"Of course!" I retrieved her clothes and handed them over, then turned away and snatched up my boots, sitting at my chart table to put them on, my back to the quarter gallery. "I wanted to tell you that Miko and I will be asking you another question this evening. That is, if you think it's been long enough."

"Yes, sir, I expected you would."

I glanced back. The door to the quarter gallery was open. Preel stood with her back to me, clad only in her pantaloons, her hair dripping as she donned the curious halter, wrapping it around the back of her neck and then her torso, finally tying a simple knot before turning to face me.

"Will you want to discuss it first?"

"Yes." I looked away, attending to my boots. "We may as well optimize our chance of getting a relevant answer. And you should have a good meal before we ask, enough to sustain you through your sleep." I stood, donned my work jacket, and tucked a dagger into my boot out of habit.

"Thank you." She went to her chest and pulled out a brush before sitting upon the bunk. "I'll just read and maybe exercise until you arrive if you don't mind."

"Not at all." I glimpsed Preel's golden manacles lying in the bottom of my cabinet and remembered one more thing I had to do before I took my watch on deck. "I'm sorry, Preel, but I think we should put on your gag while I'm out. It's just too great a risk. If someone should ask you an unexpected question, it will delay us for days."

"Oh, of course, sir." She picked it up from beside the night stand and held it out. "I don't mind. I wish I could put it on and take it off myself, but the magic won't let me."

"I thought not." She stood, turned her back to me, and held her wet hair out of the way.

I leaned in to tie the ends beneath the heavy wet curls, breathing in the scent of soap and clean skin, a heady perfume so close. I hastily finished the knot and stepped back. "There. I'll be back for lunch. If you'd like to take a turn on deck this afternoon, I'll be happy to escort you. The fresh air will be a nice change from a stuffy cabin."

She whipped around and nodded enthusiastically, the crinkle of her eyes showing her hidden smile.

"I wish…" I stopped and swallowed, curiously not sure what I was going to say. "I wish you didn't have to wear that gag. I like the sound of your voice."

Preel cast her gaze to the floor and retreated to the bunk. Sitting, she picked up her brush and started running it through her hair, first teasing out the tangles, then taking longer strokes. Her eyes remained fixed upon her lap.

"I'm sorry," I said, realizing that I was staring at her like a dolt. "I'm not used to having someone living with me, so…you'll have to tolerate my foolishness."

Preel looked up and shook her head, her brow furrowed. She pointed to the bunk, the books, my hammock, then clenched her hands and bowed. She was thanking me for the merest of considerations, simple courtesies that would be expected by anyone. *Anyone who's not a slave.*

"You're welcome, Preel." Deeply touched by her unwarranted gratitude, I stepped into the corridor and closed the door behind me. "Hemp!"

He stepped out of the galley door, his mouth so full that he could barely spit out the word. "Sir?"

"Post a guard. I'll be on deck."

"Aye, sir."

I strode past him without another glance and proceeded out of the sterncastle into the light of day.

The first of the two dog watches—the foreshortened watches that fall during the time of the evening meal—came far too soon for me. I don't know why I faced it with such trepidation, but my nerves were drawn as tight as bowstrings. The delight of my forenoon watch had been Boxley, bright-eyed and as enthusiastic as a young pup on her first hunt. She soaked up knowledge like a sponge soaks up water, smart and eager, a refreshing change from my other midshipmen. Afterward, I ate a light lunch with Preel during which we barely spoke a word, then walked her around the deck, pointing out this and that while she nodded and smiled with her eyes. I think she enjoyed the fresh air and sunshine. For my part, I felt constrained by the morning's awkwardness. It didn't help that the eyes of the crew followed our every step, standing the hairs on the nape of my neck on end. I would have given a finger to hear their thoughts.

Scourge sailed on an even keel, broad reaching under topsails and reefed courses on a southerly course toward no set destination. The seas were mild and the horizon clear, so I assigned Midshipmen Quiff and Kivan to command the two dog watches while Miko and I went to my cabin to eat dinner and discuss our pending question with Preel.

Bert—may the Gods of Light bless her to live forever—served the three of us marinated saddle of mutton with mint glaze, garlicky potato mash, and greens stewed with bacon that brought tears of culinary bliss to my eyes. We paid proper homage to the meal, content to postpone conversation. With my stomach straining my belt, we sat back, Miko and I sipping a heady Marathian red, ready to finally discuss the pending question.

"I think we've narrowed things down nicely," I began, ticking points off on my fingers. "We ask for a coastal location, someplace we can sail *Scourge*, where we can find someone capable and willing to accept payment or barter to remove the enchantment. The only way it can really go wrong is if we don't get an answer at all."

"I had a thought about that this morning." Miko leaned back in her chair, staring at her empty plate. "We should consider what we'll do if the answer is Haven."

"Bugger! I hadn't thought of that." Good thing I wasn't trying to do this all myself. "Jhavika *might* be able to release the enchantment, not that she ever would. We just don't know what she can do."

"That *is* a possibility, sir," Preel agreed. "You could exclude Haven from your question, but you'd have to be careful about the wording. Also, asking for the *closest* location would probably be wise."

"I don't know… At this point, I wouldn't mind being as far away from Jhavika as possible."

Miko chuckled. "I hear the Shining Sea's nice this time of year."

I shot a scowl at her.

"Also, sir, you should be specific about the enchantment in your question," Preel cut in. "We don't know if there might be some other minor magic working on you. Asking simply to remove the enchantment could get the wrong answer."

"I don't have any other spell on me that I *know* of, but you're probably right." I considered the result of that grim prospect. "Returning to Haven thinking I'd broken Jhavika's hold on me, when I actually hadn't, would earn me a lifetime of pain."

"Or a very short one," Miko agreed. "This is even more complicated than I thought it would be."

"I know." I considered all the things that had to be included into the question, working out the phrase in my head. "Do you know, Preel, if there's any limitation to the *complexity* of the question?"

"The only limitation I know of is that it must be a single question. You can't ask for answers to two unrelated things, even about the same subject. Someone's favorite food *and* favorite color, for instance." Preel pursed her lips, moistening them with her tongue. "If you ask for the nearest location you can sail to, excluding Haven, where you can find someone both capable of *and* willing to accept payment to remove the compulsion Jhavika has placed on you, that *should* work."

"I would think 'willing *and* capable' two different questions." I said

"They are close enough, I think. One answer will satisfy both aspects." Preel nodded sagely. "Yes, that's usually a good gauge of phrasing. I think that's a safe question."

"You're good at this," Miko complimented.

"I have answered a great many questions," Preel said with a frown. "Hundreds…"

I wondered how anyone with such a resource at their disposal could ever give it up. Would Preel be as addictive as grog to a drunk? If she chose to stay with the ship, become a member of the crew, what would our future hold? Would we become slaves to our own questions, always wanting to know more? Would I become as bad as Jhavika? Had Preel's previous masters sold her to break their own addictions?

These were questions I might ask her later, but now we had more pressing puzzles to solve.

"Very well. I think we have our question." I nodded to Preel. "You'll be out all night, so you should probably use the head."

"Yes, sir." Preel got up and went to the quarter gallery.

When the door closed behind her, I whispered to Miko, "Have you heard anything about Preel from the crew? What are the rumors?"

"Nothing mutinous that I've heard. A few still think she's a witch and that you're charmed." Miko grinned at me. "Maybe you are."

"I would have said I wasn't under *any* enchantment a week ago." I downed the rest of my wine and considered the possibility. "Not likely. If she could charm people, she'd never have become a slave."

"Aye, you're probably right." Miko looked amused. "She *is* charming, but I suppose it's not magic."

Dusky curves in starlight... "I can't argue with that."

The door opened and Preel returned to us, a subtle smile on her lips. I wondered if she'd overheard us.

"I'm ready, sir."

"Good." I stood and gestured to the bunk. "Get comfortable."

"Please don't forget to put the binding back on my mouth afterward. A careless question..."

"Right." I picked up the silken bond as she lay down on the bunk and shifted to get comfortable.

"Ready, sir."

"All right." Again, I felt an unaccustomed reticence, as if using Preel's talent was something to be abhorred. *I'm not hurting her*, I told myself. *The gods gave her this ability for a reason.* I took a breath and asked my question. "Where is the nearest place we can sail to, other than Haven, where I can find someone both capable of and willing to accept payment or barter to remove the enchantment Jhavika has placed on me?"

Preel's back arched and her eyes rolled back, showing stark white. Her voice, a harsh rasp that sounded so wrong coming from those sensuous lips, sent chills up my spine.

"Valaka." She collapsed.

"Well, that seems clear enough," Miko said with a grimace.

I couldn't blame her. *Valaka...of all places.* "Yes, it does." I leaned down to place the silken gag once again over Preel's mouth, but hesitated for a moment. Such a lovely mouth, it seemed a shame to cover it. I brushed her lips with my thumb, just a bare touch, and felt instantly guilty for taking the liberty of touching her while she was insensate. I affixed the gag in place and turned back to Miko. "And it brings up all kinds of new questions."

"Like who in Valaka, other than on of the fucking *dragonlords*, can do this for you, and what do they want in payment?"

"Exactly." The dragonlords didn't rule the island, but they had the power to do so if they so chose. Fortunately, they didn't crave that kind of power. They were obsessed only with the magic of the

Serpent's Eye and its lure to dragon-kind. I sat back down and lifted the decanter to fill Miko's glass, but she shook her head.

"I've got first watch and that meal already has me sleepy."

I checked my pocket watch, surprised that so much time had flown past. "You still have a couple hours. You should get some sleep anyway." I filled my own glass.

"After learning *that*?" Miko waved a hand at Preel. "Valaka... Damn, just saying the name of that place gives me the shivers."

"Me too." I sipped and frowned, then reconsidered my downward spiraling mood. Valaka wasn't the end of the world, and the answer could have been much worse. "But *someone* there can break Jhavika's hold on me. All we have to find out now is who they are and what they want."

"Right." Miko chewed her lip in consternation. "You don't suppose it *is* one of the dragonlords, do you?"

"Odea's tits, I hope not." The dragonlords wielded magic, of that there was no doubt, but they were notoriously reclusive, ill-tempered, and reportedly mad to boot. Close contact with the Serpent's Eye for too long was said to have driven them over the edge. I knew what else the magic of the Serpent's Eye did, and being within a hundred leagues of it made me nervous. "It'd be my luck..."

"But you asked for someone willing and capable, so..."

"Yes, I did." I downed my wine and sighed. "Well, obsessing on it won't get our answer any faster." I rose and called for my steward. "You can clear, Hemp. Give Bert my compliments on that meal."

"Aye, sir." He started for the table, then noticed Preel unconscious on the bunk. "What happened to her?"

"She's fine, Hemp, just exhausted. She'll sleep until morning. Just tend to the dishes."

"Aye, sir." He cleared the table, muttering as he left.

"I'll order a course change and grab a couple hours sleep, if you don't mind, sir." Miko started for the door.

"May as well wait until your watch to change course. We're in no rush. We can ghost downwind through the slot between Ton Chi and Black Point." I stretched to alleviate the discomfort of the meal and sighed. "We've got days before we can ask another question. I'd rather spend them at sea than moored in Valaka."

"Good point." Miko made a face. "I'll wait. Goodnight, sir."

"Goodnight." I bolted the door behind Miko and got ready to bed down.

The sun was just setting, so the stern gallery windows framed a horizon darkening from pink to blue to deep cobalt. I donned a nightshirt and climbed into my hammock, swinging gently with the roll of the ship. The sky darkened, and the first stars winked to life. Before the light had entirely faded, I shifted to my side and watched Preel breathe, wondering at my fortune, bad and good. Was knowledge of one's own slavery truly better than ignorance? Was a truthsayer a blessing or a curse? Only time would tell.

I stood the midwatch, and when I woke again to take the forenoon, Preel still slept. The question must have been more taxing than I'd thought, regardless of the simple answer. I left a guard on duty and ordered Hemp to bring Preel breakfast when she woke, but only to remove her gag long enough for her to eat. I also warned him not to speak to her or mutter foolish questions while in her presence at the risk of her safety…and his life, because I'd kill him if she came to harm. I prayed that he took the warning to heart.

Thoughts of Preel plagued me during my watch, threatening to interfere with my duties. Boxley's insatiable thirst for knowledge, so gratifying yesterday, now wore on my nerves. After three hours of endless questions, I finally snapped at her to leave off and study her mathematics. That, of course, made me feel guilty, so Miko and I did a noon sighting with the girl at the watch change.

Hurrying below, I opened my cabin door to a rainbow of disarray. "What happened here?"

Preel started from where she knelt in front of her open trunk. Multi-hued piles of silk were mounded on the cabin sole around her feet. Sweat glistened on her skin; she'd apparently been exercising. Her brow furrowed, she held out a handful of her clothes and pointed to spots of mold and mildew on the fine silks.

"Moisture must have gotten into the bottom of the trunk." I waved it off. "Don't worry. I'll have Hemp launder them."

Preel tapped the silk band girding her mouth. She wanted to say something.

"All right." I untied the gag.

"Sir, Hemp shouldn't have to wash my things. I can do it if given water and soap."

"Hemp can do it. It's his job."

"But...he's *your* steward, sir, not mine." She frowned and looked down. "And I don't think he likes me much."

"Hemp doesn't like *anybody* much, Preel." I lifted the silk gag again. "His job is to keep this cabin in order, including your clothes while you're staying here. Let me put this back on and you just watch."

"Yes, sir." She turned obediently.

As I fixed the gag in place, I noticed that sweat from her exercise had darkened the clothing she wore. I went to the door and called for my steward.

"Sir, your lunch ain't quite on yet. I'm sorry, but..."

I waved off his apology. "Not about that, Hemp. Do you have Preel's clean clothes? Damp got into her sea chest, so she can't wear any of those, and the ones she's wearing are soiled."

"*Damp?*" Hemp looked horrified, well acquainted with the damage damp and mold could do to clothing. He stepped forward and stared down at the piles of clothing, the chest, and the tiny specs of mildew. "Devils and fishes swallow me whole! I never thought to... I'm sorry, sir! I didn't unpack it all when she came aboard, and I just took what was on top the other day. It's not a proper sea chest, you see. Not jointed well and made of common *green*wood, not cedar

225

as it should be. I never thought to look down the bottom. It's all got to be cleaned, of course, and I'll scare up a proper chest. This ain't fit for stove wood!"

"Good. And bring in her clean clothes so she can change."

"Her...um..." Hemp wrung his hands. "They're not clean yet, sir. I figured a slave could wait—"

My temper flared. "Hemp, Preel is my guest in this cabin. She might have been a slave, but she's not anymore, and she's performing an invaluable service for *all* of us. You've put my hospitality in question."

"I'm sorry, sir! I'll get these done straightaway." He fumbled the clothes into the chest.

"Wait!" I went to my locker and pulled out a clean nightshirt. "Here, Preel, go to the quarter gallery and hand out your soiled clothes. You can have a rinse and wear this until your things are clean."

Her eyes widened momentarily, as if she feared my nightshirt.

"Don't worry. Nobody will come in, and your things should be clean and dry by tonight."

She nodded and dashed for the quarter gallery. In moments, the door opened a hand-span and her arm extended with her sweat-damp clothes. I took them and handed them to Hemp.

"Don't you worry none, sir, I'll have this done in two shakes!"

"You better." I'd known Hemp would react like this. He took pride in his work. Preel would have no more trouble from my surly steward.

By the time I'd removed my boots, Hemp was back with lunch. He laid out two place settings silently and efficiently.

Before he left he asked, "Shave today, sir?"

"Tomorrow for the morning watch." I scratched my stubbly jaw. After dressing up like a hired trollop for Jhavika, I was reveling in my unkempt appearance.

"Aye, sir."

Hemp left, and I sat down to lunch, a salad of greens topped with fresh fruit, turtle soup, and a plate of cakes as an after-meal sweet. Starved, I lifted a ladle to fill my bowl, then paused, glanced at the quarter gallery door, and mentally kicked myself. I'd lectured Hemp on Preel's new status as my guest, but I wasn't treating her that way myself. I put the ladle back and poured two cups of the greenberry wine Hemp had chosen, then sat back and waited. There was no humming from the quarter gallery this time, of course, since she wore the silk gag, and I found that I missed it.

Finally, the door opened and Preel edged cautiously out into the cabin.

I had to smile; my nightshirt came down to her shins and fit her like a tent fits a pixie. "Sorry I don't have anything that would fit you, Preel, but I thought this would be preferable to wearing your soiled clothes." I gestured to the other chair and the place set for her. "Please eat with me."

She nodded and took her seat, turning so I could remove the gag. I put the band of silk beside my plate.

"I hope you're all right." I lifted my glass to her. "You seemed a little flustered."

"I was...upset, sir." She picked up her glass and sipped. "I wanted to show you that I was grateful for everything you've done for me, to dress in something nice while I ate with you, but my clothes were ruined. Now I look like I'm wearing a sack."

"You look charming, even in a sack," I told her with a smile. "And your clothes aren't ruined; Hemp's had years of practice in getting mold stains out. They'll be fine. Now, have some salad. I've got to get some sleep before my next watch, but I'd like to...just talk with you. The answer you gave last evening was...interesting."

"Valaka." Her eyes flicked hesitantly to mine. "Did the answer...please you?"

I laughed aloud. "I was pleased that we *got* an answer. The answer itself, well, let's just say that's the interesting part. I'd like to hear what you know about Valaka."

"I've never been there, sir, but I've read somewhat."

"Well, I've *been* there, but probably know less than you in the arcane context."

We ate while we talked, starting out with benign things like how long the trip to Valaka would take. The conversation veered from prosaic to speculative as we discussed the legends of that strange city and its denizens. I admitted to my trepidations about the dragonlords. Preel had heard only that they were wielders of magic and obsessed with the Serpent's Eye—the magical maelstrom that centers the Serpent Isles—and dragon magic in particular. We both agreed that it would be wise to phrase my next question to exclude them from the list of those who might lift my enchantment. I used great care not to ask any questions, falling into the pattern of asking for her opinion, which she said was safe. If I asked what she *thought*, her talent would not be invoked.

I regretted when the meal drew to a close. I could tell that casual conversation came hard for her—no wonder, when her entire adult life had been spent as a slave—but her knowledge was so broad and so far beyond my own, I soaked up every word that fell from her lips.

"I want to encourage you to speak your mind, Preel," I said as I finished my last bite of cake. "If you want something, ask for it. If I do something to offend you, say so. If I'm about to make a mistake, warn me. You're intelligent and educated, but neither helps us if you don't speak up."

"I'll try, sir." She bit her lip, pearly teeth pressing hard. "It's...hard to get used to, asking for what I want, I mean."

"Well, you've got some time to practice before we get to Valaka, so feel free." I stood and called Hemp in to clear the dishes. "I'm going to wash up and sleep for a while, Hemp."

"Aye, sir." He nodded politely and left, still contrite.

Would that it will last...

I washed my face and hands, brushed my teeth, donned a nightshirt, and considered my scruffy appearance in the quarter gallery mirror. I decided to let Hemp wield his razor every morning, if for no other reason than to honor my cabinmate.

When I exited the quarter gallery, I found Preel perusing my books, leaning down to study the spines, pulling out one after another to consider. The light from the stern gallery windows caught her just so, silhouetting her shape through the thin linen of my nightshirt. I looked away and busied myself rigging my hammock.

"Sir?" Preel was suddenly behind me, holding up the silken gag.

"Oh, right." I sighed as I took it from her. "I really hate this thing."

"It protects me, sir. I don't mind, but..." She bit her lip again. "...could I ask you something before you put it on?"

"Of course."

"Are you *sure* you wouldn't rather sleep in your bed? I *am* beholden to you, and I feel bad about displacing you from your comfort. I can sleep on the floor, or in the hammock, or..." Her gaze lowered. "...or share it with you if you wish."

A knot formed in my gut. It would have been so easy to say yes, to lay with her in my bunk and take her in my arms, to feel her silky skin against mine, to taste those beautiful lips...but I couldn't.

"Preel..." I put my hands on her shoulders and felt her trembling. "You needn't feel beholden to me, and you shouldn't offer yourself up as...compensation for what I've done for you. You're doing something for me in return. It wouldn't be right for me to take advantage of you."

"But...you said..." She looked up at me, and her dark eyes nearly shattered my resolve. "...you said I look adorable and charming. You think I'm...attractive, don't you?"

"Of course. Far *too* attractive, truth be told, but you're still coming to understand what it is to be free, and I'm..." *What?* My body was willing—I thanked the gods that my baggy nightshirt disguised just how willing—but my mind overrode my baser instincts. To take advantage of her thus, would just be wrong.

Chris A. Jackson

"You don't want me." Her gaze fell. "After what happened with Geit."

"*No*, Preel, it's not that. I just don't want you to do something you don't want to do out of indebtedness. I'm *captain*. If I said yes, it would be too close to an order. I'd be no better than Geit."

"No, sir!" Preel looked up at me then, her eyes suddenly brimming with tears. "No. Never. I'd *never* think that of you."

"Good." I released her shoulders and lifted the silken band to bind her mouth to keep her from saying what I so longed to hear. She stood very still while I tied it in place. "Now, you read or relax or do whatever you like while I sleep."

Preel nodded, and a tear spilled down to dampen the white silk.

I turned away and climbed aboard my hammock, facing away from her. Closing my eyes, I begged for sleep while listening to her soft feet shuffle about the cabin. She was pacing. I'd upset her, but I'd be damned if I knew how to make it right.

A pen scratched on parchment, then a finger lightly touched my shoulder. I opened my eyes to find Preel standing beside my hammock, holding a note in her hand. I read the elegant script.

You are very chivalrous for a pirate, Captain Longbright.

I smiled at her. "Not the rapacious scoundrel you—"

Her fingertips pressed against my lips. Preel shook her head, and her smile once again reached her eyes. She turned away then and let me sleep, but dreams of silky skin and sensuous lips plagued me until I woke.

Chapter Seventeen
Valaka

Fear, not lust, avarice, or ego, is the dominant poison of the human mind.
The Lessons of Quen Lau Ush

From the diary of Kevril Longbright –
What is superstition in a world where magic can twist one's offspring into abominations? I've read legends of powerful lords and wizards sailing into the Serpent's Eye in search of its source, the core of wild magic that draws dragons like a magnet, to harness that energy. One in a hundred is said to have survived unscathed. Fearless fools. There is nothing wrong with being afraid of something that can destroy you. Not being governed by fear is called courage. Never was my courage so tested as by one dusky-skinned truthsayer.

Slow sailing drives me mad. I had to constantly remind myself not to trim sails for optimum speed and efficiency. I didn't want to arrive in Valaka before it was safe to ask Preel another question. *Scourge* ghosted along in moderate winds under reefed sails, the crew lounging and laughing at our sedate pace. As hard as that was, however, living with someone I found physically alluring, but could not touch, was harder by far. Controlling my baser urges in the company of my cabin guest tried my every nerve.

Despite my unease, we fell into a simple routine during those few days. Hemp would wake us in time for breakfast before the forenoon watch. I'd lunch with Preel in the cabin at midday, and we'd stroll the decks for an hour or so after. She would spend the afternoon reading or exercising while I saw to the less-demanding duties of navigation and the instruction of my midshipmen in officer-like conduct and mathematics. I would stand the first dog watch, then dine with Miko, Preel, and sometimes a midshipman. Boxley might be progressing well in mathematics, but her table manners were straight out of the lower decks. While Miko took the first evening watch, I would read and catch a couple hours of sleep. Then I'd stand the midwatch, sleep through the morning watch, and start again.

Strangely, I found the quiet hours of the midwatch most difficult. My mind went places I didn't want it to go. More than once, upon returning to my cabin in the small hours of the morning, I stood beside the bunk and watched Preel sleep, counting her breaths, memorizing the curves of her body under the sheets. Once she must have tossed in her sleep and the blanket had been pushed down to her waist. As the ship rolled, moonlight swept across her satin curves like frothy surf caressing a dark-sand beach. I pulled the sheet up carefully, thankful that she didn't wake, and resolved to have Hemp sew a nightshirt for her to sleep in.

I should have assigned her a cabin of her own and put a guard on her door, but I couldn't make myself give the order. It was too risky to let such a treasure out of my sight. At least, that was what I told myself.

I never thought I'd be happy to see Valaka, but by Odea, I'd have welcomed an encounter with a sea drake at that point to relieve my building frustration. The crew muttered oaths and made warding signs as we ghosted into Valaka Bay. Most had been here at least once; the rumors and tales initiated those who hadn't.

I'd been here too many times in my youth to worry much about the stories of curses. All over the world children are born with deformities—whether due to curses, magic, or some cruel twists of nature, who's to say—but Valaka certainly has more than its share. About one in five newborns in Valaka are so horribly malformed that mothers have been known to drown their babies and fathers to murder their wives for begetting such abominations. Scholars generally agree that it's due to the proximity of the Serpent's Eye. They call the deformed the Serpent's Children, bestial chimeras of human and any manner of creature from sea or land, no two alike.

Here, the deformities only afflict the newborn, and the malformations aren't spread by touch. If so, I'd have succumbed long ago. But Valaka Isle only skirts the archipelago. Few indigenous people inhabit the inner Serpent Isles, for as you venture closer to the perpetual storm at its center, adults are afflicted as well. Upon the isles nearest the Eye, it's said even the trees are deformed by the magic, some so changed that they crawl about and feast on each other. Only dragons seem to be immune, or so it's said. I've never asked one.

"I despise this place," Miko muttered as we maneuvered *Scourge* through the returning fleet of fishing smacks. "Makes my skin crawl."

"True enough." I noticed the coxswain of one of the smacks gripping the tiller of his craft with a long, ropy limb reminiscent of an octopus' tentacle. "We'll anchor at the east end of the bay and take a launch ashore. I don't think the crew'll be champing at the bit for shore leave."

"Don't bet on that, sir." Miko made a face. "I heard Hemp talking about some of the local brothels."

"Seriously?" Valaka sported as active a red-veil district as any seaport, and some of the brothels catered to twisted tastes. I'd frequented a few in my youth, thoroughly altering my view of carnal

233

relations and acquiring an aversion to seafood for a while. I wasn't eager to revisit those dens, but far be it for me to dictate to my crew. *To each his own...* "If anyone wants to go ashore, they go in groups of four or larger, and armed. I hope we're not here long enough to need provisioning."

"We're good there, sir. Bert's got a full larder. We may need water and fresh produce if we're here more than a couple of weeks though."

"That's easy enough, but let's hope this doesn't take *weeks*." I pointed to a gap in the anchorage. "There. Furl topsails and bring her in under stays'ls. Put a leadsman in the forechains."

"Aye, sir."

We eased into position between a narrow two-masted ship that had 'smuggler' written all over her, and a beamy junk awaiting a berth, dropping anchor in six fathoms. We swung on the lazy breeze and slack tide, unfortunately downwind of the city. The reek wasn't as bad as Haven, but the fetid tang of rotten fish wrinkled my nose.

"Secure the ship, post watches, and feed them. Tell Wix to dole out a double ration of grog with my compliments."

"Aye, sir." Miko passed the order and I got a lazy cheer as I descended the steps to the main deck.

In the sterncastle, the scents of cooking food overpowered the reek of shore. I stopped at the galley and leaned though the open door. Bert stood before the massive stove tending a skillet of simmering sausage, onions, garlic, and spices, her massive frame jiggling like pudding as she manhandled the heavy pan.

"Roberta, if you weren't wed to this galley, I'd take you as my bride."

"And it'd be the fourth offer I got today!" Bert laughed and grinned, her round face florid and streaming with sweat. "Off with you, now, or I'll chop you up for stew!" She brandished a spatula.

I laughed and headed aft. Bert had become the bright spot aboard *Scourge*, the one person everyone liked and many idolized. Good food invariably has that effect on people. I swept the great cabin with my eyes as I entered and didn't see Preel, but that didn't concern me overmuch. The guard was still at the door, so she couldn't have gone anywhere. I clattered around loudly enough to announce my presence and turned in surprise as the starboard-side quarter gallery door opened. Unlike the port-side quarter gallery, which functioned as a head, I used this compartment for storage. There was no reason for Preel to be in there, or so I thought.

I opened my mouth to ask her why she was poking about, but stopped when I saw the spyglass in her hand. "Having a look at Valaka?"

Preel nodded and tapped the silk band, an eager look in her eyes. Turning, she lifted her braided hair out of the way, and I quickly untied the gag. We'd settled into a comfortable association during the trip, and she'd stopped being reticent about asking to speak to me. She also acted less like a slave and more like a guest in my home. Unfortunately, I still acted like an ass every time the light caught her just so.

"Yes." Preel gestured out the quarter gallery windows. "I couldn't see from the other side and didn't think you would mind. It's odd; the city looks…disorganized, like nobody knew what to build where."

"It's old." I doffed my jacket, then rinsed my face and hands. "Many of the buildings used to be temples and monuments. You know how people used to worship the Serpent's Eye as a god?"

"Yes. Wars were fought between the different cults."

"Which destroyed temples and rearranged the city every time one cult fought another. Now that most of the religions have died away, many of the temples have gone to ruin or been torn down. Some have been built over, but the locals avoid others like the plague."

"What about the higher neighborhood on the hill? The houses are beautifully painted."

"That's the Children's Quarter."

"The misshapen ones?"

"Yes. Many are shunned by their families and move to live with others of their kind. They tend to paint their homes in bright colors, though I'm not sure if it's symbolic of anything. The locals avoid them and the Children keep to themselves for the most part, though you'll see them here and there." I didn't want to tell her about the ones I'd seen performing in the red-veil district. "Valaka isn't as bad as Haven for outright violence in the streets, and there *is* a government and city watch. It's still a dangerous place, though, as most larger cities can be."

"I see." She raised the spyglass and peered at the nearby junk through the windows.

"Don't worry, Preel. You're safe here."

"Oh, I know, sir. I'm just..." She closed the spyglass and sighed. "I'm *bored*, I guess. I'd welcome a little danger to get out of...I mean off the ship for a bit."

"I can't blame you, but Valaka's not a place you want to go without an escort." I shrugged helplessly. "I'll take you on deck later and you can look, but we'll be asking you another question tonight, so I can't offer you any more than that for now."

"Yes, sir." Preel handed me the spyglass and sat down on the edge of the bunk, clearly morose. I couldn't really blame her; save for our brief walks on deck, she'd been cooped up in this cabin for more than two weeks now. "You wish to know who here can remove the enchantment?"

"Yes, other than the dragonlords." I'd been worrying about that a lot the last few days. "We could be here on a false errand if they're the only ones who can help."

"You asked for someone willing to accept payment to help you, so whoever it is should indeed be willing."

"That's true." The dragonlords didn't have a reputation for philanthropy or even much inclination to trade their magical skills for gold or services. That didn't sound willing to me. "That might rule them out already, but I think we should craft the question to exclude them."

"That's probably wise." Preel stood and paced the floor, tapping her lower lip with a finger and frowning.

"Something else is bothering you, Preel. Please, tell me what it is."

She stopped and looked at me, then down at her hands. "I…am worried, sir."

"About..."

Her lower lip protruded, then vanished as she clenched it between her teeth. "I serve only one purpose. I answer your questions. You don't need me for anything else, yet you keep me *here*." She gestured to the cabin about us.

"Preel, we spoke of this. It's too dangerous for you to—"

"Then assign a guard to me or give me a weapon and teach me to fight!" Her eyes snapped up, as dark and hard as obsidian. "You say I'm to be free when the enchantment that binds you is lifted, but you do nothing to prepare me for freedom! I'm little more than a slave here."

She's chafing, I realized. *A fledgling impatient to fly, but she doesn't know how far the fall is.*

"All right." I went to my locker and picked out one of my smaller daggers. The thin golden chain of Preel's manacles still gleamed in the bottom of the cabinet, and I considered how much easier this would have been if I'd never agreed to free her. *Easier, but not better…not for her, and not for removing this damned enchantment.* Closing the cabinet, I turned and extended the dagger to her hilt first. "Our agreement was that you would be free when Jhavika's hold on me was broken, but you're right. You should have more freedom now, at least to get used to it."

"Thank you, sir." Preel looked at the dagger strangely, as if frightened of it, then wrapped one slim hand around the hilt. Slipping it partway out of the sheath, she stared down at the honed steel, then resheathed it.

"What you have to realize, Preel, is that if you choose to stay aboard *Scourge*, you'll *still* be under my command. Until then, you can go anywhere on the ship you like under two conditions: you take that dagger with you, and you go accompanied by either me or a guard."

"Yes, sir." She frowned even more deeply, but nodded. "Thank you, sir."

"Don't thank me yet." I wondered if I'd just made a mistake by arming her. "Until this enchantment is lifted from me, our deal's not settled, and you'll be staying here where I can protect you."

"Oh, I...didn't mean I wanted..." She looked like I'd slapped her. "I'm sorry, sir. I don't want to seem ungrateful. I'm just..."

"You've had a taste of freedom, Preel. It's natural to want more."

"I *do* want more, sir." The corner of her mouth twitched up and she lifted the sheathed dagger. "You told me to tell you what I wanted. Will you teach me how to use this?"

"It's simple." I drew my own dagger from my boot. "You put this end..." I pricked my finger with the tip. "...here." I pressed my finger to her bare abdomen, just below her sternum. "Angle it up a bit and jam it in to the hilt. Do it right and you're done."

She looked down at the dagger in her hands. "You make it sound easy."

"Killing is as easy as falling overboard, Preel." I sheathed my dagger. "It's living with it that's hard."

"How...many people have you killed?"

"I don't keep count." I clenched my jaw. "Some, like Geit, deserved it. Others didn't."

"Oh." Her gaze fell again. "I didn't mean to pry, sir."

"Don't concern yourself, Preel." I pointed to the dagger in her hands. "And keep that hidden. You're not a fighter; you'll only have a chance to use it if it's a surprise."

"Yes, sir."

"Good." I sat back down, considering her for a moment. I couldn't tell if I'd improved her mood or worsened it. "Now, what would you like for dinner? I'll be asking you our question afterward, and you'll be out for the night, so it's your choice."

"Oh, I don't care." Preel sat down on the edge of the bunk and put the dagger aside. "Everything Bert makes is delicious, and I've been eating too much." Her hand drifted to her smooth belly. "I'm getting fat."

"No, you're not." I smiled at her. "Well, think on it and let me know." I rose and lifted the silken gag. "Now I've got to go see about letting some of my crew ashore so they can spend their money."

"Yes, sir." She stood and turned, and I tied the silken band over her mouth.

Miko was right; several of the crew wanted time ashore. Wix had explained the rules to them, but they weren't green and they were used to spending shore leave in Haven. They were also superstitious enough about the legends of Valaka to mind their cups and tankards. To my surprise, Miko came to me and said that Boxley asked if she might be allowed to accompany one of the groups.

"She's a bit young for that, isn't she?"

"For a trip to the red-veil district, yes, but..." Miko shrugged. "She's curious, sir, and nothing's more dangerous than a boy or girl her age who's told they're too young. If you're going to deny her shore leave, don't tell her it's because of her age. She'll just rebel."

"I suppose." I considered for a moment before deciding on a different tack. "Call her up."

"Yes, sir." Miko sent a sailor after my newest midshipman.

"How old *is* she, Miko?"

"She says thirteen, but I don't know if she's telling me the truth. She's skinny for her age if she is."

"Is she...I mean...has she come into her cycles yet?"

"Yes, and that's part of the problem. She's got a headful of what she *thinks* a woman's supposed to be, and a body that's changing

Chris A. Jackson

before her eyes." Miko chuckled. "I'm sure it's much the same for boys."

"Oh, it's similar, but it happens later." I thought about my own puberty and cringed. "I don't want her to get into trouble, that's all, but you're right. She'd jump ship if I told her no because she's too young. I've got a better idea, I think, if you're willing to help."

"I'm game, sir."

"Good." I paced until Boxley arrived.

"Sir!" She snapped a salute, looking very young in her midshipman's jacket and breeches.

"Miko tells me you want shore leave."

"Yes, sir."

"You know Valaka's a dangerous place, don't you?"

"Oh, yes, sir. I've heard all the tales." She seemed unconcerned, which was just what I'd feared. "Can't be much worse than Haven, sir."

"Maybe not *worse*, but dangerous in a different way. I'm not about to fill your head with rumors and tales; you've heard enough of those already. And I'm not going to tell you that you can't go, but I *can* set some rules, as I do for *all* my crew."

She bounced on her toes, fairly bursting with elation. "Yes, sir! I'm fine with rules, sir!"

"You better be." I scowled at her, but it had all the effect of a fly offending a dragon. "You'll go ashore in the company of Miko, one bosun's mate to be assigned by Master Wix, and at least two more veteran crewmembers willing to accompany the group. We're here to conduct business. If you create a row that disparages *Scourge* or me, I'll have Wix take the skin off your back with the cat. Is that clear?"

"Perfectly clear, sir!"

I wondered from the look in her eyes if she'd heard a word I said. "Very good. Off with you then."

"Thank you, sir!"

I waited until she was gone to fix Miko with a level stare. "You know what I want you to do, don't you?"

240

Miko smiled coldly. "Put the fear of the gods into her?"

"No, the gods won't scare her nearly as much as an evening in some of the seedier dives in Valaka." I remembered my first night here and suppressed a shudder. "Don't let her get hurt, but let her see enough to learn what she *needs* to be afraid of."

"I can do that, sir."

"And be careful yourself, please."

"I'm always careful, sir." She grinned dangerously. "And don't worry; this place scares the shit out of me."

"Good." I waved her off. "See that we have at least two watches aboard at all times and arrange for boat crews to ferry our people back and forth. Anyone goes missing, you let me know. I'm going to ask Preel our next question right after dinner."

"Oh, very good, sir." Miko sobered. "You're going to try for a name?"

"Yes, excluding the dragonlords."

"Good idea." She shuddered and turned to go.

I paced the quarterdeck until afternoon, watching our boats take the few crewmembers ashore who wanted to go. When eight bells struck, I handed the watch over to Kivan and told her to keep an eye out for our people. Then, on a whim, I asked her why she hadn't asked for shore leave.

"*Here*, sir?" She looked mildly horrified. "No, thank you. I've been here before and have seen enough of Valaka, sir."

"Not all the tales are true, you know."

"Oh, no doubt, sir, but you never know which ones are true, and which ones aren't, until you wake up one mornin' with tentacles for hands and a forked tongue." She shivered and made a face. "I'd rather not take the chance."

"Such wisdom from a midshipman is both surprising and laudable, Mister Kivan." I gave her a nod and a smile.

"Thank you, sir." She saluted and I left her to her duties.

Kivan would make a good officer one day if she'd just buckle down and give it some real effort. I'd hoped that adding Boxley's enthusiasm to the berth would stimulate the others, but I'd seen little evidence of success yet.

When I entered the great cabin, I found Preel seated on the bunk reading. She dropped the book and stood, an eager look on her face.

"Is something wrong?"

Preel shook her head and went to my chart table. She lifted the spyglass from the rack of instruments and pointed up, pantomiming using the spyglass to look afar.

"You want to go on deck to look at the city?"

She nodded.

"All right."

And so I spent the remainder of the afternoon showing Preel the sights of Valaka from the quarterdeck. I pointed out the ancient crumbling temples, the colorful awnings of the shops lining the market district, the alchemists' shops with their mortar-and-pestle signboards, and the seedy waterfront. I rehashed the tales I knew of those who had worshiped the Serpent's Eye and their resultant mutated offspring. Preel knew more of the dragonlords and their obsession with the magic of the Eye than I did, but had never seen their grim keeps, so I pointed out the high-walled castles and towers jutting from clefts in the mountains. It all seemed much more real and menacing here than it had far out at sea.

Hemp had gone ashore, so when four bells struck and the watch changed, one of the scullery swabs came up to tell me that dinner was ready. I escorted Preel below, removed her gag, and asked, "So, how did you like the spyglass tour?"

"Valaka is *interesting*!" She hurried to the quarter gallery and spoke through the open door as she washed her hands. "I wish we had time to learn more about the old culture. There's magic here I've never learned about, and more alchemists than anywhere!"

"Maybe after we're done lifting this enchantment, we can risk a trip ashore." I furrowed my brow at the haphazardly set table. Instead of plates and eating utensils, each setting consisted of just a small bowl of water and a folded linen napkin. A tray of fresh sliced meats, cheeses, fruits, and vegetables dominated the center of the table alongside a large covered bowl. "This is different."

"I sent Bert a note." Preel grinned as she took her seat. "You said we could have whatever I wanted for dinner, and this is a dish I remember from home. It's called *huvi*. You dip things in the sauce and eat them with your fingers."

Lifting the lid of the bowl, I sniffed dubiously. "Do you know what's in it?"

"Not everything, but Bert knows all *kinds* of foods. It's spicy." Preel picked up a slice of ham, layered it with cucumber, dipped it into the sauce, and popped it into her mouth. "Mmm, it's just as I remember."

I sampled the dish. My mouth lit up with tangy spices and a slow, back-of-the-throat burn that had me reaching for the carafe of light wine. "It *is* spicy!"

"Do you like it?" Preel ate another bite and accepted a glass of wine.

"I'm still deciding."

After several more bites, I decided that I did. I also decided that I liked sharing the dish with Preel. She instructed me on the proper etiquette; double dipping was strictly forbidden unless the people eating were very close, the bowl of water was for rinsing the fingers, and only the right hand was used for the food, the left handling everything else necessary, including the glass and napkin. The overall flavor varied with the food being dipped, and I found the cool, light fare satisfying without being heavy. We didn't finish the bowl since Bert had, as always, served too much. When we were both full, we sat back with another glass of wine and spoke of the pending question.

"Other than excluding the dragonlords, I don't see how it can go wrong."

"Things can *always* go wrong." Preel frowned. "If you ask for a name and the answer is a common one, you've gotten nowhere. If it's someone that nobody knows, you've got to find out who and where they are. If the answer indicates someone who is impossible to find, say a prisoner or a recluse, you have another problem."

"I didn't think of that." I poured myself another glass of wine and offered the carafe to Preel. When she shook her head, I said, "You may as well, you're going to be sleeping all night anyway."

"Well then, yes, please." She held out her glass and I filled it. "So, finding this person could require more than one question."

Which meant remaining in Valaka for days at least, not a prospect I relished. "Well, I think we'll try for a name first. Then, while you recover, I can ask around to find out where this person can be found."

"Didn't you say Valaka was dangerous?"

"It is dangerous." I gave her my best piratical grin. "And so am I."

"But not a rapacious scoundrel." She smiled and sipped her wine.

"Well, not *usually*..." I laughed, and Preel followed suit. I liked her laugh very much. "That's the first time I've heard you really laugh."

She blinked in surprise. "I...think that's probably the first time I *have* really laughed in...a very long time."

"You have a nice laugh, Preel."

"Thank you, sir."

We finished our wine in silence. Preel's eyes danced with the lamplight as she eased back in her chair, three cups of wine apparently lulling her into a state of relaxed bliss. I was glad she could have a little pleasure, considering the ordeal I was about to put her through. The scullery swab came at my call and silently cleared the dishes away. When the door closed behind him, Preel sighed and smiled at me.

"You seem happy," I said.

"I am." Her smile turned pensive. "Another first in as long as I can remember."

"Good."

"I should change before you ask me your question, Captain." She stood, wobbled a little, and giggled. "I have to pee and I've had too much to drink."

"Not too much, but definitely enough." I chuckled at her.

"Enough to make me happy." She took an unsteady step and reached out for the back of my seat for balance. She stopped to look down at me, and a new expression swept her face, a bold look I'd never seen before. "And enough to ask you…"

"Ask me what?"

"For what I *really* want."

Preel leaned down and kissed me, delicately at first, then with a rising urgency, a hunger that took my breath away. Her hands nested in my hair, pulling me in, her lips and tongue devouring me. With shaking hands, I reached up and pulled her closer, returning her ardor with a desire that had been building in me for weeks. When our lips finally parted, I found myself drowning in those dark, bottomless eyes.

Oh, gods, I can't do this! Not now! Against all my instincts, I pushed her gently back. "Preel. I don't want to take advantage—"

"I *know* you don't." She unwound her fingers from my hair and stepped back, wobbling again. "But once I'm a free woman, Captain Longbright, and there's no question of who is beholden to whom, I'll show you what I *really* want from you."

My mind was blank, void of any kind of rebuttal. "All…all right."

She wove her way to the quarter gallery and closed the door. I snatched up the decanter and downed two full glasses wine, willing the liquid to dissipate the heat of the unexpected encounter before she came back. I had an enchantment to dispel. The last thing I needed was a romantic complication. *When it's all over, Kevril… When we're both free.* I steeled myself as the quarter gallery door opened.

Preel stepped out clad in the night shift Hemp had sewn for her. It covered her modestly, but the thin fabric left no question of what she wore, or didn't, beneath. She went to the bunk without a word and lay down, her hands folded on her stomach, her eyes fixed on the overhead.

"Ask your question, Captain."

I stood, picked up the silken gag, and went to the bedside. Preel gazed up at me, and it was all I could do not to lay down there beside her. *Odea's tits, sometimes I truly hate being captain...*

"Who in Valaka, other than the dragonlords, is capable of and willing to accept payment or barter to remove the enchantment placed upon me by Jhavika Keshmir?"

Preel's eyes rolled up and her back arched. "Brekka!" she rasped, then fell limp, her breathing labored, but easing quickly.

I watched her for a moment, then placed the silken binding over her mouth, loath to conceal the lips that I'd finally tasted. Carefully I pulled up the sheet to cover her, judging the night warm enough not to need the blanket. I then turned down the lamp, drained the decanter into my glass, downed the contents, and went to my door.

"Hemp!" I remembered the moment his name left my lips that he was ashore, probably up to his hipbones in some well-proportioned trollop. The scullery swab materialized before I could correct my error.

"Sir?"

"Call the officer of the watch and have an armed guard posted outside my door. I'll wait until one arrives."

"Aye, sir!" he scampered off, and a burly foremast jack arrived moments later.

"Foist, isn't it?" I asked him as he saluted.

"Aye, sir."

"Stand here. Nobody goes in but me. Understand?"

"Aye, sir." Foist crossed his ropy arms. "Nobody."

"Good man." I clapped him on the shoulder, comforted by the fact that I may as well have been trying to budge *Scourge's* keel timber.

I went on deck and began to pace. As the night deepened and eight bells struck, I relieved Quiff and continued my pacing. Miko returned from shore leave with Boxley draped over her shoulder and a grin on her face.

"Mission accomplished, sir." She handed my young midshipman over to a foremast jack before saluting. "Drunk off her ass and scared shitless."

"And you?"

"Sober as a magistrate, sadly, but ready for duty."

"Get some sleep. I'll take your watch." I still had thinking to do.

"Did you get an answer?"

"Yes. A name." *And a kiss that knocked me senseless...* "I'll talk to you about it over breakfast."

"Very good, sir." She saluted and went below.

I resumed my pacing.

Chapter Eighteen
Needles and Haystacks

The flesh does not often mirror the soul.
The Lessons of Quen Lau Ush

From the diary of Kevril Longbright –
Humans have strange preconceptions: anything beautiful is good, while anything ugly is evil. I've been fooled more than once by a pretty face and was once treated with kindness by someone truly vile to look upon who could have justifiably held me in contempt. I really should learn not to judge a book by the quality of its binding.

By the time Miko relieved me for the morning watch, I must have walked ten miles around the quarterdeck. Footsore and exhausted, I told her to assign the forenoon watch to one of the midshipmen and meet me for breakfast in the great cabin. I went below without another word, dismissed the guard, and entered my cabin. Preel lay exactly as I'd left her, sleeping soundly.

I stripped and donned my nightshirt, used the head, and drank some water to ease the dull headache brought on by too much wine. After rigging my hammock, I started to climb in, truly intended to, but found myself standing beside the bunk instead, staring down at the truthsayer.

I watched Preel breathe for a while, my mind still spinning with the events of the previous night. With any luck at all, she wouldn't remember the kiss. She'd had plenty to drink, after all. I brushed my fingertips along the silken band that covered those mind-addling lips. *No!* Tearing myself away, I strode to my hammock, swung aboard, and fell asleep with the ease of exhaustion.

Hemp, bleary-eyed from shore leave, woke me sometime later. The scents of food and blackbrew filling the cabin were enough to roll me out of my hammock...barely.

"Shave today, sir?" He poured tea and started placing two settings.

"The way your hands are shaking, you'd cut my throat."

"As you wish, sir."

Trying not to stare at Preel still peacefully sleeping in my bunk, I went to the head, relieved myself, washed my face to wake up, and changed into trousers and shirt. When I came out, Miko was there, too, looking as bleary-eyed as either me or Hemp.

"Have a cup of blackbrew before you fall down." I gestured her to a chair as I sat and started loading my plate with eggs, sausage, fried potatoes, and toasted bread.

"No, thank you, sir. I've already had too much." She sat and buttered a piece of toast. When Hemp had finished fussing and left us, she asked, "So, you got a name?"

"Yes," I said around a mouthful. "And that's all I got." I hooked a thumb at my bunk. "She just said, 'Brekka' in that croaky voice and passed out. I excluded the dragonlords from the question, so now all we have to do is find this person."

"Shouldn't be *too* hard." Miko finished her toast and buttered another, ignoring the rest of the food.

"Not if it's a wizard of some kind and reasonably well known, I guess." I refilled my cup. "I'll take Wix and a couple of solid sailors ashore this morning and start asking questions. We'll find this Brekka."

"You hope."

"Yes, I hope." I gestured to the rest of the food. "Just toast this morning?"

"Trying to convince my stomach that I'm human." She smiled weakly.

"I thought you stayed sober last night." It wasn't like Miko to get drunk while watching over a green midshipman on shore leave.

"I did, but we had a couple of platters of spiced oysters. I must have gotten a green one." She nibbled toast and shrugged. "It'll pass. I think Boxley'll be better off this morning for having emptied her guts last night."

"How'd she do?"

"Well enough." Miko considered her toast and put it down. "She gets happy and a bit too friendly when she drinks. It was good she was in company she could trust. A couple of sailors from Ton Chi tried to pick her up, and she might have gone with them if she'd been alone. She'll have a better respect for strong drink and strange ports when she wakes up."

"Good." I finished my blackbrew and wiped my mouth. "Get some sleep and look in on Preel when you wake. I'll tell Hemp to feed her when she wakes up. She had a bit too much to drink last night as well."

"Oh?" Miko looked surprised.

"Preel's...having some trouble with the idea of being a free woman, I think." I wasn't about to tell Miko about the kiss. "She'll get used to it."

"I hope so." Miko took her leave, and Hemp came in to clear the dishes. I told him to post a guard and look in on Preel while I was ashore. "She'll probably sleep halfway through the watch at least, but she'll need food when she wakes."

"I'll have Bert put something aside for her." Hemp seemed very quiet this morning. Not a surly word out of his mouth. I wasn't sure if that boded well or ill.

"Did you have a good time ashore last night?"

"Oh, aye, sir. Just a bit spent this morning." He flashed a sidelong grin. "The ladies of the red-veil district were downright frisky, they were."

"And you spent your very last penny, I suppose."

"Well, I don't know what *else* in the heavens or hells I'd spend my money on." He paused at the door. "Man's got needs, after all."

"As long as you had a good time and didn't get knocked on the head." *Or contract the pox.* "Tell Wix he's going ashore with me. Have him pick out two more to go with us."

"Aye, sir."

Hemp left and I readied myself for a trip ashore. I picked out a cutlass, two daggers, some money, a clean jacket, and stomped my sore feet into boots. I'd regret last night's pacing today, but there was nothing for it. I finally stood and glanced one more time at my bunk.

Preel breathed deeply, her eyes flicking about beneath her lids. I wondered what she dreamed and if she would remember last night.

"A man's got needs..." I brushed a lock of hair from her forehead and left the cabin.

I don't know if having Wix at my side was an advantage or a disadvantage in my search for this mysterious worker of magic. He's intimidating as hell, which is useful for keeping daggers from sprouting from my back, but some people respond poorly to his presence. Good or bad, I knew one thing for certain; I wasn't about to go ashore without him. Valakans aren't known for their hospitality to strangers. He met me on deck flanked by two dour sailors: a foremast jane named Tansy who bore a scar across her forehead from some long-ago boarding action, and one of his bosun's mates, Camel, nicknamed for his hunched shoulders and constant chewing and spitting of tobacco. It's a wonder the locals didn't flee before us.

We started our search at the waterfront, not because it was the most likely place to find a wizard, but because it was where we landed and the least alienating part of the city. Waterfronts are similar just about everywhere: busy with trade; crowded with longshoremen, sailors, trollops, and cutpurses; and lined with warehouses, pubs, chandleries, and whorehouses. The Valaka waterfront differed from Haven in that the streets were cleaner and less choked with squalor. The pubs and whorehouses were closed this early, and the longshoremen, though surly and suspicious, seemed honest enough when they said they'd never heard of anyone named Brekka. Even the promise of coin got us nowhere.

We worked our way up the hill looking for more likely sources. After a dozen or so shops, apothecaries, provisioners, and one tannery specializing in shark-skin leather—I swear by Odea, the smell of that place curled my nose hairs—midday found us with nothing for our effort but sore feet. I caught the scent of food and directed my escort toward a corner tavern, *The Twisted Tail,* its entranced framed by pillars sculpted in the shape of spiraling dragon tails. The pillars had probably been scavenged from one of the old temples; the carvings had the look of the old architecture. Inside, a burly young man was hefting chairs off the tables and righting them onto a floor still damp from mopping and smelling of lye.

"At least it's clean," Wix muttered, wrinkling his nose.

"Too early for a bite and a tankard?" I asked the broad-shouldered woman swabbing the bar with a rag.

"Door's open, ain't it?" She looked us over, evidently decided we weren't plague carriers, and pointed to a table. "Fish in a blanket's all we can whip up quick, unless you want to wait."

"That'll be fine, and four tankards of your best ale." I sighed as I eased my weight off my aching feet and into a chair.

"Thank you, sir." Wix sat with his back to the corner and glared around the bar yet-empty of patrons.

"Got to have something to kill the pain." I grimaced and flexed my toes. "I need new boots."

"Pacin' the quarterdeck half the night ain't got nothin' to do with it, sure."

So Wix knew I'd paced, and he knew me well enough to know that when I paced, I was troubled. Well, I had reason enough to be troubled.

The burly youth delivered our tankards with a bowed head and hastened back to his duties. The bartender polished mugs. From the kitchen came the hiss of something hitting a hot griddle, followed by the scent of frying fish.

"So, this Brekka's a wizard of some sort, sir?" Tansy asked, sipping her ale.

"I have no idea. I don't even know if it's a man or woman, just the name, and that it's not one of the dragonlords." I sipped my ale, a heavy brew with a sharp tang. Not bad, but if this was the best *The Twisted Tail* had to offer, I wasn't impressed. "All I *do* know is that this person can remove the… enchantment that I told you all about."

"And that girl, Preel, gave you the name?" Wix asked.

"Yes. She's been very helpful." I wasn't going to elaborate on Preel's talent, not here.

"She looks full recovered from…what happened." Tansy frowned and shook her head.

"She's coming along. She's had a hard life, and Geit wasn't the first one to abuse her." I gritted my teeth and sipped my ale.

"Twice cursed," Camel muttered.

"Twice?"

"Aye, sir. Once with this ability that put her in chains and again with her looks." He frowned and spat into a nearby spittoon. "The pretty ones always have a hard time of it."

"True enough." I considered what Jhavika had forced her beautiful slaves to do for her. They'd been two of the most graceful dancers I'd ever seen, true artists, and she'd used them only to sate the lust of her important friends.

"Which is why I'm so blessed by all gods high and low!" Wix raised his tankard and grinned his horrible grin. "Ugly as a canker and bad-tempered to boot! Nobody'd make *me* a pleasure slave unless they've got a likin' fer pain!"

We all laughed and drank, and I secretly thanked Wix for breaking the somber mood. "Well, whoever this Brekka is, we'll find out eventually and convince—"

An ear-shattering crash brought all four of us out of our seats, my cutlass half-drawn and Wix's daggers in his meaty fists. Whirling, we found no assailant, just the lad who'd brought our ale standing board-stiff and staring at us, the floor at his feet littered with shattered plates and food. The boy staggered back a step, but his eyes weren't on our weapons...they were on me.

"Beeka?" The word issued from his mouth with a stream of spittle.

"Drofee!" The bartender's bellow snapped the boy's rapt attention as she hustled around the end of the bar, her face blanched. "What in the names of the gods..." She glared at our bared weapons and then at the broken platter, fried fish, peppers, and flatbread scattered across the floor. "What's going on here?"

"Just a misunderstanding. No harm done." I motioned the others to put their weapons away and sit. Raising my hands in a placating gesture, I addressed the bartender, but fixed my gaze on the boy. *Beeka?* The word bore a vague semblance to the name of the person we'd been seeking all morning, but it was the lad's reaction that spoke volumes. "The boy called out the name of someone we've been looking for. I'd like to ask—"

"You'll not ask anything of Drofee, 'cause he can't answer you!" The woman turned to the disturbed boy and waved him off. "Get a broom and mop." The boy hurried off.

"I don't understand why—"

"No, you *don't* understand!" She rounded on me, her glare as sharp as any blade. "Drofee *can't* answer your questions!"

"Then maybe you can. We're looking for someone named Brekka. The name seemed to upset him."

"I can't help you. Finish your ale and go." Muscles bunched like walnuts at her jaw.

"But we haven't even paid you for—"

"There's no charge and nothing for you here. If you want answers about *that* one, you'll have to go uphill and ask the Children. Just leave us be."

Her stony glare brooked no argument, but at least she'd provided some direction. I didn't relish visiting the Children's Quarter much more than the dragonlords, though. "Very well." I motioned to the others, then dug in my purse for a silver imperial and dropped it on the table. "For your trouble."

She still frowned, but seemed somewhat mollified. "Good luck to you, then, but have a care. The Children of the Serpent don't like questions."

"Seems *you* don't like 'em neither," Wix grumbled, glaring down at his spilt ale before he turned for the door.

Outside, Tansy asked, "What'n the Nine Hells was *that* about, sir?"

"I don't know, but that boy sure pitched a fit when I mentioned the name Brekka." I shook my head and started up the hill. "Damn, I wish she'd have let us ask him a few questions."

"I think she was tellin' the truth, sir. You wouldn't get no answers." Wix wiped the spilled ale from his trousers and frowned. "The boy had no tongue. I'm thinkin' he's a Serpent's Child. No tellin' for sure, but some parents remove the evidence when deformed babies are born. You saw they look like mother and son, didn't you?"

Now that Wix mentioned it, the two did have the same build and facial features. "But if the boy knows something…"

"Oh, he *knows* something, right enough," Wix agreed, "but we won't get an answer from him. He was scared. I think this Brekka might be trouble."

"Well, his mother said we should ask uphill. If her son's actually a Serpent's Child, maybe she's right."

"Any chance we could stop for a nibble somewheres, sir?" Camel's homely face screwed up in a pained expression. "The smell of that food had me all set sharp for a bite."

"We'll find a street vendor on the way." I lengthened my stride, my aching feet forgotten. "Come on."

We made our way up the twisting, narrow streets, pausing briefly at a street cart to devour a dozen spicy sausage wraps, avoiding the oysters that had brought Miko low. A half dozen more blocks on, well up the hill, we entered the district where the Children of the Serpent lived.

As Preel noted from the ship, the Children paint their homes in bright colors—reds, yellows, oranges—intense, high-energy hues, often clashing and garish. Sometimes the colors were worked in abstract patterns, and other times the artwork was ornate and explicit. One fine mural boasted a long, sinuous dragon slithering around a door frame, each scale painstakingly rendered in a different hue. The colors were remarkable. We passed a downspout carved as the head of a nightmare serpent: eyes of red staring out from green scales, toothed mouth framed by purple barbels so lifelike they seemed to actually writhe.

"Kinda purty," Wix said as we strolled past. "In a dragony sorta way."

I couldn't disagree. The area was poor, but beautifully decorated and clean. It seemed as if the general populace had exiled all the Children into a ghetto to isolate the ugliness of their deformities, but the Children, perhaps in defiance, had made their would-be prison a thing of beauty.

It became abundantly clear, however, that we weren't welcome.

Doors and windows closed as we approached, twisted or scaled faces turned away, hobbling forms ducked around corners or behind elaborately painted doors. The music from an open-air market stilled as we passed, like birds going silent in a forest, the shoppers scurrying away. A few bolder residents met our curious eyes, but nobody spoke, open resentment evident in their distorted features. The answer to my question might indeed reside here, but getting it wouldn't be easy.

Only one, a flaxen-haired figure of slim, feminine stature, didn't react to our approach. Her attention remained so focused on her work—a mural of a sea-drake, its long, scaly body rendered in vibrant and exacting detail—that she seemed not even to notice as we strode up behind her. She wielded tiny brushes in both hands, dabbing first at the paints on a narrow pallet suspended around her waist, then on the wall before her, coloring and recoloring, breathing life into the static image.

I raised a hand to bring the others to a halt and stepped closer. Perhaps by starting a casual conversation, I could ask her a question about Brekka.

"That's beautiful."

"Ugly!" The voice was high, a child's, and strained. "She's ugly, and she'll eat you!" The brushes didn't slow.

What she said was partly true; sea drakes were fearsome creatures to be sure, the bane of the sea and the death of many a sailor, but they had a sinuous majesty. "Oh, I don't think it's ugly at all. I've seen a sea drake, and you captured it perfectly. I like the colors."

"Her colors are blood and meat and bone! She hungers and thirsts always!" The voice lowered. "What do *you* know of colors?"

"I'm no artist, but I know what I like."

"What *you* like?" Her tone mocking now, she turned.

The tangled mop of blond hair framed a totally inhuman visage, eyeless and split from brow to chin by a vertically oriented maw edged with rows of dagger teeth. The orifice gnashed and snapped, parting to reveal a gullet lined with more cruelly hooked teeth. Anything that went down that hole would never come out again. The figure's cloak folded back below the neck to reveal a deformed infant's head and two small arms protruding from its chest, baby-like hands holding the tray of paints. Sagging breasts rested on the infant shoulders, and saliva dribbled from the monstrous mouth onto the infant head. The gnashing maw above seemed incapable of articulate speech, but the infantile mouth spoke clearly.

I recoiled reflexively.

"What do *you* know of ugly, with your pretty faces from downhill?" The infant-face sneered at me.

"Captain!" Wix's huge hand closed on my shoulder and dragged me back. His other held one of his daggers. "Stay back, you foul thing!"

"*Foul?*" the creature shrieked, the infant face contorting into a mask of disgust. "Oh, *foul*, am I, pretty ones? Go back downhill and stick your pretty faces up your pretty asses!"

"Wix, put the blade away." I pried his meaty hand off my shoulder and addressed the Child. "We aren't here to hurt or insult anyone. You *do* paint beautifully. We just came to find someone."

"Go away." The infant face turned and suckled one of the sagging breasts, milk dribbling from its chin as it spoke. "Pretty ones don't belong here with the Serpent's Children."

"We're looking for someone named Brekka," I persisted.

The infant eyes widened. "Her? No, you don't want to find *her*. Now go away." The figure started to turn.

"You know her?" I reached out to grasp the shoulder. "Look, I'll pay you for—"

The mop of blonde hair whipped around and the horrible jaws snapped, closing only a hair's breadth from my hand. I jerked away and stumbled back a step.

"Stay back! Don't touch or she'll eat you!" The infant face seemed more distressed than angry.

"Look, we don't want to hurt you. We just need to know about Brekka. What's your name? We'll pay you for your time and—"

"*Captain*, we got trouble." Camel's hushed tone brought me around.

A dozen armed Children had ventured from hiding, their misshapen faces glaring, monstrous limbs gripping blades and clubs as they closed in from all sides.

"Looks like we finally got their attention." Wix brandished his daggers.

I turned back to the creature we'd been speaking to, but she had scurried off, hunched over. "Wait!"

She didn't turn, but hurried along the wall she'd been painting, slipping between the advancing Children with a speed that belied her rolling, unsteady gait. The others closed in, tightening their ranks. Rage, resentment, and outright hatred burned in their eyes.

Tansy and Camel drew steel, and Wix pulled me back until the wall nudged my shoulders. I found my cutlass in hand, though I didn't remember drawing it. Outnumbered four to one, we didn't have much of a chance, but with our backs to a wall, at least they couldn't flank us.

"We don't want trouble."

"Don't care what you want or don't want." A hulking creature in the fore, his arms like chitin-armored trees and sporting lobster-claw hands, grinned maliciously. "You come here with your pretty faces, harassing poor folk, calling them vile names... You've made your own trouble."

"We weren't *harassing* anyone!" I drew a dagger as well. "Nobody has to die here."

"Oh, that's a matter of opinion." The man grinned and clacked his pincers threateningly.

As they approached, their ranks closed further. If we held our ground and fought shoulder to shoulder, the worst we would face was two against one. We tightened our line, Wix to my right and Camel to my left with Tansy to his.

"Don't be a fool! We only came here for information."

"*You* were the fools for coming here in the first place, and you'll never leave," the burly man growled an instant before he lunged.

Their attack wasn't very well coordinated, but it didn't have to be. We couldn't retreat and we couldn't maneuver; brute force would do the job. But four seasoned pirates are a force to be reckoned with, and we met the attack with steel.

I fended off a nail-studded club with my cutlass and caught one of claw-man's snapping hands with my dagger. The claw closed on the blade, and the tempered steel snapped. I released the hilt and ducked under the clacking member. My right hand worked on its own, riposting with a slash that opened a deep gash in the club wielder's neck. He dropped the weapon and stumbled back, clutching the spurting wound and giving me a moment to draw another dagger from my boot. I heard a crunch beside me, and Camel grunted and went down. I drove my boot dagger into claw-man's gut and his knees folded, but the claw that had broken my dagger snapped onto my leg as he went down. I roared in pain as the meat of my thigh was crushed in that iron grip. Slamming my dagger into the joint at the base of the hand, I twisted savagely. The claw came free from the arm with a spray of blue ichor, but remained clamped on my leg.

Camel had crumpled to his knees, clutching a bloody mass of broken ribs. Tansy stepped over to cover him, closing the gap, her cutlass and dagger both red, but her sword arm dripping from a deep gash. Wix had felled two Children, the spikes of his daggers dripping gore, but didn't have a mark on him. The Children stepped back from the melee, obviously reconsidering the wisdom of the fight. Five of their number lay dead or dying at our feet versus only one of ours.

"Now, I'll say it again, nobody *else* has to die!" I pointed my cutlass at those in the fore. "We came here only to talk."

"Nobody here will talk to you, pretty man." The woman who'd spoken lowered her dagger and stepped forward to check one of her fallen comrades. As she knelt, I realized that her legs bent the wrong way, her feet cloven hooves. She rose and stepped back, blind hate plain on her face. "Take your questions someplace else."

"We're looking for a woman named Brekka." I saw recognition in several faces.

"I *said* nobody will talk to you. Now *leave*!"

I cursed under my breath. My leg hurt abominably, Camel lay in a spreading pool of blood, and we'd gotten nothing for our pain. Slipping the tip of my dagger into the joint of the claw clamped onto my leg, I cut the tendon that held it in place, and it fell away. Blood flowed down my leg inside my pants and into my boot. I wiped my dagger clean and sheathed it, but kept my cutlass ready.

"Wix, help me with Camel. Tansy, cover us."

My bosun and I hefted Camel between us and we limped away, Tansy covering our backs with two bloody blades in her hands. Camel groaned weakly, blood flecking his lips as well as drenching his chest. Blood squished in my boot with every step. Two blocks away from the fight, I called a stop.

"I've got to tie up my leg, and your arm's still bleeding, Tansy." We lowered Camel to the street. "Do what you can for Camel, Wix."

I checked my leg and cringed. The wounds were deep, the meat of my thigh crushed until it had split. Slitting my pant leg and cutting the fabric it into two broad strips, I tied one around my leg. Tansy did the same to her shirt sleeve to bind her arm. Wix knelt beside Camel, a rag pressed to the gaping hole in his chest.

"Can we stop the bleeding?" I handed my bosun the other wide strip of my pant leg.

"Dunno how, sir. His chest is open." Wix stuffed the rag into the gaping wound and started to bind it in place. Camel shuddered and coughed blood. "A lung's been flayed."

"Well, we can't leave him here." I wiped my cutlass and sheathed it. "Let's get him back to the ship and we can—"

"Hyly."

All three of us whirled at the child's voice, startlingly close. The woman-creature who had been painting stood there, the hood of her cloak pulled low and the front fabric held together by human-looking hands so that only the infant face and arms showed. It looked as if a deformed woman held a child.

"What?" I asked, harsher than I'd intended.

"Hyly. You asked my name. It's Hyly." Her large infant eyes flicked back and forth between us. "You…were wronged. You didn't mean to harm us. The others didn't understand."

"No, they *didn't* understand." I waved Wix and Tansy back and risked a step closer to her. "They attacked us and my friend was hurt badly."

"And you killed Uelek, Donse, Malaka, and Caetra. Loence and Balla will live." She pointed to Camel. "Your friend will not."

I stared at her. The certainty with which she spoke chilled me. "How do you know?"

"I don't, but she does." The baby arm hooked a clumsy thumb upward. "She can *smell* it."

"Captain!" Tansy's urgent tone brought my attention back to my comrades.

Camel's color had gone bad. He bucked, struggling to breathe, then stilled, his mouth gaping silently, a frothy pink bubble of blood forming and popping on his lips. Wix looked up at me and shook his head.

"Your friend is dead, Captain. Don't seek Brekka or others will die as well."

Wrenching my gaze from my dead crewman, I stared at the child-face, biting back my temper. "Are you a prophet as well?"

"No, but I know of Brekka. The witch will take more than she gives. She always does." The baby face frowned. "I'm sorry for your friend." Hyly turned to go.

"Tell us where to find Brekka. I need her help." I hated the desperation in my voice, but this was my only hope for freedom.

Hyly paused, but didn't turn. "In the temples of the abandoned gods. The one with the great dragon's maw for a doorway. People say it's haunted, but it is not. Not like the others. Brekka lives there, but she doesn't like visitors."

"Thank you."

Hyly turned to face me again. "Don't thank me and don't tell Brekka my name." She walked away. "She's already taken enough from us."

I turned and helped Wix and Tansy carry my dead crewman back to *Scourge*. We had what we came for, but the cost had been steep.

Chapter Nineteen
The Witch's Abode

The warm welcome of a stranger oft hides malice.
The Lessons of Quen Lau Ush

From the diary of Kevril Longbright –
Gauging people has always been my weakest skill. I suppose
that's why I'm not a gambling man. I can never tell with any
measure of certainty when someone is lying to me, when
they might have ulterior motives or hidden purposes. One
day, I would wager, that weakness will cost my life.

We buried Camel at sea.
Our misadventure convinced me to take a step back and
approach this situation with the caution it deserved. Or maybe it was
the two gashes in my leg that Bert doused with wood alcohol and
sewed up with catgut.
Preel was awake when we got back, and the distress on her face
when I came in leaving bloody footprints on the deck warmed my
heart. There's nothing like having someone care about you to lift
your spirits. She sat on the bed and stared as I leaned back in a chair
with my leg up and Bert worked on me.

"You're lucky, Captain." My cook drew a stitch tight and cut the thread short. "A bit deeper and it'd have cut the big artery. We'd be wrappin' *you* in canvas and shufflin' you off to a watery grave."

"I'll take lucky." I tilted the bottle of spiced rum again as she started another stitch. I was almost drunk enough to blunt the pain to a tolerable level…almost. "Camel wasn't so lucky."

"Case in point." Bert drew the last stich tight and snipped it short. "You lost a bit of blood. You should take a couple of days with your leg up. I've got some bread-mold tea brewin' to keep the fever down. I'll send it in with Hemp."

"Thank you, Bert." I tilted the bottle again.

"Thank me by keeping that leg up." She glared at me and snorted a laugh. "Bloody damned pirate."

"That I am." I raised the bottle to her as she turned toward the door. A knock sounded as she reached for the latch, and Miko came in.

"Captain, we've cleared the harbor. Tansy's arm is tended and Camel's been wrapped up in his hammock with ballast stones." Her forehead wrinkled at the sight of my leg.

"Good." I adjusted my seat and winced. "Northerly tack under reefed tops'ls. We're in no rush. We'll bury Camel at sunset."

"Aye, sir." She peered at the wounds in my leg. "What the hell did *that*, anyway?"

"A Serpent's Child with lobster-claw hands and a really bad temper." I pointed to the chair across the table and she sat. "We tried to question someone and a dozen of them jumped us. The strange thing is, the one we tried to talk to found us after and…apologized."

"For the attack?"

"Yes." I took another pull from the bottle and tried to remember exactly what Hyly said. "She told us where to find Brekka, but warned us that the witch doesn't like visitors. And if we went, not to mention her name."

"Sounds like this Brekka's not a very friendly sort."

Chris A. Jackson

"It does." I looked to Preel. "But I asked Preel who would be *willing* and able to remove the enchantment. If she doesn't take visitors, that's not very willing."

"True," Miko said.

Preel nodded.

I drank.

Hemp knocked and entered with a pot of tea smelling of an unappetizing combination of herbs and moldy bread. "Medicine for the captain."

"Just put it on the table, Hemp."

"Bert says you should drink that whole pot, take a lie down, and keep yer leg up, sir." He put the tray down and looked dismayed at my bloody, mutilated trousers, blood-sodden boot, and the smudges on the rug.

"Sorry about the mess, Hemp. I'll drink the tea."

"Aye, sir. Let me just take your other boot. I'll get the blood out somehow. Your trousers are a loss, I'm afraid. The rug…"

"Right." I wrenched off my other boot, wincing when I moved my damaged leg. The stitches seeped blood. "Probably ought to wrap this up."

"Bert said to let it air. Gotta see if it starts to fester."

"Fine." I wrinkled my nose at the smell of the tea and waved him out. "Odea save me from cooks and stewards."

"And Serpent's Children with nasty tempers," Miko added.

"Right." I started to take another pull from the bottle, but Preel clapped her hands twice, loud and sharp. "Yes, Preel?"

She pointed to the bottle and shook her head, then pointed emphatically to the tea pot.

"And truthsayers," Miko said with a chuckle. "Best take your medicine, Captain. We won't be needing you on deck for a few watches anyway."

I glared at the both of them, but corked the bottle and put it down. "So much for a captain's authority." I poured a cup of the rancid-smelling tea and grimaced. "I hate this stuff."

266

"Then don't get cut, stabbed, or lacerated by Serpent's Children with bad tempers, sir." Miko chuckled again at my expense and stood. "Anything else?"

"We'll go see this Brekka when we get back." I sipped the nasty brew and forced down my gag reflex. "But one other thing that creature said comes back to me now. She said that Brekka had...taken enough from them already."

"Taken what from them?"

"She didn't say." I glanced to Preel. "Maybe it would be worth asking Preel, but we've got days before we can, and I don't want to wait that long."

"Either way, this Brekka doesn't sound very friendly."

"I don't need her to be friendly." I downed my tea and reached for the pot. "I just need her to remove this blasted enchantment."

"Too right, sir, but we'd best be careful. Magic's a double-edged sword, they say." Miko left.

I sipped tea and tried to think through the haze of rum. Preel got up from the bunk and took the bottle of liquor from the table to the cabinet. She returned, tapped the silken band girding her mouth, and knelt with her back to me.

"All right." I untied the knot in the back and dropped the gag on the table. "How are you feeling?"

"I'm fine, sir." She sat down where Miko had been, then licked her lips and cleared her throat. "I'm sorry you were hurt."

"Not your fault." I sipped the vile tea and made a face. "And I've been hurt worse."

"And I'm sorry for last night." She looked down at her clenched hands in her lap. "I drank too much and..."

"So, you remember." I poured the last of the tea into my cup, trying not to smile.

"I remember being foolish." Preel clenched her hands hard enough to blanch her knuckles. "I'm not free yet. I didn't mean to...act that way."

I don't know why her regret felt like a knife in my gut, but it did. "No harm done."

"I'm sorry if I…embarrassed you."

"You didn't embarrass me, Preel. Don't worry. Alcohol makes some people bolder." I downed my tea and lifted the gag from the table. "Now, I should lie down and get this leg up before Bert comes in here and gives me twenty lashes for insubordination."

"Yes, sir. Please, take the bunk. You shouldn't try to manage the hammock with your leg."

"All right." I affixed her gag and accepted her help to the bunk. There, however, I realized that I still wore my blood-soaked trousers. If I lay down in them, I'd soil the sheets. Pulling them down over the stitches would hurt like hell and risk snagging one. The pants were a loss anyway, but I didn't have a blade handy. "Preel, where's your dagger. I need to cut these off."

She fumbled in a slit in the billowy leg of her pantaloons and came out with the small dagger I'd given her. I was pleased she kept it close. I cut the side seam of my trousers and pulled them off. Preel took them, and I lay on the bed. The stitches were seeping blood.

"Fetch a towel from the quarter gallery, please. I don't want to get blood on the bunk."

She hurried out and returned with a towel, placing it carefully under my leg. I lay back and she drew the sheet up over me.

"Thank you." Her eyes finally met mine, the regret and embarrassment in them another knife in my gut.

With a nod, she turned away and picked a book off the shelf, sitting at the table to read. I closed my eyes and tried to rest despite the scent of Preel on the pillow plaguing my every breath.

The following morning, we dropped anchor in the exact spot we'd left, and I ordered two boats into the water. My leg was cool and dry and walking didn't pain me much, but when Miko offered to reconnoiter this abandoned temple Hyly told us about, I took her up on the offer. I did make one stipulation.

"Take Wix with you and have him pick a squad."

"Not very stealthy."

"And not very *healthy* to go without some swords." I gave her my 'I'm the captain and I'm giving you an order' look.

She gave me her 'I'm not an idiot' look. "Good *point*, sir."

"I do have them occasionally."

"But that was a truly horrible rhyme. You've been reading bad poetry again."

"Poetry's good for the soul, Miko."

"I'll stick to wine, women, and song, thanks."

"Remind me to loan you a book of poetry dedicated to those *very* three things."

"Can I sing it to a beautiful woman over a glass of wine?" She cocked an eyebrow speculatively.

"You're hopeless."

"And proud of it, sir." She sketched a sarcastic salute and turned to yell for Wix.

I watched my first mate, bosun, and a half dozen sailors head toward the docks, wondering if we'd be making another trip into deep water to bury someone tonight. I paced the quarterdeck until my leg started to throb with my heartbeat, then assigned Quiff to watch for the shore party and send for me when they returned.

Hemp intercepted me on my way to my cabin. "Thought I'd let you know that Preel's at it again, sir. Whirlin' around the cabin like a dancer with no music. Don't know if she's quite right in the head, but I didn't think you'd want to…um…disturb her."

"Thanks, Hemp." My steward might be a nag, but he was sharp enough to note that something had changed between me and my guest. She had barely looked me in the eye since her apology for kissing me. I didn't know if she was embarrassed or afraid that her boldness would prompt me to expect more from her. For my part, I didn't know what to say to her, so I'd been avoiding my cabin all day. "I'll just have a sit down in the wardroom. Fetch me a pot of blackbrew and a biscuit, would you?"

"Straightaway, sir!" He headed for the galley, and I made my way to the wardroom.

Kivan and Boxley were sitting in the corner, giggling over a pot of tea and something on the table. They bolted up from the table like I'd caught them doing something evil.

"Sir!" Kivan looked horrified. "Sorry, sir, we were just…"

"Relax." I waved them back to their seats. "I just need to put my leg up."

"Sir, we'd best be at our duties." Kivan nudged Boxley and they exchanged a glance.

"She's right, sir." Boxley scooped a thin book off the table and slipped it under her jacket.

"Mathematics?" I ventured, taking a seat and propping my leg on a chair.

"Um, no sir." Boxley looked horrified. "Just something I picked up ashore."

"Oh?" Miko hadn't mentioned any trips to booksellers, and Boxley was being evasive for the first time since I'd brought her up from the lower deck. "I thought you were too busy carousing to be interested in books, Boxley."

"I…was just…we stopped on the way, and I just…thought I'd buy something I could keep. It's just a bit of fun, sir." Her face flushed. "Light reading."

"Nothing wrong with light reading. I've been known to do a little myself."

I waved them off. When two young female midshipmen were evasive about a book, there was little doubt about the subject matter. I'd have Miko talk to them about keeping that book to themselves. I wouldn't want any of the foremast jacks to get the wrong idea, or worse, the *right* one.

Hemp delivered blackbrew and biscuits with several slices of a sharp highland cheese I favored. By the time I'd finished the last crumb, my leg felt better, so I got up and ventured back on deck. The weather was turning foul to the south, burgeoning clouds over the mountains promising rain. I opened my mouth to order the ship secured for weather, but saw that Quiff had beaten me to it; he might make an officer after all. He snapped a salute as I mounted the steps to the quarterdeck.

"I was just going to send for you, sir. The launch just left shore." He pointed and handed me a spyglass. "Looks like everyone's aboard."

"Good." I raised the glass and focused on the launch. I saw no blood and no one missing, the best news I'd had in a week.

I met Miko at the boarding hatch. "Well?"

"Found it with no problem, sir. Not many people go to that district. We didn't see a soul."

"Hmm. I wonder if I'm being sent on a pixie hunt."

"Might be, sir, but *someone's* been there recently." She squinted at the city. "Most of the temples have been vandalized or razed, but this one hasn't. The doorway's been cleared of rubble. I didn't see anyone watching from inside, but that doesn't mean there wasn't."

A curtain of rain started to descend from the hills toward the city.

"I think I'll wait until this squall passes to go ashore. No sense getting soaked."

"Aye, sir."

"Tell Wix I'll take the same shore party with me, minus you, of course."

"Of course." She didn't look happy, but relayed my message.

The problem with my plan was that the deluge wasn't a simple squall. It rained all day and into the night, which was just as well. My leg hurt, and Bert cursed me when she had a look at the stitches, prescribing more vile tea and a poultice. I spent the afternoon in the great cabin with my leg up, reading and avoiding eye contact with

Preel. She handled the confinement better than I did, quietly reading on the settee beneath the stern gallery windows. We ate dinner with Miko, but there wasn't much conversation; there was nothing to discuss. My declaration that I'd go to speak with this elusive Brekka in the morning, rain or shine, met with scowls of disapproval from both of them. I told myself I didn't care; it's not a captain's job to make *everyone* aboard happy.

The rain didn't let up, but it matched my mood perfectly. After breakfast and more poking and prodding from my cook, I assembled my soggy party and we rowed ashore.

The rain-soaked waterfront paid us little interest. Cutpurses and trollops don't like the rain, and the longshoremen were too busy to care about a few unfamiliar faces. The walk to the old temple district didn't tax me overmuch, and Wix pointed out the dilapidated temple they'd found the day before.

It was hard to miss.

The area didn't get much foot traffic; crumbled stonework and refuse littered the once proud avenues, creating a maze and hazardous footing. It wasn't a place for tourists. Few of the abandoned temples still stood. Most had been flattened, salvaged for cut stone, or razed to scorched skeletons. Brekka's abode was one of the few that had been repurposed. The stonework had been gouged and chipped, surely, but the structure looked intact. The steps to the foyer were clear of rubble, though that little bit of maintenance did nothing to make it look welcoming. The head of a great fanged dragon that framed the temple doors, grinning down in unmarred splendor, didn't help in that regard. If it ever came to life, the beast could have devoured the entire city.

Wrought of solid stone and bronze long tarnished by the elements, the toothed visage towered to the height of four men, its fangs as long as a tall man's leg. The doors, solid bronze by the look, sported bas relief depictions of huge sea drakes dragging ships into the depths, tearing them to bits, and swallowing men whole. It was enough to give a sailor nightmares. Two of my squad muttered oaths under their breath, and I forced my hand to relax on the hilt of my cutlass.

"Just a pile of stone." I started slowly up the steps. "No need to get nervous."

"Not the stone what bothers me," Wix said. "It's what's inside."

"Hopefully that'll be a witch named Brekka." I paused for a moment at the doors. They sported no knockers, latch, or even a keyhole. I settled for drawing a dagger and rapping the pommel thrice upon the metal.

We waited.

After a while with no answer, I knocked again, louder and longer.

As I considered a third attempt, a heavy clank sounded from within. We all tensed, hands on weapons, but I raised a forestalling hand. One of the massive doors moved inward, the ancient hinges groaning. It opened barely wide enough to show the pale face of a man within.

He blinked and squinted at us. "Who are you and why do you pound on this door?"

"My name is Longbright. I'm captain of the *Scourge*, a free trader out of Haven." I saw no reason to lie gratuitously, but I wasn't about to tell the door guard we were pirates. "I need to speak with Brekka."

"Why?"

"I have a business proposition."

"Business?" The man frowned. "What type of business?"

"The kind that involves enchantments."

The man wrinkled his nose. "I'll ask her if she's interested."

The door closed with a clang.

"Not very friendly," one of my squad said.

"You expected tea and biscuits?" Wix glared at the man.

"Oh, I'd *like* that. Can we have some of Bert's tartberry jam, too?"

The others chuckled.

"Shut your gob, Palter, or I'll shut it for you." Wix's glare stifled the man's humor.

We waited in silence.

Finally, the door groaned open again. The pale face peered out as if surprised to find us still standing there, then the aperture opened wider.

"Just you," the doorman said, pointing one finger at me.

One finger and a thumb were all he had on the hand. He was a Serpent's Child. Maybe that was what Hyly meant when she said Brekka had taken enough from them.

I frowned at him and shook my head. "My people will come in with me." Call me craven, but I wasn't about to go in that dark place alone.

The doorman glowered, but then nodded. "Only into the hall."

"Fine." I didn't know what the hall was, but at least I wouldn't have this seemingly impregnable barrier between me and my crew.

We stepped inside.

If the exterior of the temple had seemed foreboding, the interior descended into the downright macabre. Fetid-smelling oil lamps cast a sickly green light onto row after row of tall columns. Each one bore sculpted images of draconic beasts ravaging men and women, scales and fangs, gaping mouths, and gnashing beaks all rendered in exquisite detail. As we followed our guide between the columns, I tried to keep my eyes from straying, but the sculptures were so lifelike I expected them to start moving, screaming, writhing, and devouring. Motion at the edge of my vision drew my gaze, but closer inspection revealed only stone, still and cold.

"Such a *cheery* place," Palter quipped in a tremulous voice.

"Clap it shut," Wix ordered.

Once my eyes adjusted to the gloom, I again spied flickering motion in the shadows. Though more animate, these were just as twisted and misshapen as those depicted in stone. Serpent's Children edged forward around us, as pale of hue as the doorman, haphazardly armed and armored. Obviously, Brekka kept them as guards. The witch business must be profitable to keep so many.

Breaking free of the intimidating forest of columns, we entered a lofty hall. The floor descended into an octagonal depression, while massive pillars at each corner supported a vaulted dome. The pillars and dome glittered, the lamplight reflecting off the mosaics covering their surfaces, even more gruesome scenes rendered in tiny colored stones. An off-center crack in the dome admitted a dim shaft of diffuse sunlight and rain, which pattered down to wet the floor.

Here our guide stopped. Again, the finger jabbed at me. "You come with me. The others stay here."

"I prefer to stay with my people." I glanced at the dozen or so Children that hung around the chamber's periphery.

"Too bad. This is *Brekka's* home and you're *her* guest, pretty face." The man's lips peeled back from dagger-like teeth that rivaled the sculpture framing the foyer. "You'll do as *she* wants or you'll be on your way."

I couldn't insist, but I could certainly make it clear that I wasn't happy. "Wix, if I'm not back in a quarter glass, take this place apart."

"It'd be my pleasure, sir." My bosun grinned at the Children, every bit as gruesome, and unswervingly sincere in his claim. Wix enjoyed mayhem like nothing else. I'd give long odds against anyone trying to keep him from laying waste to a few guards.

"Lead on," I told my guide, "but the sand's flowing."

"This way, Captain." The doorman turned and started off.

My nerves singing and my hands on my blades, I followed. We didn't have far to go. Down a corridor, one wide flight of stairs, and another longer and branching hallway, my guide stopped at a pair of heavy wooden doors artfully reinforced with bronze. He worked a key the size of my palm in the lock and pushed. A pungent reek and the light of hundreds of candles ushered me inside.

One glance told me Brekka's expertise resided in the art of alchemy. Pots and bowls, jars and crucibles, mortars and pestles, distillation coils, and stoppered vials containing a thousand different components vied for every available surface. Small cages and glass bowls housed creatures of all descriptions, some alive and others dead. Some I'd never seen before, and most I never wanted to see again. An entire shelf seemed dedicated to various organs, digits, and other body parts preserved in cloudy liquid. Some of them moved.

I was so engrossed in the surroundings that I barely noticed the alchemist.

"And what business does a ship's captain have with Brekka?" The source of my salvation—I hoped—turned to face me.

If asked, I couldn't have pinpointed her age or described any particularly distinguishing features, other than an unruly mop of dark hair streaked with threads of silver, and that her left eye shone like a pearl, utterly sightless. She wasn't young, but she wasn't wizened either, standing straight and moving with ease. Nondescript gray robes covered her modestly and might have hidden any number of secrets. If she was a Child of the Serpent like her guards, she bore no outward signs. Her hands, at least, sported the usual number of fingers, though stained by her trade. At the moment, those stains were crimson, for she held a short, curved knife in one hand and a dead lizard in the other.

"I'm under an enchantment that I wish to have removed or broken."

"And what makes you think Brekka can help you?"

"Are you Brekka?" I found her manner of speech off-putting, though her voice was friendly and melodious enough.

"Yes."

"Then suffice to say that I have it on good authority that you can help me."

One dark brow rose. "*Whose* authority?"

"That's not your business."

"It *is* my business, as a matter of fact." She turned her attention back to the lizard. The knife explored the tiny corpse and finally freed the desired organ. This she deftly removed and plunked into a vat of liquid before dropping the eviscerated reptile in a bucket. "I like my privacy, Captain Longbright, and I like to know how people learn of my…services." She reached into a jar teeming with more lizards and snatched another one, quickly dispatching it with the knife.

"I learned of your services from a person of particular magical talent." There was nothing under the Seven Heavens that would force me to tell her about Preel. "Can you help me or not?"

"Not without knowing the nature of this enchantment and what you're willing to offer in return for my services." Another organ plopped into the jar, and the tiny corpse fell into the bucket. "Do you know who cast this spell on you?"

"Yes, but she's not a worker of magic. She used an enchanted scourge, a cat-o'-nine-tails that allows the wielder to compel any whose flesh the lash has tasted. Whatever command she gives me, I'm bound to follow."

Brekka looked back at me, her single sighted eye wide. "Interesting!" She wiped her bloody hands on her robes and put the knife on her workbench. "And do you know from whence this scourge came? How it was made? Who made it?"

"No."

"Then I can't help you." She flicked a hand dismissively. "Brewing a potion to remove an enchantment is like sailing through fog, Captain. Just blundering along at full speed without direction is apt to get you killed, as you undoubtedly know. I need details, information, specifics, or I'm just fumbling around with no hope of success."

I thought of Preel's talent. "I may be able to find these things out for you, if you agree to help."

"And what will you offer in compensation?"

"I have money, a ship, and a few baubles I've picked up during my career." I pulled from my boot one of the jeweled daggers that I'd brought for just this purpose and held it so that the light gleamed on the ruby pommel, then handed it over hilt first. "Consider that a retainer. Do you agree to help?"

Brekka examined the dagger, pursing her lips as she squinted at the gem with her good eye. "I agree to *try*. This will do as a partial payment, with the full price contingent upon the difficulty of the task. To determine *that*, I need further information about this enchanted scourge."

"Very well. What *specifically* do you need to know?"

"I must know what materials it was crafted from. For instance, if it's leather, which I suspect, from what creature? I must know what *specific* enchantments it possesses. Knowing who made it would also help."

I gritted my teeth in frustration. "It'll take me some time to get this information." *If I can get it at all.* Preel had said that questions about enchanted artifacts were difficult for her to answer.

Brekka shrugged. "I'm in no hurry, Captain."

"Very well, I'll find out all I can about the scourge and come back with your answers."

"Before you go…" Brekka brandished the jeweled dagger. "A small amount of your blood will serve as a base component for the potion."

I narrowed my eyes, wary. "How much blood?" I knew little of magic, but I'd heard tales of wizards casting foul enchantments with a person's blood.

"Just a few drops." She produced a small glass tube and held forth the dagger I'd given her. "A pittance."

"Fine." I held out my thumb.

Brekka grabbed the digit—her hands were cold—sliced the tip with a surgeon's efficiency, and squeezed several fat drops into the tube. When the tube was half full, she released my hand and nodded respectfully.

"See? No lasting damage, and I now have a place to start while you get my information." She turned back to her bench and corked the tube, placing it in a rack with many others. "Come back when you have answers to my questions, and we'll discuss payment."

"Very well." I considered how many questions I'd have to ask Preel. Two at least, maybe three. "A week, maybe twelve days."

"I have no pressing engagements." Brekka smiled thinly.

I nodded and left. There was nothing else to say, though a jeweled dagger and a dram of blood seemed a steep price for such a nebulous answer as "I'll try."

Chapter Twenty
The Flesh of Dragons

There is nothing more fickle in the world than magic.
The Lessons of Quen Lau Ush

From the diary of Kevril Longbright –
I don't know why, but I've never handled being at the mercy
of others very well. Being injured or ill always makes me feel
unduly helpless, as if those caring for me would take
advantage of my infirmity. This isn't a holdover of
childhood experience. In fact, the only time my father ever
showed any gentleness to me at all was when I was
recovering from some injury, usually one inflicted by his
hand. I don't know if this was the product of his guilty
conscience or not. If so, it didn't stay his hand the next time.

By the time we got back to the ship, my leg hurt like hell, I was
shivering from the rain, and my mind was spinning with the
questions I would have to ask Preel.

Miko met me at the boarding hatch. "Sir?" Worry wrinkled her
brow. "Bad news?"

"Not that bad." I winced as I heaved myself up the last rung of the boarding ladder and suppressed a shiver. The unending damp had given me a chill. "We found Brekka, and she's willing to bargain, but she needs information." I shivered again. "Let's talk it over in my cabin in a quarter glass. I need a pot of blackbrew and something hot to eat. Preel should hear this, too."

"Aye, sir." Miko barked orders to stow the boats as I strode aft.

I doffed my hat and weather cloak at the wet locker, but rain had somehow invaded my clothes. My jacket felt heavy and my shirt stuck to my skin. Hemp stood at my door beside the guard I'd posted. For once I was happy to have him fawn over me. He took my weapons as I stepped into the cabin, muttering about the damp causing rust. Preel sat by the stern gallery windows with a book in her lap. She met my eyes with a questioning expression as I handed my jacket over to my steward.

"We'll talk, Preel. Brekka has some questions I'll need you to answer."

She nodded and went back to reading.

Hemp fussed over my jacket for a moment as I sat and started on my boots, then gave me a startled look. "Sir! You got a fever!"

"I have nothing of the kind. I'm just wet from the rain."

"No, sir. Jacket's dry on the outside, but the lining's wet. Your shirt's soaked through."

"Rain must have gotten down my collar, then." I managed the first boot, but couldn't bend my injured leg to get the second one. "Help me with this gods-damned boot!"

"Aye, sir, but..." He took hold and pulled the boot off with some difficulty. "Sir, *listen* to me. Yer leg's swole up, yer shirt's soaked with sweat, and yer face is pale as cheese! You got a fever!"

I jerked back as a slim hand touched my brow. I hadn't noticed Preel's approach. Her brow furrowed as she insistently pressed her hand to my brow. She looked worried and nodded to Hemp.

"Oh, for the love of all the Gods of Light and Darkness, I'm not *sick*!" I lurched up out of the chair and dragged off my damp shirt.

"I'm wet from the rain, and my leg's swollen because I just walked a league on it!" I strode for the quarter gallery. "All I need is a pot of blackbrew and..." The deck lurched under my feet. *Bloody rolly anchorage!* "...and something to eat."

I slammed the door behind me, braced myself against the damnable rolling deck, and pissed out the scuttle. Rain hissed against the windows, the bay outside beaten flat by the deluge. Not a wave or ripple married the velvet surface.

No swell, no roll, no waves, so why is the deck pitching?

I released my grip on the hand-hold and nearly fell over. Shaking my head, I washed my hands and face in the icy water from the pitcher, then steadied myself and peered in the mirror. The face staring back was as pale as the moon on a cloudless night, my chest sheened with sweat, and my hair matted against my skull. Reaching down, I felt my injured leg; the pant leg clung tight against the flesh and felt warm to the touch.

"Son of a motherless pox-ridden..." I fumbled with the door latch, stepped into the cabin, and glared at Preel and Hemp. "Okay, you're right. I've got a fever!" I took two steps and the world started to fade to gray at the edges. Fortunately, I was quite familiar with the feeling that precedes unconsciousness. *Have to thank old dad for that one...* I managed to make it to the bunk before the gray darkened to black and closed in.

I woke to the unmistakable sensation of someone trying to take off my pants.

I blinked my eyes open to find both Preel and Hemp attending to the task. That struck my fever-addled mind as strangely erotic and disturbing at the same time. Pain lanced through my leg, blunting both responses and tearing a yelp from my throat.

"Hang on, will you!" I swatted at their hands. "Let me help. I'm not an invalid!"

"Beggin' the captain's pardon, sir, but you are *so* an invalid!" Hemp glared right back. "So lay back and quit fussin!"

"I can take off my own gods-damned *pants*!" I hitched up my hips, and the two of them pulled my trousers down from the waist, turning them inside out to avoid snagging my stitches. The light bandage I'd wrapped around my leg was stained, but not with blood.

Hemp wrinkled his nose and put a hand on the puffy flesh around the bandage. "Hotter than a ten-imperial…" He paused and glanced at Preel. "Well, it's fevered. I'll get Bert."

"Do that." I shivered and pulled up a blanket.

Preel stood beside the bunk, looking down at me with frightened eyes.

"Oh, don't worry. It's just wound fever. I've had it before." I waved her away. "I'll be fine in a couple of days. Sooner, with Bert tending me."

Preel shook her head, her furrowed brow telling me that the silk gag concealed a frown. She fetched a cup of water and handed it over, then stood there with hands on hips, waiting for me to drink.

I did, more to humor her at first, but discovering halfway through that I was parched. "Thank you."

She nodded and took the empty cup, her stern expression undiminished.

Bert and Hemp bustled back in, the former with her bag of surgeon's implements, the latter with a pot of tea. I could tell by the smell it was medicine, not the blackbrew I craved.

"Fainted, eh?" Bert scowled at me.

"I didn't *faint*! I got dizzy and lay down."

"He fainted," Hemp said

Preel pantomimed the same, tipping one flat hand to clap the other like a falling tree.

"Shouldn't't've walked so far on it, and in this damp. I told you to let it air." Bert retrieved a pair of shears from her bag and pulled the sheet aside. She cut the bandage with one snip, sniffed it, and frowned. Her plump fingers pressed around the stitches while she muttered under her breath. "Don't think it needs to be lanced, but it's hot as a ten-imperial trollop, for sure."

"Told ya," Hemp said.

"I'll fix up another poultice. You drink every spot of that tea, captain, or I'll drill a hole in your head and pour it in!" Bert started packing up her bag.

"I'm hungry."

"That's good. I'll bring some soup."

"I'm hungrier than soup."

"You'll get soup." My belligerent cook left without another word.

Preel pulled the sheet and blanket back up to my chest, and Hemp handed me a steaming cup of the vile brew from the pot.

"Bloody damned nursemaids…" I tried to bolster myself up to drink the tea, but couldn't manage the pillow one-handed. Preel was there in an instant to help. "Thank you."

I sipped the steaming brew and grimaced. By the time I finished the pot under the watchful eyes of my steward, Bert was back with a bowl of soup and a nasty-smelling poultice. Thankfully, once applied and wrapped with clean linen, the smell diminished enough that I could enjoy the soup. It took the edge off my hunger, but didn't really fill the void. When Hemp left with the empty bowl, Miko came in.

She assessed my condition at a glance and scowled. "You sick, sir?"

"The leg flared up." I waved her to a chair and beckoned Preel to another. "You need to hear this, too, Preel."

I filled them in on my meeting with Brekka, providing as many details as I could recall. Preel, especially, might have revelations about the alchemist that I would never think of. When I mentioned the information Brekka had said she needed to brew an effective potion, Preel fetched parchment and pen from my navigation table and started taking notes. When I finished, she stared at the page, her brow furrowed in thought.

"What about this old temple?" Miko asked. "Were they actually…worshiping there? The Children, I mean."

"I don't know. They didn't seem to be. The central hall didn't look like any temple I've ever been in. More like a small arena." I described it in detail, from the shape to the high vaulted ceiling with rain pattering through a crack to the lurid mosaics.

"Maybe they used to do sacrifices there, or held ritualized fights," Miko surmised.

"Neither here nor there, is it?"

"I suppose not, but I'm curious how Brekka keeps these Children loyal, considering what Hyly said. Religious fanaticism?"

Preel tapped her parchment, scrawled something, then turned to show us. She'd circled the word "Alchemist," then underlined the word "Drugs!"

"Maybe," I agreed. "Maybe both. That'd be a potent mixture: drugs and religion."

"Too right, sir." Miko turned to Preel. "So, how many questions will it take, do you think?"

Preel shrugged, considered her notes, then held up two fingers, then three, then wiggled her hand in uncertainly.

"That's about what I thought." I waved the two of them away. "We've got a couple of days to think about the first one, and I need to get back on my feet, which means rest. We can talk about this again tonight over dinner, if Bert decides to feed me something besides soup and bread-mold tea."

"Right." Miko grinned ruefully and stood. "Get some rest, sir."

"I will." I was feeling better already, but tired. "Wake me if anything comes up."

"I will." She left.

Preel went to my navigation table and began studying her notes and scratching more. I lay back and closed my eyes, my mind spinning with images from Brekka's temple, her laboratory, and our meeting. Poised on the edge of sleep, I wondered why I couldn't remember exactly what she looked like.

The rain eased by the following evening, and I was walking around the cabin, thoroughly sick of being sick. Preel had barely left my navigation table, working tirelessly on our next question. The greatest difficulty was deciding what to ask first. Preel knew her talent better than Miko or I, so when she suggested we first ask who crafted the scourge, even though it didn't make much sense to me, we took her suggestion seriously.

"If we know the name of the crafter, it will help us phrase the following questions." Preel tapped a pen to her pursed lips and reached for her cup. She sipped tea while Miko and I enjoyed fine brandy. I think intoxication frightened her now.

"Brekka seemed less concerned with the crafter than what it was made from and what enchantments were placed on it." I rubbed my eyes; it was late and we were all tired. "I don't see how knowing who made it helps us."

"If it's someone we can track down, we could just *ask* them what materials and enchantments they used to make the scourge." Miko spread her hands and smiled. "All our information in one shot!"

Preel shook her head. "It's less about finding the crafter than it is about phrasing the next question. Consider this: if you ask me what Jhavika's scourge is made from, the question pertains directly to a powerful magical artifact. My talent must pierce that artifact's magic to discern the answer, which often doesn't work. But, if we have the crafter's name, you could ask me what materials they used in making the scourge. That allows my talent to simply look back in time and see what happened, not into the artifact itself."

I furrowed my brow. "But we could phrase the question like that without knowing his name, and not waste a question."

"We could try, sir, but remember the problem with ambiguity. You have to refer specifically to Jhavika's enchanted scourge in the question. The phrasing could be tricky."

"She's got a point." Miko emptied her glass and frowned.

"But if we phrase it as 'Jhavika's enchanted scourge,' that should be specific enough. It's not like she has two of them."

"True." Preel tapped her pen to her notes. "But it would be easier if we knew the crafter's name, and Brekka *did* say she wanted to know that, too."

"Wait! What if—"

"No questions!" Preel interrupted, forestalling Miko's incaution.

"Sorry. Right...um...so consider that we don't know if only a single person crafted the scourge. If you asked who made this ship, for instance, you'd get a list of names as long as my arm."

"That's *right!*" Preel frowned and dropped her pen on the table. "I didn't think that there might have been more than one person involved in its making."

"Neither had I." I drained my glass and reached for the bottle. Miko shook her head when I offered her another splash. Sighing, I put it down without filling my glass; I needed a clear head more than another drink. "So, we're back to asking what components went into the making of Jhavika's enchanted scourge. That seems a pretty straightforward question to me."

"It could be a very long list of ingredients," Preel warned.

"That's true, and we have to record every single one. We'll need to write it down as quickly as you say it, or risk missing one."

"Quibly's got a quick hand. We could have him take notes." Miko shrugged. "It's not like Preel's talent is much of a secret aboard *Scourge* anymore."

"I know, and that worries me almost as much as the damned witch does!" I lifted the bottle of brandy and swirled it. "Sooner or later someone's going to get drunk and talk about Preel. Then we'll have a real problem."

"I wonder how Captain Nightspinner kept the secret," Miko said.

Preel looked down at her lap. "He told everyone that I was his whore, and that he preferred his women silent and…compliant. He wasn't lying."

"Then he truly *was* a fool." I threw caution to the wind and poured myself another drink.

"Tell them the truth, sir."

"What?" I looked at Miko like she'd suggested I climb to the foretop naked.

"Tell the truth to the crew, every last one of them."

Preel looked as horrified as I did. "You *can't!*"

"Think it through, both of you." Miko raised a hand and counted off fingers. "You tell them Preel's a truthsayer. You tell them her talent's going to make them *rich!* And you tell them that if a single one of them breathes a word of this to anyone outside the crew, you'll be able to find out who did it and track them down." Miko snatched the bottle from my grasp and poured herself a dram. "And then you remind them what happened to Geit." She downed the liquor in a swallow. "*That's* the truth!"

"Yes, it is." I sipped and looked to Preel. "It's your choice, Preel. There's no place in the world that's safe for you, not even empires where slavery's been outlawed, but a ship's a tight community. If you intend to stay aboard, there's really no better way to handle things that I can think of."

Preel still looked horrified, but finally nodded. "I suppose you're right. I don't see any other alternative."

"Of course, I'm right!" Miko stood, looking pleased with herself. "I've only ever been wrong once, and that was when I thought I was mistaken!" She laughed at our disgusted looks.

"We'll ask our question tomorrow night, then, after I tell the crew." I finished my drink and stood. "Goodnight, Miko, and thanks."

"My pleasure, sir." She saluted, then turned and bowed to Preel. "And *lady.*"

Preel gaped at the gesture, but I just laughed. Miko grinned like a merchant with an exclusive trade contract as she strutted to the door and let herself out.

"Well, it's late, and my leg hurts." I started for the hammock.

"Sir, please, take the bunk. I'm fine in the hammock." Preel was up and helping me to the bunk before I could protest.

"Very well, but you don't have to help me." I'd been flat on my back most of the day, so my leg felt comparatively good. "Just let me wash up."

"Fine, but quickly." She redirected my unsteady gait to the quarter gallery. "You shouldn't be standing."

I bit my tongue on a sharp retort. Her concern really was touching, but between her, Hemp, and Bert ordering me around my own cabin, I felt ready to explode. I scrubbed my face and teeth, then hobbled to the bunk, doffed my robe, and lay down. My leg felt better the moment my weight came off it, and I tolerated Preel's hesitant attention as she drew up the blanket, turned down the lamps, and readied herself for bed. I even checked my amusement watching her first few attempts to climb into my hammock.

The crew took the news well. Avarice and fear of reprisal, both from me and from their peers, would keep their mouths shut. Quibly accepted the assignment as scribe with some trepidation. He reported to the great cabin promptly after supper, his favorite pen in hand.

"Have a seat at the navigation table, Quibly. Preel's just getting ready." She'd been in the quarter gallery for half a glass and I was starting to worry. Miko sat at the table with pen and parchment. Between the two of them we planned to record Preel's every word.

Finally, Preel emerged, looking a little embarrassed in nightclothes and a robe I'd had Hemp alter to fit her. Her hair was down, framing her face in chaotic onyx curls. It made her look very different—younger, fragile—and I caught myself staring. She hurried to the bunk, as we'd agreed that would be more comfortable for her long recovery than the hammock, her eyes cast down. I took the robe from her and stood between her and Quibly as she climbed in and pulled up the blanket.

She took a deep breath and let it out slowly. "Ready, sir."
"Good." I hung up the robe. "Quibly?"
"Aye, sir." He flexed his nimble fingers and dipped his pen.
Miko nodded and did likewise at the table.
"Okay then." I turned back to Preel.
"Promise me you won't pace around the cabin while I sleep," she said.
I chuckled and smiled at her stern look. "Very well. I promise."
She clutched the blanket up to her chin, looking uneasy, as if she'd never done this before.
"Are you all right?"
"I'm fine, sir. It's just...nothing. I'm ready."
"All right. I'll have Bert make something special for your breakfast."
"Thank you, sir." She closed her eyes.
I took a breath, recalling the phrasing of the question we'd agreed upon. "During the crafting of the magical scourge that is now in the possession of Jhavika Keshmir, exactly what materials were used in its making?"
The truthsayer's back arched, her eyes flung open and rolled up. Her mouth gaped silently for a moment as she gasped a deep breath, then that uncharacteristic croaking voice issued forth.
"Water, brimstone, a rendering pot of black iron, the rendered fat of a cockatrice, two feathers from a black vulture that died of eating poisoned grain, the heartstrings of the great dragon Noethrex, the lifeblood of twin virgins, nine claws from the great dragon Noethrex, leather made from the heart sinews of the great dragon

Noethrex, two drams of urine collected under a red moon from a pregnant bitch in labor, the dying screams of eight murdered elf maidens promised to wed, and a blood pearl weighing four ounces collected from the depths of the Serpent's Eye."

It all came in one long, tearing sentence without pause. When it ended, Preel collapsed and gasped for breath, her lips pale and her face sheened with sudden sweat. Her labored breathing eased quickly, and her color returned, but the answer had cost her dearly. I quickly tied the silken gag over her mouth.

The sound of scratching pens brought me around. When they stopped, Quibly and Miko looked up at me, then at each other.

"Well?"

"I think I got it all, sir," Quibly said, looking hopeful. "It came bloody fast, though."

"We should compare and review what you remember her saying, sir." Miko blinked and put down her pen. "The screams of dying elf maids?"

"Dying screams of murdered elf maidens, I think, sir," Quibly said, wincing as he contradicted his superior officer. "Sorry."

"Don't be." Miko shook her head. "I'd never have guessed so much went into crafting such a thing."

"Aye, that was quite a list." Turning back to Preel, I wiped the sweat from her brow with a handkerchief and tucked in the blanket. For those of us still awake and confused, I retrieved a bottle of spiced rum and three glasses from my cabinet. "Come over to the table and let's compare notes, Quibly."

"Aye, sir."

We did, word by word, and I was glad I'd brought my purser in to help. He'd done a better job than Miko, and better than my memory by far. Between the three of us, we made a list that we all felt sure was complete and accurate.

"Now the question is do I send that list to Brekka straightaway, or do I wait until I have the next answer?" I leaned back in my chair, rubbing the itchy poultice bound to my leg.

Chris A. Jackson

"I see no reason to delay, sir." Miko shrugged and sipped thoughtfully. "You needn't go yourself. I can deliver a note easily enough."

"True." I didn't relish another walk to the temple until my leg was healed.

"Might I ask a question, sir?" Quibly raised an eyebrow.

"Yes, of course."

"Does Miss Preel remember her own answers when she wakes up?"

"Yes. Why?"

"Well, I know we did a fair job of writing it down, but mightn't we ask her, too, just to make sure?"

I nodded. "Good idea. We're certainly not in a hurry."

"I agree," Miko said, raising her glass to the purser. "Well done."

"Thank you." Quibly downed his drink, grinned, and stood. "Well, I'm off to my bunk if you don't mind, sir."

"Goodnight." I waved him out, but then had a thought. "No word of this to anyone, Quibly. The crew know what Preel is, but they don't need to know what she said."

"Oh, no, sir! I wouldn't presume…"

"Good." I watched him leave and hoped he'd spoken true.

"Don't worry about Quibly, sir. Greedy as a dragon, that one."

"Aye…greedy as a dragon." I considered our list. "The flesh of a *dragon* went into that blasted thing, Miko. And a pearl from the Serpent's Eye. By the Nine Hells, dragon heartstrings, claws…"

"Makes you wonder, doesn't it?"

"About what?"

"About what that thing might not only be doing to those who are lashed by it, but to those who do the lashing." She considered her drink, swirling the amber liquid in the glass. "Dragons are notoriously greedy creatures, and you've said you never met anyone as avaricious as Jhavika."

"True, but she was that way when we were both midshipmen, too."

292

"But all she ever wanted *then* was to be captain of this ship. Now she commands you, the ship, and her own private army, and *still* wants more."

"Makes me wonder why she didn't command me to fall on my sword the moment she lashed me with that thing, instead of giving me *Scourge*." I downed my drink and pushed myself up from the table.

"Maybe she wanted more than just a pirate ship and knew you could help her get it." Miko finished her drink and stood. "Maybe the scourge—the cat-o'-nine-tails, I mean—*made* her want more."

"Maybe." I shrugged and waved her out. "If it does make her avaricious, I wonder if she realizes it."

"Telling her she's under an enchantment might rattle her cage." Miko went to the door and looked back at me. "Telling her to stick the thing up her arse is liable to cause hard feelings."

"I'll keep that in mind." I hadn't thought about that conversation yet. I'd been putting it off. "Goodnight, Miko."

"Goodnight, sir." She saluted and left.

I started to pace out of habit, then remembered my promise to Preel. Instead, I straightened up the cabin, turned down all the lamps except one over my hammock, picked out a book, and settled in. After reading the same page three times, I put the book down and rolled over to watch Preel sleep. Her chest rose and fell as her eyes flicked around beneath her lids. She claimed she didn't dream, but there was *something* happening behind that dusky brow.

"The flesh of dragons…" This didn't bode well at all.

Preel didn't wake until almost noon the following day. I was worried, but had refrained from pacing. When her eyes finally fluttered open, she lurched up out of the bunk and raced for the quarter gallery with a distressed expression. Miko and I exchanged a bewildered look after the door slammed closed. We'd been sitting at the table working on our next question, and Preel had dashed by before either of us could even say good morning.

"I hope she's okay." I stood and started for the quarter gallery.

"Probably just morning's call," Miko said. "Best give her a moment, sir."

"Oh, right." She had been in bed for three quarters of a day, so that sounded reasonable. I picked her robe off the stand and waited by the door.

Water splashed within, then the latch turned and she opened it wide enough to peer out. I handed her the robe.

"You okay?"

She nodded and donned the robe, stepping out with a bewildered look. She tapped the silk band and I obliged, slipping the knot free.

"What's the time? How long have I slept?"

Through the night and half the day." I gestured to a chair. "I promised you breakfast, but it's nearer lunchtime. Are you hungry?"

"Yes." She rubbed her face and sat, moving slowly. "That was...evidently a stressful question."

"You *did* seem taxed by it." I went to the door and called for Hemp. "Lunch when it's ready and a pot of blackbrew straightaway. Preel's finally awake."

"Aye, sir! Two shakes!"

The three of us sat and ate lunch while we discussed the list Miko and Quibly had compiled. Preel's memory of her answer matched what they had to a remarkable degree, so we decided there was no reason we couldn't send the result to Brekka as soon as possible. When we were finished eating, I penned a note to go with the list, informing the alchemist we'd have the rest of the information in a few days. Miko took both and left to deliver it.

"Thank you for lunch, sir." Preel pushed back from the table and went to her footlocker to select fresh clothes. "You'll forgive me, but I need exercise. I'm always stiff after so long abed."

"I know how you feel." I stood, wincing at the pain in my leg. It was healing, but not fast enough. "I'm tired of being cooped up here. I'll take a turn on deck and leave you to exercise."

"I don't mind if you want to stay, sir." Preel looked uncomfortable despite her claim. "I mean, it won't bother me."

"Maybe, but it'd bother me." I gave her an easy smile and headed for the door. "Take your time."

"Thank you, sir."

I left her and summoned Hemp. "Guard on the door. I'll be on deck."

"Want a chair on the quarterdeck, sir?"

"No. This damned leg needs to be stretched."

"But Bert said—"

"It's not Bert's leg." I started forward, doing my damnedest not to limp.

The following days were an exercise in patience. We had the next question nailed down to everyone's satisfaction in a day, but we couldn't ask it for at least three more. I kept having to tell myself that there was no rush. We'd found the person who could break this enchantment. Now, it was just a matter of time.

With the ship at anchor, however, there was little to keep me occupied. I exercised my leg as much as possible, drank pot after pot of Bert's vile brew to stave off fever, submitted to her examinations, and rejoiced when she finally pulled the stitches and pronounced me fit for duty. Unfortunately, that left me even more fidgety, and spending time alone in the cabin with Preel tested my nerves in ways that I'd never thought the company of another human being would.

She amazed me at every turn.

Preel fell into an easy rhythm, seemingly content to exercise twice daily, read, and casually stroll the deck with me. I had to leave the cabin while she performed her twisting exercises; I couldn't keep my eyes off her graceful movements, and staring seemed rude.

I spent those hours in the wardroom, much to the discomfort of my midshipmen. I'm afraid I took out some of my frustration on them, but it kept me busy and their mathematics improved markedly. Boxley had transformed the midshipmen's berth from a gaggle of lazy laggards to a laughing, competitive, and occasionally combative trio of young officers. When she showed up one morning with a shiner, and I asked where she'd gotten it, she told me flatly that such minor bumps and bruises were beneath the concern of the captain. I decided to let them handle their own disagreements as long as they didn't resort to blades.

The ship was running smoothly. My crew had settled into a comfortable routine of work and relaxation, sharing music, stories, and each other's company. Rauley, my new sailing master, prospered under the tutelage of Wix and Miko, happier than I'd ever seen him. Bert bought fresh provisions and kept everyone in a state of gastronomic bliss. Only the ship's captain seemed uneasy, which made it all the more frustrating.

Finally, the night before we were to ask Preel our final question, my patience reached an end.

I don't even know what set me off. Preel and I were just reading, each of us sitting comfortably with our own lamp, her on the bunk, me at my navigation table. We'd eaten dinner, chatted about nothing in particular, then I'd put the silken band back over her mouth. Silence filled the cabin like an oppressive fog. I couldn't concentrate on my book and found myself counting the seconds between each page she turned. Thirty seven…thirty six…thirty nine…thirty seven… Eventually I turned to watch her dark eyes darting back and forth, her breathing slow, one finger tapping the edge of the book, ready to turn the next page.

"I don't know how you tolerate it, Preel." I heard my voice before I realized I'd spoken.

Her eyes came up and her forehead wrinkled.

"The inactivity. The silence. The damnable *waiting*..." I lurched out of my chair and strode to my cabinet. I'd told myself I wasn't going to drink tonight, that it only made me less able to deal with the frustration, but I needed to do *something*. "It's driving me insane!" I poured a measure from the first bottle my fingers touched and bolted it down.

She clapped her hands to get my attention and tapped the silken band girding her mouth.

"I don't know if it's a good idea, Preel. I'm in a mood, and I might ask you a question inadvertently." I poured another measure of the malt whiskey.

She clapped her hands again, tapping the band insistently.

"All *right*." I went to the bunk and untied the gag.

"Sit down please, sir." She patted the bunk beside her.

"Why?" I downed half my glass and stared at her suspiciously.

"Because you *are* in a mood, and I don't want you to ask me a question by accident either." She lifted the silken band, her face solemn. "This will keep you from asking while I explain how I tolerate this...inactivity."

I stared down at the gag with trepidation, loath to be bound by magic and unable to remove the thing, even if it only kept me from speaking. I knew rationally that there was no real danger, but tell that to my nerves.

"Please," Preel said, her dark eyes pleading, "trust me."

How could I not?

I downed the rest of my drink, sat down, and let her tie the silk band around my mouth. The scent of her right under my nose didn't help my frustration. I tried to speak, of course, and found that I couldn't. I felt no discomfort, I just couldn't form words. Similarly, I had no difficulty reaching up to touch the silken band, but couldn't make my fingers pull it away or untie the knot.

A strange feeling, being bound by magic, not unlike Jhavika's control over me. It didn't hurt, it just made me compliant. I didn't like it at all.

"Odd, isn't it?" Preel asked, touching the gag with her fingertips.

I nodded.

"After a time, you get used to it. It's not like being a slave; not *really*. You never get used to that."

I tried to understand what real slavery must feel like and failed.

"This *inactivity*, this waiting that is bothering you..." Preel bit her lip as if deciding whether to tell me a deep dark secret, "...has given me some of the best days of my life."

I knitted my brow and shook my head.

Preel smiled. "I'm *safe* here with you. You've made that clear to me. I need not fear beatings or abuse, even when I'm unconscious and helpless."

My eyes must have widened at that, because her smile faltered.

"Yes, Captain Nightspinner used to do that." She crossed her arms and hugged herself tight. "Not at first, but later...I would wake up sore, sometimes bleeding. I learned to...expect it." She shivered and looked down.

I touched her shoulder and pantomimed for her to stop. I didn't need, didn't *want* to hear this.

"It's all right. Sometimes talking about it...helps." She smiled weakly. "So, what I mean for you to understand is that there are *worse* things to endure than peace and quiet. You've probably endured trials of your own in life that I know nothing about. This is how *I* deal with the waiting; I tell myself that it could be worse. I could be abused, a slave, a whore, even some foul lecher's *wife* would be worse." She smiled again, this time genuinely. "I'm safe here and I have you to thank for it, Captain Longbright. So, stop fretting, stop drinking to kill your frustration, stop worrying about what you cannot control, and be thankful that it's not a thousand times worse."

She reached up then and untied the silken gag.

"Better?" she asked, still smiling.

"Yes." By Odea I wanted to kiss her more at that moment than I wanted anything in the Seven Heavens or Nine Hells, but what she had said stopped me cold. She felt safe here, and the lecherous attention of a pirate was the last thing she needed to deal with. I couldn't shatter her trust in me, the security I'd given her. "Thank you, Preel."

"You're welcome." She held up the silken gag. "Now put this back on me, please, before you ask a silly question and make your wait that much longer."

"Right." I affixed the gag over her mouth, then went back to my book with a much lighter heart. I thought of my years under the yoke of my father, more years under the harsh stewardship of Captain Kohl, the scars on my back and my soul. *Yes, things could be a great deal worse.*

The next night, I asked Preel our final question.

"During the creation of Jhavika Keshmir's enchanted scourge, what magical effects were placed upon it?"

As always, her back arched and that raspy voice tore from her throat. "The claws of Noethrex were enchanted so that none whose flesh the scourge tastes can resist the master's compulsion. The heartstrings of Noethrex bestow the ruthlessness of the great dragon upon the master. The heart sinews of Noethrex compel the master to greatness with the avarice of the great dragon. And the blood pearl from the Serpent's Eye binds the master to the scourge for life."

Preel collapsed and fell silent. I checked her breathing and quickly affixed the gag back on her mouth.

"Got it all," Quibly said when his pen stopped scratching.

We quickly compared our versions of Preel's answer, and they agreed perfectly. I thanked my purser and dismissed him.

"We were right, sir." Miko leaned back in her chair. "Looks like Jhavika's every bit a slave to this *thing* as you are to her."

"Yes, and she's never going to give it up, either." I paced and chewed a fingernail. "She *can't.*"

"True enough." Miko sighed and shrugged. "Do you think you should tell her that?"

"I don't know." I considered that dilemma. "I don't think it'll make any difference."

"How so?"

"She's never going to stop wanting more, Miko. Not until it kills her." I chewed my fingernails some more. "Maybe it'd be better for everyone if we just rode her coattails until that happens."

"*If* it happens."

"There's only one of two outcomes, Miko. She either becomes queen of all the world or she eventually comes up against someone who kills her."

"And then *they* take the scourge." Miko frowned. "I don't know if I like the idea of that thing in the hands of someone like the God-Emperor of Toki."

"First things first." I grinned at my first mate, satisfied with our success. "We have everything we need. Write it up pretty and I'll take it to Brekka in the morning. We'll worry about Jhavika later."

"Aye, sir!" Miko left with a jaunty salute.

I checked Preel once more. Her breathing was steady, but her eyes flicked around beneath her lids. I brushed a lock of hair from her damp brow, wondering, "What are you dreaming about that you don't or *won't* recall?"

But that was another question for another time. Right now, I had all the answers I needed.

Chapter Twenty One
The Witch's Bargain

Everyone has a treasure with which they refuse to part.
The Lessons of Quen Lau Ush

From the diary of Kevril Longbright –
Why must it always be a choice between freedom and love?

After a quick confirmation from Preel that our recording of her answer was accurate, I set off with an escort to settle the bargain with Brekka. Her guards answered at the first knock.

"Captain." The same misshapen creature opened the door wide, lips pulling back in that shark grin. "We've been expecting your visit."

"Good." We strode in and, as before, my escort stayed in the central hall while I followed my guide to Brekka's laboratory. The alchemist straightened from a scale where she was weighing out some powder and faced me.

I stopped short. For some reason, I found her face utterly unfamiliar. Her dark hair and sightless eye were the same, but the rest of her features seemed just different enough that they left me wondering if I was speaking to the same woman.

"You have an answer for me, Captain Longbright?" Appearing not to notice my hesitation, Brekka brushed her hands on her stained robes.

"Yes." I handed over the scroll we'd prepared. "There are four enchantments on the scourge. Only one of the four is affecting me."

"That information will be useful." She read the note and nodded, a thin smile spreading across her lips. "Yes, very useful indeed. I don't suppose you learned who crafted the artifact."

"No. Is it necessary?"

"Not really. Just professional curiosity."

"I can probably find out, if you'd like to consider the information as part of your payment." That would be a painless price, indeed.

"No." Brekka tucked the scroll away and scrutinized me. "But I do have one more question that I require you to answer before I begin my work."

More delays... "I'm not going to answer endless questions for your own satisfaction, Brekka. Can you make a potion that will break this enchantment with what I've given you or not?"

"I believe I can, yes, but I won't begin until we agree on compensation, and I can't negotiate that compensation without an answer to this one simple question." She stepped forward, her single eye fixed upon me in a most disconcerting manner. "I must know how you came by the answers to the previous two questions I put to you."

"That's not your business."

"Then find someone else to break this enchantment." She turned away as if unconcerned with my plight, which I had no doubt she was.

I gritted my teeth. I hadn't come this far to give up now. "The same way I found you. I have in my employ someone with a magical talent that helps me learn things. That's all you need to know."

"Then you should have no difficulty finding someone *else* to help you remove this enchantment." She flicked a hand dismissively without turning around. "Goodbye, Captain Longbright."

The two-fingered grip of her guard closed on my arm.

I looked the man in the eye, then down at his misshapen hand. "Remove that or I will."

"The mistress told you to leave." His grip tightened and his other hand went to a dagger at his belt.

My other hand, however, was already on my cutlass, and I had it out and at his throat before his weapon even cleared the sheath. "Drop it!"

His lips parted to reveal his gruesome teeth, but it wasn't a smile.

"Threatening my servants isn't likely to win me over, Captain." Brekka didn't even glance over her shoulder.

"And threatening *me* is only likely to get you killed, witch." I scraped the razor edge of my sword up the man's neck, removing a day's worth of stubble. "Tell your man to stand down. We're not through here."

"Unless you tell me how you came about these answers, we *are* through here." She did turn then. "And if you kill my guard, I'll be quite cross with you."

"Tell him to stand down." I twitched my wrist and a line of blood formed beneath my blade. "Or you'll be more cross with me than you know."

She rolled her one good eye and waved a hand. "Release him and step back."

The guard let go of my arm, and I lowered my sword. He took two steps back, but kept his hand on his dagger.

"Now, Captain Longbright, if you *truly* wish to negotiate, your first step is to tell me who in your employ gave you the answers to my questions, and how they managed that feat."

I had no recourse. Killing Brekka would get me nothing and threats would only gain her enmity, which would undoubtedly raise the price of her services.

"Fine." I wiped my sword on my pant leg and sheathed it. "I have a truthsayer."

"A *truth*sayer..." The brow above Brekka's sightless eye rose. "Interesting."

"Now, name your price for the potion. I can offer gold, the services of my ship, or answers to a negotiated number of questions you can get nowhere else. What'll it be?"

"I think, Captain, that I would rather have a truthsayer of my own."

"Ha! No, Brekka. I'll not be bartering that. Her services, yes, but she stays with me."

"I do not want her *services*, Captain, I want *her*!" The alchemist's voice dripped avarice. "I want her magic! I value magic more than gold, power, or lands, Captain! *That* is my price!"

"That's too bad, because I'm not going to part with her."

"Then you don't wish to be free of this compulsion that the master of the scourge holds over you." Her negotiation tactics left much to be desired, but she got her point across.

"Then I'll find *another* alchemist to brew me this potion." I headed for the door. If I had to wait another month or so to find someone, so be it, but I'd not give up Preel.

"There is no other in Valaka who can do this for you, Captain!" Brekka called before I reached the door. "No other but Brekka!"

"We'll see." I didn't look back, and I didn't wait for my guide.

"Ask your truthsayer, then, and I'll see you when she gives you your answer." Her laughter faded too slowly as I strode toward the hall and my companions.

"Sir?" Wix must have seen the ill humor on my face. "Problems?"

"Yes, problems. She asked too high a price. We're leaving."

"With you, sir." My squad formed up with a single gesture from Wix, and we made for the outer door.

Two Children stood there. I half suspected that they'd bar the way, but they only worked the heavy mechanism that freed the doors and pulled them open for us. We made our way to the ship without incident, pause, or a word spoken between us. I fumed in silence; not only had I ruined my one clear chance of being free of Jhavika's compulsion, I'd given away the one secret I'd sworn everyone else aboard the ship to keep. For all I knew, Brekka might already be sharing the secret with others or plotting to take Preel by force.

The answer was simple: ask Preel who else in Valaka could brew a potion to break the spell. If Brekka could do it, someone else should be able to. There were dozens of alchemists in the city. *Unless she's telling the truth...* In which case, I'd be in a hard spot. I didn't relish the thought of trying to find another willing and capable of breaking this enchantment, if indeed anyone else in the entire Blood Sea could do so.

Of course, I could ask Preel, but that meant more waiting.

Preel... As we boarded the launch and Wix ordered the crew to their oars, I wondered what to tell her. I couldn't tell her that I'd divulged her secret, and I certainly couldn't tell her that Brekka wanted her in exchange for breaking the enchantment. If I did, she'd never trust me again.

Her misplaced trust...

But I had to tell her and the rest of the crew *something*.

I might not have much skill in discerning the falsehoods of others, but I have, over the years, gotten fairly good at spinning my own. I'd already told Wix that Brekka had demanded too dear a price for lifting the enchantment. But what could she have demanded that all would agree would be too great a price to pay? When we arrived at the ship, I had an idea.

Miko met me at the boarding hatch. "Trouble, sir?"

"Hell, yes, trouble. Brekka's insane and she doesn't negotiate worth a damn!" I started aft. "We need to talk about this."

"Aye, sir!" She snapped orders to Rauley to see to the stowing of the boat and followed me aft.

The guard outside my cabin saluted and stepped aside. I called for Hemp to bring blackbrew as I opened the door.

Inside, Preel was in the middle of one of her sessions, her tiny, lithe frame contorted in a manner that would have fractured my spine. She relaxed her pose, her brow furrowed in question, no doubt concerning my quick return.

"Sorry to interrupt, Preel, but there's been a setback and we need to talk." I ushered Miko in and stowed my weapons in my locker. "Brekka's asked for something I'm unwilling to do in exchange for lifting the enchantment, and she's equally unwilling to negotiate."

"What did she ask for?" Miko took a seat at the table.

Preel joined her, looking worried and all too alluring in her sweat-damp clothes, moisture beading on her bare midriff like dew on varnished teak. I felt a pang in my gut at the lie that was about to leave my lips and forced my gaze to remain fixed on hers.

"She wants us to sail into the Serpent's Eye."

"*What?*" Miko's expression told me instantly that I'd chosen my lie well. "Why in the names of all the gods would she want *that?*"

"She wants us to take her there. She seeks some magic in the maelstrom, but she wouldn't say what it was, and I don't care. I'm not sailing this ship into *that*, not if it means being a slave to Jhavika for the rest of my life!" I started pacing the cabin.

"And she wouldn't accept anything else?"

"No!" I flexed my hands at my side in honest frustration. "Take it or leave it were her only choices. She also said that we'd find no one else in Valaka able to lift the enchantment."

"So where does that leave us?" Miko asked.

A knock at the door heralded Hemp with a tray of blackbrew, toasted cheese, and biscuits. The aroma of crispy cheese filled the cabin and eased my jangling nerves. *May Odea bless Bert*, I thought as I directed Hemp to place it on the table. He poured three cups and left us without even a muttered complaint. Obviously, word of the failed negotiation had spread through the crew with the speed of a striking viper.

"It leaves us in a very difficult spot." I went to Preel and untied her gag. "We can find out easily enough if Brekka's lying by asking

Preel who else in Valaka can break the enchantment, but if the answer is no one, then we're stuck."

"You could ask me what *else* Brekka might take in exchange for lifting the spell." Preel added a dollop of goat's milk to her blackbrew and sipped. She seemed unperturbed about the setback, but then, she didn't know the truth.

"A good idea." And one I might actually employ. "But it'll take time."

"I thought we weren't in a hurry," Miko slathered crispy, drippy cheese onto a biscuit and took a bite.

My stomach growled. I sat and followed suit. The cheese had an undefinable spice to it that left my tongue tingling and wanting more.

"I don't know about that anymore, Miko. Your question about breaking the news to Jhavika made me realize that the longer we take, the harder that confrontation's going to be." I chased the bite with a sip of blackbrew and found myself reaching for another biscuit. "We've already been gone a long time."

"Will another ten days or so really matter?" Preel eyed the cheese, but refrained. She had more willpower than me.

"Maybe not." I smiled as I slathered another biscuit. "Yet another question we could ask."

"Save that one for the trip back to Haven," Miko suggested. "Dealing with Jhavika is a problem, but first things first."

"So, we have to decide what to ask first; if there's someone else in Valaka who can lift the enchantment, or if Brekka would accept anything else in payment." I ate and considered. If I asked the second question, I'd have to phrase it carefully to hide my lie. "We're only well and truly buggered if the answer to both is no. But we've got more waiting to do before we can ask."

"It could be worse," Preel said, sipping her tea with an easy smile. "We're not exactly suffering here."

"True enough." I sampled some more cheese and sipped my tea, wondering if things could indeed get much worse.

Three days later I asked Preel who else in Valaka besides Brekka was willing and capable of lifting the enchantment set upon me by Jhavika's scourge. I was worried that we might be taxing Preel overmuch, employing her talent every fourth day, but she assured me that others had pressed her harder. She lay on the bunk awaiting the question, utter trust gleaming in her eyes. Deceiving her scored my soul like a hot iron.

The answer was as harsh as her raspy voice: "No one."

"Well, *shit*." Miko lurched up from the table. "That was useless! Now we sit here for another four days before we can ask another question and *that* one might be just as pointless."

Miko's uncharacteristic response worried me as much as the answer itself. "Yes, we wait." I fixed the silken gag back over Preel's mouth and turned to my first mate. "You must be out of money or bored with the pleasures of Valaka already."

"I was bored with the pleasures of Valaka the day we arrived, sir." She started for the door. "And the crew's getting antsy. They're broke and tired of sitting at anchor."

I knew she was telling me the truth. The tide had turned on my peaceful ship a few days ago. More than one fistfight had broken out in the lower decks. Wix assured me that the crew was just relieving tension and that there was nothing to worry about, but more waiting would certainly not make it better.

"I'm open to suggestions on how to make Brekka settle for something different, Miko." I couldn't tell Miko and the crew the truth, of course. It could start a mutiny, considering that I'd sworn them all to silence about Preel's talent and told them she could make them rich. "She doesn't respond well to threats, and she only covets magic."

Miko paused with her hand on the latch and looked back at me. "What about Preel?"

I stiffened like I'd been knifed. "What *about* Preel?"

"You could offer to answer a number of questions for Brekka. Questions she can't get answered anywhere else."

I breathed a sigh of relief that I hoped looked like exasperation. "I thought about that, but I can't very well tell the witch I've got my own truthsayer, and if you're tired of waiting now, how tired of it will you be when a dozen or a *hundred* more questions are answered?"

"Good point." Miko frowned and shook her head. "Well, we better figure out something else she wants soon. We're pirates, Captain. We need to be at our job or there'll be all Nine Hells to pay."

Miko left, and I paced the cabin. She was right; we couldn't wait forever. The crew had spent their pay ashore, and ship's chores and sea chanties wouldn't keep them satisfied for long. Another four days just to find out what else, if anything, Brekka might accept as payment, when I'd already offered everything I could...or would. The answer would be the same: nothing.

Then what?

Then I'll be right back where I started. I tried to convince myself that it wasn't hopeless. Valaka was only the *nearest* place to Haven where I might find someone to lift the enchantment, so it was entirely possible that somewhere there was someone else who could free me. But each step required another answer from Preel, more days waiting, a ship to maintain, and a crew to feed. After all that, there was still no guarantee that another wizard might want any less than Brekka had demanded. And all the while, the truthsayer sleeping in my bunk would draw the attention of every powerful wizard or ruler from Chen to Mati. Jhavika knew by now that I'd fled and likely had agents aboard every merchantman sailing the Blood Sea looking for me. If I didn't break her enchantment, I'd be her slave forever, even if I sailed to the Shattered Isles and started pirating on my own. She'd continue hunting me, and if she ever brought me in, she'd order me to fall on my sword, or worse. I began to wonder if I mightn't be better off to cut my losses and take Brekka's offer.

I found myself standing beside the bunk, staring down at Preel.

"A treasure beyond price..." I brushed a lock of hair off her brow, touched the tattoo etched there, and slowly came to the realization that my options had been suddenly and irrevocably reduced to only one. In one hand I held Preel, the dove who laid diamond eggs, and in the other I held my freedom. I could have one or the other, not both.

My breaths came quicker, and my throat tightened. I'd made a similar choice once before when I left home. If I'd stayed there, I would have either killed my father or continued to be his whipping post. Despite the abuse, I still loved the man. I chose to run, risking his life against mine with my freedom in the balance. Now I risked my freedom against Preel's, with both our lives in the balance.

It seemed that the farther I ran from my father, the longer I continued being the frightful, hate-filled boy sleeping with a kitchen knife, waiting for him to come home. I couldn't live that way anymore.

Irony's a bitch.

I made my choice and called for my steward.

"Aye, sir!" Hemp rubbed his eyes, probably napping at my door until I turned the lamps down.

"Send for Wix. Tell him to put together a shore party."

"*Now*, sir?" He blinked in surprise. Nice to know I could still do that.

"Yes, Hemp. Now."

"Straightaway, sir!" He ambled off muttering to himself.

To my surprise, Brekka's doorman answered after the first knock. His pale face showed no wonder at seeing a party of glowering pirates at the door so late at night.

"I need to speak to Brekka."

"Of course you do, Captain." He grinned that threatening grin at me and opened the doors.

There were fewer Children about at this hour, but still more than my ten-squad. I examined them closely this time: their weapons, their readiness, their eyes. The dim lamplight didn't give me a very good view, but they were all as pale as the doorman. Their deformities varied, but their twisted limbs and malformed hands gripped serviceable weapons. They looked steady, not the type of down-and-out lotus addicts you see littering the gutter. If Brekka was using drugs to keep them loyal, she kept them well supplied and used something that didn't render them listless. If they were religious fanatics, however, all bets were off.

Neither option boded well.

I left my escort in the hall and followed the doorman. This time, however, he didn't bring me to the alchemist's laboratory. Instead we turned down a branching corridor at the base of the stairs, and he rapped at a gilded portal far more elaborate than the bronze and wood laboratory door.

"Yes?" called a voice from within at my guide's knock.

He opened the door and waved me through. I kept my eyes on him as I passed, quite sure that he held a grudge over our last altercation and unwilling to present my unguarded back to his dagger. Stepping to the side to put a wall behind me, I turned to face the room and stopped cold.

"Captain Longbright! What a surprise!" Brekka reclined on a divan, clad in robes of azure silk rather than the drab gray I'd seen before. Smiling at me with amusement, she raised a crystal goblet of some dark liquid in salute. "Care to join my loyal followers in their pleasure?"

Before her, arrayed on numerous thick pillows and rugs, more than a dozen men and women were engaged in some of the most imaginative and enthusiastic copulation I'd ever witnessed. But these weren't Serpent's Children. These were the most beautiful specimens I'd ever seen, women of perfect proportion, lithe and full-figured, and men with chiseled physiques wielding phalluses that would have put Maurice Malchi's impressive manhood to shame. They writhed and moaned, thrust and bucked, a veritable storm of seething, perfect flesh.

"I think I'll pass," I said, trying to hide my confusion. Who *were* these people? Brekka had said these were her loyal followers, but... *It doesn't matter. Focus, Kevril!* I tore my gaze away and centered it upon the alchemist. "I've come to negotiate your offer."

"There will be no negotiation, Captain." She smiled thinly and swirled the liquid in the goblet. "You will agree to give me your truthsayer in exchange for the cure to the spell that assails you, or you'll leave me to my work."

"Your work?" I waved a hand at the orgy taking place at her feet. "Interesting work."

"Alas, the price of devotion..." She sighed as if bored by the riotous display.

A man lurched up from his exertions. "Brekka! More! I need more!" He stumbled to her, and I noticed that his legs had begun to twist and change. By the time he reached his mistress' divan, they were bent backward, his feet deformed into monstrous claws. He knelt at her side and turned up his face to her, mouth wide.

"Yes...there's a good boy." Brekka poured a scant measure of the liquid from the goblet into his mouth.

He swallowed, gasped, and rose, his malformed legs quickly reforming into muscular perfection. He rejoined the fray with renewed enthusiasm.

"So *that's* how you pay them for their service." Physical perfection, a lure few Serpent's Children could resist. It made a twisted kind of sense. Brekka could give them the one thing they could get nowhere else. They were addicted to perfection.

"Yes, Captain, but enough about them. Are you here to meet my bargain for your freedom from this enchantment, or just to disturb my leisure?"

"I've come to implore you to think of something else you'd be willing to accept."

"As a matter of fact, I have thought of one thing that I'll accept in lieu of your truthsayer." She sat up and regarded me with her half-blind gaze.

"Yes?" My heart redoubled its cadence.

"The enchanted scourge that holds you in thrall. If you bring me that artifact, I'll give you the concoction that will break the enchantment."

I considered that proposal for a moment. With Preel's help, stealing the scourge might not be as impossible a task as one might think, but it would mean returning to Haven, which would draw Jhavika's attention, which would probably end with me falling on my sword. Killing her before she could order me to end my own life would be the only option, and that would be perilous in the extreme. But would it be impossible? There was only one way to find out, and that would cost me more weeks of waiting and questions to Preel. In the end, it might also prove fruitless.

Unless...

"The only way I could manage that would be to have the enchantment lifted *before* I steal the scourge for you. If I'm still under compulsion, I'll die trying to take it. Cure me first, and I'll get you the scourge."

Brekka laughed, low and humorless, offering the goblet to another of her followers as the woman stumbled up, her arms transformed into segmented worms. A sip sent the Serpent's Child hurrying back to the pillows, her perfect human arms reaching for another perfect partner.

"I think not, Captain." Brekka swirled the potion in the goblet. "You'll forgive me, but I don't trust you to fulfill your end of the bargain."

Trust...

"Very well." I took a steadying breath and let it out slowly. "How long will it take you to concoct this potion?"

A dark eyebrow rose over the alchemist's sightless eye, and I realized that it was *not* the same eyebrow that had arched before. I shuddered, realizing that I still couldn't fix her face in my mind's eye, even though I was staring right at her. There was something very *wrong* about Brekka.

"Six days."

"Then in six days I'll bring the truthsayer to you, and you'll hand me this potion in exchange."

"I will."

"But before I hand over the truthsayer, I'll use her talent to confirm that the elixir will banish the enchantment that holds me in thrall." I smiled humorlessly. "You'll *forgive* me, but I don't trust *you*, either."

"Of course." The alchemist nodded respectfully. "I accept those terms."

"If you know anything about truthsayers, you'll know that asking her a question will put her into a state of unconsciousness for at least half a day, and that no other question can be asked for at least four more days without risking her life." I stared her down. "She is a treasure beyond price, Brekka. Use her ill and she'll die, leaving you with nothing."

"I would sooner pluck out my own eyes, Captain."

"Very well, then, we have a deal." I turned for the door.

"Captain!"

I turned back to find Brekka now standing, her azure robes pooled at her feet. Her body shone like a pillar of feminine perfection, one hand proffering the goblet.

"Are you *sure* you won't join us?"

My lip curled back from my teeth in a sneer of distaste. "I'd sooner pluck out my own eyes, Brekka."

She laughed long and hard at that, but I didn't care. I flung open the door and stalked down the hall, the knife in my gut twisting with every step.

The choice had been made: freedom over love.
I hated myself for it, but I was used to that.

Chapter Twenty Two
Payment in Full

Lies, like cancer, consume one from within.
The Lessons of Quen Lau Ush

From the diary of Kevril Longbright –
I am many things—a liar, a thief, a murderer even—but I'm also free. The choices I've made in my life, the ones I'm least proud of, are those that have made me free. If forced to make them again, knowing what havoc they would wreak on my soul, would I change my choices? I think not.

Six days was a very long time to keep my lie a secret. Miko and Preel were, I think, suspicious. The only thing I could think to tell them was that I'd made a bargain with Brekka, and that she'd sworn me not to reveal what the payment would be. A thin falsehood.

The only truth I told, that I'd take Preel with us to confirm that the potion Brekka concocted would indeed break the enchantment, met with as much skepticism as the lies.

"I don't see why you can't confirm the potion's potency once you bring it back here," Miko said one evening as we finished our dinner.

"Because if it isn't genuine and I've already paid Brekka's price for a fake, my only recourse is to assault the temple." I shook my head and downed my cup of sweet liqueur, the perfect complement to the spicy dish Bert had made. "No, that would go poorly, Miko. The temple's as good as a fortress, and killing half her followers wouldn't put her in a helpful mood."

"I suppose." Miko sipped and regarded Preel, who had eaten the meal in utter silence. "But showing Brekka what Preel can do... That's dangerous."

"Yes, it is, but I don't see any other way." I shrugged. "I can't ask Preel if Brekka intends to double-cross me, and I can't ask her about a potion that hasn't been made yet."

"True." Miko didn't sound convinced. "I just don't like risking her."

"Neither do I." Never a truer statement left my lips. I needed to change the subject. "About crew morale... I've decided to advance some money to keep them occupied. What do you think?"

Miko shrugged. "Couldn't hurt, and if Brekka's not asking for gold, you can afford it."

"Good." I finished my liqueur and stood. "Tell them they'll each receive five imperials in advance of our next prize. That should keep them happy."

"Aye, sir." Miko finished her drink and left the cabin.

"Hemp! You can clear." I affixed Preel's silken gag while Hemp came in to take the dishes. "Would you like a walk on deck, Preel?"

She shook her head and tapped the book she'd been reading.

"As you wish. I need to stretch my legs." I headed for my door, but stopped, thinking there might be one more way I could convince Preel of my honesty. "At this rate, you're going to finish all of my books in no time. There's a bookseller in Valaka. I'd be happy to get some more for you."

Her eyes lit up and she nodded.

"Good. Just write down whatever subjects you like, and I'll go tomorrow."

Preel nodded, her smile hidden, but reaching her eyes well enough.

I smiled back and left the cabin to walk the deck, the lies writhing my stomach like a nest of vipers. I paced until far into the midwatch, wondering if I was making the right decision, but the night air, the stars, and my conscience all refused to answer.

When the day finally came, I sent Miko ahead to make sure the potion was ready. She came back to report the doorman had told her everything was ready for the exchange, and I could see the suspicion glowing in her eyes. Thankfully, she didn't ask, and didn't call me a lying bastard to my face. I put together a shore party and went to the great cabin to get Preel.

"Everything's ready," I announced as I went in.

Preel looked up from her seat by the stern gallery windows and put down her book.

I picked up a pot of makeup that Bert had concocted to hide Preel's tattoo. "Let's just put a dab of this on for the trip."

She stood dutifully, and I applied the makeup, careful to avoid smearing it into her dark eyebrows. When I was finished, only someone very close could have told the pigment was hiding something, and even then, wouldn't be able to say what.

I went to the locker to arm myself while Preel strapped on a pair of sandals and donned a cloak. While buckling on my weapons, I surreptitiously reached into the bottom of the locker to retrieve Preel's long-abandoned golden manacles, tucking them into the inner pocket of my jacket without jingling them overmuch. When I turned around, however, Preel was looking intently at me, her brow furrowed in concern.

"Don't worry." I muttered a silent prayer that she hadn't seen the manacles. "It'll be over in no time, and you'll wake up right there." I pointed to the bunk.

Preel nodded hesitantly. Not knowing how else I could assuage her fears, I escorted her out onto the deck where my detail awaited.

I'd picked them carefully, including Miko, Wix, Rauley, and Boxley in the group, as well as a dozen hardened pirates all armed to the teeth. If Brekka chose to double-cross me at the last moment, she'd find us a hard pill to swallow. I removed Preel's gag before we strode to the waiting palanquin I'd rented—a woman wearing a rune-embroidered gag would have drawn the wrong kind of attention—ushered her aboard, and re-affixed the silk gag before drawing the drapes closed. Eight burly pirates picked up the conveyance and we started on our way.

"I'm still not easy about this, sir," Miko said as we entered the district of ruined temples.

"Neither am I, but I don't see any alternative." The truth of those words pained me no less than the lies, a knife in my gut. "I'm not about to trust Brekka, and she's not going to trust me."

"I just wish you could tell me what you're giving her in exchange for the potion."

"I wish I could, too, Miko, but wishing for something never made it happen." I flashed her a pointed look. "Brekka said she'd know if I told anyone. I don't know if she's lying, but I can't risk it."

"Aye, sir."

We fell into an uneasy silence until we reached the temple with the draconic foyer. My crew lowered the palanquin, and I helped Preel down. There was nobody else around, so I left the gag on as we formed up around her and mounted the stairs. I counted them without knowing why, fifteen steps from the street to the door, fifteen steps that seemed to take forever. I gritted my teeth against my nagging conscience.

"Everyone keep your eyes open." I rapped thrice with a dagger hilt.

The door opened, and the pale face of the usual doorman peered out. His eyes took us in and fixed upon Preel. Grinning and nodding, he opened the door wide.

"Welcome, Captain Longbright."

I didn't respond and I certainly didn't feel welcome. Guards escorted us into the hall where, unlike before, Brekka awaited us. Around the periphery of the chamber stood what I assumed to be her entire force, perhaps fifty Children in all. I assessed them carefully this time and gauged them to be formidable, but not disciplined. Their weapons and armor didn't match, and some of their deformities rendered them ill-suited to formation fighting. I remembered our brief fight against the Children in their own district and felt confident that the force of solid fighters with me would prevent any foolishness on Brekka's part.

"Captain." Brekka stepped forward, once again clad in nondescript robes of modest cut, her face as undefinable as always. "I see you've brought my truthsayer."

"Your *what*?!" Miko's incredulous question heralded a roar of outbursts from the others.

"Silence!" I bellowed, turning to face them down. Preel's wide, startled eyes stabbed into my soul. "All of you keep quiet. This is the only way we can be free."

"The only way *you* can be free!" Miko's accusation hurt me almost as much as Preel's damning gaze, but I'd expected nothing less.

I rounded on her. "You really think you'd fare any better against Jhavika? That damned lash has tasted *your* flesh, too!" I raked them all with a steely stare. "All of you are her slaves, not just me! This is the only way we can be free." I turned then to Preel. Tears tracked down her face, wetting the silken band that girded her mouth. "I'm sorry."

She looked away, and I knew I'd broken her heart.

So be it.

"You have the potion?" I asked Brekka.

"It's not a potion, Captain, but an oil that must be applied to your skin." She produced a bottle of greenish liquid. "You must apply it to *all* of your skin from hair to toes. Only then will it remove the venom that the enchanted lash has infected you with."

"All right. I'll just confirm that you're telling me the truth." I pulled Preel close and untied her gag.

To this day, I don't know what saved me—reflexes honed by a lifetime of violence, perhaps, or a subconscious knowledge of what I would have done in Preel's place. As the gag came free, she jerked something from her pantaloons. Dropping the gag, I snatched her wrist just as pain pricked my abdomen. Looking down at the dagger in her hand—the dagger I'd given her—I winced. The tip of the blade had pierced my shirt and my skin beneath, but only to the depth of a fingertip. Her placement and angle of entry had been perfect, just as I'd taught her. If I'd missed my grab, the blade would have pierced my heart. Perhaps I should have let it.

"Please, Kevril." A sob escaped her lips, the very lips that had kissed mine with such passion, the lips I longed to taste again. "Don't do this."

"I have to." I pried the dagger from her hand and dropped it to the floor, then gazed into those dark, tearful eyes one more time, perhaps the last time. "Has Brekka spoken the truth in telling me that the oil she holds in her hand will remove the enchantment cast upon me by Jhavika Keshmir's scourge?"

Preel's eyes rolled up and she stiffened. "Yes!"

I caught her in my arms before she hit the floor.

"Hand her over, Captain Longbright." Brekka motioned one of her Children forward, holding out the bottle of oil.

"Very well." I handed Preel over to the guard, then accepted the bottle from the witch's hand. Reaching into my jacket, I pulled forth the golden manacles and the key. "These will keep her from injuring herself. They may have other properties I don't know of. And this," I picked up the silken gag, "will keep her from answering any questions until you're ready to ask one that matters." I handed both

321

over. "If you ask her another question too soon, even if she's unconscious, you risk her life."

"Thank you, Captain."

I turned away without another word.

The glares from my crew stabbed me like a rank of pikes. Boxley stared at me as if I'd just sold *her* into slavery, not Preel. Miko's was the most damning; I'd lost her trust completely. They'd likely abandon me if given the opportunity, maybe even mutiny and cast me overboard with my guts tied to the taffrail as I did to Geit. In their eyes, I deserved nothing less.

I couldn't disagree.

"Out!" I waved them at the door. "And not a gods-damned word!"

They complied, and I followed them out. The doorman closed the door behind us with a fanged grin of satisfaction. Maybe he thought he knew what this had cost me. Maybe he was right.

"Captain, I can't—"

"Later, Miko." I waved my crew toward the empty palanquin and hurried down the stairs.

"No, sir, you'll hear me *now*!" Miko grabbed my shoulder and yanked me around. "You're a right bastard! You sold her to save your own yellow skin!"

"Tell me you wouldn't have done the same!" I glared her down and pointed back down the deserted street. "Now get back to the ship!"

"No, *sir*!"

I wasn't expecting the blow but managed to turn my head just enough that it didn't break my jaw. My ears rang, but again, a lifetime of violence served me well. My hand caught the baldric that crossed Miko's chest and I hauled her in. Miko's strong and quick as a viper, but she's not very heavy. I lifted her off her feet, our faces an inch apart, before my vision even cleared from her blow.

"Not *now*, Miko!" I growled between bloody clenched teeth, keeping my voice a harsh whisper. "They might be watching and I can't explain this yet, but I'm not sailing away from Valaka without Preel. I had to lie to everyone. Brekka would have smoked it out otherwise."

"You're…" she stared at me in shocked understanding, her dark eyes flicking over my shoulder at the toothy maw that framed the entrance to Brekka's abode. Her eyes returned to mine, and I felt the prick of a dagger in my stomach. "Put me *down*!"

I did, none too gently.

My first mate straightened her shirt and glared at me, dagger in hand. "You'll *answer* for this, Captain!"

"Yes, I will."

"Fine!" She whirled and waved the crewmen to the palanquin. "Pick that up! Back to the ship!"

I don't know if any of the others had heard what I told Miko, but they followed orders readily enough. We were a dozen blocks away when Miko finally turned to me.

"You plan to take her back?" she asked, loud enough for everyone to hear.

Several gasped in surprise. Wix laughed out loud and called me something anatomically impossible. Boxley whooped.

"Keep it down!" I glared them all to silence. "I promised to exchange Preel for the potion, and I fulfilled that bargain." I rubbed my sore jaw and spat blood. "I *didn't* promise not to steal her back."

"How?"

"Not here. We'll discuss it back aboard."

"When?"

"Tonight, before Preel wakes up."

"She's still going to hate you for this, you know."

"Maybe." I'd considered that eventuality during many sleepless nights of late. "But at least she'll be free."

Chris A. Jackson

"We'll leave a skeleton crew aboard *Scourge*." I paced the main hold, assessing each one of my crew. Some of them were still sore at being lied to, but they were all on board with my plan to get Preel back. "We've got them outnumbered, and I'd bet my last penny that we're better fighters than Brekka's Children. If we time it right, half of them will be occupied elsewhere, not on watch, though we can't depend on it. The problem is getting in."

"That door's a right fooker, sir," Wix said. "Take a ram to make a dent in it."

"We won't need a ram." I grinned and patted my newest midshipman on the shoulder. "We've got Boxley."

"*Me*, sir?" She looked puzzled.

"Yes, you and the other midshipmen, and maybe a couple of the skinniest crew, but not too many."

"The crack in the dome!" Miko piped up, her face alight with eagerness.

"Yes." I nodded and gestured to Boxley again. "It's too narrow for a full-grown person, but I'll wager Boxley, Kivan, and maybe Rauley will fit through. They'll have to be quiet, but if they can get to the front door and work the mechanism, we're in."

"And if they aren't quiet, they're dead." Miko frowned.

"Let us try, sir!" Boxley leapt up, glancing at the other midshipmen. Quiff was clearly too big, but Kivan would fit. "Maybe a ship's brat or two with us?"

"I don't know if that's—"

"Please, sir!" Tofi forced his way through the crowd to the fore, brandishing a dagger. "Let us help!"

Three more brats joined him, and damned if they didn't all have daggers.

I looked sidelong at Miko. "More would be better, but they'd have to be *quiet*."

Miko nodded. "Four or five at the most. I'll take a team up to lower them in so they won't have to climb."

324

"Good." I looked over my unlikely burglars. "Daggers only, and you don't use them unless you have to, understood?"

"Yes, sir!" Boxley saluted.

"Kivan, you're senior, so you'll be in command once you're in. Getting that door open is your *only* goal. Got it?"

"And not getting killed," Miko added.

"Yes, sir, I got it." Kivan looked less enthusiastic than Boxley, but I needed someone with a cool head in charge.

"Good." I raked the rest of the crew with a long, even stare. "Now, I want to make clear that I lied to everyone here, but I did it because it was the only way I could see all of us getting out of this on top. If I didn't get that potion from Brekka, we'd be Jhavika's slaves forever. Even if we sailed away, she'd eventually track us down. I'm risking Preel, but I'm *positive* that Brekka won't hurt her. She's worth too much alive and well. If we pull this off, she'll wake up in the great cabin before she realizes what's happened."

"That'll take some explaining." Miko still wasn't happy with my use of Preel, but at least she agreed to the plan for getting her back.

"Yes, but that'll be for *me* to explain." With any luck, we'd be at sea by then. "We've got maybe a watch before it's dark enough for us to go. Wix, I want you to pick the skeleton crew to stay aboard. Quiff will be in command."

"Aye, sir!" Wix pulled one of his daggers and examined the spiked hilt guard. "Want to be clear on the level of mayhem we're likely to end up in the middle of?"

"We're boarding a hostile ship full of mercenaries. We have *one* goal and one goal only: get Preel out alive. Anyone who gets in our way buys a blade in the gut." I nodded at my bosun's raised eyebrow. "You've got no holds barred on this one, Wix."

"Fookin' *right*!" The bosun grinned horribly and turned to the crew. "You cutthroats get ready! We take 'em down fast and quiet until all the hells break loose, then it's a close-order boarding action."

325

"Exactly. If any of them throws down weapons and pleads for mercy, we leave them be, but if they fight, we fight to kill." I looked them all over once again. "Everyone clear on that?"

My crew mumbled their assent, grim as death and ready for blood.

The only question I didn't have an answer for was Brekka.

Chapter Twenty Three
A Pirate's Bargain

Though the transition from life to death is painless, the conditions that
initiate that transition are often not.
The Lessons of Quen Lau Ush

From the diary of Kevril Longbright –
As a youth, my father taught me to farm, to plow the earth
and sow seed, to reap her bounty, to be one with the land. It
would have been a simple life. Now I plow flesh with steel
and reap blood and gold. There's nothing simple about this
life I've chosen, but all things considered, I'd rather be the
plow than the earth.

Miko and I decided four would be best: Kivan, Boxley, Rauley,
and Tofi. Miko would take them up with a team of topcrew, nimble
and strong as apes, to lower the youngsters through the crack in the
dome. Tofi and Boxley were enthusiastic, while Rauley and Kivan
were grim and nervous. We made it clear that stealth was paramount;
one slip, one dislodged stone or misstep, would cost all their lives
and the entire plan would fail. Their only goal was to unlock the
front door.

I hated putting them at risk so, but midshipmen join in boarding actions with the rest of the crew, and a pirate can die falling down a companionway in a heavy sea as easily as on the end of a blade. At least that was what I told myself. Still, I hated it.

The rest of us, sixty seasoned pirates, made our way through Valaka's streets in scattered groups of four or five to converge upon the temple as quietly as we could. Forged by dozens of nighttime boarding actions and tempered in blood, we crept toward the fanged foyer of the temple and hunkered in shadow. I took the fore with Wix and half a dozen of my best fighters, mounting the dark steps to stand with our backs to the heavy bronze door, alert for the click of the locking mechanism being thrown open or the screams of our dying comrades from within.

We waited.

In my mind's eye I saw Miko and her team climbing up the ivy-shrouded walls of the temple's dilapidated northern wing, traversing the slate roof toward the higher dome, every step risking a dislodged tile and discovery. They must have tread softly, though, for I heard only the soft song of night insects, the occasional skitter of rodents in the rubble-strewn streets, and my own hammering heart. I imagined the four youngsters being lowered through the crack, partway at first to look for watchers below, then, with the signal tap on their ropes, dropped quickly to the floor of the hall.

Silence...

They would take cover among the pillars and shadows, sticking together, working toward the doors as quietly as they could, daggers sheathed, dressed in dark clothes, faces blackened with soot. At the door, I knew they would encounter wakeful guards. Kivan would decide how to proceed, signaling those she thought best to take the guards down while the others attended to the door's mechanism. Thankfully, there were no keys involved, just a lever that disengaged the heavy bronze bars from the wall. The sound would be unmistakable.

A shout from within stiffened my back.

I whistled a single, loud note, and the shadows of the street disgorged my main force of pirates. They sprinted for the foyer as the rest of us drew steel.

The door remained locked.

A scream, and something heavy hit the door, but still the mechanism didn't click. My knuckles whitened on my cutlass' hilt. Another scream, higher pitched. *No!* Visions of bloody children—*my* children, not Brekka's Children—surged through my mind. Then another scream registered clearer, Kivan bellowing an order, her voice shrill.

Metal grated on metal, and the bars clanged free of their recesses.

"Now!" Wix and I slammed our shoulders against the doors, a dozen pirates aiding our efforts. The portal flew open hard enough to send poor Rauley sprawling. We surged through, over two very dead guards and one small shape.

Tofi.

I forced the anguish aside —*No time now!*—and looked for the rest. Rauley was bleeding from a gaping wound to his shoulder, while Kivan and Boxley, daggers in hand, faced a score of onrushing guards.

Our force barreled past the midshipmen and met the guards in a glorious clash of steel, flesh, and bone. The Serpent's Children fought with a discordant ferocity that startled me at first, but ravening jaws and clacking pincers are a poor match for the organized and disciplined swords of seasoned pirates. With Wix to my left and Tansy to my right, each of them flanked by more swords and backed by ranks of our best pikemen, we cut through the guards with brutal efficiency.

Wix, in his glory, laid waste with both hands, blades and spiked hilt guards parting and pulping twisted flesh, bone, and chitin, his harsh laughter ringing off the walls. I worked mechanically, cutlass and dagger weaving in a dance I'd perfected a decade ago. The temple floor ran with blood, little of it ours. Injured pirates fell back without a word, their ranks filled by those behind. We fought our way to the central hall in the span of a dozen breaths, some of the Children laying down arms, others fleeing before us.

"Secure this chamber!" I barked. Then, pointing down the corridor that led to Brekka's laboratory, I called, "First team with me!"

Wix and a score of pirates dashed down the corridor on my heels. Shadows flickered across the walls, light from the torches held high by our rear ranks. We kicked in doors as we went, but the resistance was token, and none stood in our path for long. Doors slammed shut ahead of us, and bolts clacked home. *So much for Brekka's loyal guards.*

I plunged down the side corridor that led to the pleasure chamber, hoping to find the alchemist there with the rest of her slaves, so distracted with the pleasures of the flesh that they hadn't heard the alarm. I could hope, couldn't I? I pointed my bloody cutlass at the door.

"Wix!"

"Aye, sir!" He and two burly pirates barreled forward. Six-hundred weight of meat hit the stout door, splintering wood.

We charged in, steel in hand, and my hopes were startlingly fulfilled. A tangle of perfect flesh writhed on the floor, men and women fumbling for clothes and weapons, but my pirates were on them before they could arm themselves. Behind her cowering slaves, Brekka shrugged perfect shoulders into her azure robe, the material closing over perfect breasts, perfect hips, loins glistening with moisture from her recent activity.

Her sightless eye smoldered with hate. "How *dare* you invade my home!"

I barked a laugh. "I'm a *pirate*, Brekka! Home invasion is what I do best! Now, hand over Preel and we'll let you and your slaves get back to fucking, since that's what *you* seem to do best."

"I'll *kill* her before I let you take her!" she raged.

"Brave words, but really stupid." I motioned my pirates forward. "We'll just kill you all and find her ourselves."

"I'll see you all writhing in agony for this!" She backed away, her hand dipping into the pocket of her robe. "You'll die screaming, Captain Longbright!" She pulled out a vial and popped the crystal stopper.

"No!" I flailed desperately through her slaves, but too late.

As she quaffed the potion, Brekka began to melt away, her flesh transforming to liquid in a ripple from her head downward. The alchemist's robe landed in a wet heap, and a wave rose from the puddle to rush toward me. I sidestepped and slashed out, but my cutlass passed harmlessly though the wave and struck the stone floor, nicking its fine edge. I stared as the undulating puddle surged toward the open door.

"After her!" I bolted through the ranks of my stunned pirates, chasing the liquefied alchemist, not exactly sure what to do if I caught her.

"Need a fookin' swab and bucket!" Wix said, hot on my heels. The rest of my troop thundered after us.

At the intersection with the main corridor, the puddle splashed to the left, toward Brekka's laboratory. We gained a few yards on her before she reached the door, but I stared helplessly as the liquid surged right under the stout portal.

"With me, Wix!" I didn't slow, leading with my shoulder.

"Aye, sir!"

We hit hard enough to rattle my teeth, but not hard enough to fracture the door, and the heavy bronze reinforcements bruised my shoulder. Wix and I both swore and stepped back. The rest of my squad arrived, and my bosun quickly picked out the four largest pirates among them.

"Together now!" They rushed the door and the latch gave way, wood shattering and bronze screeching as the heavy door slammed open.

Preel!

The truthsayer lay atop a flat bench, dressed in her silks, the golden chain girding her wrists and waist, silken gag over her mouth, still deeply asleep.

The alchemist was once again flesh, bare flesh, for her azure gown had been left behind, but her perfect human form had also been abandoned.

Now she wasn't human at all.

I recalled the potion she'd used to bribe her guards and realized that it must have given her a human semblance. Only her dark hair and eyes were the same now. The alchemist glared at me from above a flattened nose and beak-like mouth bordered with scales and short pinfeathers. Brekka's torso resembled the throat-skin of a vulture, ruddy and pocked with patches of scabrous growths. Her legs were bent backward and ended in clawed bird feet, long talons clicking against the stone floor. Her hands were similarly clawed, but one also held a long creese. Brekka brandished the wicked blade and held it edgewise across Preel's bare throat.

I leveled my cutlass at her as my squad fanned out behind me.

"One step and the truthsayer dies, Captain Longbright!" Brekka's voice was surprisingly unchanged, though I don't know how she managed to speak at all with that mouth.

"Drop the blade, Brekka, and we'll let you live."

"Why should I trust a lying pirate? You invade my home, kill my servants, threaten my life, and you want to *negotiate?*" Her throat flexed, emitting an inhuman squawk. "I think not!"

"I never lied to you *once*, you foul creature." I thought to step closer, but the blade against Preel's throat stayed my movement. "I promised to exchange Preel for the potion and I did that! I said nothing about not taking her back from you! Now you can stand aside and let us take her, or you can die."

"I will not die here, Captain." The alchemist fumbled her free hand along the bench behind her and snatched up another vial. "I can escape any time I wish!"

"If that blade draws a scratch on her throat, I will kill every living thing in this temple, smash every bottle, jar, and flask, and raze this entire structure to the ground!" I'd never spoken truer words. If Preel died, I would raze all of Valaka if I thought for a moment it would bring her back. "You have nothing to blame but your own *greed*, Brekka. I would have bargained anything else I owned, answered any question you wished, and let you go with my blessing, but you chose the one person I couldn't part with. If you give her over to me, we'll leave you to your pots and potions, but harm her, and you'll wish a *dragon* had come to roost on your stoop."

Brekka seethed, the pinfeathers around her mouth bristling, but her single bright eye darted around the laboratory, at the amassed alchemical wealth she'd accumulated there. So far, we'd probably killed a dozen or so of her people, but she could replace their number with little effort, seducing more Serpent's Children with the promise of a lifetime of perfect pleasure. Her laboratory, however, probably represented decades of labor. She very well might be able to escape death, but she would spend years regaining what she'd made here.

"Filthy pirate!" she spat.

"Fookin' right we are, you feathery fook!" Wix grinned and stepped over to a shelf of bottles, raising one of his spiked daggers. "Ready to break some shite, lads and lasses?"

My pirates grumbled dangerously.

"Stop!" The creese lifted from Preel's throat. "You win, Captain. Take your truthsayer and be gone, but never set foot in Valaka again or your life, your ship, and your *soul* will be forfeit."

"I'll take that bargain." I sheathed my cutlass and dagger and stepped forward to lift Preel from the bench. She was very light, a feather in my arms, warm and musky. I breathed in her scent like an intoxicating vapor. "Give me the key to her manacles."

"There, on the bench." Brekka pointed with the creese.

"Wix, get the key. We're leaving."

"Aye, sir!" Wix sheathed one dagger and snatched up the golden key.

We backed out of the alchemist's laboratory and hastened to the temple door, picking up the others from the main hall, carrying our wounded and dead with us. One of my pirates had fallen to a spear stabbed through her gut. Poor Tofi, the brave little fellow, had taken a horrible wound to his throat from the doorman's fanged maw. The doorman had paid with his life, however, Tofi's dagger still lodged in his chest. Miko met us at the door, her face grim, but stoic. The cost had been dire, but we had what we came for, a treasure beyond price, far more than pirates regularly risked their lives for.

We formed up and marched back to the ship in close order. It was late enough that few people took notice, and those who did weren't about to interfere with three-score armed men and women. We boarded the boats without incident and rowed to the ship, clambering aboard with our precious cargo.

"Unmoor ship, Miko." I started for my cabin, Preel still cradled in my arms. Wix tucked the golden key in my pocket in passing, grinning his horrible grin. "There's enough moonlight to navigate out of the harbor, and I want to put some distance between us and that witch. Set a northerly course for open sea with all sail she'll bear."

"Aye, sir!" Miko started barking orders, organizing the injured, and generally doing all the things I should have been doing myself.

I had more important things to do.

I carried Preel to the great cabin. Hemp held the door open for me and closed it behind without a word or complaint. Laying Preel down on the bunk, I unlocked the golden chains and checked her over carefully. A bandage on her left wrist covered a small cut. I swore under my breath. Brekka had evidently harvested some of Preel's blood for her alchemy. I didn't know what she might do with it, but one question to Preel would answer that.

I also removed the silken gag, brushing Preel's sweet lips with my fingers. Her breathing was fine, her eyes flicking around beneath her dusky lids, dreaming dreams she would not or could not recall. I pulled up a chair and retrieved a cloth and basin from the quarter gallery, pausing to wash the blood from my hands and arms. Returning to the bedside, I pressed the damp cloth to Preel's brow, wiping away the smudge of makeup that covered her tattoo.

Then I sat down and watched her sleep.

I heard the calls of the crew working the ship, felt the motion change as she made for sea, but I didn't pay any attention; Miko knew what to do. Hemp knocked on my door and delivered a pot of blackbrew. I thanked him and handed over my weapons for cleaning, save for one boot dagger. I poured blackbrew and drank it without tasting it, watching Preel's stomach slowly rise and fall with every breath, never tiring of that slow, steady cadence, the scent of her filling my head.

Finally, sometime during the first watch, her breathing quickened and her eyes fluttered open.

A gasp of surprise, a look of terror, confusion, and finally recognition. Preel bolted up and caught sight of me sitting there, then scuttled back until her shoulders hit the bulkhead.

"What?" She blinked at me, her dark eyes wide with fear.

"You're safe, Preel."

"You! You..." Confusion returned, her hands went to her mouth, discovered the silken gag missing. She found the bandage on her wrist, but finally seemed to realize that she was back in my cabin. Her eyes narrowed, and she spat out her words. "You *traded* me. You bartered me for the potion."

Her justifiable rage wounded me more than any blade could have. "Yes, I did, and I'm sorry to have put you through that. I'm sorry I lied to you. I'm sorry I risked losing you, but I couldn't see another way." I shrugged helplessly and put my cup aside. "We took you back while you were sleeping. Now we're headed into open sea, away from Valaka." I gestured to the silken gag lying beside her on the bunk. "You're free, Preel. I'll never put that on you again unless you ask me. You're free to leave or stay as you wish. If you want to leave, I'll take you to any port you name. If you decide to stay, I'll never ask you another question that invokes your talent without your explicit consent."

"I..." She stared at me, her expression softening, and her eyes dropped as she rubbed the bandage on her wrist. "I tried to *kill* you."

"Yes, you did, and a damn near thing it was!" I grinned at her. "Lucky I'm a pirate."

"I...don't understand. You had your potion and you were free to go. Why did you steal me back? Why risk it?"

That knife skewered my gut again, just like when I left home all those years ago. "Are you *sure* you don't know?"

"Know?" She shook her head slowly. "No, I *don't* know."

Standing, I retrieved the dagger from my boot, the remaining one with the gemmed hilt, and dropped it on the bunk. "Pick it up."

Preel stared at the weapon, then finally reached out and clasped it.

I doffed my shirt and pointed to the tiny wound just below my sternum. "There. Right there, angle up slightly, just like you did before. If you don't know why I came after you, Preel, then sheathe that blade in my heart and be done with it. I won't stop you this time. You're a free woman now. You can do as you will with me."

She stared at me for a moment, then at the knife in her hand. For a second, I thought she might just do it. I don't think I would have stopped her. I'll never know.

The dagger clattered to the deck. "I love you, Kevril Longbright."

I felt as if I'd been plunged into icy water, gasping out the breath I didn't know I'd been holding. "*That's* why I stole you back."

Preel launched herself off the bunk and into my arms.

Two days at sea, our course set for Haven, Preel helped me remove the enchantment of Jhavika's scourge. I trusted no other with the task. Locking the door to my cabin, I stripped mother-naked, then consigned the bottle containing Brekka's spelled oil into Preel's hands.

"Every inch of my flesh from hair to toes, she said, and there are quite a few spots I can't reach on my own." I smiled as she uncorked the bottle "Don't miss any."

"I won't." Preel returned my smile knowingly. We'd already explored every inch of each other—an enjoyable journey for both of us—so there was no new territory for her to discover. She sniffed the bottle. "Not bad, really. It smells of herbs. Now, we should start at the top. You'll have to kneel down."

"All right." I knelt, then looked at her askance as she put the bottle aside. "What are you—"

"This is liable to be messy. There's no reason to get my clothes oily." She slipped the knot to her halter and unwound it, tossing it onto the bunk, then wiggled out of her pantaloons, her fabulous lips arching in a sultry smile. "Besides, this could be fun."

"Oh? You think so?"

"Yes." Preel poured some oil into her hand and slowly massaged it into my scalp, pulling my head forward until my lips brushed her breasts. "Very much so."

I don't think she missed any spots.

I certainly didn't.

Epilogue
Free Associations

Never underestimate the lure of avarice.
The Lessons of Quen Lau Ush

From the diary of Kevril Longbright –
In the end, it all boiled down to gold. I'm a pirate, after all.

Jhavika's spies saw us coming long before we dropped anchor. I chose to moor ship well off the broad stone quay lined with warehouses, not only because I had no cargo to offload, but to make it more difficult for Jhavika if she tried to take the ship by force. Even as my topcrew furled the last of the sails, a boat set out from the warehouse quay and headed straight for us.

"We've got company, Miko." I focused my spyglass on the launch and recognized Ty-lee. For once, he wasn't smiling. At least the boat wasn't full of mercenaries. Fortunately, although Jhavika is avaricious and ruthless, she's not stupid. "Boarding ladder port side."

"Trouble?" Miko asked, shading her eyes from the morning sun.

"Nothing I can't handle." I tucked my spyglass away and strolled down to the waist of the ship, hands folded behind my back. "Bring the launch alongside, Master Rauley."

"Aye, sir!" Though his arm was still in a sling, the wound was healing cleanly. He'd have an interesting scar on his shoulder, however. "Tansy, Vol, lines fore and aft on the launch! Fenders low. Scratch my paint and you'll pay the devil!" The young man was developing an authoritative tone that I thoroughly approved of.

The launch came alongside, and Ty-lee clambered up and through the boarding hatch. "Captain Longbright! You've been away so long we feared you'd been pressed into service by Toki!" It sounded like a joke, but I knew it wasn't.

I didn't laugh.

"I had matters to attend to. I trust Lady Keshmir is in residence."

"She is, Captain, and she's *very* eager to see you." He lowered his voice to a stage whisper easily audible to everyone on deck. "She's quite wroth with you, I'm afraid. She insists you attend her immediately."

"Please inform Lady Keshmir that I'll attend her this afternoon, no sooner. I've matters aboard I must see to."

"I'm afraid I can't do that, Captain. I was told not to return without you."

"And you can't disobey, can you?" I saw the confusion on his face and almost felt sorry for him. "Tell you what, get back in that launch, row ashore, and wait for me there. I'll be ashore this afternoon, and you can escort me to Lady Keshmir. That way, both of us do as we wish and she can't have you flayed for disobedience."

"I...suppose that would be sufficient." His hesitant assent belied his horrified expression. "But I warn you, delaying will only make her angry."

I smiled at him. "And I warn *you*, Ty-lee, I don't *care* if your mistress is angry, and I don't have time to deal with you right now. One way or another, you're leaving my ship this instant."

He took a half step back. "As you wish, Captain. I'll await you on the quay."

"Good." I watched him go without remorse for a word I'd said.

339

Chris A. Jackson

"Is pissing on Jhavika's shoes really the way to go about this, sir?"

I chuckled at Miko's question. "Maybe not, but I'll not smile at a tongue lashing from that little worm. Besides, Jhavika doesn't have a hold on me any longer, on *any* of us."

It was the truth. During our transit from Valaka, I'd asked Preel one more question, with her permission, of course. The answer had confirmed my deeply held hope; Jhavika held no sway over anybody aboard *Scourge*. Evidently, the control that Captain Kohl had enjoyed had lapsed with his death. I had been the only one aboard whom Jhavika had used the lash upon, and that hold had been severed. The crew and I were free.

"Too right, sir, but that doesn't mean she's powerless." Miko arched an eyebrow at me. "She could easily make our lives hell."

"She could, but she'd lose her private pirate."

"So, you've decided to stay with her?" That surprised her, too. Twice in one month had to be some kind of personal best for me pulling one over on Miko.

"I'll make the offer, but it's up to her." I grinned dangerously. "I'll never be *anyone's* slave again."

"Got news for you, sir, but that truthsayer in your bunk's got manacles on you right now." She laughed hard, her pearly teeth gleaming. "Though they're around your manhood, not your wrists."

"That's not slavery, Miko, that's..." I almost said it, and by the look on her face, she knew what I was going to say. *Reading my mind again...* "...something else entirely."

"Maybe, sir." She winked and turned to her duties. "Maybe."

I hustled aft to my cabin to get cleaned up and check on Preel, a spring in my step that I hadn't felt for years...if ever. I found her awake, seated at the table in a robe over her nightclothes, ravenously eating breakfast.

"Good morning!" I grinned as I strode to my cabinet, stopping to drop a kiss onto the top of her head. "I see Hemp's been doting on you again."

340

"Mm-hmm." Preel swallowed the bite she'd been chewing. "He's really a treasure, Kevril. You shouldn't give him such a hard time."

"Hemp's a scallywag and a punter of women of ill repute." I winked at her as I doffed my salt-stained jacket and shirt. "But you're right. He's also a damn fine steward. Just don't tell him I said so."

I stole a strip of bacon from her plate on my way to the quarter gallery.

"When are you going ashore?" she asked as I laved the salt from my face and arms. Our last night offshore had been blustery and wet.

"This afternoon. Why?"

"Because..."

Her voice was much closer, and I looked up to find her at the door to the quarter gallery, her robe and nightshirt abandoned on the floor behind her. My heart leapt in my chest, a flush of heat radiating outward from my stomach.

Tilting her head, Preel gazed solemnly at me as she said, "You're walking into a dragon's den today, Kevril. I want to lie with you one more time before you do."

"The last rites off a condemned man?" I took her in my arms, smiling at her glare, even though my own nerves were taut.

Preel brushed off my attempt at humor. "Stop it! Jhavika's dangerous, and she still wields that damnable scourge. One lash and you're hers again." She clutched me tight.

"Calm, love. She's also enchanted by that same scourge, remember? The avarice of a dragon runs through her veins." I held her warm body against mine and ran my fingers over the smooth skin of her back. "She'll not throw away a perfectly good pirate out of spite."

"But she also wants you in her *bed*!" Preel pushed me far enough away to glare directly into my eyes, though distress lingered behind her pique. "Don't forget that!"

"I'll *never* forget that, Preel, but you've got to trust me. I know how Jhavika thinks. I'll convince her that she needs me as a pirate more than she needs me as a bedmate. Besides, the only way she'd *ever* get me in bed again is if she used that lash on me, and that's not going to happen."

"And why not?"

"Because I'll die before I let her touch me with that thing again."

Preel drew me into a crushing embrace. "That's what I'm afraid of."

When I entered Jhavika's business office, I knew immediately that Preel's fears had been justified. I had surely walked into a dragon's den, and the wyrm was angry. If my business partner could have shot dragonfire from her eyes, I would have been roasted on the spot.

Jhavika leaned against her expansive desk, arms folded, one palm resting on the handle of the accursed scourge at her hip, her eyes smoldering. My gaze flicked involuntarily to my coiled nemesis, the instrument of my slavery, my debauchment, my helplessness. If that length of dragon flesh left her hip, I would kill her and damn the consequences. The problem was, the consequences would likely leave me skewered by her house guards.

Luckily, we were alone. She still thought I was under her control, which gave me a chance.

I stopped three long strides from her and bowed formally. "Jhavika."

"Where in the Nine *Hells* have you been?" Her voice trembled with barely bridled rage, her knuckles white on the handle of the scourge.

This was the moment when I would discover if she even knew what she had done to me. If she, too, was enthralled by the scourge, perhaps she didn't realize how the thing affected others. For all I knew, her use of the lash was a reflexive action induced by the weapon's enchantment. She might not even know what that horrible thing truly was.

"I sought out someone to remove the enchantment you placed upon me with that scourge." I pointed with one finger at the coil of dragonhide on her hip.

Her eyes widened, and her whole body stiffened. "*What?*"

Her astonishment was real enough. I'd taken her by the lee. "The enchantment is broken, Jhavika. You can no longer command me with your every whim."

"What are you *talking* about? What *enchantment?*" Her protestation rang patently false. She'd overdone it and knew it, if the tightening of her jaw was any indication. She knew perfectly well what she'd done to me, what she was doing to others, and how she was doing it. So much for giving her the benefit of the doubt.

"Don't be coy. I'm talking about the scourge you wield, the scourge that used to belong to Captain Kohl." *Now to find out if she knows the rest.* I chose my next words very carefully. "I'm talking about the artifact that has taken control of you and made you into something even *you* may not realize. It's made you as avaricious and ruthless as a dragon, Jhavika. It's controlling you, and it'll do so until you die."

Her face blanched—she hadn't known *that*—but only for a moment before her eyes narrowed and she spat, "Bullshit! How could you know anything about *any* of this?"

I understood her denial. Learning that you're a slave is humbling, and Jhavika Keshmir was not a humble person. But I'd slit my own throat before I told her about Preel. "I have my sources. Believe me or don't, I don't care, but it's true. There's no denying that I'm free of the enchantment. If you doubt it, command me."

"Come *here!*" Jhavika pointed to the floor a step before her.

I stood perfectly still. "No."

Jhavika's fingers tightened around the handle of the scourge and she pushed herself off the desk, but I was watching for it and moved first. My cutlass was out of its scabbard and at her throat before she managed to take a step. I thanked the gods that she hadn't already summoned guards. We were alone, and I needed to make sure we stayed that way.

"Don't even *think* about it, Jhavika!" I drew the jewel-hilted dagger with my left hand. If she freed the scourge from her hip, I'd block with my cutlass and gut her with the dagger. "You call for help or take that thing off your hip, and I swear by all the gods, I'll cut you down!"

"You'd die before my body was cold."

"Maybe, but you'd be no less dead! There'll be no mercy this time." That was the stick, now for the carrot. "I'm willing to continue to work with you, but I'll *die* before I'll be your slave again."

"You'll…" My words obviously surprised her, and her hand fell away from the scourge. "You'll *what?*"

"I said, I'll continue to be your partner, but I'll *not* be your slave."

"You *would?*" Her eyes narrowed, suspicion and avarice warring behind them.

"Yes, but we'd be *equal* partners or nothing. You agree to that, or I sail away and you never see me again."

Jhavika shifted her stance, then froze as my blade pressed her throat. Settling back against the desk, she scowled at me. I could almost see her thoughts, the machinations of her mind as she considered my proposal and whether I was telling her the truth. She was also probably wondering if she could use the lash on me at a later date. Finally, however, she raised her hands clear of her belt, open and empty.

"You really mean that?" she asked, her brows furrowed. "About being equal partners? After…what I did to you?"

It was as much an admission of guilt as I was ever going to get from her, and I wouldn't hold my breath for an apology. I lowered my sword, but didn't sheathe it. "Yes, even after that." I swallowed the memories of being her slave and tucked them away with all the others I loathed. "I'm in the business of *piracy*, Jhavika. It's a damn sight easier with you handing me fat prizes. Just because you're

344

spelled by a magical artifact that won't let you stop until you rule all the world doesn't mean that I won't let you make me rich. But know this," I raised my blade again, close enough to end her life with one twist of my arm. "I will never, *ever* be controlled by you again. Even if you manage to lash me with it, I know how to break the enchantment now." Not that Brekka would ever brew that potion for me again.

Her eyes narrowed. "Or I could have you killed and promote Miko."

I had to admit, she had the balls of a dragon, too. It was time to show her that I had bigger teeth than she thought. "Only if you want all of Haven to know your secret, Jhavika. I've told others, *many* others, what that scourge is, and what you're doing with it. If I die mysteriously, word will get out."

Rage smoldered behind her eyes, but Jhavika was smart enough to know I wasn't bluffing. "I don't like threats, Kevril."

"I'm not threatening you; I'm just telling you that I've taken precautions." I pointed my cutlass at the coil of dragon flesh on her hip. "Nothing will take that scourge from your grasp except death, but I'll be content to ride your coattails until then."

Jhavika barked a laugh. "Such sentimentality!"

"There is *no* sentiment between us, Jhavika. There never was." Pain flickered briefly in her eyes, and I almost felt sorry for her. Almost. I didn't know if she actually had feelings for me or if the scourge had merely egged her on for another conquest. I didn't care. "I'm in this for the money, and *nothing* else! Take the whole *world* if you can; I'll be happy to tag along. But keep your hands and that fucking scourge away from me and mine. I'm *free*. I'm going to stay that way or die trying."

Her eyes narrowed, then she nodded sagely. "You really *are* a pirate, aren't you?"

"To the bone, Jhavika."

"Very well, Kevril Longbright. We have a deal." Jhavika strode around behind her desk, opened a drawer and withdrew a bound scroll. She held it out. "If you're still up to a *challenge*, I've got a ship for you to take."

I sheathed my cutlass, but not the dagger, and stepped up, watching her other hand. If she reached for that scourge, I'd put my blade in her gut before she could blink. "I'm up to any challenge you can give me, Jhavika."

"Good." She handed me the scroll, her grip lingering a moment too long before she relinquished it. "We could have been good together, you know."

"No, Jhavika. Slavery is *never* a basis for a lasting relationship." I'd learned that lesson all too well.

"So be it." Jhavika's eyes drooped to half-mast, and her lips turned up in a sly smile. "So be it."

About the Author

Born and raised in Oregon, Chris meet his wife and soulmate, Anne, while attending graduate school in Texas. Since then they have been nigh inseparable: gaming together since 1985, sailing together since 1988, married since 1989, and writing together off and on throughout their relationship. Most astonishingly, they have not killed each other during the creation or editing of any of their stories…although it was close a few times. Since 2009, the couple has been sailing and writing full-time aboard their beloved sailboat, *Mr Mac*. They return to the US every summer for conventions, always happy to sign copies of their books and talk with fans.

Preview Chris' books and get updates on upcoming events at jaxbooks.com. Follow Chris and Anne's cruising adventures at www.sailmrmac.blogspot.com.

Novels by Chris A. Jackson

From Jaxbooks
A Soul for Tsing
Deathmask

Blood Sea Tales
The Pirate's Scourge
The Pirate's Truth (coming 2019)
The Pirate's Curse (coming 2020)

Weapon of Flesh Series
Weapon of Flesh
Weapon of Blood
Weapon of Vengeance
Weapon of Fear *
Weapon of Pain *
Weapon of Mercy *
(* with Anne L. McMillen-Jackson)

The Cornerstones Trilogy
(with Anne L. McMillen-Jackson)
Zellohar
Nekdukarr
Jundag

The Cheese Runners Trilogy
(novellas – also on Audible)
Cheese Runners
Cheese Rustlers
Cheese Lords

From Dragon Moon Press
The Scimitar Seas Novels
Scimitar Moon
Scimitar Sun
Scimitar's Heir
Scimitar War

From Paizo Publishing
Pirate's Honor
Pirate's Promise
Pirate's Prophecy

From Privateer Press
Blood & Iron (ebook novella)
Watery Graves

From Fantasy Flight Games
The Deep Gate (hardcover novella)

Check out these and more at
JAXBOOKS.COM
Want to get an email about my next book release?
Sign up at http://eepurl.com/xnrUL

CPSIA information can be obtained
at www.ICGtesting.com
Printed in the USA
LVHW081322071019
633420LV00012B/397/P